There's no time like the holidays to share love with those near and dear to you. This year, three of our favorite Arabesque authors help you celebrate the magic of the season with tales about the greatest gift of all: love.

Francine Craft,
Linda Hudson-Smith,
Michelle Monkou

GIVE
LOVE

ARABESQUE®

GIVE LOVE

ISBN-13: 978-1-58314-811-2
ISBN-10:   1-58314-811-6

© 2006 by Harlequin Books S.A.

The publisher acknowledges the copyright holder
of the individual works as follows:

KISSES AND MISTLETOE
Copyright © 2003 by Francine Craft

FANTASY FULFILLED
Copyright © 2003 by Linda Hudson-Smith

SOMEONE TO LOVE
Copyright © 2003 by Michelle Monkou

www.kimanipress.com

Printed in U.S.A.

CONTENTS

KISSES AND MISTLETOE

Francine Craft

This story is dedicated in memorial
to my beloved grandfather, Frank Craft,
who was always there for me. Rest in peace.

He brought me to the banqueting house,
and his banner over me was love.
Stay me with flagons; comfort me with apples:
for I am sick with love.
                    —*The Song of Solomon* 2:4–5

Chapter 1

On a Friday night in early September, the Rocketship Night Club in Washington, D.C., was jumping. Janet Smith, a high school English teacher, had come with her best friend and fellow teacher, Bea Barry, who taught and loved music. A melody from a lone introductory guitarist filled their ears as the musician played an old Marvin Gaye tune. He bent over his guitar as if caressing a lover, and Bea laughed and hugged herself.

"I just can't wait for you to hear Nick Redmond and his combo. You're going to fall in love."

Janet brushed back a wisp of dark brown chemically straightened, lush, and long hair from her nutmeg-colored face. Her golden brown eyes were wary. "We don't have long to wait," Janet said. "They come on in twenty minutes."

"Nick's the protégé I'm most proud of. He got his start with my teaching. He attended Howard for a while, then moved on to the New England Conservatory of Music. I have a hunch you two will be talking. Ask him about his dreams for Rhapsody." Bea tapped her fingers against her face. "But I've got an ulterior motive in bringing you here."

"Oh?"

"I think Nick's gonna love you and you'll at least like him. You two remind me so much of each other."

"I've seen his pictures. He's an attractive guy, but isn't he a little young?"

Bea shrugged. "He's thirty-one, going on fifty. He's a doll."

Janet laughed a trifle harshly. "I'm *forty*-one, remember? He's way under the age I'm looking for."

Bea's head went to one side. "Trouble is, girlfriend, you're not finding anyone."

"Ouch!"

"You know I don't mean to hurt you, but facts're facts. At least *befriend* my old-soul friend Nick. You'll be good for each other. He's such an attractive guy and I don't think he's really aware of it."

Janet reached over and patted Bea's slender hand. Bea was very dark brown with high cheekbones, liquid black eyes, and coarse, close-cut, curly black hair. A strikingly attractive woman, she was voluptuous and proud of it.

"Looking good, ladies!" Coming up to their table, Memphis Traxell, a big, bluff ginger-skinned man who owned and managed Rocketship, grinned at both of them. "You two sure add great big touches of class to my place. *Love* the knockout outfits you're wearing."

Bea grinned back at him, flirting. "Oh, this old thing," she said, parroting a line from an old movie. "I only wear it when I don't care *how* I look." Dressed in pale yellow with big diamond studs in her earlobes, she was spectacular and knew it.

Memphis leveled his gaze on Janet then and began to say

something when a very tall, rangy man with long, curly dread-locks came up.

"Nick!" Bea exclaimed. "Give me a hug!"

The man smiled, displaying big, white, perfect teeth in a bronze, long, leathery face. He was black-eyed, black-haired, and clean shaven. Janet felt her breath quickening as she looked at him, felt electricity jolting her body again and again. Nick hugged Bea, who watched with keen satisfaction as Janet and Nick looked at each other, and then she introduced them. "I think you two knew one another in some other life," she teased.

Nick took Janet's hand and murmured, "I'm very glad to meet you, Janet. Any friend of Bea's—"

"I'm very glad to meet *you*," Janet said shakily. "Bea talks about you so much." Her hand came alive with his touch. He seemed reluctant to let it go.

Nick stood there, his big body tingling. He met so many women, wined and dined them sometimes. A reticent man, he didn't often get very close, but there'd been a few women in his life. What was there about this one? He stared unabash-edly at Janet's dark brown hair, her thickly black-fringed and beautiful golden brown eyes, and the curved moist lips that begged him to kiss her.

"I have a few minutes before we go on," he told them, "and I wanted to say hello to Bea…and you…" His eyes narrowed and his voice trailed off.

"Nick could never resist a beautiful woman," Memphis said, ragging him.

Nick smiled crookedly. "Oh, I've resisted a few."

"Nick's dad was the late Oscar Redmond, jazz great," Memphis added proudly. "Oscar and I grew up together. Nick's like my own son, so you treat him right," he told Janet.

"I've never been known to mistreat anybody," Janet said easily, then to Nick, "My son loves your music…."

"Good," Nick answered. "What about you?"

Janet blushed. "I think you're a comer, but I only have two of your CDs. I think Marc—that's my son—has everything you've ever recorded. You play a mean guitar and your group's really together."

"Why, thank you, ma'am." Nick's eyes played games with hers. He could imagine that slender, curvy body with its softness pressed against his fit hardness and he was glad he worked out. He hadn't dated in a while. He was too busy.

"The man's going places," Memphis said to Janet. "You'll see. A year or two, and I won't be able to pay his price."

"That'll never happen," Nick said staunchly. His eyes went to Janet's high breasts in her long-sleeved, semi-low-cut garnet *peau de soié* dress. She wore no jewelry save one eighteen-karat gold Wittnauer watch. She had a smattering of freckles across the middle of her face and those golden brown eyes were melting.

"Sit down!" Bea commanded.

He smiled. "No. We'll be going on in a few minutes." By then, mesmerized, he was standing close to where Janet sat. Trust Bea to come up with someone special, he thought.

Now Bea looked at Nick, smiling. Memphis excused himself and began to walk away, saying over his shoulder to Nick, "Now don't get so caught up you forget to go onstage."

Nick threw back his head, laughing, as Bea said, "Nick was my prize pupil when I taught at the Ellington School for the Performing Arts."

"She flatters me," Nick protested.

A light brown-haired, small, slender vision with stunning olive breasts spilling over the top of a tightly fitted black sequin dress swept up to their table and placed a proprietary hand on Nick's arm. "Have you forgotten your first loves?" the woman said.

Janet thought the woman looked to be about twenty-five, as beautiful as nature and modern cosmetology could make her.

Tamara Kyle. Nick introduced her, lingering on Janet's name.

Tamara eased her reed-slender body closer to Nick, and Janet wondered where the heavy breasts grew from, the rest of her was so thin.

"Nick and I go back forever," Tamara murmured.

"You're a great group," Janet complimented them.

"We're trying," Nick said.

"Nick, we'd better go. The guys're looking at us, beckoning us back."

Nick nodded and Tamara's eyes narrowed as she saw the way Nick looked at Janet. Her fingers tightened on his arm. "Honey?"

For a moment, Nick looked annoyed. He leaned over and touched Janet's hand. "I'm so glad to have met you. I'll see you later." He said goodbye to Bea then and he and Tamara moved away and back to the bandstand.

"Star light, star bright, first star I see tonight." Bea chortled. "You're shaking, love."

"You've got a great imagination."

"Oh, and I guess I'm imagining the way you and Nick couldn't quite get your breath, either of you. Tol' ya!"

"Told me what?"

"Don't play dumb. That you'd be drawn to each other."

"You're crazy now where you're usually unusually sane. I'm forty-one, love, and this youngster is *thirty*-one."

Bea expelled a harsh breath and pressed her case. "He looks older than his age and you look younger. I told you he's an old soul. He was born to older parents and he worshipped his grandmother, who had quite a story to tell. You'll love Grace, his mother."

Janet leaned back, holding up a long, slender hand. "Whoa! You're moving ahead at the speed of light. Girlfriend, get ahold of yourself. Besides, it looks as if wunderkind has his hands full with the great Tamara."

Bea shrugged, said thoughtfully, "They once had something going on and they work well together, but he's moved on...."

"*She* certainly hasn't."

"Stop making excuses. Do you like him? Or should I ask, *don't* you like him?"

"He's nice enough. Charming. Well mannered."

"And a hunk."

"I've never been particularly attracted to hunks, especially *young* hunks."

"You might try something different. I've been worried about you, Janet. Your ex, Casey, isn't getting any nicer to you. Your son, Marc, is growing up—and out. You work with your English students—"

"Along with Marc, the loves of my life."

"You need a new distraction. Give Nick a chance."

Janet looked at Bea in wonder. "You're pleading his case. Why?"

Bea shook her head. "No, I'm pleading yours. You're forty-one and you're lonely."

"I'm not..." Janet began to say, but she didn't finish. Instead she licked her lips. She *was* lonely. She sought to change the subject. "I think you like Memphis more than you know, and he's attracted to you."

Bea shrugged. "I've *known* Memphis a long time. The

woman he was about to marry ran off with his daughter's money. Now, his motto is, trust no one but God."

"Memphis is a great guy. That story makes me sad."

"Not half as sad as it makes me."

As they talked, the room had filled up. Nick's combo, Rhapsody, came on in pulsing spotlights beamed across the stage at angles—mostly pastels and beautiful. Nick stood before them in jet-black-beaded velvet. He and Tamara seemed to fit together. Nick introduced the combo, Tamara first. Tamara played guitar and, with Nick, was a lead singer. One other guitarist, a saxophonist, and a keyboard player. You knew to look at them that they'd be hot.

The lights dimmed and the combo played something soft and sensuous, another old Marvin Gaye tune. Nick sang in an indescribably beautiful silken baritone. His voice caught huskily on the sensual lyrics and Janet wondered if she imagined that he looked at her. Did he sing to her? She stared ahead, certain that every woman in the room thought he sang to her alone.

The audience was Rhapsody's from the beginning. Janet thought it was not music they played, but magic, and Nick's group was going to the top where they deserved to be. Entertainment columnists were busy saying it.

The room was hushed when they finished and out of nowhere came the long, lonesome wail of a virtuoso saxophone, playing the bone-deep, weary blues. In a few minutes Nick joined in with his guitar. The crowd went wild. Memphis passed and winked at Janet and Bea, gave them the A-okay sign. Janet sat thinking she had been caught up before in Nick Redmond's music, but she had missed something. The man was superlative, not just good. She hated to hear the song end.

"Uh-oh." Bea drew a deep breath.

Tamara stepped to the microphone. "Love you all," she

courted. "Now, I'm going to sing a song Nick and I wrote together. You'll remember it. 'A Love to Last Always.'"

The crowd cheered and the intimate black velvet voice beguiled them. It was a hot song, written and delivered in passion. The smooth cadence of Tamara's vibrant contralto held them.

Janet smiled grimly. "I said it before. Your young guy's taken."

"That's over," Bea insisted. "Trust me."

Rocketship was located in the Adams-Morgan section of D.C. and was only ten blocks away from Janet's apartment. She pulled into her underground parking space, greeted a security guard on duty, and rode the elevator to her apartment on the eighth floor.

Going in, she felt wired. Catching sight of herself in a full-length mirror in her living room, she smiled. Lonely? She didn't feel lonely anymore. It was warm for September; the air-conditioning was still on. Wouldn't it be wonderful, she thought, if Nick were older, a *real* possibility for her? As it was… She shrugged. She worked with young people, was fond of many of them. Bea had suggested that she and Nick at least be friends. Well—

She sat on an ivory glove-leather sofa and looked around her, keenly mindful of her body that felt more alive than it had in ages. Okay, so Nick Redmond was a hunk. She came in contact with plenty of hunks. He had more going for him. Charm. Talent. He seemed to have depth. She groaned. Why couldn't their ages have met somewhere in the middle? Five years wasn't too bad, but *ten* years… She shook her head. No way.

Her three-bedroom apartment was large, well put together with the help of a decorator. As a master's-level teacher, she made a fair salary and her parents had left her a sizable inheritance. Casey, her ex, had coolly explained that, being well-off, he didn't want his son or his son's mother deprived in any way. She had protested that she had plenty, at least until Marc was through college and whatever additional training he wanted. Domineering, controlling Casey, who had made her life and their son's hell, had explained that he wanted to help. "I want my son to love me, more now than ever. I've made mistakes. Maybe it isn't too late."

Thinking of Marc, Janet smiled and her eyes went to a large photo of him on the end table. He was staying with Casey this weekend and was excited about a high school football game they would watch in Virginia Sunday. Removing her watch and putting it on the end table, she heard the grandfather clock chime one o'clock. She needed to go to bed because she had a writing session with a group of students the next morning. They were working on a book about the successful lives of several people who had overcome formidable odds. Some of the students showed so much talent. She pushed herself and them and they were all proud of the results. This same group had worked on projects before, but this one was special. They intended to look for a publisher.

Only then did she concentrate on her apartment. The living room was done in curved ivory couches, dark brown glove-leather chairs, and extensive pandanus-wood bookcases. Books were everywhere. The plush dark aquamarine carpet felt good under her feet. Touches of red, yellow, blue, and aquamarine accented the décor. It was a calm, peaceful, engaging room, reflecting her personality.

She always smiled at the thirty-gallon aquarium with its bubbles and fancy lighting. Two big golden goldfish swam and flipped about. Getting up, she went to them. "Hot dogs," she chided. One flipped high as if in agreement.

Two waist-high Egyptian urns stood on either side of a long bookcase. Her glance lighted on a large and beautiful carved white jade music box that sat on a curved antique light oak table. It was one of her most prized possessions. Her father, a merchant marine captain, had given it to her as a high school graduation present.

"Value it," he had said. "It comes from Taiwan and is thought to have once been a gift from an emperor to his empress. They were very much in love and had a long and happy life with many children. Jade is said to denote the meaning of life and to bring luck and happiness."

She had always held the precious gift in her heart, a reminder of how much she had loved her father.

Getting up, she walked over to the paneled entertainment center and sliding back a panel, looked for and found one of Marc's many CDs by Nick's group. Their name described them; they *were* rhapsodic. She put on several selections, then walked into her bedroom and began undressing. Pulling back the trapunto-quilted deep rose velvet bedspread, she stroked the rose Egyptian cotton sheets. The wall-to-wall window carried a valance that matched the bedspread. Ivory silk and nylon sheer ninon billowed from the windows. She opened the blinds and gazed out on the peaceful streets with their many lush green trees, awaiting the fall change of color.

She had had only two glasses of wine at Rocketship, but she felt slightly dizzy with excitement. Closing the blinds, she went to her closet and selected a dark rose jersey-fitted robe and gown she hadn't worn in a very long time. She even took down the rose-quilted mules that matched the outfit. "Nothing wrong with looking good for myself," she whispered, and then she chided herself for being silly. Softly and slowly she said to herself, "I can't go back to his age and he can't come up to mine." Besides, there was Tamara, who worked with him and obviously wanted him badly.

She undressed and began a prayer that lasted until she had finished going through the apartment, turning off the CD player, cutting out the lights, and climbing into bed. She always missed Marc when he stayed with Casey. In bed, she sat propped up on pillows, wide awake. Without realizing she did so, she began to hum one of the Marvin Gaye tunes Nick had sung that night. In the darkened room, she reached over, opened the night table drawer, and took out a small vial of lemon verbena essential oil. Dabbing a bit on her wrists and on the pillows, she closed the vial and put it back. The herbal oil often helped her sleep. She thought about calling Bea, but decided against it.

She drifted into a seamless, happy sleep in which she walked through fields of wildflowers, brilliant colors and pastel, wild roses, and wild violets. Big, swirling white clouds hovered. She was alone and she didn't want to be alone, but oh, it was lovely here. The enchanting dream went on and on.

It was a while before she realized the telephone was chiming with melodic bursts of sound. Groggily she picked it up.

It was the night desk clerk. "Mrs. Smith, you have a visitor." The desk clerk's voice was warmly respectful. "A Mr. Redmond…."

Janet sat bolt upright. Nick! Why was he here? The luminous dial on her clock radio reflected two o'clock. Oh, Lord, her eyes were going to be puffy with sleep. She thought about saying she couldn't see him. Her hand touched her soft, silken jersey gown. Had she divined his coming?

"Send him up," she said, "and thank you."

Frantically getting into her robe and mules, she snapped on the lights and went to the mirror. Just awakening was not her best time. She patted her face, decided to stay as she was. He was quick in getting there and she hovered near the door as he sounded her chimes.

When he came in, they didn't speak for a moment. He looked at her, his breathing ragged. Finally he said, "Hello, Janet, and forgive me for disturbing your sleep. You look beautiful."

His piercing black eyes probed her body, searched her very soul. The crisp coal-black dreadlocks framed his handsome bronze face. "I had to come," he said. "I had to know you're real and not a dream. I want you to know I'm *not* a player."

Shocking herself, she couldn't speak and she leaned toward him, heavy with sleep, yet more alive inside than she had ever been. Oh, Lord, she thought fretfully, he was going to think she was easy; then it was like a dream.

It happened in slow motion. His arms went around her, then one arm dropped to her middle back. He held her very tightly before his mouth came down on hers. Through the robe and gown's thin jersey she could feel his hard, muscular body against hers. Her mouth gave way under his tender onslaught and his tongue was inside her mouth, lazily flicking hers for a precious moment; then his lips were against hers so hard her mouth hurt. She pulled him even closer as wildfire swept through them both. Her body burned with pure consuming desire and she felt his hardness assaulting her every sense. This was madness, she thought. This had to stop, but she crept even closer. It didn't have to stop just now.

Momentarily letting go of her body, Nick took her face in his long, sinewy fingers and lightly pressed the pad of his thumb into one outer corner of her mouth. She was avidly responding to his body that begged her for any crumb, and he was ten feet tall. He kissed her very gently then, barely grazing her lips, a slow, tantalizing kiss.

When Janet could get her wits about her, she pulled back.

"I can't say I'm sorry," he said as he stood looking down at her. "I got carried away, but I'm not sorry."

To her surprise, Janet found herself saying, "I'm not sorry either. It's only kisses, Nick. Your generation takes such things lightly."

Nick laughed a low throaty laugh. "*My* generation? We're the same generation, Janet. I know a lot about you from Bea. She encouraged me to come to you this morning."

"Oh, she did, did she? I'm light-years ahead of you."

"Then you can afford to be kind. Clear your calendar because I'm a stubborn man and I intend to see a lot of you. I have powers of persuasion a politician might envy."

Janet drew a deep breath and caught his hand. When she spoke, it was as if to a far younger person than she. "Come and sit down, Nick."

He followed her to a sofa. "I like your aquarium," he said. "I've ordered one. You or a decorator have put together a stunning place."

"Thank you. I'm mostly to blame."

They sat and Nick closed his eyes as he leaned back, and then he took her hand, squeezed it, studied it. "No rings," he finally said. "Bea told me you were divorced. Thank God for small favors."

He swallowed hard as he kept wanting to kiss her again, to feel that sensuous softness melt into him, melding with his own rock hardness.

"Do you believe in fate?" he asked her.

"Sometimes, but I'm a pretty pragmatic person."

"When I saw you tonight, something came together in me. In the back of my mind, all my adult years I've had a mental image of someone like you. You remind me of people I've known and loved. My mother will tell you that when you meet her."

Janet looked at him and laughed with surprise. "I hardly think your mother would approve of us."

His eyes nearly closed. "You don't know my mother. But you will."

"Nick?"

"Yes."

"You're a romantic—and you're young. Find someone your own age, or closer in age, anyway. Forget about me. Forget the kisses."

Again his hands held her face, forced her to study him, study the bronze skin and his intense look.

"Can *you* forget the kisses?" he asked softly, then demanded, "*Can* you?"

She thought about his question for a long while before she answered, still surprised at herself. Where was her trusted reticence, her reserve? "No, I'll never forget the way we kissed each other. It was beautiful."

"Then, don't rob us of more like that."

She hunched her shoulders, seeking a lighter vein. "For all you know," she said, "I could have had a lover here."

He shook his head. "You looked too lonely at Rocketship to have a lover. Look to the future, Janet. When you're ninety-one, I'll be eighty-one. It won't matter then. It doesn't matter now."

"Wishful thinking won't make it so."

"And your thinking it matters doesn't make that so, either. We're deeply drawn to each other. *Both* of us. It's not just me. See me again; see me often. Give me a chance to plead my case. I'm going to insist on it. I'm not going to let you go."

Janet sat with a sense of wonder filling her. Her body felt relaxed and heavy. "I can't stop you," a romantic inside her that matched the one in him told him.

"Good. That's a start. Bea's right. We've met in some other life."

"You're hopeless," she teased him.

"No, I'm full of hope for us."

She sat up, thinking how much she wished they were lovers and he could spend the night. "I think you know I want to stay longer," he said, "but I'll let you get some sleep."

His eyes fell on the white jade music box. "Exquisite," he told her.

She told him about the background of the music box. "It plays 'O Holy Night.'"

"Great choice," he commented, "and that's a great story."

"I display it from about this time of year through the holidays."

"Are you a holiday person?"

"Oh, yes, I love the whole season. What's your favorite thing about it?"

He thought awhile and chuckled as his eyes held hers. "After the wonderful spirit of the season, mistletoe," he told her. "*Kisses* and mistletoe."

She smiled. "Then I don't need to be flattered. Kisses are your groove. No wonder you're so good at it."

He was silent a long moment. "Our kisses were special, Janet. *Very* special. I've never felt anything move me like what moves me tonight. I think it was special for you, too. Our kisses will get deeper and ever better, but that was the beginning." He shook his head, closed his eyes. "And God, what a glorious beginning."

Chapter 2

Next morning, Janet met five of her senior English students at Horton High in upper Northwest. She had brought doughnuts and Danish pastries, and had fixed varied sandwiches for the group of them. Now at nine o'clock, five bright, eager faces and bodies fanned around her: Monk, Daryl, Eileen, Lily, and Myra.

"Hey, I know you said you would," Monk, a lanky seventeen-year-old bar of chocolate, said, grinning, "but I never expected this spread."

The girls oohed and aahed, got paper flowered napkins Janet had brought, and began eating.

Janet smiled. "Don't rush, but let's get it together and get our show on the road."

She quickly scanned her mind about the project they worked on. Monk and Myra had come to her with the suggestion that they write a book, selecting people who had overcome severe adversity and succeeded. The school year had just begun and they were still in the selection and planning stage. They would meet each Saturday until the project was completed.

"Listen," Monk said urgently to the group, "I've got an idea. We've been calling this thang of ours *'Overcoming Adversity.'* I think a catchier title would be *'Don't Let Anything Keep You Down.'* Then put *'Overcoming Adversity'* in parens. What think you?"

The group mulled it over a few minutes as they relished their food. "I like it," Janet said. "Why don't we take a vote?"

All five hands went up. Monk usually won. He was one of the brightest students she had ever taught. Now he grinned widely. "All *right!*"

The prim, calla lily-colored Myra, who favored Monk, sat up straight. "My mom's got a friend who's an editor in New York for a small publishing firm. I heard her mention our project to this lady over the phone and Mom told me the lady liked the idea. So maybe we've got a publisher."

"Way to go, babe," Daryl, the only other boy in the group, said, supporting her.

Janet smiled at their vivid enthusiasm. This was going to be fun. Now she said, "Thanks for checking about, Myra, but we've got a long way to go before we publish."

Myra shrugged. "We can always self-publish."

The food was quickly finished and the boxes stacked to be taken outside. Lily went out to refill the big stainless steel water pitcher, took a while, and came back with a carton full of six sodas from the hallway soft drink machine outside the cafeteria.

"You're reading my mind," Eileen, the third of three girls, said.

Janet shook her head. "I'll take mine home for my son. I let him drink them from time to time, but I've sworn off."

Monk groaned. "The health police are going to kill us. Give me Wendy's and Popeye's and McDonald's. There's nothing I like better than a Slurpee Coke or Seven-Up." He closed his eyes. "Just leave me with my grub and let me die happy."

Janet looked at him, laughing. "You're too young to be throwing your life away on fast food. I hope you're hitting the salad bar with a vengeance."

Myra grimaced. "He does, you know. He's a regular veggie animal. He even eats spinach salad and asparagus."

Janet bit her bottom lip. "Then thank heaven for that."

Brown plastic-covered writing tablets the group had assembled were opened. Janet got up and went to the blackboard.

Picking up a piece of chalk she wrote in her fine script, *Suggestions for people to be studied.*

Daryl held up his hand. "I've got a prospect who goes to my church. He's a deacon and his name's Ward Cater."

Janet wrote the name, then asked, "Background?"

"He's one of ten children and his father died when he was young, thirteen, I think. Three years later, his mother become bedridden with complications of diabetes. She had always worked to support the family. Then Ward had to go to work and he took what he could get."

Janet wrote and summarized.

"We'll go into this more deeply later," she said. "What further steps did he take and what was the outcome?"

Daryl hunched his thin shoulders. "The great outcome was that the church helped and he kept working and finally was able to go to college, taking care of his mother, his sibs, working, *and* studying. Lucky for him, he's a computer nerd. Now he's got his own business and he's *flying*. He's married and buying his family and his mother a new house and he does make the long green. He's gonna be livin' large."

"Love that story," Eileen said. "It sure gets my vote as one of the top picks."

Each student had someone in mind. They spoke briefly and Janet wrote each person's selection on the blackboard. "You know these aren't cast in concrete," she said. "I think each of you should make two selections and—"

"You gotta make a couple, too," Monk said.

"I'll consider it, but it's your project."

"*Our* project," Myra said firmly.

Around eleven, they were winding down making plans for the next week. "Hey," Monk said, "it'd be a good thing if we got the people we select to come and talk to us. That way we could get their karma."

"Sounds good to me," Janet said and the others agreed.

At a light tap on the door, Janet wondered who it was and called out, "Come in." Her heart began a wild staccato drumming as Bea stood in the doorway, with Nick's tall form behind her.

"Hey, hey!" Monk chortled. "It's the gee-tar wizard, my man Nick Redmond."

Nick grinned widely and looked directly at Janet, who wondered if others could hear the thunder of her heartbeats.

"I knew it was about time for you all to wind up," Bea said. "Nick was visiting and I thought about lesson plans I'd left unfinished in my desk." She glanced at Janet, looking roguish.

"You told me and I see from the blackboard what you're working on. My friend here would be a good candidate. Talk about adversity."

"You—and adversity?" Daryl's tea-brown face had frown lines. "Man, you're the coolest guy we know. Talk to us."

From the time Nick and Bea had entered, Myra had gone into a trance. Now she murmured to herself, "Talk about your African *gods!*"

"Sit down. We're willing to stay awhile longer," Daryl told Nick and Bea, then looked at Janet. "We can, can't we? I know I got nowhere better to go."

Nick was the flame, his students and Janet were the moths, and Janet thought, *I am the biggest moth of all. He really is charming.* His kiss so early that morning clung to her mind, wouldn't let her go, and suddenly she thought, *I won't see him again. The students know he belongs to them. He's on their wavelength.*

"Tell us about this adversity you've had," Lily said. "Tell us a little bit anyway. You know for sure we're gonna ask you back. I've got every CD you ever cut. Love ya!"

"Thank you," Nick said humbly. He and Bea sat down.

"Talk!" Monk demanded.

Nick stroked his chin. "I won't go into details, but my father died when I was a teenager—fifteen—"

"Yeah, I read your dad was Oscar Redmond, jazz wonder," Monk said.

"He was and he was a great dad. The year after he died, I was thrown from a horse and sustained spinal injuries." He hesitated, remembering. "The doctors said I'd never walk again…."

The students' faces were full of consternation and sympathy. "What a bummer," Daryl said.

Now Nick said, "My mom wasn't going to let that happen. She prayed with me, worked with me, tutored me. I went to almost daily physical therapy. It was two years before I took my first steps, but we hung in there. I've got a very slight limp."

"I think you're perfect," Lily breathed as Janet and Bea and the others laughed.

"And I think you're all perfect," Nick said gallantly. His eyes swept them before his glance rested on Janet.

"You don't need to write the summary of his story down," Lily said, making a fainting gesture. "I've got it written in my heart."

Nick gave Lily his widest smile as Janet sat reflecting that customers in Rocketship had been nearly hysterical over this man. Now the students were—what?—well, *worshipping* him. She didn't care that much for celebrities. What few she had come across had been vain, egotistical, but Nick Redmond certainly seemed different. Looking at him, she couldn't help wondering how his wickedly curved, hot mouth would feel in the hollows of her throat, on her breasts. She blushed vividly as the thought fastened in her mind. Bea grinned at her as if she knew exactly what she was thinking.

"You *will* come back?" Lily asked. "I study the saxophone and I know your group has one saxophone player. Tell him I may be moving him aside one day."

Nick laughed heartily. "I'll do that."

The students seemed reluctant to leave when the door opened. Casey and Marc came in. Janet's eyes went to her lanky, all-spice-brown son with his close-cropped black hair and black eyes. He was a good kid and she was so proud of him. "Surprise, Mom," he said in his still changing voice. "Dad and I are going out to White Flint Mall. We thought you just might like to tag along."

Janet shook her head. "I have other plans, but thanks for asking. Let me introduce you two to Nick Redmond."

"Heck, I'd know you anywhere," Marc told Nick as both grinned and shook hands. "You a friend of Miss Bea?"

"Yes, I am."

"Nick, I want you to meet Marc's father, Casey Smith." Janet deliberately presented Casey to Nick, giving Nick the advantage. Was it a mean-spirited thing to do? Well, Casey was no stranger to mean-spirited things.

For a moment, she thought Casey wouldn't shake hands. He hated entertainers, but he finally extended his hand, saying gruffly, "Nice meeting you."

The lone security guard, on duty when someone was in the school on weekends, swung in and briefly greeted them, asked how much longer they'd be staying.

"We're leaving shortly," Janet told him.

Casey frowned, looking anxious when he saw Bea and Nick would be staying until Janet left.

"May I talk with you a moment?" Casey asked Janet.

She nodded and followed him out into and down the wide corridor. Stopping near a window, he studied her intently and she glanced at him. Casey was a reddish brown, dark red-haired man with a fairly tall, stocky body and a grim expression. His brown eyes were flat. Why had she married him? They hadn't been in love, but he had pursued her relentlessly. A contractor, he bought, renovated, and sold family homes and apartment buildings and was fairly wealthy. Real estate was his passion; he had little time for people.

Now she faced him and his smile was downbeat, crooked. "You look happy, Janet. Would the clown in your classroom have anything to do with that?"

Janet came back at him. "Don't be juvenilely jealous, Casey. It doesn't add anything."

"He looks way too young for you and you haven't answered my question."

"I won't answer your question," she found herself saying without intending to, "Have you ever known me to be interested in younger men?"

He licked dry lips. "I can't say I have, but that's the past. Women's lib's ruined you chicks. You think every man's fair game. Don't make a fool of yourself. You've got a son to consider."

She was going to let him have it again. "Thanks for the excellent advice I always get from you," she said sarcastically. "Give me credit for being pretty levelheaded."

Chapter 3

That afternoon Janet lay on the couch in stonewashed blue jeans and a red T-shirt, one barefooted leg propped along the couch back. She worked with a batch of lesson plans for the week and knew she should sit at a table, but lassitude had overtaken her. Was Nick Redmond as handsome as he seemed? She realized then that she wasn't all that taken over his physical looks. No, it was the charisma of the man, the intelligence, the bone-deep sensuality. Her blood still ran hot from seeing him that early and later morning.

She picked up the phone on the first ring, said hello, to hear a melodious older woman's voice. "You don't know me, my dear, but I'm Grace Redmond, Nick Redmond's mother."

"Oh, hello!"

"I hope I'm not interrupting anything."

"Nothing that I can't go right back to."

"Good." The woman hesitated a moment. "Nick's talked to me about you. He seems quite taken with you."

"I met him only last night."

Grace chuckled. "My son has always known what he's wanted and gone after it."

"I was very impressed with him. Great personality. Wonderful voice. He's going places."

"I expect so, but he's not just interested in fame and fortune; he wants a *life*."

Janet laughed. "Don't we all?"

"Nick tells me you're an English teacher at Horton High. I retired as a guidance counselor for a high school in Montgomery County, Maryland. Now I work part-time with at-risk kids, runaways, abandoned kids.... I'm coming into Adams Morgan tomorrow shortly after noon. I want to pick up some material from an art gallery. I was going to wait to ask you, but I don't get into D.C. much. Are you free? Could we have lunch—your choice of places?"

Janet felt pleasantly surprised. "I'd like that very much. You sound like an interesting person to know. Why don't *you* choose a place?"

"All right. What about El Bodegon, the Spanish restaurant? I like their food."

"Oh, so do I. Do you like flan?"

"Love it. Could I pick you up?"

"It's not too far from here. I'll meet you there. Is one o'clock okay?"

"Perfect. You don't seem like a stranger at all. You're charming. I don't wonder my son is in a rush to know you better." She laughed a little. "I must say I'm a little surprised. Nick is usually reticent. I look forward to seeing you. I'll be wearing a gray and small-white-flowered suit. I'll park and meet you in front of the café."

Janet described herself and what she would be wearing, then said, "I'm so glad you called."

"I'm glad I called, too. I was going to delay a few days, but life is so short and when you get older, it's shorter. See you tomorrow."

Janet paced the floor, reveling in the deep plush carpet about her feet. She didn't think Nick had told his mother about coming by the night before. Nick probably hadn't told her Janet's age; as Bea said, she looked younger. But she didn't intend to hide it at all. If Mrs. Redmond didn't approve, so much the better, because Janet thought she didn't need this younger man baggage.

She flopped onto the couch. The lesson plans could wait until later; she was too keyed up. Going to her bedroom closet, she examined clothes and selected a navy crepe fall suit with deep white faille cuffs and a matching white collar that folded over and buttoned down. It was one of her favorite outfits, but she felt it was a bit dressy for these casual-wear times. Grace Redmond could be her ally about talking some sense into Nick.

When the phone rang again, she answered with a gay lilt.

"The more I see you," Nick began and stopped. "Remember that song?"

"Oh, *I* remember it, but it came along before your time."

"Rub it in. I've got total recall for songs I hear and like and I've liked that one a long time. My mother will be calling you, Janet. I asked her to meet you. Give her a few days."

"She just called."

Nick laughed. "Atta girl, Ma."

"She sounds interesting. We've having lunch tomorrow at a nearby restaurant."

"Thanks, Janet." His voice was husky.

"For what? I like pleasant weekend lunches. You call her 'Ma'?"

"Yeah. If you like weekend lunches, I'd like to treat you to a few in a number of special places. What's your favorite cuisine?"

Janet thought for a moment. "There're so many. One of them is Spanish. Any good American food. Soul food. Candied yams and deep-fried catfish, collard greens, crackling corn bread, all the heart attack foods, but I only eat them once in a while."

"You're coming in on my territory. I'm a good cook, Janet. I think I can please you in many ways."

"I hear music in the background. You're rehearsing."

"We are. We've got a couple of new songs. I've started working on a song: 'What I Want From You.' I'll sing it for you when I get further along on it."

"I'll wait impatiently."

"You mean that?"

"I do. I love music—and you're the best."

A high, lyrical voice in the background called Nick's name, said, "You're holding up production."

"Tamara?" Janet asked. "Don't let me keep you."

"Yes, Tamara, who can really be a spoiled brat."

"You work with your group," Janet said slowly. "They're your friends. Don't let me hold up production."

"You can hold up anything I have."

"I like your mother."

"You're going to like her even better. You two are alike. Oh, she's much older, but you're so much alike."

"She's not that much older."

"She is, you know. Stop aging yourself."

Tamara called Nick again and the edge to her voice was unmistakable.

"Go," Janet told him. "I'll understand."

"You're sweet. We're working late tonight. Would you and Bea like to come by again?"

"Thanks, but I'm bushed. I did some cleaning."

"Let me come by tomorrow afternoon or evening, whichever is best for you."

"Either is fine."

"Do you like zoos?" he asked.

"Love them, especially the pandas."

"Good, because I want to take you and Marc. He's a great kid."

"We'll talk about it," Janet said evenly, "and thank you for liking Marc. He's hung up on you. Now go, Nick. I don't want to read about a murder at Rocketship."

He chuckled. "I guess I'd better. See you tomorrow."

"You're a lovely young woman," Grace said immediately on meeting Janet. "I'm good at connecting people with their voices and I got you just right. I'm so pleased to meet you, and do call me Grace."

Janet laughed happily. "You're *so* attractive." She admired the smartly coiffed medium-cut silver hair and the unlined, soft mocha skin. Grace wore the gray flowered silk-and-cotton suit with a model's flair. Small silver dome earrings hugged her shell-like ears.

Inside the elegant restaurant with its white damask, its silver and china and crystal, Grace asked for and was given a seat near the windows. "I like to watch the passing throng," she said. The restaurant sat near a couple of pale gray-barked sycamore trees.

They sipped white wine and nibbled on corn sticks. Grace kept looking at Janet and smiling. "Nick said you have a son."

"Yes, I'm divorced. My ex shares custody."

"I always wanted a daughter. Do you want more children?"

Janet looked at her levelly. "It's getting late for that. Marc's a handful. I'm going to be frank. I'm forty-one. Did Nick tell you that?"

Grace smiled drolly and nodded. "Yes. He's thirty-one. Ten little years."

"You sound like Bea."

"A wise woman."

"You'd have no problem with my getting closer to Nick?"

A beautifully composed Grace answered her forthrightly, "None whatever. Times change, Janet. The world is moving on. Men have always courted and married much younger women. Nick's different. He's so mature. He's always known what he wanted. He's an old soul."

Janet nodded. "That's what Bea says about him."

"Are you attracted to my son? Oh, I know you just met, but are you attracted? He certainly is. He's never asked me to intercede with someone before."

Janet's breath came swiftly. "I'd be lying if I said I'm not attracted. He's not just a hunk, he's an unusual man. Be proud of yourself."

"I am. He took it so hard when he lost his father. When he was so badly hurt and the doctors said he wouldn't walk again, he never gave up."

"He gives you so much credit."

"We worked together. We always have. He's wanted me to marry again, but there has been no one I've wanted."

Janet held her glass too tightly, her fingers pressing against the stem. "I've got to think it over carefully."

"He's going to keep pressing you—hard. He believes in fate. Do you?"

"Sometimes. Not always."

"Were you in love with your husband? Did your breakup hurt?"

Janet shook her head. "I wasn't in love. I wanted to get married. All my friends were getting married and I wanted at least one child."

"That's understandable. My relationship with my late husband and with Nick has been so precious to me. Be honest with him, Janet." She leaned forward. "He's a very honest man. Tell him you need breathing room, space, time to make up your mind. He usually has a gift for choosing what's right for him. I trust his judgment."

Now Grace stopped and smiled slowly. "My, my, here I am rushing you too. I want to relieve your mind on the age count though. His paternal grandmother was a nurse and she married a man twenty years younger than she—back then, people were scandalized. He was a powerful, fiery minister and she was a petite beauty. My husband loved his stepfather and they were all happy. She outlived her husband by fifteen years. Nick and she adored each other. So you see, there are reasons he's attracted. Oh, you're tall, lissome where she was tiny, but the similarities are there."

The waiter served their dinner of stuffed leg-of-lamb with mint jelly, couscous, asparagus with hollandaise sauce, summer squash, and a colorful garden salad. They ate in companionable silence for a while before Grace asked, "What are you doing this afternoon?"

"Not much. Why do you ask?"

"I'd like to take you home with me to the house where Nick grew up. I think you'd love it out there. Stay only as long as you like. There'll be other times and I'll bring you back early, if you choose. I'll understand if you're too busy."

Janet knew instantly that she wanted to go. "I have lesson plans I can do tomorrow," she said. "I'll do it. Thank you for asking me."

"Thank *you.*"

They were both too full to eat the sliced strawberry and heavy cream-covered flan, so the waiter packed a box and they took it with them.

Out on the highway, Grace drove her Porsche expertly, hitting Wisconsin Avenue going toward Rockville. Grace lived a few miles out in the countryside. Finally, they pulled into a yard surrounded by a tall, white picket fence. Trellised roses were everywhere.

"How charming!" Janet exclaimed, taking in the old-fashioned white country house with its gingerbread trim. There was a wide hall in the middle and four big rooms on each side. A front porch with carved banisters stretched across and wrapped halfway around the side.

"Nick always loved it out here. I wanted him to live with me, but he values his independence."

They sat in a blue, plastic-cushioned swing on the front porch with a massive oak nearby. "I'm going to take the flan inside," Grace said. "Should I show you the house now, or would you prefer to wait?"

"I think I'll wait a little while," Janet told her. "It's so wonderfully peaceful out here. I certainly don't get enough country air."

Alone, Janet sat thinking the place was like Nick himself— special. Out in the yard there was a fieldstone fishpond and big golden goldfish leaping about. She was lost in thought when Grace came back with an album of photographs.

"I thought you might like to see these."

Janet loved looking at photographs. Now she and Grace sat

side by side in the swing, leafing through the heavy pages. She had seen photos of Oscar Redmond, an attractive, gifted, proud, and highly intelligent man. Grace had retained so much of her youthful beauty. And Nick. Oh, he was adorable from the naked baby picture taken as he lay on his stomach on a white polar-bear-skin rug, to his calm, sincere gaze as a younger man.

"And this," Grace said, pausing at a picture of a spirited black horse, "is Darby." Her voice was strained as she spoke. "We all loved Darby. I don't know how it happened. He was usually so surefooted, but he stumbled on a fairly large boulder, Nick told us, on a new woodland path. Our son's injuries were devastating." She was silent a long time. "But with so much hard work, he finally recovered. At first, doctors thought we might lose him. Then as I told you, they didn't think he'd walk again."

"I'm so sorry," Janet murmured. "He was lucky to have parents like you two."

Grace shook her head. "He was lucky to be born the person he was. Nick is a fighter. Now can you understand why I believe in what he wants for himself? He has a nearly divine gift for making the right choices. Oh, he's made a few mistakes. There've been people I thought he'd be better off without, but they always parted company and he went on with his life."

Janet wondered then about Nick and Tamara and how deep that relationship went. Did Grace like Tamara?

Grace flexed sturdy fingers. "I'm very proud of my son. I love him very much. He is so like his father."

"And like *you*."

A joyful feeling settled on Janet as she looked at the photographs. How different this marriage had been from her own with Casey. Now Marc lived with the heated divisiveness of Casey and her, and it tore at him, which meant it tore at *her.*

"Tell me about yourself," Grace said as she patted Janet's knee. "You're such an attractive woman, so gracious… What turns you on?"

And Janet talked freely, warmly. About her son, Marc, her students, her failed marriage. How long had it been since she'd talked with anyone like this? And it occurred to her that not since her mother's death ten years ago had she opened up and talked about her life.

When she had finished, Grace smiled. "Your vivid enthusiasm about your son, your students, reminds me of myself. I'm going to a conference in Chicago in early November. I understand they've assembled a wonderful panel of experts on at-risk kids. I'm keenly looking forward to it."

Grace showed her around the five-acre place with its flower and vegetable gardens. "We wanted Nick to have a special place to grow up in."

Janet nodded. "It's very clear to me although I've known him only hours that he got the best from both of you and he passes it on to others."

"Well put. If for some reason—although I hope you will— if you and Nick don't work out, I hope you'll still want to be friends with both of us. I think I said I've always wanted a daughter. I'm like Nick, impulsive, but deeply reasonable. I, too, know what I like when I see it."

"I'm flattered that you'd ask. I find myself liking you more than I've liked anyone for a very long time."

Janet blushed then, thinking of Nick and the powerful surges of joy he awakened in her.

"I'm glad. My son has excellent taste."

They ate their strawberry-covered flan on a small sunporch

with afternoon sunlight streaming in. The dessert plates were Limoges china and Janet remarked on how beautiful the flower-patterned cutouts were.

"These were my grandmother's," Grace said. "They were not wealthy, but she saved and purchased lovely items. She loved beauty." Then, shifting subjects, she asked, "You've seen Nick perform?"

"Yes, and he's really good. I've rarely heard a more beautiful voice."

"He's sung since he was a very small boy. I think that helped him pull through the accident. Do you like his group?"

"They're very good, as well. They seem close."

Grace seemed to begin to say something else, but fell silent. Drawing a deep breath, she murmured, "It helps us know and understand people when we study where and what they came from. If you enjoyed our time together as I have, then let's do it again—soon. Don't stand on ceremony. Pick up the phone and call me anytime. You'll find me a dedicated and ardent listener."

"That statement certainly warms me," Janet told her, reflecting that she wasn't usually this ebullient.

As they drove back into D.C., Janet complimented her on the Porsche. "It was a Mother's Day present from Nick. He didn't think I was sporty enough."

Janet laughed. "I'm not a sporty person at all."

"Oh, he means sophisticated, knowledgeable. You're quiet and you're gentle and somewhat self-effacing, but you're *highly* sophisticated in the best sense of the word. You always see beyond the usual. I'd bank on that."

Chapter 4

At home that same afternoon, Janet changed to dark blue jersey lounging pajamas and fastened a narrow, beautiful silver bracelet onto her wrist. Nick was coming by at four-thirty; Casey usually brought Marc back around seven. Thinking she might as well look over her lesson plans, she sat at a table. "Damn!" she murmured. She had forgotten to pick up Friday and Saturday's mail. It wasn't like her to be so absentminded.

Glancing at her watch, she got up, went out and down to the mailbox. Opening the big box that could hold small packages, she saw they had little mail. Marc had ordered a video game from Marvel Comics and she shook the box, fervently hoping it wasn't too violent or too sexy.

She looked around the corner at the desk clerk and waved. The friendly older woman waved back and Janet's breath caught as she saw Nick being buzzed in. She stood transfixed as she waited for him, thrilling at his tall form addressing the clerk, then catching sight of her and waving.

"Janet," was all he said when he reached her, and her heart turned over. He carried a very long, narrow white florist's box, which he handed her.

"Hello, Nick. Thank you."

He grinned as he looked her over. "You look lovely. Huggable. Kissable." He smiled as his eyes nearly closed. "Edible." The last word was barely audible. "I'm early. Do you mind?"

"Not at all."

"They say being early means you're anxious, late that you're hostile and pretty much on time that you try to operate on an even keel."

She chuckled. "I've been all three. You look—great."

They walked down the wide, deep blue-carpeted hall and he stopped halfway to the elevator. "Thank you. I put myself together just for you."

Janet raised her eyebrows. He *did* look good. Navy gabardine sports jacket, dark cream English flannel trousers, and an open-at-the-throat lighter cream Egyptian cotton shirt. She admired the expensive, black tasseled Gucci loafers. He really was a hunk and he seemed totally unaware of it.

In her apartment, he went directly to the aquarium.

"Names?" he inquired.

"Flip and Floppy," she answered pertly, "and I'll tell you why. Flip is the big male, dominant, of course. He loves to come up for food and jump way up, getting at least a few drops of water on me. His mate, Floppy, also is not always the demure female. You said you had ordered an aquarium."

"Yeah. This one's nice. Would you like to help me set mine

up? If I'd known I was going to meet you, I'd have asked you to go with me to select it."

She found a very tall vase, filled it with water, and opened the packet of cut-flower life extender that came with the flower. Lifting the exquisite black-red rose and fern from the box, she sniffed the delightful perfume.

Going back to Nick, she saw he seemed restless as she told him, "Make yourself at home." She went to the already open entertainment center and loaded a few of Rhapsody's CDs onto it. As the music played softly he smiled at her.

"That's quite a compliment putting our music on."

In a few minutes Tamara's husky, sexy contralto purred a come-onna-my-house set of lyrics and Janet wasn't sure this *had* been such a good idea. The less she was reminded of Tamara Kyle, the better.

Janet found her breath kept catching in her throat. She sat down first and Nick sat fairly close to her.

"Did you hear from Ma?"

"We had lunch this afternoon at El Bodegon and she took me out to the house you were raised in. Nick, I had a wonderful time. Your mother's quite a lady."

"Talk about moving fast. I thought she'd call sometime next week. Like you, she's a busy woman. I haven't been home and my cell phone's been cut off. We often like the same people…" He paused before he finished. "But not always. Would you like to go out to dinner?"

Janet shook her head. "We overdid it at lunch, which was really dinner. We took our dessert to her house, which by the way, I love. I saw wonderful photos of you and your family. You were certainly loved."

"For which I'm grateful and try to pass it on." His voice fell and a wry smile rested on his face. "When I'm permitted."

Her heart skipped a beat. "Why don't you take off your jacket? It's warm in here."

He sat up, shucked the jacket, which she took and hung in the hall closet. Going past the table where the single black-red rose sat in majestic beauty in a tall Steuben bud vase, nestled in maidenhair green fern, she lightly touched the flower.

"Where did you find flowers on a Sunday?"

"A place in Georgetown that isn't open, but I know the owner. I leaned on him for past favors he owes me for."

"What can I get you to eat or drink?" she asked as she stood before him.

Looking at her beautifully rounded form, Nick felt his body go rigid with hot desire. Somehow he knew, felt deeply what she would be like beneath him, and a sudden vision nearly consumed him. He saw that she was trying to be cool, reserved, and in an instant he felt he knew that beneath her warm, pleasant, womanly exterior lay extraordinary passion that went far beyond the physical.

She saw a strange and marvelously happy expression on his face and wondered. Looking at his well-developed biceps and wide shoulders in the cotton shirt, she felt slightly dizzy. His face reflected more tenderness than she had ever known. To steady herself, she asked again, "Can I get you anything to eat or—"

This time he was quick on the uptake. "I went by Popeye's for popcorn shrimp, so I'm pretty full, but I didn't have dessert. Anything you've got that's sweet I'd be grateful for. What if I come with you?"

"Be my guest."

In the kitchen done in yellow enamel and stainless steel, she knew exactly what she'd serve him: Ben and Jerry's chocolate chip cookie ice cream and a chocolate swirl pound cake she'd made a couple of days back.

She told him what she proposed to serve, then asked him teasingly, "Does this hit you where you live?"

"Bring it on," he answered huskily. "I'll show you that it does."

She dished up the ice cream, ran it in the oven to thaw slightly, and sliced the cake, arranging it in and on sparkling cut glassware. He wanted only water to drink.

"Aren't you eating anything?" he asked.

Janet laughed. "Remember, I told you about the extra-delicious flan. It will be days before I crave dessert again."

"Don't watch your weight. I'll watch it for you."

"You're a very fresh man."

"And you don't like fresh men."

"I like *you*." Janet jumped a little; she hadn't meant to say that. She did and said things with this man she didn't intend to do and say.

"I'm glad because *like* doesn't begin to describe what I'm feeling."

She put her head to one side watching him enjoy his food, getting vicarious pleasure from him. "Are you always this impulsive?"

He stopped eating and looked at her. "No. I'm not sure what's gotten into me."

"You're young. Have you been deeply involved often?" She chided herself. They were *not* deeply involved.

"Only once or twice before, never very happily." He looked a bit sad now.

"Doesn't that tell you something? Doesn't it make you anxious?"

He toyed with his nearly finished dessert. "I didn't rush in those times at all. I took due time. You and I—we're different from others, Janet. Can't you feel that?"

Janet smiled. "You mean we're fated?"

"Maybe. Just open and let me in your heart a little bit. I won't hurt you."

Not until then did she respond to his statement.

"You won't *mean* to hurt me."

He had finished his dessert.

"Want more?" she asked.

He shook his head. "That was delicious and I'm brimful. You bake a sumptuous pound cake."

She sat with him a few minutes before she picked up the dishes, walked over, and put them in the sink.

"I'll wash them," he offered.

She quickly rinsed the dishes and left them in the basin. "No need. Living with Marc teaches me not to be the world's best housekeeper."

At the kitchen door they paused. She leaned against the wall, still dizzy with his presence. Her knees felt weak. He came close and propped a long arm over her head against the wall. She almost groaned aloud. Dear God, what kind of passion was this? These feelings were new to her. She was forty-one, had lived without them, didn't need them now. Every cell in her screamed *Danger!* He was going to kiss her again and she wanted to flee his magic.

But he lowered his arm. "You're scared and I don't blame you. I'm scared, too. But we need to know what we can have together...."

"If anything," she said staunchly.

"We'll see." He ran a long finger over her lips, touched the corners of her mouth. "Relax. I'm not going to kiss you again until you ask me to."

"Fair enough," she said shakily, relieved but half sick with hunger for him.

He drew a deep breath. "I want you to come over to my place soon and I'll cook for you. I told you I'm a damned good cook. You said you like soul food and I swing a wicked soul skillet. Bring Marc if you'd like."

"Thank you. He's with his father on weekends."

"Then you'll come."

"I'd love to come," she said slowly, wondering at herself. She wanted to hold back, wait, be safe. She wasn't a risk-taker and she thought with a tinge of bitterness, *Fools rush in....*

"Hey, Mom!" The front door slammed and an ebullient Marc came bounding in calling, "Mom, where are you? Dad dropped me off early." He came into the kitchen.

"Hello, Marc."

Marc's mouth fell open and he nearly dropped the packages he held. Backing up and pitching the packages onto a living room chair, he strode forward, arm extended. Nick took his hand, shook it with a firm grip. "I'm glad to see you again."

Marc finally got his voice. "Oh, man, am I glad I came home early! You're a friend of Miss Bea's."

"I am and I hope I'll be yours and your mother's, too."

"Well, I'm sure willing. Mom?"

Janet wet suddenly dry lips. "We'll see. Did you have a good weekend?"

The boy enthusiastically told her about the high school football game they'd seen and the awesome shopping malls they'd visited. "Of course," he said regretfully, "I wanted to go to the zoo. Dad *hates* zoos."

Janet ruffled the boy's hair. "I'll take you one weekend soon."

Nick cleared his throat. "I'd like to take you both. I'm off much of the day Sundays and Mondays. What d'you say?"

"Oh, *man!* You'd do that?"

"I'll do it and be delighted. I'm a panda lover."

"Me, too. Listen, Mom got me a guitar last Christmas. I'm studying all week and Dad doesn't care too much about music. Tell me a good music teacher?"

Marc was fishing; he wanted a *certain* music teacher: Nick.

Nick laughed delightedly. "Would I do?"

Marc was beside himself with joy; his eyes danced. "You'd do that for me? I know my drums, but I'm crazy about guitars and I don't know squat about them."

"Why don't you show me your guitar?" Nick asked.

Marc fairly flew from the room and Nick grinned, put his head to one side. "So, I'm insinuating myself into your life. Dinner. The zoo. Guitar lessons. Let it happen, Janet. We'll both be happy you did."

Chapter 5

It was two weeks before Nick and Janet could keep the zoo date. Marc came down with early-season flu and it lingered; he was out of school. Janet stayed with him until he felt able to be by himself. A doctor friend of a friend had come to check on him and advised that he completely heal before going back to school.

Nick came by often, even when he could only stay briefly. Once he brought his guitar and played for them. "Get well," he said to Marc, "and we'll start the lessons."

Marc was too enthralled to keep it to himself. He told Casey, who came often, too, and Casey exploded. "That musician isn't the role model I want for my son!"

"Casey," Janet had said stubbornly, "Nick Redmond is a nice man. The fact that he's a musician is in his favor. He's talented—very—and he's highly trained."

"Yeah," Casey had grunted. "And I'll bet his songs are one half step away from pornography. Trash!"

"No, Dad," Marc had protested, "Nick doesn't do it that way. He's in the sweet class. They do love songs. Soft and sweet."

"I'll bet." Away from Marc, Casey had fussed with Janet. "That guy's too young for you. What's gotten into you, Janet? You used to be so sensible. I want you to stop seeing this clown and unless you do…"

"Unless I do?" Janet's glance had been steely.

Casey had sighed. "I'm gonna have to go back to court, ask if I can get control of my son. I sure don't plan to sit by and let your debauched friends and lifestyle ruin him."

His words had struck fear in her heart. He had looked for ways to have fuller custody of Marc since the divorce. "It's not like your behavior is so perfect," Janet had shot back. "Too many women. Gambling. Drinking. You don't leave much out, Casey."

"I've changed and you know it," Casey had retorted. "Be warned, girl. Keep seeing this fool and you pay the price. What do you find to talk about with a kid like him?"

Words—cruel words—burbled to Janet's lips. *He's twice the man you are,* she wanted to tell him. *So soon Marc is sold on him and he's fond of Marc.*

Bea was always there, lifting Janet's and Marc's spirits, and Grace came a couple of times, bringing delicious chicken and turkey soup and video games. "You complimented me on raising my son," she'd said. "You've done a magnificent job with Marc."

Pleasure at Grace's words had lasted. Now this day, a Sunday, she and Nick were at the crowded Washington Zoological Park. The Washington Zoo. An excited Marc walked ahead of them. "Hey, Mom, they look like your collection," he called back as they lingered at the giraffe enclosure. "Quite a feat nature's engineered in these guys," Nick said. "All these beautiful, graceful necks…" He glanced obliquely at Janet. "And speaking of graceful, beautiful necks."

He was looking at her as if no one else were there. His eyes were kissing her all over and Janet's breath came too fast. Even her toes fairly tingled. "Let's get to the reptile house," Marc said. It was a short distance from the giraffe enclosure and once there Marc stood enthralled. In separate cages were huge boa constrictors, deadly poisonous African mambas, rattlesnakes, harmless king- and blacksnakes. Pythons. "Oh, man," Marc breathed, "what're the chances of my keeping a snake, Mom? Nonpoisonous, of course. Pete's dad lets him keep a great golden snake. He's cool."

"Who's Pete?" Janet asked.

Marc shrugged. "A little bit older kid who comes to the playground to check on his younger brother. He's neat."

"How much older?"

"Sixteen," he said as she thought: *Too much older.*

"Do you see much of him?"

"Not too much, but I see him."

"Then I think you should invite him over to meet me."

"That'd be cool. You'll like him. You like snakes, Nick?"

Nick thought a moment. "They fascinate me, going all the way back to Eden, but I wouldn't say I like them. A gold one sounds unusual."

"Wait a minute," Janet thought suddenly and turned to Marc. "How do you know the snake is golden? Have you been to this Pete's house?"

"Ah, Mom," Marc said, a little taken aback. "Trust me, will you? He *told* me about the snake, showed me a photo…"

His voice drifted off and Janet stood thinking he seemed evasive, secretive. Was he lying? She was willing to give him the benefit of the doubt, but he was at the age when he badly needed a man's guidance and Casey knew only to control, to dominate, not how to parent. And he didn't seem interested in learning.

They watched big, white, awkward polar bears amble from wallowing pond to grass, gazelles and a couple of gnus that ignored them completely. Shortly after he had spoken of Pete, Marc began to stay closer to Nick. *Am I holding him too tightly?* she wondered. *He needs a certain amount of freedom, but it's such a dangerous world these days.* Drugs. Violence. Negative sex. She wanted all the positive things for him.

They sat on a green slatted bench under a cypress tree, Janet and Marc flanking Nick. Just after noon, Janet asked Marc how he was feeling.

"If I felt any better I'd fly." He grinned and pressed Nick's hand. "Hey, thanks for bringing us. Like I said, Dad's got nothing for a zoo to do. He says the people he knows are animals enough."

Nick laughed easily. "To each his own. What would you guys like to eat? And where?"

They liked the idea of the nearby Japanese restaurant, but it was crowded, as were two other ethnic places. They finally chose a Wendy's a block or so from the zoo and settled on big juicy cheeseburgers, fries, and garden salads.

"I've got an idea," Janet said as they sat munching happily. "Let's hold off on dessert and have chocolate-raspberry café lattes at the Starbucks around the corner from us."

"I'm game," Nick said.

"You're gonna let *me* have coffee?" Marc raised his eyebrows.

"Wel-l-l," Janet said, laughing. "The server could fix you one with a half portion of coffee. How does that grab you?"

"I like the thought," Marc said dreamily.

Back in the zoo, the flamingos were first this time. "Hey, when do we get to the lovebirds?" Marc asked.

"Oh, Marc," Janet fretted, "we're way away from the birds and I'm getting a little tired. We can always come back."

"Hey, I'm not talking about real birds. I mean the lovebird pandas. They're not too far away. We've been on field trips here."

Nick stood up and reached out to hold Janet's hand and help her to her feet. At the touch of his slender, steely fingers, electricity shot through her; she looked up at him and nearly came undone. He had to stop looking at her in that special sensual way that made her senses reel, set her body on fire. And she thought to herself, a little sadly: *It's not just my body. He sets my soul on fire.*

Did Marc notice? He gave no inkling that he did. He just looked happy as he had not looked in a very long time.

Then there were the giant pandas in all their black-and-white, cuddly glory. Their big enclave with its wallowing ponds, its greenery, fountain, and many bamboo shoots that the bears munched on steadily, all seemed a fairyland. Janet and Nick drew closer and Marc came within their circle. After they had watched for a long time, reveling in the exotic byplay, the warm affection displayed by the bears, and the rotund antics of the big bodies, Nick turned to Janet. "Let's go to the gift shop. I want to get you something."

"Oh? What?"

"Don't ask questions. Just come along." He took her hand and laced his fingers in hers.

Marc laughed as if a lightbulb had gone on in his brain. "Hey, I do believe you two guys like each other."

"There're not many people I don't like," Janet said defensively as Nick looked amused.

"I know a few you don't," Marc muttered, still smiling.

In the crowded gift shop Nick asked Marc to select his gift and Marc looked for and chose a soft plastic replica of a golden snake, coiled around a tree limb.

"Thanks," he said heartily. "I really wanted this."

"You're welcome." He glanced at Janet and this time his look was bland. "Now for your gift."

"You haven't asked me what I want."

"I'm choosing for you." He pointed out a big black-and-white plush panda from the glass case, then a smaller one, and paid the clerk, who wrapped them up. "People tell us they're good-luck charms," the clerk said.

Nick laughed. "I'm counting on it."

It had been a wonderful day, Janet thought as they parked and began the trek to Starbucks. Suddenly Marc frowned. "Look, you two," he said, "I'm gonna go on home. I'm feeling a little tired."

"We'll go with you," Janet said. "Are you sure nothing else is wrong?"

"No. Nothing's wrong. I'm just a little tired. Go on. I insist."

Marc looked at Nick for support. "Make her know I'm not a baby anymore. Dr. Reid said I'd get a little tired when I began to be active again. I'll lie down and you two take your time."

Janet looked at Nick, who looked at Marc, put his hand on his shoulder. "We'll be on shortly, skipper. Be sure you lie down."

The inside of the coffee shop wasn't crowded the way it usually was. Nick seated them, ordered from the pert blond waitress, and excused himself to use his cell phone. "Damn," he said, exasperated. "I forgot to recharge it."

Janet looked at him drolly. "And I left mine at home on holiday."

"So I'll have to use one on the phone bank. Back in a minute, but I think I'll go to the men's room."

Left alone, Janet looked around her. A young couple were billing and cooing at a corner table. An old couple looked comfortable with each other. A twenties couple looked angry and quarrelsome. Others were on their best public behavior. She sat with her back to the door, so the lyrical voice brought her up short. Tamara came around the table and stood before her. "Well, well," she drawled, "if it isn't the middle-aged teacher. Caught any good tadpoles lately?"

Janet frowned. What in the world was Tamara talking about? Then it hit her. Tadpoles were a term for *boys* with older women. She brought every ounce of sophistication she owned to bear on the situation.

"First," she said coolly, "tadpoles are *boys*. Nick is a *man*. I'd think you'd know the difference."

Tamara's sea-green eyes blazed now. "Nick and I go way back and we go *deep*. Know *that*."

The light brown silken hair flowed around her face and her fair skin reddened.

Nick came back then. "Hey, Tam," he said, "what brings you here?"

Tamara said nothing for a minute. He sat down, not offering her a seat, and she bent over and kissed him full on the mouth. Nick looked startled, frowned. "Tamara, *behave*," he said sternly. Janet wondered if she'd had a puff or two of something illegal.

"What brings me here?" Tamara cooed. "Just the desire to feel your lips on mine. Forgive me. I couldn't wait. See you soon."

She gave Janet a furious look and glided across the floor in slow provocative motion and out the door. *Slithered*, Janet thought, would be a better word for it.

"I'm sorry," Nick said. "I'm afraid Tamara sees the world in her own terms."

As Nick picked up her hand, lightly kissed and stroked it, Janet remembered he had called the woman *Tam,* a pet name.

"Don't take this too seriously," he said. "We'll talk about it any time you wish."

Janet drew a deep breath. "We're friends, Nick. There's no need to discuss anything. Your past, your life, belongs to you."

The waitress saw that Nick had come back and brought the frosted café lattes. Janet ordered a decaf café latte to go, for Marc. She tried to go back to her former state of merriment. Sipping the delicious creamy froth, she licked her lips. "M-m-m, these are good."

"Janet?"

She glanced at him levelly. "Yes?"

"Don't."

"Don't what?"

"Don't pretend it doesn't matter. You and I are on the brink of something special. We've got so much already. I'll explain to you about Tamara and me and hope you understand."

Inside she cried: *When, Nick, when will you explain? You and this woman share a bond of songs written and performed for adoring audiences, and I believe much deeper things. I hope you can explain, and I hope you don't wait too long.*

Chapter 6

On a mid-October Monday morning at six-thirty, Janet came awake again. Marc was going in to school early to practice on the kettledrums he played in his school's marching band. The digital luminous clock on her radio displayed the time; she had been awake an hour before. At five-thirty she had roused to a telephone call from Horton High, her school, informing her that there had been a water-main break near the school and there would be no school that day. She had gone back to sleep. Later, an announcement came on TV. She got up, walked over to the window, and closed it.

Going back to bed, she thought she'd get another snooze; Marc always fixed his own breakfast. Musical peals from the telephone sounded; she picked up on the first ring.

"I understand from TV that you're off today." Nick's voice caressed her.

"Isn't that wonderful?"

"Listen, I've got a great idea."

"Spill it."

"Let me pick you up, bring you back here for that soul-food dinner I want to do for you. I'll get you back before Marc gets home."

"He's going to be late. Band practice."

"Hey, luck's showing me love. Does that mean you'll come? Pick you up at eight?"

"I've got to shower. Give me an hour and a half."

He chuckled. "You can shower here."

Janet laughed and her breath caught in her throat. "Yeah, *right*."

"Okay. I'll make it around eight."

Marc knocked and came in, fully dressed. He wiped cereal crumbs from his mouth. "Who was that on the phone, Mom?" he asked.

"Don't be nosey." She smiled at him, ran her hands over his soft black hair as he sat on the side of her bed, his walnut-brown face alight.

"You don't have to tell me," he said. "I am swami and swami knows everything. That was Nick, wasn't it?"

She nodded. "Horton's had a water-main break and I'm off, so I'm going over to his house for a soul-food dinner."

"Oh, man, why couldn't our school have had a break, too? I don't suppose you'd consider letting me stay home today."

"What?" she said in mock alarm. "And let you miss a chance to pound those drums? I wouldn't think of it."

Nick picked her up a little ahead of time in his burgundy Saab. They drove through light traffic out to the Maryland countryside where his big cream stucco Cape Cod house with dark blue shutters sat, surrounded by immaculate landscaping.

A black wrought-iron fence graced the premises and on either side of the front steps a large stone lion sat on its haunches.

Inside he showed her through the house immediately. It was lovely and showed a woman's touch, she thought. Tamara came to mind. At his bedroom door, her eyes half-closed and she drew a deep breath, imagining gentle love scenes between him and her on the indigo blue coverlet. The scenes he imagined were not gentle. He took her in fierce passion, ravaged her, and his body grew taut with the vision. His loins were singing an ancient male love song. What would she think if she knew? She wore a pale blue faille tunic over a long navy skirt split on the side to display her great legs. He thought she looked good enough to *be* dinner—his.

The house was a mixture of modern and old. It needed a bit more color, she decided, but it was really beautiful.

"I spend a lot of time here," he said. "I got a decorator. Ma helped. Do you like it?"

"I love it. I would kill for your Persian rugs."

"I selected those over a long period of time. Now to show you my lion's den."

"You're fond of lions," she murmured. "Doesn't that mean you're dangerous?"

"What do *you* think? One thing I know. I'd like to gobble *you* up."

They were going down a short flight of stairs to the basement. As they walked along a small corridor, he opened the door to a recreation room sparsely furnished with black leather sofas, chairs, and a big black leather and walnut bar. There was a fully equipped bandstand. So Rhapsody practiced here, she thought. *Tamara* came here. She felt tension rise in her body. He closed the door behind them and leaned against it.

"This room is soundproofed," he said, smiling wickedly.

"I could crush you in my arms, suddenly, unexpectedly, and you could cry out with fright...." He lowered his voice and with a mock leer, teased her. "No one would hear you. You'd be at my loving mercy."

Thrilling, her blood warm, she let him talk.

"Or you could cry out with pleasure as I made love to you. That couch has a queen-size bed. I would cover you with kisses and you'd let me know with your cries that you like every nuance of what I do to you."

Her lips were open a little. Was he going to kiss her? She swayed toward him, but he only gripped her shoulders. "Janet. Janet," he whispered. "I'm so glad you came."

They decided to prepare the dinner together and eat early. Neither had had breakfast, so Nick squeezed fresh orange juice, mixed it with cranberry juice, and filled two tall glasses. As they sipped their juice, they divided the chores and began.

"The baked beans, the scrumptious bread pudding—my own concoction—and the corn pudding I prepared yesterday. I was going to freeze them, invite you over on the weekend, and then the water main broke. How lucky can I get? So, here we are."

As he spoke, Janet listened and thought that since she'd met this man, feelings, sensations she hadn't known she possessed had constantly swept through her, threatening at times to take her under. She wanted to believe that he could love her, because it felt so good when she did, but a wise voice within said he was young and young people *changed*. That was one of their characteristics.

He wore a big white cotton butcher's apron over his dark blue chambray shirt and dark blue denim jeans. From a drawer he pulled out a frilly white organdy apron for her. The woman's touch, she thought wryly. Which woman? She didn't want to think about it.

His words in the soundproofed rec room kept racing through her mind. Was he dangerous? If he was, she decided, she liked the danger he posed. It wasn't as if she knew nothing about him. They had covered a lot of territory in a little over a month. She and Bea had gone back once to Rocketship to watch him perform. She knew his mother, his background. She had gone away from him, he thought. "Sometimes you're like quicksilver—elusive," he said.

"Am I?" she murmured.

"Never mind. I love everything about you."

They had not spoken of Tamara again. The night she and Bea had gone back to Rocketship, the stunning woman had pointedly ignored them. Tamara had stayed close to Nick, though, her eyes hotly adoring him, throwing everything she had his way.

"What're you thinking about?" Nick asked now.

"A lot of things," she answered simply.

"Us?"

"Yes. Some."

"Think in my favor. Show me love."

"Let me just think clearly. Lord, how I need to think clearly."

"Think romance. Deep love."

"If we want to eat before we starve, we'd better move. You promised me a soul-food dinner, and a soul-food dinner I will have."

A quick, warm expression crossed Nick's face. "I've got a lot of things in mind for you I didn't promise." Then his face got grave. "You may not like them all."

"Oh?" she said only and he went no further.

* * *

They ate at one o'clock on gaily flowered crockware. Both were ravenous for food, but there were much deeper, unappeased hungers both were well aware of.

The food was superb. Janet savored every bit of catfish fried in wheat germ and sour cream batter, green cabbage quarters, stewed tomatoes and celery, julienne carrots, corn pudding, baked beans, and macaroni and cheese. A mixture of six salad greens was one of several dishes she had prepared.

"The wheat germ coating is a deviation from soul food," he said. "Forgive me."

"It's all so delicious. This spiced hot apple cider is like none I've tasted before. I hope you'll tell me how to make it."

"Come around enough and you'll see for yourself."

"That's only fair."

When they were finished, both cleared the table. He brought out small portions of extra-rich bread pudding. "More to come later," he said.

She tasted the pudding and leaned back. "Oh, Lord, this is *ultra,*" she told him. "I've got to know what's in it."

He smiled at her. "Day-old bread, heavy cream, coconut, vanilla, golden currants, brown and white sugar, orange liqueur, and lemon sauce over it all. Isn't it special? I'm proud if I do say so myself." Holding up a hand, he said, "Wait," then explained, "I need brandy for this. You make me forget."

He got Courvoisier brandy from the wet bar, brought it back to the table and poured a small amount into the dessert dishes. Picking up a gold-plated table cigarette lighter, he snapped it open and soon blue and yellow flames brought out the aroma of the pudding.

"Exquisite," she said. "Do you smoke?"

He shook his head. "No. I like living too much."

Once finished, she leaned back. "The dinner was ultra, as I said. You're a fabulous cook." With a sense of deep satisfaction, she reflected that it was one of the nicest dinners she'd ever eaten.

After they'd put the used dishes in the dishwasher, Nick suggested they go jogging around the grounds. "We didn't stuff the way we might have, but we could use the exercise."

"I think you need to change," he said. "I'll give you a pair of my jogging sweats. They're going to be a loose fit, but…" He shrugged. "We won't be out long."

With her lost in his rolled-up long gray sweats, Nick and Janet hit the paved walks around his house. It was crisply cool, overcast. Shedding elm trees on either side of a walkway arched over the walkways and touched high up.

They jogged in silence until he asked, "Do you work out often?"

"Not really. I go to a gym with fair frequency. I keep saying I'm going to buy equipment, use it. Marc works out daily at school. He'd love fitness equipment."

"You could both come out here."

"We won't push our luck."

He stopped, turned to her. "Hell, I'd love it if you *moved* out here with me." He looked sincere, intense.

She began to jog in place. "Give me time," she told him. "Let's see how it plays out." Then she said urgently, "Nick, try to pay more attention to the age thing. It could prove to be a big headache."

"Let's go," he said suddenly. "Talk as we jog. Let me tell you about my grandmother and her marriage."

"Grace told me."

"I thought she probably had. Can't you look at it from that point of view?"

"I don't like being mocked, laughed at."

"Is that more important than being happy, having someone you want who wants you?"

She thought a long while before she answered, "You know it isn't."

They went out for almost an hour and Janet was pleasantly winded. Back inside, Nick brought out an old gray-and-white-striped robe of his. "Let's lie down and rest. You can put this on, save your clothes."

He left his bedroom as she got out of the sweats, and as with the sweats was swallowed again in his robe. She liked the mildly woodsy odor of his garment and put her face against one of the sleeves, breathing deeply. His smell was like his persona: clean, clear, direct. Natural. She got up, sat on a chair by the bed.

"Happy napping," he said as he knocked and came back in.

"Are you going to take a nap?" she asked.

"I plan to."

She looked at him obliquely. "In here?"

"Don't run, rabbit. I'll be in another bedroom or on the couch."

"We run from danger," she said evenly, "if we're wise."

He bent down, reached out, touched her face. "There're all kinds of danger, love. You can let yourself get too hungry. Starve. Janet, before we sleep, I want to talk to you; tell you some things about me—"

"And Tamara?" she asked slowly.

"Yes."

He helped her out of the chair, took her hand, and led her into the living room, where they sat side by side on the sofa. He turned to face her and she turned to face him, too.

"We were lovers," he said abruptly.

"I gathered as much."

His sigh was deep, ragged. "We were engaged to be married, but I wanted to wait, to be more successful. I didn't feel I had enough to offer a wife." He laughed ruefully. "I know now I wasn't ready to settle down." For a long while he said nothing further and he seemed to be looking back. Was he dreaming? she wondered.

When he spoke, his voice was low, husky. "She was like a fever in my blood. She was twenty-two and psychologically young even for that young age. We quarreled when I said I wouldn't marry her then and she left the group for a while. She went on a long vacation to St. Maarten and came back pregnant with a rich older man's baby. He married her and she moved to the island...."

"You were badly hurt," she said, empathizing.

"I was *devastated*. I said she was like a fever in my blood and for two years it didn't cool. There were other women, wild living, drinking too much. I did things I'd never thought of doing before. Can you understand that?"

"I can."

He took her hand, squeezed it. Head bowed, he continued. "She lost the child. It was a full-term stillbirth. They stayed together six months longer and he filed for divorce."

"She came back to you."

He shook his head. "She needed to sing again. She was torn up. It seems she really wanted the baby. We all let her come back. She's been back over a year...."

Should she ask him? "Are you still in love with her?"

He hesitated a moment. "No. At first I thought I was, thought it until you came into Rocketship with Bea. I came over to your table to speak to Bea, saw you, and the rest, as they say, is history. Do *you* believe in love at first sight?"

"It's never happened to me," she began as troubling thoughts and feelings crowded her mind. "I was physically attracted to you. You're a hunk. It happens."

"Nothing deeper?" he questioned. "Because I felt something much deeper. It really was, as Bea said, as if we'd known each other before. My mother. My grandmother. What I felt from the beginning was not simply physical attraction. I had a ravening hunger I felt some hope of filling with you."

She searched her own mind as he spoke and knew full well that much more had happened early on than she had let herself realize. She wasn't going to deny it any longer because the feeling was hovering over her like a guardian angel.

Looking at him levelly she felt a hint of tears. "I said love at first sight has never happened to me. I guess I should have said it's never happened to me—*before*."

Nick's eyes on her were warm, compelling. "That's my girl," he said and hugged her tightly.

They moved to his bedroom again. He pulled back the spread on the king-size bed to reveal deep blue sheets and they lay side by side for a long while.

"This is a very big bed." Janet breathed deeply. Surprising herself, she said, "We could *both* take naps on it."

"Are you sleepy?"

"No. Are you?"

"Not even a little bit. I'm used to jogging."

She moved up on the bed and propped herself against the big firm bed pillows. "I've got to begin formally interviewing you about how you overcame adversity in your life. We've talked, but I've got to make notes. The kids were cute, giggling when they said I should take you as my project."

"I'm willing anytime. More chances to be with you. Why

don't you take me as your total project? As for healing from the injury, I've told you I could never have done it without Dad and Ma."

"You're a strong man."

"I get that from them, too." He propped himself on one elbow. "You're so tense, Janet. How'd you like me to give you a clothes-on massage?"

Startled, she looked at him. "You know how to give a massage?"

"Obviously, if I offered to."

"Where'd you learn?" It was something the sensuous, sensual Tamara would know. She pushed the thought roughly aside. She didn't need this grief.

He laughed. "I haven't lived in a monastery. Massages can be a lifesaver in my business. I'm not an expert, but I'm pretty good. Janet, your eyes are getting a little cool on me. I'll tell you where I learned."

She sat up and put her hand over his mouth. "*Don't* tell me. I don't want to know. I don't care. It's not that I don't care about *you,* but if we're even just going to be friends, we've got to develop trust between us."

"Amen to that," he said heartily. Then, "Lie on your belly."

She turned over, straightening the big robe that bunched under her as his long, marvelously effective fingers began with her shoulders, moving up to her neck, her scalp, then slowly back down. It felt wonderful.

"I've never wished I could purr before," she said.

"Good. That means I'm giving you pleasure. Something tells me you haven't had enough pleasure in your life. You're kind of uptight."

"You're relaxed enough for both of us."

"Not always," he said, stroking more deeply, kneading her

flesh under the robe. "I've had my uptight moments, too. Since I've known you, I've had a hell of a lot on my mind."

"I'm sorry if I cause you discomfort."

"Don't be. You bring me much more joy. I just wish I could get you to believe in us the way I do."

He stroked her hips, her long legs with sweeping movements, pausing to press his fingers deeply into the muscles.

"You should be naked for me to really do this well. I'd put a sheet over the parts I wasn't massaging. You need this...."

"It certainly *feels* great," she said slowly, not commenting on being naked.

She was aware then that his voice had become softer, huskier. In the quiet room she could hear him breathing. Lost in thought, she didn't hear him at first and he had to say it again. "Turn over."

Blushing now, she turned and drew the robe around her. His eyes lingered on the swell of her breasts, her narrow waistline, and her wide hips as his eyes had lingered on her heavy buttocks. Mentally, he had stripped her from the very beginning; the robe was just a formality.

As he massaged her, his hands cupped her breasts in the robe for a brief moment until she protested, "You aren't being businesslike at all, Redmond. You couldn't keep customers, handling them like this."

"I'm only interested in keeping *one* customer."

She laughed at his mock leer.

As his hands left her hips, she suddenly trembled. Would he move to her inner thighs? She fought her desire to have him stroke her secret places, enter, and rise up mightily inside her; she held her breath.

His hands moved past her mons veneris quickly as he chuckled. "Don't worry, rabbit, I'm not going to jump your bones. I'm not going to sneak my way in."

She blushed vividly as he stroked and kneaded her front thighs, then her calves. He lifted her feet, placed one against his cheek, and kissed it, his tongue teasing the instep. His touch got to her deepest recesses, sent wild thrills coursing through her.

"How romantic you are," she murmured.

"The better to please you, my dear. Your perfume always turns me on. What is it?"

"Two kinds. Sometimes it's French lavender. Today it's Ralph Lauren."

"My compliments to the perfumer. You turn me on higher than at any time I can remember."

He finished and, leaning back, asked her, "How would you rate my massage?"

She answered without hesitation, "On a scale of one to ten—twenty."

Nick threw back his head, laughing. "Call me anytime. You've got my number." He sat on his haunches on the bed then looking pleased with himself. Reaching over, he switched on an expensive small CD player and the sweetness of Borodin's *Nocturne* surrounded them. She smiled, remembering that an old pop tune, "This Is My Beloved," had been taken from that song. Then he stretched out, rolled over, and caught her mouth beneath his. His kiss was so hard it hurt her mouth for a moment, so sudden and so deep it shocked her.

Since that first kiss, he had been gentle, tender. Now his tongue probed her mouth ruthlessly. She felt something inside her give way, wanting him with a fierceness she couldn't believe. She was responding wildly to him. One of them had to hold back, she thought frantically. But nothing in her wanted to hold back.

Pushing aside the top of the robe, he stared at her beautiful breasts in the pale blue lacy slip she wore. He shuddered as he pressed the side of his hot face to them. Her hand crept to the back of his head, pulling his crisply dreadlocked head against her as hard as she could. She heard his heart pounding as hers fluttered crazily. Then she was falling, falling, and nothing but this man mattered anymore.

With pained reluctance he came away from her then and again propping himself on an elbow looked down at her. He shook his head. "As much as I want to make love with you, I won't press you," he said gently. "I'll wait until you love me the way I love you, and, my darling, even that is not enough. I want you to come to me, tell me what you want, and I'll move heaven and earth to get it for you. Tell me what you want and I'll do it for you. *Anything* and *everything*. I love you, Jan, body and soul."

She saw the sincerity on his face and it moved her greatly. "We've known each other such a short time."

He looked at her closely for a moment. "Relationships can be quickly built and be altogether valid—and last."

"You're so much younger."

"Not all that much. I know what I want. I always have. I'd like to see a lot more of you. Are you willing?"

"It couldn't hurt, but you didn't respond to the age thing."

"Because I don't believe it matters between two people like us. So quickly you're already in my heart. I want you in my *life*."

She was there more than an hour after that. They dressed, talked quietly, and sat in the living room in companionable silence before he took her home. As she got out of his car, he told her, "Thank you."

And she responded, "No. Thank *you*."

Back at his house, the place suddenly seemed empty without her. He was a man who liked being alone at times and he had seldom craved company, but he craved it now. *Her* company. Her presence and her fragrance filled his rooms. Dreams of her filled his mind.

He walked to an end table and picked up a photo of the three of them at the zoo. Janet. Marc. And him. He held the photo a long moment. He wanted Janet as his wife, Marc as his son. But damn it, she couldn't get past the age thing. In the back of his mind, he began to plan a blitz to change her mind. Then he knew that blitz had begun almost as soon as he'd met her. Today, it had grown a whole lot deeper.

Chapter 7

"You look happy, my dear, positively glowing, and thanks for meeting me. I won't keep you long."

"I *am* happy," Janet replied. "I guess you're happy, too, over your coming trip for the Chicago conference."

"I am. I plan to have a ball."

The two women sat on a park bench near Horton School. The area was resplendent in the red and gold and green foliage of late October. It was chilly and Grace pulled her full-length navy sweater-coat around her. Janet was comfortable in a smart, natural-colored wool suit.

Janet couldn't help noticing that Grace looked a bit sad. "You don't have to worry about time," she said. "One of the other teachers and I swap favors. She's supervising in the cafeteria in my place. You have something special in mind, don't you?"

"Is it that plain? You're very perceptive."

"I can be." She smiled and added, "When I care about people."

"Thank you for caring. How're you and Nick coming along?"

Janet didn't hesitate. "I'd say wonderfully well. I told you about the soul-food dinner he made me. He's come to be close to my heart...." Her voice trailed off.

"But you have doubts. I thought telling you about his grandmother would help."

Janet looked at Grace and a smile spread across her face. She reached over and took the older woman's hand, squeezed it.

"I'm a forty-one-year-old fuddy-duddy. I've always cared too much about what other people think." She stopped, frowning. "But I'd be lying if I said it doesn't scare me that it won't last, that he'll find someone nearer his own age in the end."

"That's understandable." Grace paused a moment. "I'm assuming you know about him and Tamara. Nick's pretty up-front."

"Yes, he told me."

"I'm glad. I've said I haven't always approved of what he did, but he's an independent soul. Tamara's one of the people I haven't approved of. She's vain, egotistical, selfish, and I don't think it has anything to do with being young. I'm betting she won't change."

"She loves him."

Grace shook her head. "Tamara Kyle doesn't know the meaning of love. Nick was never truly happy with her the way he's been with you."

It might be sharing too much, but Janet found herself telling Grace, "Nick said she was like a fever in his blood."

For a moment Grace looked startled; then she laughed harshly. "I couldn't have put it better. He was edgy, driven as long as they stayed together. At one point, I thought she'd *make* him marry her, but he can be stubborn. Still, when she married someone else, my heart nearly broke for him. Janet, watching him was more painful than when doctors said he'd never walk again. I never stopped having hope then, but I nearly lost hope when Tamara hurt him so."

"I'm sorry. He may not be over her."

Grace seemed to hold her breath. "I've never stopped praying that he's over her. I was furious when she came back to Rhapsody, when he, when *they* took her back, but I'm his mother, not his keeper."

"Did you get along with her?"

Grace thought about the question. "I was civil, courteous. From the beginning I didn't care for her. She was *not* what I wanted for my son and I shuddered at the thought of that selfish girl raising a child. What if something happened the way it happened with Nick? But I didn't meddle, and God saw fit to have it be otherwise."

"Something's on your mind now. Is it about Tamara and Nick?"

"Heaven forbid," Grace said heartily. "I just had the strangest feeling of *needing* to talk to you. I follow my hunches and you're not just perceptive, I think. You *divine* things, don't you?"

"My mother used to say I do."

"I do, too. It's one of the reasons I am so fond of you."

"That makes two of us being fond of each other."

Grace picked up a small shopping bag from the bench. It bore the logo of an exclusive dress shop, and she opened it. She withdrew a tissue-wrapped package and handed it to Janet, saying, "It's one of my most treasured possessions. My late husband and I celebrated our tenth wedding anniversary in London. He bought me so many things. Here, open it."

Janet unwrapped the tissue and gazed at the exquisite Royal Doulton china basket of multicolored roses. The basket, the petals, the leaves were fashioned with incredible detail. "This is so beautiful!" she exclaimed. "No, Grace, it's too precious. I can't accept this."

"You can—and you must. This gesture should tell you what you mean to me. I want you to remember this always."

A chill ran the length of Janet's body.

"What is it?" Grace asked her.

"I don't know," Janet told her. "I had the strangest feeling, and I have *no* idea what it means." She felt tears gather in her eyes and looked away from Grace.

"Janet, look at me."

Janet faced her, eyes brimming with tears. Grace took her hand.

"We have so much to say to each other when I get back, and I'll call you while I'm there. The holidays have always been a big thing with us. Beginning with Thanksgiving, or even before, I want you and Nick and Marc to come over. We'll cook together—Thanksgiving, Christmas, New Year's. Oh, my dear, what a wonderful time we will have...."

Grace's face was radiant now, dreaming. "I really must go," she said reluctantly. "I've got a jillion things to do, gifts to buy for friends in Chicago." Then suddenly her eyes filled with tears. "Janet, if you and my son don't work out—no matter how much I want that—if you two don't work out, I want us to be friends. And I have no right to ask it, but I want you to keep on being friends with him. He needs you. Will you?"

Without hesitation, she said, "Believe me, I will. Nick loves me, at least for now, and God knows I love him, probably forever. Thank you for asking."

The women stood up then and began to go their separate ways, but a few steps away Grace turned and said, "I *will* be calling you."

As each neared the end of the park at opposite ends, Janet turned and looked back and found Grace looking back at her. Both waved and took a moment before each turned and continued on her way.

Walking, Janet reached into her tote bag and touched the tissue that covered the china flowers. It was a treasure no less exquisite than the woman who had given it to her.

At Rocketship around four that same afternoon, Nick sat with his guitar on his knee, waiting for Marc, who knocked loudly on the locked front door. Memphis, the owner, let him in, extending his arm for a high five, which Marc promptly submitted.

"Afternoon, Mr. Traxell," Marc said, holding his guitar in front of him.

"Afternoon, young fellow. Glad to see you. Any son of a friend of Bea's…" His voice trailed off and Marc looked at the big man, surprised. He sounded a trifle choked.

"Hey, Nick!"

Marc seemed to bound toward him and Nick stood up, waited for Marc to reach him, then brushed the boy's flat-grained black hair with his hand. "Hey yourself, Marc. Ready? I've got some points I want to give you that will make all the difference in your playing."

"Oh, man, thank you. Is it true you're going by Mom's school Monday to perform?"

"It's true. One day we'll come to your school, if you request our presence."

Marc's mouth flew open and his voice came out a squeak.

"You *would?* Oh, man, that'd be the neatest. Way cool." His wiry body jumped at the thought.

"Let's talk about guitars and music," Nick said, drawing the boy onto a padded bench.

"Yeah," Marc responded, all eager body and flashing eyes.

"Guitars are like people," Nick began. "They respond wonderfully well to good treatment. Your guitar has a soul—yours—and if you ever hope to make the kind of music I think you want to make, you've got to cultivate that soul."

Nick got up, lifted his guitar from another bench and brought it back, then sat down and laid the guitar on his lap.

Marc stretched out his hand. "Okay if I touch it?" he asked humbly.

"Sure. Go ahead."

The boy stroked the satiny smooth finish of the blond-brown guitar with the big grace notes painted on it. A Gibson guitar. His eyes were dreamy. "It's so beautiful," he said. "It cost a lot, didn't it?"

"Yes, it cost a lot, but your guitar is fine for learning. There's so much to come, Marc. Oh, yes, you're learning the basics, but strings and tuning pegs, the choice of picks and fingers, they're only elements of playing. You'll develop your own special technique as you go along.... You show me so much promise and I'll guide you all the way in."

Marc's eyes were shining now; he could hardly contain his joy. "Thanks, Nick. You're awesome."

At a loud banging on the door, a frowning Memphis strode over and opened it.

"Yeah?" he asked the short, ginger-colored youth who stood there, covering discomfort with bravado.

"Hey, man, I got a friend I seen coming in here. I need to talk to him."

"This friend you followed in got a name?"

"Yeah. Marc. Marc Smith."

Memphis thought he didn't like the kid's looks and wondered what his connection to Marc was. "He's getting a guitar lesson," Memphis said. "I'm not sure he'll want to be disturbed."

"Please. It's important."

Memphis's eyes narrowed as he thought: So, the little punk could be civilized.

"Okay. Five minutes or so. Like I said, the kid's busy. You got a name?"

"Yessir. Pete Brooks."

Memphis's presence hassled the youth, who hung back. "I won't be more'n a few minutes."

Nick and Marc had their backs to Pete and he walked over, cleared his throat.

"Excuse me. Marc," he mumbled, "c'n I see ya a minute?"

Nick stopped talking and looked long and hard at Pete. He said to Marc, "Cut it short. I've got a little less time to spare than usual."

Nick frowned, thinking he didn't like the discomfited look on Marc's face. He didn't seem afraid of this kid, just wary. "Okay," he said, "I'll let you two talk a few minutes, but I want to get back on track."

"You bet," Marc said and Nick got up, walked away from the boys.

"How'd you come to come in here?" Marc questioned Pete gruffly.

"Ah, man, I saw *you* come in here and I wanted t'tell you I'm comin' over to your school tomorrow. I'm real excited. My music teacher said today I'm gettin' good on my bass fiddle. I had t'tell somebody. Mebbe Nick'll talk to me. I really dig his stuff."

"You do? You never said so. I thought you liked rap and the hard stuff."

Pete's wink was slow, provocative. "You don' know ev'ry-thin' about me, man. I'm a real s'prise package. See ya aroun'."

He left as abruptly as he had come, and Nick came back. "Your friend's a little older than you, isn't he?"

"He just made sixteen."

"And you just made fourteen a few months back. What's the attraction? Where'd you meet him?"

"Labor Day. His school and my school marched in the parade. He admired how I played the kettledrum and he's *great* on bass." Then sounding older than his age, he said, "I guess he's a rough diamond, but he's really good on those drums."

Nick pressed it. "Has your mom met him?"

"No, but she wants to. I'm going to take him around."

"You don't have him there when she's not at home?"

"No way. I'm going to introduce him to her soon. He hasn't got many friends."

Nick thought wryly that he didn't wonder.

The lesson ended shortly after that. Workers began to drift in to get ready for the supper crowd, then Rhapsody's performance at ten. Marc had been hoping for a glimpse of Tamara, but she'd left earlier. He licked his smooth, young lips. That was one hot, fat-to-death babe.

Chapter 8

By twelve-thirty the following Monday Janet was tense with excitement, and Horton High students were jubilant. They had thronged to the gym and seated themselves on folding chairs, waiting for a group they adored, Rhapsody.

She saw the group come in with Nick and Guy Whisonant, who strummed the second lead guitar, and Tamara walking a little ahead of them. They carried their instruments and had smiles all around. With astonishment Janet saw that Nick carried a very tall clear glass vase of bloodred roses like the one he had brought her early in their relationship. He had asked her to be near the gym door.

She almost missed it, but she caught the edge of the venomous look Tamara gave her and her heart nearly stopped. Nick said to his group, "Go on in and get warmed up. I'll be with you in a few minutes."

Turning then to Janet, grinning, he handed her the roses.

For a dizzy moment she was afraid he'd kiss her, but his eyes narrowed and he stopped short. "I'm taking us public," he declared. "If we're going to be married…"

"Nick!" Janet sputtered. She was spinning out of control. He smiled wickedly. "Get used to hearing me say that. You'll be hearing it often. Being proposed to becomes you. You're glowing."

She was suddenly bashful, her voice seeming to stick in her throat. "Thank you. They're beautiful. I want to take them to my room."

He nodded. "Okay, but first, something's haunting me and I want to get it off my chest. Janet, when I called you last night, we talked about this Pete kid Marc's been seeing. I don't want to meddle, but I don't think you're taking it seriously enough. Lean on Marc to bring him by or stop seeing him. I don't think you're going to approve. Marc's come to mean a lot to me, the way his mother means a lot to me."

He looked really bothered as the sounds of the group warming up enlivened the gym and spilled out into the corridors.

"I will," she told him.

At the sound of Bea clearing her throat behind them, they both turned and faced her merry countenance. "Well, what have we here, friend?" Bea chided Nick in mock indignation. "We're supposed to be throwing roses at *your* feet, Nicholas, not the other way around. You've got it bad, hon."

"I can't seem to stop trying."

"One thing you're loaded with is taste," Bea complimented him. "Janet, love, do you want me to put those gorgeous posies in my room? Or give me your key and I'll take them to yours."

"I'll do it," Janet said quickly. Nick was looking at her thoughtfully. "And I'll be right back. Good luck, Nick. The kids really love you."

"It's a two-way street," he said gallantly. "I'd like that same kind of feeling from someone else I know."

Flustered then, Janet began the trek up the corridor to her classroom. Deep in thought, she walked swiftly. Going public. *If we are going to be*—had he said *married?* He had teased her often; this time he seemed so intense.

"Beautiful roses," a calm, masculine voice intoned, and she looked up into the molasses-brown face of Mr. Childs, Horton's principal.

"Aren't they?"

She was one of his favorite teachers. He had been sympathetic when her marriage had broken up and he liked the way she raised her son. "An admirer? You certainly deserve an ardent one."

She laughed lightly. "People are often kind."

"I don't mean to butt in, but I happened to be passing by and saw the gentleman hand them to you. I wish you both all the best. It's been too long since I've seen you really happy. Life is short. Live with that in mind. You're going to say I'm an awful snoop, but is this serious?"

Janet reflected that it was not just anybody she was talking with. Mr. Childs had been unusually kind when she and Casey broke up; his wife had offered her solace. He wasn't being nosey; he was interested.

"Don't get your hopes up," she said softly. "There's baggage carried here."

"Isn't there always? Nick Redmond's father was a jazz great. Nick's group is one of the best influences on kids. Antidrug, antiviolence, a belief in commitment. I've long thought about giving him and a few others an award for their help with youngsters, the impact they've made on community life. What is it you considered baggage?" he asked frankly.

Janet drew a deep breath. "There's a ten-year age difference between us."

With twinkling eyes, he told her, "I'm thirty years older than my second wife, as you probably know, and we're happy. We're now an equal-opportunity society. Take advantage of it, my dear."

His words lifted her spirits, but they didn't change her mind.

He turned around to go toward the gym, then paused. His eyes on her were kind. "Think about it, Janet. At least give it a royal try. Now, hurry and put the roses up and come back to hear a good man, a good group perform." He smiled again. "Oh, I've got kids who like music and I listened hard when Miss Barry suggested bringing Rhapsody here. I don't mind telling you I'm looking forward to this concert."

Tamara was onstage, singing and strumming her guitar, when Janet came back. Bea saw Janet and moved from the row ahead to take a seat beside her. "You—ah—look discombobulated," Bea said. "Is Nick putting the heat to you again?"

"It isn't funny, Bea."

"Oh? If it's sad, I'd give my eyeteeth to have that kind of sadness in my life."

Janet tapped the back of her hand against Bea's arm. *"You,"* she said.

Rhapsody was in fine form. Today, the music was effortless, smoothly romantic, compelling. Nick looked handsome, overwhelmingly masculine in tight black leather enhancing his bronze leathery skin. Tamara was in dark red silk jersey that draped and clung to her slender, curvy figure. Her lovely pale face was skillfully made up and her light brown hair flowed in waves over her shoulder. Her movements were just this side of suggestive as she looked at Nick. When he sang in his flawless silken baritone, Tamara joined in, adoring him, her husky contralto blending with his haunting voice. Watching them, Janet felt her heart turn over as shards of pain pierced it. Unbidden, what he had said at his house surged to mind: "She was like a fever in my blood." Today, Nick had brought her, Janet, bloodred roses. He had once called her "Jan," then hadn't called her that again, but he called Tamara "Tam" often. Had she imagined that he had said today, "If we are going to be married…"? *Going public.* Her mind seethed with anxiety as she watched the stage closely.

And she wondered: had the fever really cooled?

Guy Whisonant took the stage then. A slender, wiry chocolate-brown man, he let his guitar know who was its master. He played and sang a slightly risqué mellow tune and the audience swooned.

Then Tamara stepped up to the microphone. "I'm going to sing one of our signature songs," she announced. "You've heard it before. You'll hear it again." And she glided into "Where Do We Go From Here?" Finishing the first set of lyrics, she walked over to Nick, and Janet saw a surprised expression cross his face as she reached up and lightly kissed him full on the lips.

"Sing it with me?" she asked him. "It was always one of our best. *Please.*"

In that crowded room, Nick's eyes found Janet and he smiled. Janet could only manage a faint smile.

"I'll bet my boots he's a player," a student sitting near Janet and Bea said. The girl with her shrugged. "I hear he's pretty square. A straight arrow."

"Don't believe everything you hear," the first girl scoffed.

Nick announced and came on with a medley of favorites. After a Smoky Robinson song he stopped and began a fervent riff with his guitar. It was electrifying and the crowd went wild, but they were not terribly noisy, just giving voice to their enjoyment. The others joined in, gracefully embellishing his lead. Then Nick put aside his guitar and sang again. He was adored, he was loved, Janet thought. Surely he didn't need *her*.

The concert lasted only an hour and a half, but the students clamored to have it go on longer. Mr. Childs started toward the stage, but Nick was on the mike. "Love you, too," he told them, "but we've got to move on. We're coming back...."

"When?" A cry went up.

"Soon. I promise. Now back to class and education, which is supreme. Study hard and be all that you want to be."

He blew them a kiss and the rest of the band blew them kisses, which they rapturously returned. Nick was caught up then in autograph requests and panting adoration from some of the girls.

Mr. Childs's voice was firm on the microphone. "Monitors in place," he commanded. "There will not be time for autographs. Please proceed to your next class in an orderly fashion. Behave like ladies and gentlemen *if* you want Mr. Redmond and Rhapsody to come back."

Several voices shouted, "We'll be cool. Come back soon, Nick! Tamara!" They set up a chant then of "Nick! Tamara! Rhapsody!"

Then Janet watched with two other teachers as the students began their procession to classrooms. Nick and the band packed up, but Guy finished hurriedly and walked over to Janet. "Give me a minute?" he asked.

"Of course."

"I'll make it quick. We're pretty crowded here." He seemed so earnest. "We don't know each other that well, but Nick and I go back to Ellington School together. We both founded

Rhapsody, as you probably know, although he was always main leader."

"Yes, I do know. You've got a wonderful group."

"We think so. Janet, I just want to beg you to work things out with Nick. He really cares about you. Don't let frivolous things stand in your way. My buddy's happier since he met you than I've ever seen him. He's had some rough breaks. Do you love him?" He waited for an answer.

Her heart was too full, but she managed to say, "Yes, I love him."

Guy smiled widely. "Then I'm glad. *Make* it work. *Let* it work. And I'm there for both of you. See you later." He touched her shoulder and walked back to his group.

She heard the arrogant, rasping voice behind her and turned, asking, "What are you doing here?"

Casey's eyes were icy cold. "I guess I'm just in time to see you make a fool of yourself. I saw Redmond give you the flowers."

"Beautiful, aren't they?"

He clenched his teeth. "Marc told me Redmond's group would be here today. You're acting like a fool, Janet. You saw the way that tart kissed him on the mouth. She's his type. You sure didn't use to be."

Quite evenly Janet said, "She's like you, Casey. Arrogant, selfish. Incapable of real love."

His voice was guttural now. "You think you can hold a candle to a woman like that? Young, juicy, with the world at her feet?"

"Could I interrupt a moment?" Nick said pleasantly, looking down at her.

"Be my guest." Janet's wide smile matched his even as she wondered how to explain that kiss Tamara had pressed on him.

She realized then with a start of horror that Casey had

been drinking; the mint had suddenly stopped hiding it very well. And Casey was a mean drunk.

"This is as good a time as any to say it," Casey barked. "Stay the hell away from my son, Redmond. I don't want you teaching him the guitar. He's got his drums and I don't give a damn about them, but I don't want you near him."

"I'm sorry you feel that way," Nick said pleasantly. "I think the world of Marc. Musically he's very talented. Don't crush it."

"Don't tell me how to treat my kid!" Casey exploded. "I could kill Janet for fooling around with you, bringing you to her apartment with my son. I'm warning you, Redmond."

Janet's glance at him didn't waver. "I have full custody of Marc," she said, "with good reason."

Fury seemed to blaze from Casey's every pore. He took a step toward Nick with his fists clenched, but Nick took it in stride, looked at him easily. He never looked for fights, avoided them when he could, but he knew he could take Casey down.

And Casey knew he was no match for the younger man. "Things're going to change," he shot at them. "I'm not about to let a punk like you ruin my son. You can depend on that." He looked daggers at Janet. "As for you, Janet, I'll be dealing with you on my own terms. Let this clown go or suffer the consequences."

Casey stormed away, his shoulders hunched with fury. Janet thought she would have felt sorry for him if she were not so angry with him.

Nick's eyes on her were grave with concern. "I'm sorry," he said. "I'll stop by tonight."

Janet shook her head. "Not tonight, Nick. I need to think. Casey's just part of the baggage we each carry. Tamara's kissing you kind of shook me up."

"I can see why. I've asked her not to do it. It's just her mean spirit, just her way of socking it to you. She knows I love you and she knows how much. Don't let her come between us." His voice was fierce with passion. "Don't let *anybody* come between us."

Then in a much gentler voice he said, "As you know, I'll be going away so soon, the first week in December, and I won't be back until two days before Christmas. November's going to fly. We'll be gone nearly a month. Sweetheart, we don't have time to quarrel, and we sure as hell don't have time to doubt each other. What we've got is too precious to lose, my darling."

Janet and the five students who were working on a book delineating stories of those who had overcome adversity met for a short while after school. Monk, Myra, Lily, Daryl, and Eileen all looked charged this afternoon.

"Wasn't that one cool concert?" Monk asked. "Enjoy it, Mrs. Smith?"

"I did." She felt her body grow warm.

Myra grinned, then giggled. "What did you do with those roses I saw Nick give you? Is he a friend? I know he was here a few Saturdays back."

"He's Miss Barry's friend, a family friend," Janet offered easily.

Monk looked at her speculatively. "Do you have a beau, Mrs. Smith? You're still a good-looking chick. Marc's fourteen. Did you have him when you were young?"

Janet frowned a bit. "My, aren't we curious today?" But she was pleased.

Lily cut in. "You *could* be as young as my mother. She had me when she was fifteen. Now she's thirty-two. She'll soon be thirty-three."

To Janet's relief, Monk cut in, ending the discussion on age. "My man, Nick," he said, strumming an imaginary guitar. "He's my hero."

Eileen shifted in her chair. "How're you coming along with interviewing Nick for our book? I'll do it if you don't have the time."

Myra looked at Eileen obliquely. "Oh, I'll just bet you would. He's a celebrity and I think Mrs. Smith could handle his story best."

The group agreed. "I'd interview that hunk any place, any time," Eileen said, blushing. Eileen was really a very bashful girl.

Now Eileen was really in a playful mood. "You never said what you did with the roses," she reminded Janet.

Janet raised her eyebrows. "Imagine that."

They talked a short while longer and the students trooped out. Janet waited for fifteen minutes before she went to her personal closet and took the roses from a shelf. Deeply inhaling the lovely fragrance, she covered the vase and the flowers with a white plastic grocery bag from the top, then another from the bottom, and set out.

At the end of the hall on her way to the parking lot, she burst out laughing. The five students were huddled together and they smiled sheepishly at her.

"Oh, man," Monk said. "We waited. We thought we'd get another glimpse of the roses."

Janet said truthfully, "I'd show you, but I've got to get somewhere in a hurry."

She said goodbye then and walked on. She was headed home to have a serious talk with Marc about his new friend, Pete. Was Nick, for all his youth, being a better parent to her son than she was?

Chapter 9

In the elevator of her apartment building, Janet smiled at a fellow passenger and felt happy. It had been a great day. She should have stopped by a Chinese restaurant to pick up the food Marc had asked for, but she wanted to talk to him as soon as possible. They could go out for Chinese food the next evening.

She unlocked the triple locks, opened the heavy oak door, and frowned. The apartment was dark. Wasn't Marc home?

"Marc," she called. At a muffled response from the direction of his bedroom, she relaxed. Nick's admonition about Marc's friendship with Pete had made her nervous, determined to confront him immediately.

"Why are you in the dark?" she began to call out as she snapped on the hall light. With the room illumined, she walked to the antique table and switched on the lamp. She would put the roses on a nearby table that would display them well. A sliver of a puzzle crept to mind; something was out of place.

It only took a few seconds to realize that the white jade music box was not on the antique table. Had Marc moved it? She frowned with irritation. She had asked him never to handle it.

Putting down the vase of roses, the tote bag, and her purse, she walked back to Marc's room and knocked on the door.

The muffled sound again. She thought he invited her in. Pushing the door open, she found him huddled on the side of the bed, his head bowed.

His sturdy young body was outlined in the hall and living room light. She went to him, beginning to be alarmed. "Sweetheart, what's wrong? Are you ill?"

"I'm not ill," he said in a choked voice, "just sick about something." She stroked his shoulders. He was so tense.

"What are you sick about?" She would ask him about the music box later.

"Your music box is gone."

"Yes, I saw. I thought you'd moved it. Did someone break in?"

He gave a short, hard laugh. "Yeah, someone broke in all right. Mom, I wouldn't blame you if you punched my daylights out...."

She pressed the side of her hand into his shoulder. "Don't mistreat yourself. I taught you better than that. I'd never strike you. What happened, Marc? Pull yourself together and talk to me. Do you mind a little light?"

"No."

She turned and switched on his night-table lamp, which flooded the room with low, soft light. She saw then that his eyes were reddened and his face was slightly swollen with crying. He looked terrible and she sat on the bed beside him. It came from the depths of her as she hugged him tightly. "I love you. Always remember that."

He nodded. "I know you do." The words spilled out then.

"It was Pete, Mom. You said you wanted to meet him, but he never wanted to come around. Like a jackass I bragged to him about the nice things we had here, thinking that would make him interested…"

When he had hesitated a long time, she stroked his back and said, "Go on."

"Well, today he told me he wanted to come and meet you. I said you didn't like kids in the apartment when you weren't here. He said he didn't feel well and needed to rest a few minutes, that he'd meet you and explain to you." He drew a very deep breath. "His eyes popped out of his head when we came in. He went wild over that music box. He asked me if it was expensive and I said it was. Bear with me, Mom. I'm hurting about this. I was stupid…."

Where was it leading? She touched his face. "Don't call my sweetheart names."

"Well, he said he was really hungry and I fixed him a sandwich, got him a big Coke. We talked about school, and then he said he thought he was getting the flu. His sister had it. He saw the drugstore on the corner and asked me to get him some medicine, asked me to lend him the money to pay for it." He broke off, shuddering. "Maybe you love me, Mom, but I was *stupid*."

"Forgive yourself. You were trying to do the right thing. I wouldn't have it any other way. You'll learn to be more careful. Use this as a lesson."

His voice, his demeanor was a little calmer now. "The drugstore was crowded and it took me a while. When I got back, he was gone. He took that blue afghan you had on the couch. I guess he covered the music box with that. Are you going to call the police?"

"I'll decide. Probably not. You know I don't want you to

see him again. If you two should meet, tell him the friendship is over."

He laughed harshly. "I'd like to find him and beat him up.
You love that music box."

"Don't talk like that." He sounded too much like his father.
"You're right. I love the music box and I probably will have
a hard time finding a replacement, if ever. But *you're* safe,
Marc, and you're what matters. Pete might have hurt you."

"Yeah, I know that now. I let him bully me. I know that, too."

Marshaling her thoughts, she asked, "Why did you feel you
needed him? He's so different from the other kids you're
friends with."

His eyes on her grew haunted then. Did he know why he
needed Pete?

"We met at a parade where we beat drums for our schools.
I didn't like him at first, but you met Nick and Dad hates Nick.
Right from the start, Dad asked me a lot of funny questions
about you and Nick. He said he'd take me away from you."
His voice had grown flatter now, hollow, but he rallied as he
said, "I like Nick, really *like* him. I like the way he talks to
me, teaches me the guitar. Dad never listens to me and he yells
all the time. He's messing with my mind. He keeps threatening to take me away from you.... Can he do that?" Anxiety
was palpable in his young body.

"I don't think so. I'd fight him. There were reasons why I
was given custody."

Marc turned to her, desperation on his face. "But you don't
know, do you? Mom, why don't you and Nick get married?
He's crazy about you. That way, he'd be my stepdad and boy,
wouldn't that be cool? Why don't you ask him to marry us?"

Janet laughed and hugged him. "You're an optimist, love."

"Don't you love him?"

Guy had asked that same question earlier today and she had been honest. She wasn't about to lie to Marc.

"I love Nick," she said sadly, "very much, but sometimes love just isn't enough."

His eyes on her were somber. Wanting to soothe him, she said, "You'll understand one day when you're grown up and in love."

Chapter 10

Janet, Nick, and Marc got to her apartment about dusk. In a merry mood after dinner at an Outback Steakhouse in Virginia, they had another trip to make that night. It was Sunday and Grace was coming home. She had called to say her nurse friend, Millie, wanted to drive down from Chicago and stay a few days. They planned to arrive around seven. Nick, Janet, and Marc would drive to Grace's house to welcome her back, carrying the homemade double-cheese, pepperoni pizza Grace loved.

Grace had called from her cell phone earlier in the afternoon. Everything was on schedule and she would call when they reached home. She had bubbled over with excitement. "All three of you are going to love the gifts I've bought you. Millie and I shopped ourselves weary. I'm going to drive now. Love you and see you soon."

She had talked a few minutes with Nick. When he hung

up, Nick said, "The old girl's happy. She's really looking forward to the holidays, but no more than I am."

He had caught her hand and squeezed it. Something had gone through her that she couldn't fathom. He had frowned. "What is it, love?"

She had hugged herself and said slowly, "I don't know. Goose going over my grave. Something. One thing I do know, I had too much steak, too much blooming onion, too much of that delicious thunder dessert."

"Marc and I packed it away, too. From time to time I read that lab rats live longer when they eat little. Test after test. A lot of scientists think that also applies to people."

Marc rolled his eyes. "I'm a growing boy. Don't expect me to eat less."

He sat beside Nick, who ran his hand over the boy's hair. "We'll make allowances for growing boys," he promised.

"You know," Janet said, "the late Hans Selye, who specialized in stress reactions, held that overeating is the single most stressful thing we can do."

Nick nodded. "Somehow I don't doubt it."

Marc sat upright, anticipating. "Mrs. Redmond said she'd bring me a big box of chocolate turtles. I hope she didn't forget."

"Don't you dare ask her in case she *did* forget," Janet told him.

"Aw, Mom," the boy protested, "I know how to be a gentleman. You keep telling me. Some of it's got to rub off on me."

"Good." Janet grinned at him, thinking he really was a good kid. And she wished she had a whole family to offer him.

"Mrs. Redmond said she'd teach me to make that fudge I'm so crazy about," Marc said suddenly. Then, "Nick?"

"Yeah, Marc."

"Man, you were lost in thought."

Nick turned and smiled at the boy. "Yes, I was."

Looking at his dear face, Janet wondered what Nick thought about now. It was the first week in November. She cleared her throat. "Are you almost ready for your West Coast gig?"

"Almost. We've got a few loose ends to tie up."

"But you'll be back for Christmas?" Marc asked, the timbre of his voice higher with anxiety.

"You can bet on it."

Marc left the room and Nick looked over to the antique table, noting the empty space where the white jade music box had been. "It's a damned shame," he said. "That box was so special to you."

"Yes, it was. I'm just so grateful Marc didn't get hurt fooling around with that little jerk. Nick, thank you for not mentioning the theft when Marc is around. He feels so bad about it."

"He told me he did. We talked about it. Like you, I assured him it wasn't his fault and yes, I'm glad, too, he didn't get hurt."

"Thank you again and again for warning me about Pete. I might have waited awhile."

Nick reached over, took her hand, and laced their fingers together. "You and Marc are my first priority, Jan. Nothing matters more to me."

When Marc came back, beaming at them both, Janet asked him, "Is your homework all done?"

"Yesterday. I'm way ahead of you. Gee, I'm glad Dad had to be away this weekend and I could stay with you two. He went to Atlantic City with a lady he told me he likes."

"Oh?" Janet hoped Casey had found someone.

Marc roamed the room restlessly. "Why doesn't she call?" he asked. "It's after seven."

"Give them some space," Janet responded. "Don't be like your father, exacting every minute, everything on strict schedule."

Marc laughed. "Boy, do you know Dad!"

As if on cue, the phone warbled pleasantly. With a sigh of relief, Janet picked up the receiver.

She had to strain to hear the hushed, choked voice on the line.

"I'm Millie, Grace's friend, and I hope you're Janet. Something *terrible* has happened. We just got in and Grace had a heart attack. I've called an ambulance. Her doctor lives nearby and he's coming right over. I think they'll be taking her to Adventist Hospital in Rockville. Is Nick with you?"

"Yes. My God." She fought to keep her composure.

"I don't need to speak with him. Please wait until I call you back in a few minutes so I can be sure of the hospital they're taking her to."

Nick's face turned ashen when she told him. He stood up, needing to move, to *act*. Tears stood in his eyes. She went to him, took him in her arms. "Oh, my darling," she told him, "be strong, as you *are* strong. There's so much that the doctors can do now. Let's kneel and pray."

Marc was shocked into silence. The three of them knelt in front of the couch. Janet offered a prayer for the three of them to help Grace; then each offered a silent prayer.

The call came from Millie in less than ten minutes. "We'll be going to Adventist," she said.

"I know the way," Janet said. "How is she?"

"Not well, I'm afraid. Her skin is so pale. I'm glad I was here. That's got to make a difference. Pray endlessly the way I will. She *has* to make it."

"Mom, I'm going with you."

"Sweetie," Janet began, "I think you'd better stay here. I'll tell the security guard to keep an eye on you. We'll be back as soon as possible."

Nick shook his head. "No, let him come with us. He doesn't need to be alone now."

Janet looked at him quickly. He seemed so quietly authoritative. It was as if Marc were *his* son—his and hers. The boy looked at him gratefully and went to take their coats from the hall closet.

Janet drove, thanking God for the light traffic. They parked in the big hospital lot and rushed in. Spotting Millie immediately, Nick went toward her with Janet and Marc. They stopped short. The misery on her face told them before she could speak. Then she whispered hoarsely, "She died before they could begin to work on her."

Marc clung to first Janet, then Nick in the aftershock. Her doctor was there and explained that Grace's heart had been failing for some time.

"She never said," Nick responded sadly.

"I know," the doctor said. "She saw a specialist once and he warned her to get treatment. I warned her. She never wanted to be a burden to you."

Scalding tears burned Nick's eyes. "She never *could* be a burden. I would have taken care of her for the rest of my life."

"So would I," Janet offered quietly. He looked at her gratefully.

Millie stepped up then. "There are things to be done, but I know best how to do them and do them swiftly. What funeral home would she have preferred?"

Nick told her and she nodded. "I can handle the rest. Go home and get some sleep. There's nothing any of us can do now. She would have wanted it this way—quick, painless. She's with her beloved Oscar now."

"Thank you," Nick told her, "but we can't let you handle this alone. We'll stay, take you home. One of us can drive your car."

"But the boy has school tomorrow," Millie protested. "It will soon be his bedtime."

"No," Marc told her. "I want to stay too. We'll *all* stay."

As they waited for the funeral home to pick up the body, they sat in Grace's room. Nick pulled the cover back and kissed her face and told her, "You always did everything to help make my world. Why couldn't you let me help you stay alive?"

He sat on a chair and his big body heaved with dry sobs. Janet had never seen anyone suffer like this. Bitter grief enshrouded him and he stopped his voice from breaking.

There were papers to be signed. They stayed until the administrative work was nearly done, until the funeral home's collapsible carrier held the body. It was nearly twelve then and Marc's head drooped with weariness.

They took Millie to Grace's house. "This is where I want to be," she told them. "I'll stay until after the funeral. I can help you make arrangements. God, I've *got* to keep busy."

"You've got to give yourself time to grieve," Janet continued.

"Millie, please feel free to stay as long as you wish," Nick said hollowly. "My mother will be buried by my father's side. He'll know she has come to him. She wanted to be buried quickly. No frills. A simple memorial service." He stopped his voice breaking, asking Millie, "Will you be all right?"

Quietly, the short, sturdy woman told him she wanted to be alone. Both Janet and Nick said they'd call her and she had their numbers. "We'll be back and we'll bring you food. Just deal with your loss as we have to deal with it."

They stood outside Nick's car in the crisp night air. Marc was asleep on the back seat.

"I'll take you two home," Nick said, "and I'll call you later when I get home." His voice had gone dead and her heart bled for him.

"No," she said suddenly, fiercely. "You won't need to call me because you'll be *with* me. Nick, I want you to stay with us."

"Thank you, my darling, but it's okay," he said sadly. "I've had a lot of body blows in my life. I can take this, too. Casey will make your life hell if I stay."

Without hesitation she said firmly, "Believe me, Casey's got his own baggage even if I haven't talked about it much. I want you to stay, Nick. I'm *insisting* that you stay. You say you love me, love Marc. God knows we love you. Let me do this for you. Grace would want this for you. You don't need to be alone."

Chapter 11

For the next two days Janet watched Nick anxiously, only relaxing when she saw that he held up very well. She took a week of emergency leave; he took temporary leave from Rocketship. He slept in her guest bedroom and she went to him when he seemed too restless, only to have him say each time, "Thank you, love, but I'm all right. I'll weather this." He was quiet, brooding.

After Grace's funeral and burial they came back to Janet's apartment, where he stood for a long while looking out the windows at gray, rain-threatened skies. Earlier, at the funeral, the sun had been high.

Finally, he turned to her. "She loved bleak weather," he said. "She felt it was God's way of letting us know that the world is not always a hospitable place."

She put her arms around him, and his big body drew closer to hers. "It would be so much harder if I didn't have you," he told her. "Do you know what you mean to me?"

She nodded. "I think I do and you mean everything to me."

Marc prepared a light meal of soup and salad and sandwiches. The boy ate well; neither of the grown-ups wanted much food.

"The lunch is good, Marc," Nick complimented him. Marc got up and came to Nick's side. "I'm so sorry, Nick, and I'm so glad you're here with us." He hugged Nick tightly as tears stood in both their eyes.

Late that afternoon, Marc did a lot of homework. At eight o'clock he came to Nick's room, where Nick lay on the bed while Janet sat in an easy chair.

"Look, guys," Marc said somberly, "I'm bushed and I'm gonna take a bath and turn in. I've got to get an early start tomorrow. I won't wake you when I leave. Now, Nick, if you want me to, I'll stay home if Mom says it's all right."

"No," Nick said. "Thanks, and I really appreciate your wanting to stay, but you go to school. I'm going to be fine."

After the boy left, Janet went out to the living room, put Schubert's "Ave Maria" on the CD player, and set it to keep repeating.

Coming back, she sat on the edge of the bed beside Nick and took his hand. "Sweetheart, there are several things I want to do for you that will ease your physical pain. Please go along with me."

He smiled sadly. "Just tell me...."

Going into the kitchen, she prepared a valerian infusion and set it to steep. Then in the bathroom she drew very warm—nearly hot—water into the tub, and poured in baking soda and Epsom salts. Huge white bath towels lay on a bench by the tub. She had bought massive bunches of French lavender early Monday, and the soothing odor permeated the apartment.

"'Ave Maria,'" he said as she came in the door. "Did you know that was one of Ma's favorites?"

"I know," she answered. "It's one of mine, too."

He soaked in the tub for a half hour, dried off, and pulled on boxer shorts and a terry cloth robe. He came out of the bathroom looking a little less tense.

"Put on your pajamas," she said, "and lie down. I'll go out for a moment."

In the kitchen she checked the valerian infusion, strained it, and poured it into a small china pot. A tablespoon of honey and a few squeezes of lemon juice. She poured the liquid into a thermos cup, carried it to his door, and knocked. Telling her to come in, he sounded weary, drained. He sat on the side of the bed in his pajamas.

"Please throw back the spread and lie down," she told him.

He did as she asked, unquestioning.

She began with him as he had once begun with her, at the shoulder, then his neck and scalp. Her slender, capable fingers worked his scalp, then moved to his face, and back to his neck, shoulders, and slowly down his tense body. He lay on his back and she handled him firmly, deeply, yet tenderly, finally moving to his thighs, calves, and feet.

"Turn over," she said gently; he did as she asked.

His back was especially affected; the muscles were knotted. She spent a while massaging him there. He was so tense, but he began to relax.

"Where did you learn to massage like this?"

"You taught me, remember?" Her fingers kept kneading.

"How could I forget? I'm a very good teacher."

Finishing, she lifted the cup of valerian infusion from the ~~covering~~ and handed it to him as he sat up. He drank ~~···ly~~ never pausing until it was all gone.

"I needed that," he said. "Did you and Ma talk about herbs?"

"We talked about almost everything," she said.

"You're so much like her. I guess that's one of the reasons I love you so much."

Looking at him, she felt her heart was so full she couldn't speak.

After a moment, she got a white leather, gold-lettered Holy Bible from the night table. "I want to read something to you that will bring you comfort. What would you like me to read?"

She was taking the very best care of him. Nick closed his eyes as he felt her in the deepest part of his soul.

"You choose," he said.

"Ecclesiastes?"

"Yes."

"The Bible has such gorgeous language," she murmured. "Are you very familiar with it?"

"I've read it through four times. I once considered becoming a minister." He was full of surprises. She found the chapter she sought, chapter two, and began to read:

To everything there is a season, and
a time to every purpose under the heaven:
A time to be born, and a time to die.

She read through eight more examples of purposes and times and stopped, reflecting, letting *him* reflect. He drew very quiet then, hardly breathing until he echoed, *"A time to be born, and a time to die."*

He sounded as if he was choking on his tears.

She saw him lean toward her, saw the terrible grief break on his face. Putting the Bible on the nightstand, she took him in her arms and held him against the violent onslaught of his

ragged sobbing. Opening her robe, she pressed his hot face
that was wet with acid tears against her bared breasts. And she
held him hard against her, with her heart drumming powerful,
healing sympathy and love. His grief was cutting him to
ribbons and she could hardly bear it, but after a long time the
sobbing slowed.

"I'm going to sleep in here beside you," she told him. "My
son will understand. This robe is light, noncumbersome. I'll
keep it on. It's a big bed." He felt deeply grateful.

"Please remember," she said slowly, "that all these years
you knew her precious love. Be grateful, my darling, for what
she was able to give you. You're like her. And she's part of
you forever."

The valerian coursed through his bloodstream, made his
eyelids heavy, his muscular body relax. He slept then and she
got up and went about the apartment, turning off lights, cutting
off the CD player. She looked in to find Marc dead to the
world, snoring lightly. Leaving a night-light on, she lay beside
Nick in the still room. It was raining quite hard now. Her grandmother had often said that it sometimes rained after funerals,
that it was God's way of washing away the sins of the dead.

It was nearly midnight before she slept. At two-thirty in the
morning Janet roused sharply to the door chimes. She sat up.

"I'd better go to the door with you," Nick said.

"I'm sorry it woke you. Listen, love, I'm sure it's Mrs.
Pride. She's eighty-nine and lives alone. She gets panic attacks
and comes to me to help her. She usually calls, but sometimes
she's too terrified and she just knocks. She never stays long,
she just needs to hear a friendly voice."

"Okay. Leave the door open a little just in case."

"I will." And going out she did as he asked. Drawing a deep

breath, she looked through the front door viewer. Casey stood there, swaying.

Enraged, she unlocked the door and before she could get the chain off, he barked, "Let me *in,* Janet. We're gonna *talk!*"

Keeping her voice down, Janet grated, "Don't come in here, Casey. You've been drinking. I'll talk with you down the hall."

"What if I *push* my way in?" His low laugh was harsh.

"I'll have you arrested. You've got a rep at police stations all over the city for bad behavior when you're drunk."

Looking at his ex-wife through narrowed eyes, Casey knew she'd do as she threatened and going to jail wouldn't help him in a custody fight.

Taking the locks off, she went into the hall and gently closed the door. She led him down the hall to a nearby alcove, where he stared at her with bloodshot eyes.

"Redmond's here, isn't he? You've got on a sexy robe, sexy color. You're sleeping with that bastard and my son's in there. Want me to tell you what that makes you in my mind?"

She slapped him hard then, across the mouth, and he reeled with disbelief. Grabbing her arm, he shook her. Trying to pull away, she found herself in his steely grip.

Willing herself to calmness, she told him, "I'd never do anything to hurt Marc. Can you say the same?"

"I've had you followed. I know Redmond's living here."

Her voice shot through with icy contempt, Janet told him, "If you've had me followed, then you know Nick's mother was buried today. He's staying until he can get over some of the grief, not that it's any of your business. You're despicable, Casey. How *dare* you come here so soon after her funeral? You miserable *cur!*"

His voice rose more then, furious and guttural. "You're gonna pay for this. No woman plays strumpet before my son and me."

"Let me go, Casey! You're hurting me!"

She was going to twist away if it killed her. Then Nick was there. "Let her go, Smith. Now!"

Nick's voice was so cold, so deadly that it shook Casey. Liquor never let him be the man he wanted to be. Slowly he released his grip and Janet moved away to Nick's side. He put a protective arm around her shoulders. Casey turned swiftly and snarled at them, "You haven't heard the last of this. By God, you're both going to pay for this, and, Janet, I'm going to see you get what's coming to you."

Chapter 12

Next morning, Janet came out of the bathroom wrapped in a pale blue terry cloth bathrobe. They had slept late. She found Nick in the kitchen sitting at the table with a pitcher of freshly squeezed orange juice mixed with cranberry juice and a covered basket of hot buttered raisin bagels. Touching his shoulder she asked, "How do you feel?"

He took her hand and pressed it to his lips. "Jan, thank you for last night and thank you for all you've done since Ma died." His voice was husky with emotion.

"I care about you, sweetheart," she said sadly, "so much. I wish I could take away at least some of the pain."

"You have."

She sat at the side of the table by him and he studied her carefully. "Pale blue becomes you," he told her. "You're a beautiful woman, my love, more beautiful than you know."

"Thank you. You were sleeping soundly when I got up. I'm

sorry about what happened last night. I was so furious I didn't want to talk about it. I'm glad you heard what was going on and came out. You stopped what could have been a nasty situation."

"I think I know where Smith's coming from. He's an insecure man who doesn't want to share his son's love with another man. I'm sure he thinks we're sleeping together and maybe that hurts."

"It's none of his business. We're divorced."

"Oh, I know, but I suspect not in his heart."

She hadn't told him about Casey having them followed, but Nick said, "We could never keep it under cover, my staying here with you and Marc. I'm sure Casey knows people here. People recognize me. There would necessarily have to be gossip. People talk and sometimes they're overheard. Smith really loathes me."

"He's envious. He'd like to be half the man you are."

He looked somber. "I'd be envious, too, if he had you and I didn't. You're a precious woman for a man to have." His eye fell on a piece of pink paper near the bagel basket. "You had a call."

"I thought I heard the phone." She picked up the paper. Judge Hamilton wanted her to call. The judge had handled her divorce from Casey. She swallowed hard.

"Do you think Smith's already making good on his threat?" he asked. "From what little you tell me about him, he's never going to stop trying to get custody of Marc."

"Over my dead body," Janet grated.

"Whatever I can do to help, you know I'm solidly with you."

The phone rang on the edge of the table. Janet picked it up to hear a pleasant woman's voice. "Mrs. Smith, this is the nurse at Marc's school. He wants to come home and I think he should."

"What's wrong?" Alarm bells went off in Janet's head.

"He complains of a headache and a queasy stomach. He has no temperature and no other serious signs, but there *is* some flu going around. I think he's upset about something. If you're going to be there, I'm going to send him along."

"Please do, and thank you."

She told Nick. "Poor guy," he said. "He's done everything he could to help me. I like the way you're raising him, Jan."

"Pray that I manage to keep him."

"You will."

She called Judge Hamilton then and set up an appointment for two-thirty. "I'm flexible," he said, "and if you can't make it on such short notice, I'll understand and schedule for tomorrow."

"I'll make it," she told the judge. She hardly breathed as she asked him, "Is this about Marc?"

"I'm afraid it is. I've asked Mr. Smith to be here, too. I want to talk with you both. He's making some troublesome allegations, and I want to hear your side of this. I'll look forward to seeing you both at two-thirty in my chambers at the courthouse."

"What is it?" Nick asked and Janet told him.

"Apparently you were right. Casey didn't lose any time."

Nick took her hand, squeezed it. "Sweetheart, I'm not going to stay the whole week, let alone two weeks. I'm going back to Rocketship tomorrow afternoon. I wanted to go today, but I'm still numb."

"Please don't," she whispered. "Go back to Rocketship if you feel you have to, but you *need* to be here with me, with Marc and me. A couple of days more can't matter for what Casey's trying to do...."

"I couldn't take it if I hurt either one of you."

She was pleading now. "Say you'll stay at least a couple more days. Please."

Nick knew now that they had firmly bonded. She was heart of his heart, soul of his soul.

"Okay," he finally said, "God knows I *need* to stay."

Janet went to the door at light chimes sounding and Marc stumbled in. Janet hugged him. "The nurse called. Where do you hurt?" Nick came out of the kitchen and stood with them. He touched Marc's arm.

The boy didn't hesitate. He flung his book bag aside, threw his coat on a chair, and told them, "Dad's messing with my mind again...."

"How?" Janet demanded.

"He came by the school today and we talked in the counselor's office. He says he's going to take me away from you. He asked a lot of crazy questions about you and Nick."

"Questions?" Janet frowned and thought she already knew the answer.

"Yeah, like where did Nick sleep. Mom, I'd never tell him or anybody yours or Nick's business."

"It's all right, darling. I'm sorry."

"I hate Dad," the boy burst out. "I wish he was dead!"

Marc wasn't crying; he simply looked as if he'd explode with anger.

Nick went to him, put his arm around his shoulders. "Let's sit down, Marc."

The man and the boy sat on the sofa and Janet sat on the other side of Nick.

"You think I'm terrible to say I hate him, but I do."

"It's okay," Nick assured him. "Your father loves you and you love him. You're very angry and I can certainly understand that. He wants the best for you...."

"He tried to turn me against you and Mom. That isn't right."

Nick nodded. "No, it isn't, but hatred, Marc, is not the

answer and it's the other side of love. Your father's hurting and he's striking out blindly. It will be years before you understand what makes him act the way he does, but you can look forward to understanding him one day."

"Never!"

"One day you'll change your mind. You're from his seed. He helped to give you life. I'm going to ask you to do something that will be hard."

"What? Does it have to do with Dad?"

"Yes." Nick looked now like the minister he had said he once wanted to be. "Forgive him, Marc, as God forgives you, forgives us all. This, too, is something you won't understand now, but you will later. Try not to hate him, because hatred corrodes you inside. We can't forget, but we *can* forgive."

Marc had listened carefully. "You sound strange," he said. "All right, I'll try not to hate him, but I don't love him the way I love you."

Nick's eyes on him were warmly embracing. "I love you and we both know that, but you do love your father. Search your heart and you'll know it. Your mom's going out. After you lie down a bit, what do you say we walk in the park, let a few autumn leaves fall on us, and be back by the time she returns?"

"Yeah," Marc said as his eyes lit up. "I'd really like that."

Judge Leonard Hamilton stood up as Janet entered his chambers. He was a small man, impeccably dressed, his skin, hair, and eyes nearly of the same medium brown hue.

"Mrs. Smith." They shook hands. "I won't keep you long. Mr. Smith hasn't arrived."

"Oh, yes, I have," Casey said from the doorway.

When they were informally seated, Judge Hamilton began,

"You say, Mr. Smith, that you want to reopen the case that gives custody of your son, Marc, to your ex-wife?"

"I do, Your Honor." Casey's voice was gravelly. If he had been drinking, it didn't show.

"Would you mind saying again what you told me on the phone?"

"Sure. Not at all. My ex is going around with a clown half her age. Now she's moved him in with her and my son. It just happened and I want to stop it now."

"Mrs. Smith?"

Janet drew a deep breath. "It's true, but not in a harshly judgmental way. I'm forty-one and Nick is thirty-one, a very mature thirty-one…." Thinking of Nick and his shepherding and comfort of her son that morning, Janet felt warmth like sun rays surround her. She felt it now. Nick was as mature as his mother and Bea thought he was and she wanted to marry him. The judge saw the beatific smile spread across her face and wondered. He had always liked her.

"How long have you known this man?"

"Since September."

"Not very long, but things sometimes develop quickly. He is now living with you and Marc?"

She nodded and explained that Nick's mother had just died and he had taken it brutally hard and needed them. The judge nodded. "It seems a compassionate thing to do."

"I don't care about trumped-up reasons," Casey blurted out. "She's carrying on with another man before our son and I won't let it happen."

Janet sent him a furious glance, then turned to the judge. "Your Honor, the man in question and I aren't lovers. We love each other and we're friends."

"Do you think you will marry?"

"Yes," she said firmly, surprising herself as Casey shot her a murderous look. He had only one response to Nick: blind, unreasoning anger.

The judge leafed through some papers on his lap. "I've had one of my social workers check out a Mr. Nicholas Redmond." He nodded at Janet. "That *is* the man in question?"

"Yes, Your Honor."

"Mr. Smith gave me his name. At first glance," the judge said, "he seems to be a man of integrity and honor. Solid background. His father was a great, celebrated jazz musician, his mother a school counselor. The young man's group called Rhapsody is going up. Their music is in good taste. He and his group are involved with doing what they can to help schoolkids and the community. I intend to check further, but at first glance, I'm impressed…."

"Judge." Casey seemed evil to Janet now. "Ask her about a tart who plays with that band and kisses this Nick on the mouth in public."

The judge tapped his glasses and looked at Janet. "Is this true and if so, doesn't that bother you?"

She shook her head. "They were once engaged to be married, but they broke up. She married someone else, then divorced him. No, it doesn't bother me. The music world can be different and he *does* have a lot of integrity."

A bemused expression crossed Judge Hamilton's face as he looked at Casey, asking, "Mr. Smith, you don't regard women very highly, do you?"

Casey shrugged. "I used to regard this woman highly, but not anymore."

"I'm sorry to hear that," the judge said evenly. "You want to reopen the case, Mr. Smith, and I advise against it. I checked Marc's school record and he is thriving. You have excellent visitation rights. I would handle the case and I would rule against you." The judge stood up. "I'm afraid I must move on." He shook hands with both of them. "Be grateful that you have such a splendid lad."

Chapter 13

By Monday of the last week in November, Janet breathed more easily. Nick was definitely beginning the slow healing process when he rang her door chimes that morning. He had gone back home; she and Marc had prepared frozen meals for him. He had visited often, as they visited him. Now, Marc was away on a two-day field trip to New York with his teacher and fellow band mates.

Going to the door, she let Nick in, raised her face for his kiss. "You're cold." She stroked his leathery bronze face. "What's in the package?" she asked, eyeing the wide, flat white box.

"A present for you."

"Ah, that deserves another kiss."

She was surprised then at the passion, the sudden intensity of his kiss. "You're such a great kisser," she told him. "I don't wonder that your favorite things at Christmas are kisses and mistletoe. Have you always had plenty of both?"

"Not always, but I could and did dream. Now, I've got you and I intend to make up for lost time. Open your present."

"Let's sit down a moment," she said. They sat on the love seat and she turned to him. "Thanksgiving's only a few days away. Let's stay here, Nick. I'll do the cooking and you can rest. I sense some weariness in you as you get ready for your L.A. gig. And you're still grieving...."

"Fair enough. Thank you for being so thoughtful, but I'll help. Now, by Christmas, I should have enough energy to do all the desserts and the corn bread and sausage stuffing." He ran the back of his fingers over her face. "Ah, love, what a glorious Christmas we'll have."

Just thinking about the coming holidays gave her goose bumps, filled her with warmth. She said then, "When you talked with Marc while he was so upset, I began to realize just how mature you are.

"Your guitar lessons for Marc, cautioning me about Pete. Really listening to my son—and me. I feel so different about you now than in the beginning."

His eyes embraced her. "Does this mean you can see us as a married couple?"

It was what she had wanted him to say, but she still held back. "Maybe." She didn't look at him. "I'll open the package now."

He looked a little hurt, but hopeful, wondering if he was ever going to be able to make this woman his.

Untying the box, she opened it and the tissue paper inside and lifted a gossamer sheer and lacy black gown from Saks Fifth Avenue, gasping at the beauty of the garment. "Thank you." Smiling and suddenly shy, she asked him, "Shall I model it for you?"

"Come here," he told her. She went to him. He pulled her

down onto the love seat and into his lap. "As lovely as the gown is, it's your silken brown *skin* I need to see and feel."

Her heart beat too fast as she leaned against him.

He held her, then, slid her to one side of the love seat, got up, went to the hall coat closet, and pulled two folded sheets of paper from his inner overcoat pocket. He came back. "Remember I told you I was writing a song for you. It's turning out well and I'm making it the lead song on the album we're cutting in January. I'm nearly finished, but there're a few rough edges. Would you like me to sing it to you?"

Eyes sparkling, she told him, "You know I would."

He sat on the rug in front of the love seat, facing her. He handed her the sheets and she read the words quickly. Looking at her face, adoring her, he cleared his throat and in a clear, husky baritone that was his now-growing-famous trademark, began to sing:

What I want from you—
Bone-deep kisses that set my soul on fire,
passion and loving that feed ev'ry desire.

What I want from you—
Wellsprings of caring that fill both our hearts,
a lifetime of sharing that never departs.

His eyes narrowed and he breathed more deeply, caressing her with his glance as a thrill shot through her.

What I want from you—
Flame-filled ecstasy; you're part of my soul.
Love of my life, you're a jewel to behold.

He stopped then for a long moment before he finished:

What I want from you—
is everything and I will give my
everything to you.

The melody was so gorgeous, and he sang with so much feeling, that when he sang the last words, tears stood in her eyes.

Afterward, Janet wasn't sure how they came to be in her bedroom. She only knew that she felt a heated longing for him that seared her very soul. She was still not used to feeling like this, but she didn't want to stop, wasn't *going* to stop.

She went into Nick's arms. He slowly began to undress her, quenching for the moment a raging need to take her quickly, so desperate was his need. She heard the words from her lips, words linked to a former time with him.

Close to him she whispered, "You once said you wanted me to come to you, tell you what I want—anything and everything…" She paused, suddenly holding back.

A wide grin spread across his face. "Yes, and I meant it, *mean* it." His eyes blazed fire as he reached for her.

"No, *wait*. You're such a generous man, but what I want from you is what I already *get* from you. Love and respect and affection—so many things. You cherish me and I cherish you. We've already got so much."

"You're right."

"We've got so much."

His smile was wicked then. "I also asked you to tell me something else…."

"Oh, yes," she murmured. "You asked me to tell you what I want you to *do* to me." She drew a quick breath and blushed vividly as she went even closer to him, and lazily ran the wet tip of her tongue back and forth under his ear. He shuddered with powerful thrills coursing through him as she told him in honeyed cadences all the intimate, delicate, delicious actions she wanted him to perform.

Their next kiss was long and deep with the heavy hardness of his male member pressing against her, demanding entrance to her willing body. "Kissing you is like nothing I've known before," he told her. "You've come to hold back nothing from me. I feel I go into your very heart and soul, and God knows you go into mine."

"I'm glad. Your kisses and you have opened a new world for me and that's *so* important."

"It is," he agreed. Then, "Why are you looking at me like that?"

"Like what?"

"You've got a strange Mona Lisa smile."

She bit her bottom lip, felt shy and bold at once. "Well," she began, "if we're going to be married…"

"Oh, Jan, my darling sweetheart. Don't tease me. Do you mean it?"

"Yes, I mean it. I want to marry you, belong to you, be with you for the rest of my life." He pulled her to him, and his mouth on hers was merciless in its ardor.

Leaning against him, she said softly, "I just told you what I want you to do to me and I never could have done that when I first met you. I'm changing. I feel almost wanton, but it's just with you."

His thumb traced her jawline tenderly. "You're not wanton, but if you were I'd love and welcome it. You're coming to feel your womanhood, going deep into yourself, discovering your sexuality along with your life. It makes me humble that I'm a part of this. Jan, you're dealing with a man who loves you more than life itself. Yes, you've changed and I cannot begin to tell you how much the new you turns me on."

"There's only one thing," she began.

"Which is?"

"I want to wait awhile to get married. I'd like a beautiful September wedding."

"That's a long way off, and waiting's going to be hard, but I'll give you all the time you need. Let's pick out your ring before I leave next week."

"Could we wait until you come back? I want to take a lot of time. Do you mind?"

"No way do I mind. I've got my heart's desire now. I can wait for anything, except we're losing time. I want to make love with you so bad I hurt."

Pulling his head down to hers, she teased him, "Then what are we waiting for? My body's screaming for you."

She turned the covers of the bed back and the pale blue sheets complemented the satiny brown of her skin. It was quiet, no music, only street sounds. The warmly spicy aroma of French lavender, like the bunches she had bought to soothe him while he first grieved, filled the air.

As he laid her back, she sat up again, asking, "Wouldn't you like some music? And what?"

He shook his head. "I don't want you away from me that long. I'm starved for you. We don't need music. I just want to hear you breathe, cry out…"

She smiled. "The neighbors—" she began. And he placed his hand over her lips. "Scream if you want to. I'll cover you."

As they kissed, ravening hunger hit them both. Then his mouth went to the warm, brown mounds that were her breasts. Her nipples contracted and pebbled as he sucked them gently, then moved his mouth over them. "They're so beautiful," he told her. "*You're* so beautiful."

She was bold now, secure with him. "Remember," she told him. "*Anything and everything.*"

"You've got it."

Pulling her gently into a seated position on the bed, he knelt before her and put his arms around her waist. Pressing his face into the bottom of her belly, he nipped her and she jumped. "Did I hurt you?" he asked.

"No. I was just surprised."

He kissed her belly, then the lower length of her, patterning her with the tip of his tongue. Hot kisses. He came back up her body with tantalizing kisses until he reached her center.

She trembled wildly as vivid thrills swept through her. She stroked the crisp, black dreadlocks and his face, her fingers urging him on. "I want to give you everything," he whispered. "Just tell me what you want...."

Shakily she responded, "You seem to know what I want before I need to ask for it." After he kissed her gently and moved down again, she moaned deep in her throat and pressed his head into her body. "Oh, Lord, Nick," she cried, "what are you *doing* to me?"

He raised his head, and his eyes were tender with concern and the edge of challenge. "It's your call," he told her. "Tell me to stop and I will."

She didn't want him to stop. This was new territory for her, enthralling, exciting, and she gloried in it. When she spoke it was torn from the depths of her heart. "My darling, I love you, love you."

What she had told him she desired, he set out to do for her. She would want for nothing as his own beloved. His hot mouth trailed kisses down her body. His tongue went to her navel indentation, her belly, then lingered again at her female center. His kisses at first were butterflies, lightly touching her body, then growing more demanding. For a brief moment she stopped him, reached into the night table drawer, and took out a thin roll of latex. Working together they smoothed it onto his rigid shaft.

He stormed her body then as she opened to let him in, wrapping her legs around his back, gasping for breath at the sheer ecstasy she felt. He went in slowly, easily, hot and throbbing in the wet sheath he entered. Her inner walls clutched him tightly, caught and held his shaft with powerful desire.

The air around them shimmered with excitement and intensity. He thought her face, reflecting fused love and desire and passion for him, was the most beautiful sight he had ever beheld.

There was so much more he intended to do, but the splendor of the woman under him was too much and he exploded, fireworks and raging, stormy oceans in his loins. And he heard her cries of pleasure and placed the side of his hand over her mouth as he had said he would. Every fiber of his being leaped to attention as they began a thrilling joint ascent to glory.

In all her life she had known nothing like the joy that filled her now as her tight sheath drew him, held him, then convulsively shuddered for long moments and began to voluptuously grip and relax, grip and relax. Then she lay quietly under him, shaken like a rag doll until she was limp.

Later, lying beside him, she asked, "Don't you want a snack or a drink? You know I keep good wine, all kinds of cheeses."

"No," he assured her. "Right now I've got only one hunger, one thirst, and you're taking care of both."

They were quiet then, resting, until he rolled over, got to

his feet, and pulled her up. His body outlining hers was hard against her softness. He put his face in her hair, then nuzzled her neck, inhaling the faint fragrance of Shalimar bath oil she had touched on certain pulsing spots.

He held her tightly against his wide, muscular chest where she nestled as torpor lay on and in her like a pearly veil. Her skin grew luminous with faint perspiration. So they were one, she thought, perfectly blended. Melded. This ecstasy could not last, but while it lasted it was sheer heaven. And it would come again and again.

He stood at the pinnacle of the highest mountain with her at his side. And the fire in his loins made him feel like an African god. At that moment, he thought he knew the meaning of his music, of his *life*.

Later, still hungry for each other, he lay on the bed with her again, pulled her on top of him, and caught his long fingers in her hair, gripping the heavy mass, bringing her mouth down hard against his for a very long while.

This time he got up and got a condom from his pants pocket and again they were a team smoothing it on. He squeezed her fingers and smiled at her before he touched her lips, then very lightly traced her lips with his index finger. She trembled—with him, her lips were one of her most sensitive spots.

They were slower now, basking in ecstasy. "Do I please you?" he asked her.

"Yes and yes and endless more yeses. I never hoped to feel what I'm feeling with you."

As she straddled him, Nick's big hands caressed her firm, heavy buns, cupped them, and she thrilled to his loving touch.

"You're so damned special," he told her. "I've always known what I want and seldom failed to get it. I'm relentless when I want something the way I want you."

"You said you wanted me to love you the way you love me. I already *do,* Nick. I think I did the day you said it."

He crushed her to him, held her, again stroked her jawline with his thumb. "You're like an oven in there," he teased her. "And Lord, does it feel good!"

She laughed, relaxing with the compliment. "I'm lightly heating something in my oven—something wonderful and powerful."

"I feel powerful with you, inside you."

Very quietly she murmured, "And I feel powerful with you inside me."

Pulling her catercornered on the bed, he raised her arms over her head and held both her hands in one of his.

Looking at him with limpid eyes, she asked softly, "Am I your prisoner?"

Gravely he answered, "For the moment, yes, but I want you free."

After a short while he released her arms and slipped into a deeper place, touched her womb, and was gripped by muscles controlled by desire and love and caring. He stopped and panted for a few minutes, fighting his body's ache to spill his seed into her. "You want to wait," he said, "but we ought to hurry and get married. I want at least one child with you."

The thought of bearing his baby kindled fires like nothing else he had said had done.

"I want that, too. But remember I've got a son."

"We've *both* got a son—Marc. He's a great kid, Jan, savvy. He knows there's more than enough love to go around."

He worked her now, easily, expertly. His loins were bursting with fervor, his heart pounded. He could not remember a time he'd felt the glory of his own body entwining with a soul mate. Moving rhythmically, his strokes were smooth, perfect, and he felt the beginning this time of erupting volcanoes in his loins, in his body, in his very being.

As he caught her close and kissed her with nearly violent passion, a tidal wave of pleasure took her soft body and she felt the sweeping waves begin and spread until they were rippling feverishly through her. This man had her heart. This man had her body. This man had her soul.

"We're really good together," he said after a while as they lay side by side. "The way I knew we'd be. I just needed a chance to prove it to you."

Almost sadly she told him, "I've never felt what I've felt with you from the beginning."

And he responded, "You take me places I've never been. I've wanted a love like this and never thought I'd find it."

They did not speak of Tamara or Casey.

As they lay there, Nick propped himself on one elbow and gently kissed Janet's breasts. "Hey, you're drifting off. I'm supposed to be the one who falls asleep while you fret and want more stroking."

"We're different from other people. You know that now."

He seemed to probe her heart as he said tenderly, "My little rabbit has grown up. You're not running scared anymore."

"That's because you make me feel so secure in your love. I finally know that it really doesn't matter that I'm older than you, that you're younger than I am. You're mature, Nick, the way so many people never are."

His eyes on her were somber. "I'm light-years ahead of

you, my love. I've known that a very long time. All that matters is the way we're drawn to each other, the deep, deep feelings we have for each other, and the way we fit together."

Chapter 14

The second week of December, Janet found things humming along nicely. The spirit of Christmas was in the air now, school programs for the season were being set up. The choir sang carols in the hallways just after lunch each day. School would be closed all Christmas week.

She hadn't heard from Nick as much as she wanted to, but he had explained that he was very, very busy. She sat at her classroom table after school hoping he was taking care of himself.

Her writing group trooped in—Monk, Daryl, Lily, Myra, and Eileen—and took seats at the table.

"This will be another brief meeting," she began. "I just want to tie up any loose ends so you can continue to work on our project during the holidays if you wish. We will not meet again until mid-January."

Monk's hand went up and she acknowledged him. "I keep thinking about the title for our book: *Overcoming Adversity.*

It'd be so much cooler to call it *Don't Let Nothing Get You Down*." Janet smiled; he had mentioned the title before and she found it appealing.

"We'll certainly consider it," she said. "Does anybody else have a different title in mind?"

No one did.

Eileen pulled her small eyeglasses down on her nose and peered at Janet. "Have you interviewed Nick Redmond any more?"

"I have. After Christmas, I'll have lots of information to read you."

Eileen rolled her eyes. "Now if you tire of talking to him, I'd be glad to take over."

"You already have a chosen subject."

"I'd give that one up in a heartbeat," she said as the class laughed.

"Mrs. Smith?" Monk's pleasant face was beaming.

"Yes."

"You're all lit up. Like I told you before, I saw the flowers Nick brought you here. Do you and the maestro have anything cooking?"

Janet ran her tongue over her teeth in a closed mouth. "That's pretty personal, don't you think?"

"You ask us personal questions all the time," Lily countered with a little pout.

"Only when I need the information, and this certainly isn't information you need."

"I think you two are going to get married," Eileen said pertly. "You make such a great couple. I saw you coming out of a movie theater, holding hands. I spoke to you but you had eyes only for him."

"I'm sorry. You know I would have spoken."

"I know. And you know something else, you're all lit up these days. You look divinely happy. Nick Redmond is what I want Santa to bring me for Christmas."

The girls giggled and the boys guffawed.

Janet couldn't help smiling. "I think we can wrap this up."

"Just a few more minutes," Monk said. "You're our favorite teacher and we enjoy shooting the breeze with you."

So Janet talked with them a short while longer, then demurred that she had to go.

As Janet gathered her things preparatory to going home, Bea came in. She walked over to Janet and lifted Janet's chin with her forefinger. "You know, girlfriend," she said, "I've been meaning to tease you and I don't want to pry, but you look like a woman who's been touched up around the edges."

"Oh, you," Janet said, laughing.

Bea stretched out her hand to display a multicarat diamond ring.

"How beautiful," Janet said, hugging her. "I'm so happy for you and Memphis. When does it happen?"

"We're not waiting too long." Janet had told her about Nick's proposal and she had been overjoyed. Now she said, "By the time you finally get ready to tie the knot, I'll be your matron of honor rather than maid of honor."

"You'll be great either way."

Bea paused a moment. "Maybe it's none of my business but, honey, I wouldn't wait too long if I were you. Nick wants at least one child...."

"He told me."

"And you want that too?"

"Very much." At Bea's words, a vision came to her mind of Nick and her on his bed, on her bed. He had written a song for her, sung it to her. She felt an edge of hunger for his presence and his big body now.

"I'm going to run," Janet said. "Nick's been calling early and I want to be there."

"I'll bet you do. You look wonderful, Janet. Nick's brought something into your life I was afraid you were never going to get. And *I* was Cupid."

"For which I'll owe and thank you forever. And Memphis has brought into your life what I've always wanted you to have."

"Say it again." Bea laughed, leaned over, and kissed Janet's cheek.

At home, Janet found Marc sprawled on the couch watching a TV game show.

"Don't say it, Mom. I'm doing my homework next. This is almost over. Hey, get in the Christmas spirit."

"You won't say that when you're grown up and earning half what others earn."

Marc grinned sheepishly. "I forgot to tell you I told Dad you and Nick are getting married."

"And?"

"He just looked kinda sad. Yeah, and I guess he looked angry, too, but he didn't *say* anything."

"How unlike Casey not to comment."

"Boy, I'm glad about you two. Nick's a really cool guy. Mom, Dad asked if I could stay with him Christmas Eve, but I want to be with you and Nick. Do you mind?"

"No, sweetie. We're looking forward to your being with us."

Marc laughed delightedly. "Nick said we're gonna shop the city empty. Boy, I can't wait."

"You need to get your father something special to make up for not spending Christmas Eve with him."

"Yeah. I need you to help me. How come you're so concerned about him?"

"He's your biological father. He gave me you."

"I heard you and him and Nick in the hall that night."

Janet drew a swift breath. "You heard?"

"Yeah, I woke up when he was ringing the doorbell and half yelling when you let him in. When Nick got up and went out, I cracked the door. I was going to make Dad let you go, but Nick was cool." His thin, teenaged voice went down an octave, mimicking Nick. "'Let her *go*, Smith!' Boy, was he ever cool!"

"Yes," Janet said thoughtfully. "He *was* and *is*."

With Marc deep in study in his room, bolstered by a salad plate full of chocolate chip cookies, Janet had settled down to muse when the phone rang. She whispered to herself, "I got here just in time."

But it was not Nick. A hotly sensual woman's voice said hello, then asked, "Janet? Do you know who this is?"

"I'm afraid you'll have to tell me."

"Tamara Kyle."

Janet nearly dropped the phone. "Why are you calling?" She didn't intend to play games with the little flirt.

"Well, I'm alone and I'm very happy. Janet, do you remember a song called 'We'll Be Together Again'?"

Janet thought a moment and remembered; she said so.

"It's a favorite for Nick and me. It's way before our time, but the sentiment fit so well."

"It's before my time, too."

"Oh? I guess I feel that not much is before *your* time. Nick and I are making a recording of that song—a single—to be released next spring. He's here in L.A. with me now and we're getting closer, the way we were, the way we're meant to be. Be kind to yourself and let him go. I don't intend to hurt him again."

The open line hummed then; Tamara had hung up.

Later, Janet picked at a TV dinner. Marc had gotten his own food. Her face was set in a steady frown by the time Nick called, but she found herself smiling when she heard his voice.

"Jan," he said, "I'm sorry I haven't been able to call you as often as I meant to."

"It's okay. You called often at first. I've called little because I wanted to give you a chance to dig in. How are you feeling?"

"Pretty good, but my schedule is hellish. Guy got a great chance to play in Spain, so he's leaving day after tomorrow. There's preparations for the album that'll be released in spring and a great company wants us to make a video. The club is packed every night. I get tired just thinking about it."

"Don't forget," she said quietly, "you've got grief work to do."

"Lord, do I know it," he groaned.

She wanted to tell him about Tamara's call and couldn't. Instead, she asked, "How's Tamara?"

He was silent a moment. "Funny you should ask. Tam's fine. She's taking over a lot of Guy's duties and she's helping me write our songs with a genius edge. They're crazy about her out here. I don't know what I'd do without her, and I think she's finally growing up."

He was vividly enthusiastic about Tamara Kyle and his voice had lost its lazy cadence. He sounded warm and excited. They chatted awhile longer and she was aware that he made no specific references to the love they shared. Instead, he seemed almost absentminded.

After too short a time, he said, "I've got to go, hon. So much to do and so damned little time. You take care and we'll stay in touch." He had called her "hon," not "love" or "my darling."

She hung up and felt a coolness creep along her spine. Was something wrong, and if so, what? Why hadn't she told Nick about Tamara's call? Because, she quickly realized, he hadn't wanted to hear Tamara criticized. He seemed to think she was the greatest thing since Noah's Ark. She tried to crowd the words from her mind, but they welled up with a life of their own. *She was like a fever in my blood.*

She jumped, unaware of Marc until he spoke. "Who was on the phone, Mom?"

"Nick."

"Hey, I wanted to talk to him. Why didn't you call me?"

Her voice sounded edgier than she intended it to be. "I have no way of reading your mind."

"I'll call him."

"No, don't." She added softly, "Honey, he's very busy. It'll probably be hectic from now until he gets back here."

Marc relaxed then, chortling, "I'll call him just for a minute another day. Boy, are we going to have us a great Christmas!"

Chapter 15

On Wednesday of the week before Christmas, Janet knew a strange sense of dread and impending doom. Horton High was gaily decorated and the students were full of joy. It was the merry season, but she couldn't shake Tamara's call and Nick's seeming preoccupation, his effusive praise of Tamara. The words of the song "We'll Be Together Again" kept running through her mind; the words took on a special meaning now.

She had bought all her presents, sent Christmas cards. Nick's present was a sinfully expensive natural-colored cashmere cardigan like one he had admired on one of their shopping trips. She had had it exquisitely wrapped; now she and Marc and the present eagerly awaited his coming.

Later, at home, Janet let herself into the apartment and found Marc standing in front of the table where the white jade music box had rested. Sprigs of mistletoe and holly were placed across the table. He didn't look up as she came in, but he greeted her.

"Hi, Mom."

"Why so pensive, sweetie?"

He looked at her then, sighing. "I was thinking about your music box. I've started saving money and one day I'll get you another one. Mom, I'm so sorry."

She put her bags on a chair, went to him, and hugged him. "It's all right, Marc. We lose things in this life and we go on without them. I don't need the music box. I've got *you.*"

He smiled then with pleased relief, saying, "You look tired. Listen, I'll do us some dinner. We've got frozen meatballs. Some whole-wheat spaghetti…"

She patted his cheek. "I'm not terribly hungry. You go ahead and fix the spaghetti for yourself. Just do me a chicken salad sandwich on plain, warm rye, a green salad, and there's some ambrosia in the fridge."

"Sure thing."

Going to her room, she undressed, feeling Nick's beguiling presence all around her. That bed— She blushed with pleasure at the memory of Nick and herself lying erotically intertwined. Slipping on a stonewashed denim jumpsuit and scarlet blouse, she went back into the living room.

Copies of *Heart and Soul* and *Emerge* had come in the mail that day. She sat on the couch leafing through the magazines when the door chimes sounded. Going to the door she found Anne, one of the apartment complex desk clerks, standing there.

"I've got a FedEx letter for you, Mrs. Smith. I meant to stop you when you passed through the lobby. You just slipped by me. I'd have called, but I had other packages to bring to this floor."

Janet's heart leaped. Was the letter from Nick? She didn't look at the return address because she wanted to keep hoping. "Wait a minute," she told the young woman, "I'll get my purse."

Anne waved a hand back and forth emphatically. "No,

don't. You're *so* generous during the holiday season. Let me do my part."

Janet closed the door and leaned against it. She walked quickly to her bedroom and only then did she look at the return address and her breath nearly stopped. *Tamara Kyle.* Sitting weakly on the edge of the bed, she opened the cardboard envelope and withdrew a newspaper clipping and a compact disk. The label on the record proclaimed a song recorded by Nick Redmond and Tamara Kyle, "We'll Be Together Again."

Only then did she let herself look at the newspaper clipping. Her head swam and she could barely focus as she read the headline of *R&B Record,* a small specialty newspaper: Old Celebrity Sweethearts to Wed. She forced herself to read the glowing account of the engagement announcement for Nick and Tamara. On the photograph Nick and Tamara kissed like the kisses Janet remembered all too well. Nick's praise of Tamara, his new warmth when he spoke of her, pierced Janet's brain. Nick didn't call every day now, but if he didn't call today, she had to call him. *So old loves really do die hard,* she thought.

A light knock sounded. "Hey, Mom, wash up. Soup's on."

She went to the door, but didn't open it. "You go on and eat, honey. I've got a headache. Put my food in the warmer and the fridge and I'll eat later. And thank you."

"Sure, Mom. Listen, are you okay? You sound like you're crying."

"I'm all right, really. Thanks for being concerned. You eat well now."

Nearly an hour later, benumbed, she went into the kitchen, took out her food, ate a few mouthfuls, and put the rest in the garbage disposal. She didn't want Marc to worry about her if she left the food untouched and she always wanted to let him know how much she appreciated his tender signs of caring.

Nick called later than usual and from the beginning she recognized stress in his voice.

"Janet, how are you?"

"I'm holding up. How are you?"

"I'm okay. Listen, it's hard saying this, but I won't be coming for Christmas after all. The earliest I can get there is the Sunday after." Then, urgently, "Janet, we have to talk."

"We're talking now, Nick," she said evenly. "Just tell me whatever you want to tell me." *Yes, tell me,* she thought, *that you've gone back to your first love, your 'Tam' who's come to mean so much to you again. You've never stopped loving her.*

Taking a deep breath, he continued. "There's so much I've got to do. Out here I've had time to think, even if my—*our* schedule is hellish. Janet, you're going to feel cheated, be disappointed, but believe me this way is going to be best. I want you to understand. That's what I've admired most about you, the way you understand, go with the flow."

"Do I, Nick?" she asked bitterly. "It isn't always easy."

"Believe me, I know."

She wanted to tell him about the clipping and the CD as she had wanted to tell him about Tamara's call, but she couldn't. Her throat was raw with heartache. When she spoke her voice sounded harsh to her ears. "Can't you give me some idea of what we need to talk about?"

He paused to consider her question, then answered, "I'm the world's lousiest at communicating over the phone. Just be patient. I'm asking you to wait, give me a little time, a little space."

"Sure, Nick. I'll give you all the time, all the space you need."

"Thank you. I'll be calling again before Christmas." There was an awkward silence between them. She thought he sounded strange, drained.

"All right," she said.

"Goodbye, Jan."

She waited for him to hang up and reflected that he had called her "Jan" this time, where for a while during the past two weeks he had only called her "Janet." *Tam.* A shudder went through her. She ached with tension.

That night in bed she never closed her eyes, but lay awake and dry-eyed with scalding tears dammed inside her. Around one-thirty, she decided she would call him, demand that he tell her what was going on. She sat up in bed, turned on the bed lamp, put the phone in her lap, and dialed slowly. His voice mail cheerfully spoke to her. "Nick Redmond here. Please leave a message, your name, and your number. I *will* get back to you."

She didn't leave a message, realizing belatedly that he'd just be closing up at the club. Her mind was so befuddled. At two-thirty, she dialed again and got the same message. This time she asked that he call, said it was urgent. She got up, went to the bathroom for a glass of water. In her bedroom again, her bed was her enemy, fighting her. She had to go to work today.

At four o'clock she dialed and got the same recording— left the same message. He should be home by now, she thought. Then at five-thirty, nearly ready to begin her day, she called and when the recording began, "Nick Redmond here," she hung up.

She heard Marc get up and go into the bathroom. He was going in to school early for band practice. Exercise was out of the question, although God knows she needed it. She didn't want to go to school today, didn't want to go out of the apartment. What could she teach? She needed someone to teach her how to heal a broken heart.

At seven, she heard Marc call goodbye and leave. She should get up and put the chain on the door, but she lay still, emotionally paralyzed. She knew it was obsessive, excessive, but she *had* to call again and she dialed with trembling fingers.

She couldn't decide whether to leave yet another message or simply hang up, but she didn't have to make that decision. Tamara's silken voice came on the line. "Tamara Kyle here. Nick's away for a few days, but I'm sure I can help you. Nick and I are a team again. Please leave a message...." She sounded sky-high with happiness.

For a few moments Janet gripped the phone with cold, stiff fingers, then hung up as if she held hot coals.

She sat on the edge of the bed, her heart like lead, weighting her breast.

"Where *are* you, Nick?" she whispered.

And a virulent, anti-Janet inner voice—a voice like Tamara's—viciously goaded her. "You're asking the wrong question. Don't ask *where* he is when you really want to ask *who* he's with, and you already know the answer to that."

Forcing herself up, she swung her sore legs over the side of the bed, thinking it was going to be a long and hellish two days before Christmas vacation began.

Chapter 16

Christmas Eve

Around nine that morning, Janet moved restlessly around her bedroom. Every bone in her body hurt. Had it only been six days since she had talked with Nick? It seemed a lifetime. Her face in her dresser mirror looked drawn, bereft. Marc knocked on her door and came in.

"Mom," he said, "I'm leaving early for Dad's. He's buying himself and me some threads, treating me to a couple of good video games, and hey, we're putting our heads together and getting you a fabulous present." He hesitated now, noting that her face did not light up. "Listen, I can come back, spend the night with you, and we could both go to Dad's for dinner tomorrow. He told me he wants you there, too."

"You spend the night with your father," she said firmly. "I

think I've just got the beginning of a bug. I'll be okay. Sweetie, I'd like to drive you to Casey's. I need to get out and do a little shopping. Let me just throw on a few clothes. You get your breakfast."

He grinned. "Been there, done that. Aren't you going to eat?"

"A breakfast bar, some orange juice."

Later, Janet and Marc pulled up at Casey's elegant marble, castlelike apartment complex on Sixteenth Street across from Malcolm X Park. Casey renovated and sold houses, but he hadn't owned a house since their divorce. He seemed to her to be punishing himself with taxes and investments. But who knew what Casey was looking for.

They sat in silence in the car for a few minutes, then Marc leaned over and kissed her on the cheek. "I'm really sorry Nick isn't going to be here for Christmas, Mom. I miss him. But he'll be on next week, and we're still going to have a ball. Bye now. I'll call you."

He got out and she drove away thinking her son was growing up so fast and she was so proud of him. What she had known with Nick had seemed a blessing for Marc's sake as well as hers. The mean-spirited and critical Casey hadn't been much of a father. How was she going to tell Marc that Nick was marrying Tamara? And *when* was she going to tell him?

As soon as she got in her favorite gourmet shop, Bea saw her, came to her, hugging her tightly. "You look terrible," Bea said. "Still no word from Nick?"

Janet shook her head. "I'm sure he doesn't have time to call. Coming marriages consume your energy."

"Honey, don't."

Memphis Traxell came to them, greeted her. "Hello, Janet." He hugged her and his big body felt so warm, so comforting. He liked this woman and thought it a damned shame what Nick had done to her. He'd thought he knew Nick as a straight shooter. Was he losing his skill at reading people? He and Bea were so close she would have told him. Now he said, "You and the boy ought to have dinner with us tomorrow. You don't need to be alone."

"I'm going to insist on it," Bea urged her.

Janet looked from one to the other. "Thank you both, but I've *got* to be alone. I need time to think, to sort my feelings...."

Memphis nodded. "I can understand where you're coming from. Listen, I'm going pickle shopping over on aisle nine, give you ladies a chance to talk." He patted Janet's shoulder, said fiercely, "You hang in there, you hear?"

The space near the bakery counter was empty. Janet and Bea moved to the back and Bea said miserably, "I know Nick Redmond, the whole family, or *thought* I knew him. He's in love with you. I do know that."

"Was."

"It doesn't end that suddenly. I could kill Tamara Kyle, the little b—witch."

"She loves him, they have a history together. That explains a lot."

"Oh, that woman," Bea scoffed. "Remember, I've known her a long time. Nick is a comer. He'll likely be famous soon. He's a hunk, and I'll bet he's a fantastic lover. He's certainly gentle enough, tender enough, caring..."

Janet felt pure pain stab her heart and it made her want to double over as Bea scoffed. "The only person Tamara knows how to love is the face she sees in her mirror."

"She lost a child. That must have hurt."

"I know and I'm sorry, but don't defend her. She isn't worth it."

Driving home, Janet let her car window down, let the cold wind sweep in. It was a gorgeous day with azure skies and fat, white cumulus clouds. She wanted to drive and drive and drive on the road to nowhere.

In her apartment she ached all over as she put her packages away. She wanted to lie down and couldn't, so she drew a hot bath, poured in oatmeal and baking soda, reflecting that she had done something like this for Nick when his grief had been unbearable. She wanted now to be away from the remembered sound of his affecting voice, the vision of his fit and muscular body, his personal woodsy smell that magnetized her. And yes, his warmth, his deep, deep sexuality and sensuality that went to the marrow of his bones.

She stayed in the tub a long time before she got out and blotted herself dry. Going into her bedroom, she went to her lingerie drawers and took out the gossamer sheer, black lace gown Nick had given her. Holding the silken garment to her face, she whispered to herself, "Don't be a masochist. Let him *go.*" Folding and putting the gown back into the drawer, she gently closed it.

It was one-thirty then. She slipped into the rose jersey pajamas with the harem trousers that Nick had often admired, even fastening a gold bracelet onto her wrist. A pair of matching rose mules with curved heels would do it. There, she thought, she looked too nice to be alone. Picking up a large sprig of mistletoe from the antique table, she took it into the kitchen, where she got a thumbtack and pinned it to the wall. Was it a coincidence that it was near the spot where Nick had often pressed her against the wall and kissed her so ardently? Shrugging, she thought she had always tacked mistletoe on the walls. It hadn't begun with him. Mistletoe and kisses. Nick's special gentle, tender, hot kisses. Kisses and mistletoe.

She nearly cried aloud with pain and torment, and she knew then that she would not let herself hate him. The hurt went deep and yes, she was searingly angry, but what they had known was too wonderful to destroy with hate. All her life, she would remember and treasure what she had had with him.

It was late before she straightened up the apartment, grateful for something to do. The aroma of French lavender wafted pleasantly. She had thought about putting Christmas albums on the CD player, but she craved quiet to lick her wounds.

In the living room she went to a table and touched the beautiful porcelain basket of roses Grace had given her one day in the park. She missed her so much.

And picking up a photo of Nick, Grace, Marc, and herself on the front porch of Nick's home, she felt sadness spread through her like a sickness.

There was still a link to Nick. She checked on his house twice weekly; he hadn't asked her not to. And she had approved the rental of Grace's house. She was certain he would now cut those ties with her.

They had made love only twice—once here in her bedroom and shortly after at his house. The ecstasy he had awakened in her had been incredible, was still incredible. Nearly whimpering, she wondered how to stop the tides of wondrous memory that washed over her.

It was four o'clock when Marc called, excited. "Mom, we shopped most of the day. You're gonna love what Dad and I got you. Hey, Dad wants to talk to you."

Casey's voice was gruff. "Janet, I'm sorry about your disappointment, but I warned you about Redmond. He's too young for you. He's *wrong* for you. Can't you see that? We could try again for the boy's sake. We brought him into the world."

"I don't want to talk about this," she said evenly.

"Okay, but we will later. Listen, the boy and I bought you a great present and I know how you like to open your presents on Christmas Eve. To be truthful, I'm a bit hungover and don't want to drive or I'd bring it over...."

"Were you drinking when you were out with Marc?" she asked sharply. "I've asked you not to drink too much around him."

"Hey, don't take your disappointment out on me. I'm sorry Redmond isn't coming the way he lied and said he would."

"No, you're not sorry, you're gloating, but that's all right."

"As I was saying, I'm sending your present by Matt Holiday, the taxi driver I use to deliver packages. You know him. It shouldn't be too long now. Merry Christmas, Janet."

Stiffly she wished him a merry Christmas and hung up. Facing Casey's scorn, she found hurt a wild thing in her breast. She should watch a Christmas program, listen to music, *anything* but this dreary suffering. And with that word came Nick's mellifluous baritone drawl saying, "Anything and everything." She nearly went under.

Sitting in a rocker-recliner for a long while, she willed her mind to blankness, and she welcomed the sound of her door chimes. That would be Matt, the taxi driver, with her present. But the only present she wanted she wouldn't get. She had always been a strong woman, she thought, and she *would* survive. She had a son to love and raise.

"Hello, Matt," she greeted the pleasant young man who held out a wide, flat gold box. Taking it, she thanked him.

"Hello, Mrs. Smith. I don't see enough of you."

She smiled. "Would you like to come in and I'll get you a glass of eggnog?"

"I'd love that, but I'm rushing. You're my last run. My wife and I are having a candlelight dinner in front of the fireplace."

"How wonderful," she began as he looked at her anxiously.

"Are you all right?" he asked.

"I'll be fine," she said sadly. "Merry Christmas, Matt."

He touched her shoulder lightly. "You don't seem to feel well and I'm sorry. Do you need me to get anything for you? I can take the time."

"No. Thank you, but I really am all right."

He left then and she stared at the big dusty rose Christmas tree decorated with dark red satin balls; pink angel hair covered the branches. She and Nick had picked it out before he left for L.A.

It was only a moment before the door chimes sounded again. Matt was probably returning to add a message from Casey he'd forgotten. She tried to smile as she opened the door, saying, "Yes, Matt."

In the open doorway Nick caught her to him, holding her painfully close as he buried his face in her hair. "Jan. Jan," he said over and over. Then he released her, asking gently, "Aren't you going to invite me in?"

The room spun and he had to steady her.

"Come in," she said dully. He bent to pick up a large and shiny white plastic shopping bag.

"I got a friend to bring me in on his private jet. I had to come. I've been going crazy wanting to see you and explain how things have gone out of control."

He set the bag beside the antique table and she thought he

smiled a little, but she wasn't smiling. Oh, God, her body felt like cold, dry stone. Going close to her he told her, "The apartment smells wonderful and you look, smell, *are* wonderful."

He took her in his arms and kissed her then as she held herself rigid, closed against him. He looked puzzled, but said only, "How's Marc? And *where's* Marc?"

"He's spending the night and much of the day tomorrow with his father," she answered.

Nick looked painfully contrite now. "Look, Jan, I hated like hell disappointing you and Marc, but things just got out of hand. I'm really sorry."

"It's all right, Nick," she said almost gently. "Life happens and we *can* take it if we try."

He drew a deep breath, walked over, and sat in a big, stuffed chair. Spreading his legs, he opened his arms and crooned to her, "Come to Papa, baby."

She looked at him with amazement, willing herself to keep her distance.

With a sense of horror, she saw that he was trying to be friends. Did he want her *blessing* for him and Tamara? Then with the start of outrage she wondered: what was *with* this man?

But her need for him was too strong to resist and she found herself going toward him as his waiting body beckoned and his eyes compelled her. He drew her down onto his lap and again he kissed her. Again she resisted.

After a minute he lifted his head, pleading, "Hey, let me in, Jan. I'm freezing to death out here."

Sudden fury hit her then as scalding tears filled her eyes. Choking, she managed to say it. "Let you *in,* Nick? When you're going to marry Tamara?"

"Like hell!" he exploded, his breath coming fast. "I'm going to marry *you,* if you haven't changed your mind. And by God, if you have, I'm going to lock you up and throw away the key."

She was losing her bearings. Joy and disbelief tangled and raced madly inside her. "But Tamara called," she began, "and she sent me a news clipping about your engagement and a CD of a song you two had recorded." She felt she was babbling and tears filled her eyes.

Grimly he said, "She took that song from the album to be released."

"Wait," she said, starting up. "I'll get the whole thing for you."

His big hands pulled her back. "I've seen that clipping," he said shortly, "and Tamara's no longer with Rhapsody. She's gone out as a single—as of yesterday." His mouth was set in a straight, hard line. "When did she call you?" he demanded.

She told him more about the call and he tilted her chin. "Why didn't you tell me?"

She shook her head. "I couldn't. You praised her so much. You seemed to be falling in love with her again. It sounded to me that she was telling the truth. You said we had to talk, that I'd feel cheated, be disappointed…"

"Let's hold the disappointment a few minutes. I said you'd feel cheated because you're planning a big wedding and I want us to get married *now.*" He spread his hand across her stomach, and her heart leaped with joy. "Sweetheart, if we're going to put a baby in there, we need to get started. I was born when Ma was forty-one. You'll be a year older, and I want to protect you, make sure you stay okay. *Are* you going to feel cheated?"

She put her face against his and cried. "How could I feel cheated when we have each other? But you once said Tamara was like a fever in your blood."

"And fevers sometimes kill," he muttered. "Let me tell you

what *you* are in my blood, Jan—peace and contentment, yes, and fulfillment. You're everything I want in a woman, and a wife."

"And you're everything I want in a man and a husband."

He smiled sadly then. "I was driving myself ragged doing all the things I told you about on the phone. I told you from the beginning I'll always give you anything and everything you want, if it's at all in my power." His smile was tender, warm with passion. "And I'll always do whatever you want me to do to you. My dad wanted to and tried to give Ma whatever her heart desired and she returned the favor." His eyes misted. "They were the happiest couple I've ever known."

Janet stroked his face. "A beautiful love story was what your parents lived." She placed a hand along his cheekbone. "When I decided we had to talk, after I got the CD and the news clipping, I called you all night and got your voice mail. Then I called early the next morning and the message was that Tamara had taken over."

"My God, I wouldn't have thought even Tamara could be that rotten. I blame myself. Like I've told you, I'm a wretched communicator by phone. I've got to do better."

She wrapped her arms around his neck and kissed him then, her tongue lightly caressing his, letting him all the way in, and his soul thrilled at the wonder of her kiss, but after a moment, he drew slightly away.

"You need to know the rest. I went to the hospital at two the Thursday morning you called and left messages. Tamara hooked her answering machine to my phone. She got an editor friend to run the newspaper story while I was in the hospital."

"Why were you in the hospital?" she asked in alarm.

"A raging and dangerous viral infection the doctor had warned me about possibly getting if I didn't slow down."

Her heart hurt for what he'd suffered. "My poor baby. Why didn't you tell me? I would have come to you, taken care of you."

"I know and I couldn't let you do that. It would have given Casey most of the ammunition he needs to try to take Marc away from you. I wasn't going to let that happen. Let me tell you the rest. If Guy had been there he would have known and told me what was going on. The other dudes in our group hesitated to come to me.

"Finally, Mitch—the club owner—came to the hospital and told me the whole story. I had been unconscious for two days...."

"Oh, my God, I'm so sorry." She kissed a corner of his mouth. "And I thought you didn't care anymore, that you were leaving me for Tamara."

"I read Tamara the riot act when I found out. She owned up to everything. She never told me she'd called you, sent you that garbage. No, sweetheart, I'm not leaving you. You've got me on your hands for good."

For long moments, he trailed kisses over her face, then down her throat and into the pulsing hollows.

"Aren't you hungry?" she asked him.

"Starved, but I need you more than I need food." Her body grew warm with his saying it. Gently he pushed her to her feet and got up. "Now I'll explain what I meant by saying you'd be disappointed."

He strode to the antique table, lifted the big shopping bag, and took out an enameled plastic box. "Open it," he said.

She did as he asked, lifted, and gasped at the white jade music box that was a near replica of her stolen one. Putting it in place on the table, she couldn't speak, could only put her arms around his neck and draw him tightly against her, feeling the hardness of his body outlining the softness of hers.

Still holding her, he said, "That's what I meant when I said

I thought you'd be disappointed. I was going to tell you I was looking even if I couldn't find you a music box. And it was hell looking. Finally, I found an antique dealer with ties to Hong Kong who thought he could help me, but nothing happened. On the day before I went into the hospital he called and told me he'd found a box he thought I'd like. He sent it over and I approved. The only thing is it plays 'Silent Night,' instead of 'O Holy Night' as your other music box did. Do you like it?"

"No," she whispered, "I don't just like it, I *love* it. This is the most exquisite gift I've ever gotten."

He pulled out a large sprig of mistletoe from the bag, held it over them. Grinning, he said, "My favorite Christmas things," and kissed her long and passionately. Finally he told her, "We've got to call Marc."

"A little later we'll call him," she murmured.

She took his hand and led him into the kitchen, showed him the mistletoe she had hung. He pressed her against the wall under that mistletoe and spread a hand on either side of her face. Her knees went weak with wanting him, with loving him. His mouth on hers was alternately gentle, tender, exploring, then more demanding—hot, searing kisses that healed.

When he lifted his head, gravely looking at her, she told him, "When you put your hands on the sides of my face I feel sealed in from the world with you, and time just stops."

"It stops for me, too," he said huskily, "when you do it to me. Some people just have hot bodies, sweetheart, hot meaning to me the deepest of feelings. You've got a *hot* body, a hot heart, a hot *soul*." He laughed a little then and his eyes got dreamy.

"What're you thinking?" she asked him.

"That in a few minutes we're going to know each other

again in the biblical sense. I'm thinking how *good* we are together. I'm thinking how we respond to each other with ecstasy I was beginning to think would never happen to me. You're getting to love my body, Jan, the way I loved yours from the beginning. We've added our hearts and souls and spirits to that and we've got the whole universe.

"I'm thinking you better keep me around because you're sold now on making love with me, having a life with me—a life and my baby. And yes, we can keep each other warm."

She was torpid now with wanting him inside her. It was Christmas Eve and she had everything she'd ever dreamed of. Nothing was going to stand in the way of that.

When he kissed her then it was with fierce hunger that matched her own. She let herself flow into him as he raised his lips from hers only long enough to whisper, "Merry Christmas, my precious darling."

About the Author

Francine Craft is the pen name of a Washington, D.C.-based writer who finds writing a wonderful pastime. A native Mississippian, she has also lived in New Orleans and found it the most fascinating place on earth.

She attended Alcorn College, Tougaloo, and Hampton University, and has held a variety of interesting positions. Her books have been highly praised by reviewers.

Francine's hobbies are prodigious reading, photography, and songwriting. She enjoys spending time with her soul mate.

She loves to hear from her readers. You can write to her at P.O. Box 44204, Washington, D.C. 20026. If you wish a reply, please enclose an S.A.S.E. Or contact her by e-mail at francinecraft@yahoo.com, or visit her Web site at www.francinecraft.com

FANTASY FULFILLED

Linda Hudson-Smith

Chapter 1

Ashleigh Ayers blushed and smiled as Darius Early, Thomas Early's thirty-year-old handsome nephew, kissed her on the cheek. With dark hair and even darker eyes, standing at five-eleven, Darius had a nice physique. His fashionable attire was an impeccable fit and he possessed an overall clean-cut appearance. Darius's uncle, Thomas Early, was Ashleigh's wealthy benefactor and her saving grace.

Surprised to see him at the cruise ship, *Forever Fantasy*'s baggage claim area, Ashleigh looked puzzled. "I won't ask what you're doing here, since I'm sure Uncle Thomas must've sent you. I guess he didn't get my postcard telling him Lanier and I had a ride home."

Darius shook his head. "I'm sure he didn't. Otherwise, he wouldn't have sent me. I can see that your bags haven't come around on the carousel yet. Have you been waiting long?"

"Just a few minutes. The luggage hasn't come around, only boxes and bulkier items."

Observing Ashleigh from the other side of the carousel, Austin Carrington, professional quarterback for the Texas Wranglers, was doing his best to curb his jealousy. Ashleigh had accepted his offer of giving her and her best friend a ride home versus calling a cab; it looked as if his plans had been thwarted. He had to wonder what Ashleigh's relationship was to the man.

Despite the challenge standing before him now, his heart rejoiced at all the wonderful things that had transpired between him and Ashleigh on the special Valentine's Day southern Caribbean cruise. Her encouraging words of the previous night suddenly came to mind. She'd told him that she had no doubts about his sincerity and that she was certain he'd meant every word he'd said to her out on the deck. The speech he'd made to her had come from the bottom of his heart. Integrity had always been important to him.

"This Valentine's Day can be the first of many celebrations that we'll have as a couple. You'll never again have to go through any more hell, not when heaven is right here beside you. Heaven is what you'll always find in my arms. Paradise doesn't have to end with this cruise."

Austin recalled the slight apricot coloring that had crept into Ashleigh's champagne-gold complexion during his speech. A good part of their evening had been spent under the stars, basking in all the wonderful and tender moments they'd shared in over the past fourteen days; several true confessions had also been made.

Deciding to just introduce himself to the man who dared to kiss Ashleigh in public, Austin started across the room, his confidence high. After all, it hadn't looked as if it was a passionate kiss. He couldn't find out who the guy was by standing around wondering. Instead, he had no choice but to take the risks that came with asking. He couldn't deny his need to know.

"Darling, I'm so thrilled to see you," a female voice called out.

Austin closed his eyes and prayed that the sweet but sickening sound of his ex-fiancée's voice had only come to him in his subconscious mind. *This can't be happening, not right now.*

"Darling," Sabrina Beaudreaux cooed again, "I've missed you so much." Dressed in a bright yellow dress with her head covered by a magnificent black and yellow wide-brimmed hat, Sabrina looked cool as a spring morning and very relaxed. Before Austin could turn his six-foot-three athletically built frame around, Sabrina was in his arms, kissing him full on the mouth.

Sabrina leaned into him as she looked into his ebony eyes. "I've been terribly miserable without you, Austin. I hope you've had a chance to really think things through. I pray that you've had a change of heart so that we can start to work out our differences." Her lips claimed his, making it impossible for him to respond.

Austin quickly stepped back from her. "Please don't do this, Sabrina," he managed through clenched teeth. "This isn't the time or the place for one of your demonstrative displays. This isn't going to work. The decision I've made regarding our engagement is final."

Without discretion, her small hands went to his belt and then moved down to his lower anatomy. He moved away before she could complete her mission. Stealing a glance across the room, Austin saw the disturbing look of disbelief on Ashleigh's face. Although she was a good distance from him, the unmistakable pain in her eyes was visible. He also felt her anguish.

Unable to meet Austin's seemingly imploring gaze, Ashleigh turned and looped her arm through Darius's. "Let's get out of here." *I can't take seeing Austin for another minute.*

"Slow down, Ashleigh. Why are you suddenly moving so fast? What's wrong?"

Ashleigh managed a believable smile. "Nothing that a few days of rest won't cure. It has been a very long trip."

Unaware of what was actually going on, or that anything was truly amiss, Darius complied with Ashleigh's wishes by steering the luggage cart toward the exit.

"How *is* Uncle Thomas, Darius?"

"Other than the fact that he missed talking to you on the phone every day, he's fine. He can't wait to see you and hear all about the cruise. I was told to invite you and Lanier to dinner next week. He thought you'd be too tired to make it over to the house this week."

"I'll be there. I'm sure Lanier will want to come, too. She loves Uncle Thomas almost as much as I do. And we all know how she likes to wander around inside and outside his estate."

Ashleigh looked over her shoulder and saw that Austin was still with the woman that she assumed was his fiancée. She'd only seen a photograph of him and her in the local newspaper. The large hat the woman wore made it hard for Ashleigh to make a positive identification. Who else but a lover or a soon-to-be wife would kiss him in such a passionate way?

Had Austin kissed Sabrina back or had it just looked that way? Maybe he'd missed her, too, and hadn't realized it. Perhaps seeing her again had sparked his passion anew. He had been engaged to her. So much for her and Austin seeing each other on a regular basis, as planned. It was obvious to Ashleigh that Austin still had some serious issues to deal with. But, so did she.

Ashleigh turned away just as Sabrina pulled Austin into her embrace again, hoping Lanier wasn't going to hold them up; she couldn't wait to clear the terminal. Her heart wasn't feeling very joyous at the moment and her spirit had already plummeted as low as it could go.

As though Lanier had somehow felt Ashleigh's anguish, she suddenly appeared, smiling from head to toe, as she eyed Darius. "Seeing you here makes me think our postcard to Mr. Early got lost in the mail. Always a pleasure to see you, Mr. Darius Early."

He grinned at Lanier and her flirtatious ways. "The feeling is mutual, Miss Watson."

After rewarding Darius with an engaging smile, Lanier turned to Ashleigh. "I hope you weren't worried about me. Quick bathroom stop before hitting the road. Where's Austin?"

Ashleigh discreetly pointed Austin and Sabrina out to Lanier. "As you can see for yourself, Austin Carrington is otherwise *engaged*."

Lanier looked at Ashleigh with empathy. "Don't jump to any conclusions. Please give Austin the chance to explain himself. I can almost bet you that he didn't plan this little reunion. If he did, I don't think he would've offered to take us home."

"Don't worry about me, Lanier. Austin has been straight up with me about her, yet I got close to him anyway. It looks to me like she's not about to give up on him no matter how he feels about her. Someone is going to get badly hurt. And it just might end up being me."

Lanier hugged Ashleigh to comfort her. "I don't think you'll ever have to regret the closeness you shared with Austin. Dallas told me that he knew his brother's heart. Where you're concerned, Austin is wearing it on his sleeve. That's how both Dallas and I see it."

Ashleigh stole one last guarded glance at Austin before exiting the building. Sabrina still had his undivided attention. And Austin didn't seem at all upset by what was taking place.

It wasn't so along ago that his undivided attention had belonged to her, Ashleigh mused. Because of all the unbelievably incredible events that she'd experienced since the ship first set sail from Galveston Island, Texas, she'd had mixed emotions about them staying in a relationship once the cruise ended. Now that she and Austin had been reunited after twelve years of being apart, she didn't want them to ever separate again. On the other hand, she wasn't sure if their relationship could survive in the kind of world he lived in.

Austin Carrington was a superstar, one that traveled constantly. As a dedicated social worker, Ashleigh could never see herself as a prim and proper socialite. Her current obligations and commitments wouldn't accommodate a continuous traveling schedule for some time to come. Ashleigh and her best friend, Lanier Watson, had just purchased a large home on Galveston Island, which they'd named Haven House. Raised in foster homes themselves, the two young women planned to take in as many foster kids as the house could comfortably accommodate. The old but sturdy house needed to undergo major renovations, which was going to take lots of money and hard work to accomplish in a mere nine and a half months' time.

Ashleigh and Lanier hoped to hold their grand opening celebration for Haven House during the week of Kwanzaa, a week that held significant meaning for both women.

Forgetting all that she and Austin shared was going to be the hardest part, since it looked as if it just might be over for them now. Remembering the last couple of nights of their shipboard romance came way too easy for her. Ashleigh didn't even need to close her eyes to conjure up one of their most unforgettable evenings. Her thoughts instantly took her back to paradise.

It didn't look as if the Valentine's Day dance aboard the *Forever Fantasy* cruise ship was anywhere near coming to an end. It appeared that everyone was making sure that this Valentine's Day cruise would be an unforgettable one. Ashleigh's topaz eyes drank in the animated atmosphere as she and her extremely handsome date rejoined the lively party. The music was still in high gear and the dance floor was just as crowded as it was before she and Austin had gone out on deck for a breath of fresh air.

No one seemed to notice or care that it was already well after midnight.

Austin smiled at Ashleigh as he led her back to the reserved table, where he'd left his mirror images seated with Ashleigh's best friend. Austin was the eldest brother of a set of triplets. Dallas, a baseball star, was the middle brother, and Houston, a basketball superstar, was the youngest. The identical triplets had been born only minutes apart, twenty-eight years ago.

Austin pulled out Ashleigh's chair before seating himself. "Doesn't look like we put a damper on the party people with our disappearance. I don't think we were missed at all. I wonder where everyone has run off to."

Ashleigh pointed toward the dance floor. "There are two of the MIAs. Your brother's and my best friend's feet are burning up the carpet. It looks to me as if Lanier has finally decided to succumb to the charming Dallas. They look to be even cozier than before we left."

"Dallas and Houston will be leaving the ship tomorrow. So maybe Lanier decided to just go for it. Dallas is definitely hoping to see her again onshore. He's really taken with her."

Austin looked at Ashleigh with a glimmer of hope in his ebony eyes. "Speaking of onshore, I'm thrilled to death that we've decided to continue our relationship after this big party boat docks back in Galveston in a few days."

"I'm happy with our decision, too, Austin, glad that we agreed to take things slow."

He covered her hand with his. "Since we've declared our undying love, promising to be each other's forever Valentine, what about a private celebration in my cabin?"

She leaned over and kissed him full on the mouth. "How long do you plan for this celebration to last?"

"I'm shooting for the rest of our lives. But since you're talking about here and now, I'd say it's entirely up to you."

"What if the decision was solely up to you, Austin?"

He fingered one of her copper-brown curls as he kissed the tip of her nose. "If that's the case, we'll be celebrating the sunrise from the cabin balcony. Since it's not up to me, let's not make a decision one way or the other. We'll let one moment lead us into the next. Fair enough?"

"I really like the sound of that, Austin." Her hand caressed his cheek. "It's still so hard for me to believe that we've found each other. You were my foster brother for years and then a cruel twist of fate tore us apart for twelve. Destiny has now brought us back together again."

He engaged her in a lingering kiss. "I've always felt that we were meant to be, but our four-year age difference made it a *forbidden fantasy*. I was right all along." He put her wrap around her. "We can continue our conversation in the cabin. I'm ready to be alone with you."

Before Ashleigh and Austin rose from the chairs, Lanier and Dallas appeared at the table and reclaimed their seats. Lanier's mahogany skin shone brightly from a slight sheen of sweat. It appeared to Ashleigh as if the couple had danced their bodies and feet into a state of fatigue. It was confirmed for her when Lanier instantly removed her shoes.

Austin stood and reached for Ashleigh's hand. "Ashleigh and I have a little private celebrating to do." He helped her to her feet. "We're in love. But I'm sure that our confession comes as no surprise to anyone. We'll fill you guys in on all the details later. You two take good care of each other in our absence. Good night."

Lanier was so happy that Ashleigh had succeeded in winning the heart of her childhood hero. She also knew that having Austin's love was the very thing Ashleigh had always lived and breathed for, yet Ashleigh never really thought it would happen. Lanier stood and gave Ashleigh a warm hug. She then offered heartfelt congratulations to both Ashleigh and Austin.

Ashleigh wished they could've satisfied the curious look on Dallas's face that night, but Austin needed to share with his brothers in private the news of who she was. Although they had both become very suspicious of her true identity, Dallas and Houston were bound to be shocked to learn Ashleigh was their little foster sister all grown up now. Back then Ashleigh had fondly been called Sariah by the nuns at the orphanage. Sariah was her actual middle name.

While Ashleigh was hoping she could get away before Austin exited the building, time seemed to stand still for her as she waited for Darius and Lanier to bring the car around. After mouthing a silent prayer, asking to be spared any more personal pain, Ashleigh closed her eyes, but just for a brief moment. She wanted to wait until she was at home in her own bed to relive the last most spectacular night she'd spent with Austin inside his cabin.

* * *

By the time Austin had finally made the decision to just walk away from Sabrina, he saw that he was too late to talk to Ashleigh. Just as he stepped outside the terminal, Austin had gotten only a passing glimpse of Ashleigh seated inside the dark BMW as it pulled out from the curb.

Sabrina rushed up to Austin. "Why did you walk away from me like that, Austin? It was rude of you. I wasn't finished talking to you."

"You mean like this?" Austin asked, walking away from her again, as fast as his long legs would carry him.

"Austin Carrington, if you care anything about your career, you'll stop and listen to what I have to say. My father owns your career and your future, lock, stock, and barrel!"

Seething with anger, Austin stopped dead in his tracks. He slowly pivoted around to face Sabrina as she closed in on him at a menacing rate. "Your father owns my what?"

She stepped back a pace or two, wary of the anger in his eyes. "You know what I mean."

He shook his head. "No, I don't! Please enlighten me, Sabrina."

She nervously shuffled her feet. "I was only trying to get your attention, Austin."

"Well, now that you have it, let me explain a few truths to you."

Austin took hold of Sabrina's arm and steered her over to a metal bench a couple of feet away from where they stood. They both sat down, but on opposite ends of the seat.

He turned to face her. "Sabrina, we both know it was a mistake for us to get engaged. There was never any time for us to really think about what we were doing or even feeling. Everything happened so fast between us...."

"Austin, you certainly weren't protesting the progression of our relationship back then."

"Not vocally. I unwittingly got caught up in a fantasy world that you and your dad had created. The head coach's daughter married to the star quarterback. It's not love that I feel for you, Sabrina. It didn't take me long to figure out that I was about to marry someone I wasn't in love with. When I overheard your best friend, Gloria, ask you what you'd do if I got injured and could never play football again, your answer was painful to me. But it also became crystal clear to me what I felt for you and what your true feelings for me were." He winced at the memory. "That particular conversation occurred on the very night of our engagement party. 'I'll just dump him and find me another superstar!' Sound familiar, Sabrina?"

Sabrina's mouth fell open. "I had no idea you'd heard that. But I was only joking with Glo. Both Glo and I had had a little too much wine that evening. I never meant any of it."

"Sabrina, I have to go. Talking about this now won't change anything. Be safe."

Austin hated leaving Sabrina behind like this, but he knew the whining and the tears would come next. He'd never known her not to throw a tantrum when things weren't going her way. Sabrina had a strong will, which grew even stronger when she wanted something she couldn't have. Before he'd left on the cruise, she'd made it clear that she wanted him back, that she'd go through the gates of hell to achieve her goal. He believed in her tenacity but not in her worthless causes.

"My man has to be an active sports machine. No player riding the pine can ever hold my attention for very long. The competitive edge is what turns me on. A man can't be competitive if he's seated on the bench. If Austin wasn't the best quarterback in the NFL, I'm not sure I'd have given him a second look, even as fine as he is. Money, more money, and a competitive spirit are the only things intriguing to me, in that exact order. Don't hate me for being brutally honest."

The overheard words still cut him to the quick, yet he'd felt an overwhelming sense of relief that night. Sabrina had confirmed for him that he'd been right about her all along. Her viciously selfish comments had allowed him to break off the engagement with a clear conscience. Even with all the money Sabrina had at her immediate disposal she was a self-proclaimed gold digger. The sports hero was second to the mean green, yet one didn't work for her without the other. She simply had to have both. It was bad enough that he'd overheard her outrageous conversation with her girlfriend, but several of his teammates had heard it as well.

As he continued to move farther away from Sabrina, his thoughts quickly turned to what Ashleigh must've felt when she'd seen him locked in Sabrina's embrace. Probably the same dreadful way he'd felt at seeing another man kissing her cheek. Although he was glad that Ashleigh hadn't been left stranded, it bothered him that he'd broken another commitment to her.

Removing her clothes from the suitcases was like unpacking her memories. Ashleigh hated doing it. She no more wanted to put her things away than she wanted to hang up all the new memories she and Austin had recently made.

Him kissing his purported ex-fiancée so passionately wasn't a good omen, not when Ashleigh was considering a future with him. How do you know the kiss had been passionate? It could've just looked that way. He could've hated it for all she knew. But he might also have loved it. Would she ever know for sure? *Only if he comes to you and volunteers the in-*

formation, came the sobering voices inside her head. Ashleigh would never ask Austin what the kiss had meant to him no matter how badly she wanted to know. Her thoughts were certainly provocative ones.

Such delicious pleasures, secret treasures, and forbidden ecstasy were over way too soon for them. She could easily have spent the rest of her life in paradise with Austin Carrington.

Had forever been shattered at the port of entry?

A warm shower had Ashleigh sleepy, but thoughts of Austin were keeping her wide awake. Too vulnerable to journey into the days aboard the ship, Ashleigh instead thought about the business challenges that she and Lanier were faced with. They had to make this challenging venture work. Too many kids needed good homes and so many people were counting on them to make Haven House a success story.

Two ex-foster kids opening their arms wide and exposing their fragile hearts to kids just like themselves best described Ashleigh and Lanier's mission of mercy. With no one to represent them and to truly care about their welfare, many foster kids fell by the wayside or simply slipped through the cracks. "Not the kids that come to us," Ashleigh vowed. "Love and understanding are what they'll find within the safe confines of Haven House.

"Ugh," Ashleigh moaned, thinking of all the work that had to be done on the old place. Humongous in size as it was, with well-appointed space, fixing it up would prove to be a major challenge. But it would be fun, too. She and Lanier would see to that. Several of their social worker friends had already agreed to help. Even a few of the social workers on the cruise had also offered help.

It was going to be okay, Ashleigh told herself. Not only

would many children find a home there, she and Lanier would finally have a place they could truly call home, a home where no one would ever again use and abuse them, a safe haven where they'd both truly belong.

Thinking about Thomas Early made Ashleigh realize how much she'd missed the older gentleman and their daily conversations. Uncle Thomas, she thought, her eyes aglow with the warmth and affection she felt for her very generous benefactor. Instead of her and Lanier going to his place for dinner, she thought they should invite him over. He loved her fried chicken. Remembering how much she'd loved Angelica Carrington's fried chicken caused Ashleigh's thoughts to rebound to the Carrington home and Austin. Angelica was the triplets' loving mother and her long-ago foster mother. Beaumont Carrington was the proud father of three superstars.

Knowing she would lose herself to Austin and their memories, Ashleigh got out of bed and crossed the hall to Lanier's room. Lanier had moved out of her apartment and in with Ashleigh before the trip in hopes of saving money until they could get settled into the new house.

Upon seeing Lanier on the phone, Ashleigh was about to turn away, but Lanier gestured for her to stay by pointing toward the easy chair in the corner of the room. Even though she hadn't intended to interrupt Lanier's conversation Ashleigh took a seat anyway.

Being alone with the memories of Austin kicking up a storm in her mind wasn't what she needed right now. Thinking of Austin also made her think of Sabrina, which was something she could do without. Still, Ashleigh was aware that Sabrina and Austin had unfinished business. Sabrina or not, her and Austin's relationship wasn't finished yet either, not by a long shot.

Patience on her part was what was needed now. If Austin

came to her, Ashleigh felt sure that she'd know one way or the other. He'd never leave her just hanging even if he decided to stay with Sabrina. Austin wasn't the type of man to leave a woman to wonder without explanation. Ashleigh could count on him to finish what he'd started, no matter his decision.

"Okay, Ash, I'm all through. I gather that you can't sleep. What's on your mind?"

The romantic glow in Lanier's eyes made Ashleigh sit up and take notice. "Who was that you were just talking to, Lanier? If you don't mind me asking." A wry grin crept onto Ashleigh's full lips as she silently took a wild guess.

Lanier's sweet smile came quickly. "Dallas Carrington. I can't believe he called so soon. I thought it might take him at least a couple of weeks. You know how men love to play juvenile games. *Make her wait so she'll really want you by the time you call* is the tired philosophy that some males have the nerve to believe in."

Ashleigh wrinkled her nose. "I'm glad you said *some* males. We can't fit every man into the same mold. I believe the cast was thrown away after the triplets were formed. The man simply can't live without you, girl. You sure have done a complete turn-around where Dallas is concerned, but I'm really happy to see you at least give him a chance. I hope you're ready for him because I think the brother is for real, genuine fourteen-K."

"Try twenty-four-K." Lanier put the pillow up to her mouth and muffled her giggles. "He's real enough, all right. Now I've got to get real. I keep asking myself if he's really what I want. Is he the kind of man that won't leave me bitterly disappointed in love again? I don't know, but it looks like I'm about to find out. We've decided to go for it and hope the dice continues to land on the lucky sevens and elevens. We're going to explore an onshore romance."

A smile gently spread across Ashleigh's face as she leaped onto the bed and embraced Lanier with a crushing hug. "That bit of news makes me so happy. I wish you two nothing but the best of everything."

Lanier kissed Ashleigh's cheek. "Thanks, friend." Lanier waited until Ashleigh settled into a relaxed position before stating what was on her mind. "Have you changed your mind about continuing to see Austin?"

Ashleigh scowled. "My mind may be changed for me if he decides to go back to his fiancée. I'm waiting to hear from him. You warned me not to jump to any conclusions and I'm trying hard not to. But now I'm just not sure if there can be an us anymore."

"I know the scene at the port upset you, Ashleigh. It would've made me crazy, too. Please remember that you didn't go to the designated meeting place you and Austin had discussed. You couldn't wait to get out of the terminal, so you don't know if he ever made his way there or not. In fact, you don't know if things have changed, period. You convinced me to give Dallas a chance, but you're not heeding your own advice. Have you thought about how he might've felt if he'd gone to the rendezvous point only to have you not show up? How fair would that be, Ash?"

"I don't think Miss Sabrina would've let him get away long enough to meet me there. She was a clinging vine. You don't know for sure that he went there, either, Lanier. I saw enough to make me wonder. But I know this. I won't be in a relationship with a man who's torn between two lovers. Austin needs his space right now. I have to see to it that he gets it. He'll be too busy worrying about my feelings to take care of his own if I don't insist on him taking time to sort things out. If we're supposed to be together, we'll be there for each other when the timing is right. I've waited twelve years to have him back in my life. I can be patient a little longer."

Lanier shook her head, smiling. "I don't know about you sometimes. You are amazing, especially when it comes to accepting things for what they are or even how they may seem. I know you don't want to lose Austin, so why are you making it so darn easy for Sabrina to try and win him back? By removing yourself from the game, you're leaving her a clear path to the man you love, to the man I truly believe loves you."

Ashleigh sucked her teeth with impatience. "I can't look at this as just a game, Lani. I understand that love is like a game to some, that someone has to lose, that someone has to win. But if I'm going to win Austin's love, I want to win his heart fair and square. No bending the rules of fair play, no wily charms, no games of sex and intrigue. As the newcomer, the best thing I can do for all concerned is to take a step back and simply observe. Who Austin chooses has to be left strictly up to him. Knowing the kind of man Austin Carrington is, I'm confident that he'll make the right choice. It'll definitely be the one his heart chooses for him. Mark my words."

Chapter 2

Mystified as to their mission, Ashleigh stared openly at the local male and female police officers that stood at her front door. "Yes, I'm Ashleigh Ayers. But what's this all about, Officers? Why are you here?"

"You are under arrest, ma'am. You should secure your place, because you're going to have to come down to the police station with us."

Ashleigh looked horrified. "Arrested! I don't understand. What is happening here?"

"All I can tell you is that someone filed a complaint against you for stealing precious items while you were a recent guest on a cruise ship," the male officer said.

Scared stiff, Ashleigh felt her eyes bulging with disbelief. "That cruise ended two weeks ago and the issue of the stolen item, not items, was settled long before the cruise ever came back to Galveston. The ship's security officer, Tio Webster, also returned the owner's watch to him. Who filed this bogus complaint against me? This is so unreal." Was Austin behind this?

The young officer shook his head. "For the last time, you need to lock up your place, Miss Ayers. The nature of the charges will be explained to you down at headquarters."

"Can I at least call someone?" Ashleigh wailed in distress, looking like a frightened doe. "My roommate will be worried to death if she doesn't hear from me before it gets late."

"You'll get to make a call once you've been fingerprinted and booked," the female responded. "You have to be processed in before any phone calls can be made."

Once the apartment was secured, the female officer administered the Miranda. As the male officer handcuffed his detainee, Ashleigh nearly died inside as she looked all around to see if any of her neighbors were witnessing this atrocity. The pain and embarrassment of being arrested were devastating blows to her reputation and she thought this could also kill her chances of getting important government backing for Haven House. She couldn't believe what was happening to her, so sure this had to be a nightmare despite the fact she was wide awake.

As she was led to the waiting police cruiser, Ashleigh knew that all she had to rely on to get her through this horrendous injustice was God and the power of prayer, a mighty awesome pair of tools. *God,* she silently prayed, *please take hold of my hand and preserve my sanity.*

It puzzled Ashleigh when the female officer had led her to a cell without first being fingerprinted or photographed. Though she hadn't relished the idea of either occurrence, especially taking the mug shot, she was deeply fearful of having been locked up without due process. No one knew where she was, which meant that the officers could keep her as long as they wanted to. None of this made sense to her as she sat huddled in the corner of a cold, damp cell looking totally bewildered. Never in her wildest dreams had she ever thought she'd land in jail. Tears threatened but she was determined not to cry. More concerned with the effect the arrest could have on Haven House than anything to do with her, she continued to pray fervently.

Nearly an hour had passed when another male officer, one Ashleigh hadn't seen before, came to her cell. When Ashleigh was told that she had a visitor, she nearly cried out loud her thanks to the Creator. As she was led to a nearby waiting room, she couldn't help wondering who could possibly be there to see her. Perhaps one of her neighbors *had* seen her being taken away. *God forbid!* As she gave it another thought, she hoped that someone had witnessed her arrest, someone that knew her, especially if it meant they might be there to secure her release.

Then Austin Carrington, her handsome hero, walked into the room.

Ashleigh nearly toppled him over as she leaped into his arms. Her emotions suddenly broke free and all she could think about was that she was now safe in Austin's strong arms. She had totally dismissed the earlier thought that Austin could be behind her arrest. Ashleigh held on to Austin for dear life as she stood there trembling within the strength and comfort of his arms.

Startled momentarily, Ashleigh looked up when she heard the door reopen. Standing before her, looking terribly formidable, were the same two arresting officers.

The male officer put his hands behind his back. "Mr. Carrington, can you identify this woman as the one who stole your property aboard the ship?"

Austin looked Ashleigh dead in the eyes. "She's the one, but she actually stole the precious item from me long before we boarded the ship. I just didn't know it for sure until then. Would it be okay if I have a few moments alone with Miss Ayers? Once we've talked over this matter between us, we can then best decide her fate."

Without comment, straight-faced, the two officers left the room.

Ashleigh's mouth had fallen wide open. Glistening tears fringed her lashes as she whirled herself out of Austin's warm embrace. "What in the hell is going on? What are you trying to do here, Austin? The matter of your stolen watch has already been settled and you damn well know it. This is ludicrous. Do you know what indignities I was made to suffer? All over a piece of jewelry that was returned to you weeks ago." The rage in her eyes was daunting. "What are you trying to pull off on me, Austin Carrington? Please tell me what the hell is going on with you. Have your lost your mind?" Ashleigh practically threw herself down on the straight-back chair.

He saw that quelling her anger might not be so easy. "You're not here because of my stolen watch, Ash. You've pilfered something way more precious than an expensive watch." Austin stepped up to Ashleigh and pressed his finger into the center of her chest. "My heart, Ashleigh. I had you arrested for stealing my heart. Not only have you stolen my heart, you've added insult to injury. I've been calling you constantly since we docked and you have ignored every serious attempt I've made to try and communicate with you. So, I had to resort to taking drastic measures. Desperate people do desperate things. I was desperate to see you."

Ashleigh could've been knocked over with a feather. She

was angry, flabbergasted, horrified, all at the same time. That he had gone through such great lengths in order to see her, not to mention the melodrama he'd created, left her speechless. She'd always known that Austin was an amazing person, but this was something she couldn't even fathom him doing. Ashleigh didn't know whether to be totally flattered by his ingenuity or completely outraged by it.

"I can't believe you staged all this just to talk with me. I thought you needed space after what I witnessed at the port, so I called myself giving it to you. I just wanted you to have time to come to grips with what you wanted without any influence from me, Austin. As much as I hate to admit it, I can see how I'm in part to blame for this nutty situation. But, Austin, couldn't you have found an easier way than this to communicate with me? You had me arrested!"

Looking a tad chagrined, he shrugged. "I'm creative by nature. What can I say? If you called yourself giving me the space you thought I might need, why weren't you able to figure out that time away from you was not what I wanted after hearing the numerous messages I left?"

"I guess I wanted you to be sure about everything. But I can now see your point."

"I hope so, woman. I've nearly gone crazy thinking about you and conjuring up convincing ways to make you see that I was desperate to be back in your life."

Ashleigh simply couldn't deny her deep enchantment with Austin and his crazy notions. Then her laughter suddenly bubbled up in her throat and broke free. "This is so incredible! How did you think up something so unbelievably creative and then manage to pull off such an astonishing feat? Are those two officers imposters or what?"

Feeling relieved by her laughing reaction, he grinned

broadly. "They're definitely the real things, Ash. They just happen to be close friends of mine. Ron and Regina were already off duty and on the way back to the station when I asked them to bring you here." Austin pulled her up from the chair and brought her into his arms. "Now you know how desperate I was to get back with you. You already made up for the sunset you reneged on during the cruise, so how do you plan to make up for the latest missed rendezvous? Why weren't you there, Ashleigh?"

So, Austin had shown up at the designated meeting place, even after seeing her leave with Darius. Ashleigh felt giddy with relief. He had cared enough to show up.

Prickling thoughts of why she hadn't gone there to meet him suddenly sobered her. "I think you already know the reason why, Austin. Don't you?"

He sighed heavily. "I know how things must've looked to you. I'm sorry for that. I had no idea Sabrina would show up there. That we're no longer engaged should lend some credence to why I didn't expect to see her at the port. However, Sabrina has always been totally unpredictable. I should've at least considered the possibility of her showing up. I can say that her meeting the cruise ship didn't surprise me completely. And I'm afraid she's a sore loser."

Ashleigh frowned slightly. "If I lost you, I'd be a sore loser, too. But is she a dangerous loser? Is she capable of bringing harm to you, Austin?"

Spoiled rotten, Sabrina was capable of almost anything. But he wasn't going to tell Ashleigh that. The last thing he wanted to do was have her fearful of Sabrina. However, if Sabrina found out about him and Ashleigh, and then started making threats, he'd have to rethink his decision. Sabrina was the last person he wanted to talk about, now that he had

Ashleigh right in front of him. But Miss Ayers needed answers. And he was sure she had many more questions.

"No doubt she'll try to hurt me professionally. Her dad is only the head coach of my team. At any rate, I don't think that'll work. Every team in the NFL will be hounding me should the Texas Wrangler organization decide to release me, which won't be too easy to achieve. My Wrangler contract is sealed in cement for the next six years. The money is also guaranteed."

The two officers suddenly popped back into the room. Austin immediately introduced his friends to Ashleigh. Ron and Regina had expected Ashleigh to be fuming mad at Austin, so when they first entered the waiting area, they were surprised to see the couple embracing.

Regina approached Ashleigh and extended her hand. "I don't know about you, but I'd kill to have a man who cared so much about me. When he told us his plan, we thought it was crazy. But we couldn't turn him down, not after we realized he was dead serious and how desperate he was to talk to you. We're sorry we put you in handcuffs, but we had to make it appear real."

Ashleigh glared fiercely at both Regina and Ron. "Yeah, I just bet you two are. But I'm not going to feel the least bit sorry for any of you when you receive the papers from the very *real* lawsuit I'm about to file against you and the city. What you two did for your friend was a blatant misuse of tax-payers' money. You're nothing but rogue cops on the take. I hope the superstar millionaire football hero paid you hand-somely to put your jobs on the line like that. Now you're going to have to pay me. A quarter of a million dollars seems like a fair dollar amount. That should cover defamation of charac-ter, public embarrassment, false arrest, not to mention pain and suffering at your hands and the pain caused by those flesh-tearing handcuffs."

Everyone looked astounded when Ashleigh stormed out of the room, leaving the door standing wide open. Austin looked as if he'd just taken a direct hit to his midsection. If he'd been in doubt about their future before, it looked to him as if his unusual plans had sealed their fate of being permanently apart.

Austin punched his fist into the palm of his other hand. "Guys, I'm sorry. I didn't expect her to react like that, at least, not once she learned the truth. Ashleigh looked terribly upset. I've only seen her this agitated one other time, which also had to do with the infamous watch incident that had occurred during the cruise. Looks like I miscalculated this one, big-time."

Ron looked troubled. "Do you think she'll really file a lawsuit, man? Our careers would really be hurt by something as serious as that. I kinda thought she'd be flattered as hell."

Ashleigh popped back into the room. "Officer, it seems that your male ego is as big as your friend's. Flattered indeed! As for the lawsuit, that all depends on you three. You all can convince me not to sue you by offering up a very generous charitable donation to Haven House, a safe, loving home that my friend and I are opening up to take in foster kids." Ashleigh laughed to show that she'd only been giving them a dose of their own bitter medicine. But she was serious about the donation and she didn't pull any punches about that.

"Count me in," Ron said. "Sounds like a very worthy cause."

Regina smiled at Ashleigh. "I'm in, too. You had me worried, Ashleigh. I guess I now know a little bit of how you felt when we hauled you off to jail. That you might actually bring a lawsuit against us had me really worried. We meant no harm. But I guess that depends on which end of the hand-cuffs you find yourself on." Everyone laughed.

Austin put his arm around Ashleigh. "It seems that we have everything settled. Now that you've blackmailed everyone into donating to Haven House, including me, I'm going to take you back to the safety of your home, Ashleigh." Austin kissed her on the forehead. "I'm the one to blame for all this. If you want to sue somebody, it should be me. But I'm not sorry for figuring out a way to get you to talk to me, even if it was a bit unorthodox."

Ashleigh bumped him hard with her hip. "A bit! Oh, but you're going to get yours soon enough, mister. You can count on it. I'm not through with you yet."

"Sounds like an exciting threat. I can't wait for you to deliver on it."

Lanier's eyes were wide with disbelief as Ashleigh gave her a detailed synopsis of what had occurred to her earlier in the day. Seated on the side of Lanier's bed, Ashleigh had fun further dramatizing the already over-the-top scenario of her arrest, since Lanier was intently hanging on to her every word. Lanier loved juicy stories and Hollywood-type gossip. She also loved reading every printed rag sheet she could get her hands on. To her credit, though, Lanier was very much a champion and a sucker for fairy-tale endings. She and Ashleigh definitely had that in common. For two women who'd known so much hurt and disappointment, they never failed to try and locate the silver lining in all situations, even the worst of the worst.

Lanier grinned. "I guess you'll have to answer all my burning questions later."

"Why's that, Lanier?"

"Your phone is ringing. You'd better run for it. It just might be the person who's the very topic of our discussion." Lanier couldn't help laughing at the perplexed look on Ashleigh's face.

Ashleigh shot across the hall and practically snatched the phone off the cradle. *Please let it be Austin,* she prayed, catching her breath long enough to speak into the mouthpiece. With her heart beating way faster than it should be, Ashleigh pulled back the white comforter.

Ashleigh then settled down in bed, loving the heavenly sound of Austin's lazy Texas drawl. She listened as he told her he'd gotten home safely and that he wanted to talk with her again before going to sleep. Then he mentioned the sweet kiss they'd shared before he'd left.

Her thoughts immediately took her back to the port, where she witnessed the passionate kiss between him and Sabrina. She scowled hard at the memory. "The kiss between you and Sabrina. Were you the initiator?" Unable to believe she'd voiced her thoughts, Ashleigh put her hand over her mouth, wishing she'd bitten her tongue.

"After kissing you for nearly two weeks, how could I ever think of kissing someone else? Are you telling me you don't know the power that your kisses have over me?"

A smile lit up her eyes. "How much power?"

He grinned. "Only you would ask that question. Enough power to light up the entire universe. That's how electrifying the feel of your mouth is to me. Kiss me now, Ashleigh."

She looked puzzled. "That's going to be a little difficult considering we're not even in the same vicinity, let alone the same room."

"Use your mind, girl. Just close your eyes and I'm there. I never want to be more than a thought away from you." He paused momentarily, listening to the kissing sound coming from the other end. "I really felt that one. Give me another one. Make it a wet, passionate one this time."

Ashleigh giggled out loud. "Are we having phone sex, Austin?"

"Not yet, babe. We're just a minute or two into the foreplay. What are you wearing?"

Even though she was alone in the room, Ashleigh blushed. "I'm not telling you that!"

"Okay, I'll tell you what I envision you wearing. A sexy black lacy see-through top, cut low, curving around your bare creamy shoulders. The top, no bra beneath, is cropped right at the midriff, leaving your perfect belly button exposed. Your black lace pajama bottoms, slung low on your hips, are fashioned with leopard piping. The matching drawstring is begging to be tugged loose. Your hair is free, cascading down your back like a sparkling waterfall. You're stretched out on the bed and your legs will part only for me, enticingly."

Ashleigh had closed her eyes seconds into Austin's fanciful description. She was now so hot and bothered that she had to fan herself with a magazine. "You have to stop this, Austin."

"Why? Are you feeling hot and moist?"

"Austin, you're going to make it difficult for me to sleep tonight."

"It shouldn't be too hard for you if you imagine me sleeping atop you, inside you."

Not only were her palms sweating, her entire body felt moist and hot, which was somewhat of an understatement. She felt as if her flesh was on fire. The more intimate parts of her anatomy ached to be caressed by Austin's thrilling touch.

"Austin," she breathed raggedly, "can we change the subject?"

"Can't cool off, huh? I can assist you in that. I can cool

you off and heat you right back up again in no time at all. Go ahead and enjoy the delicious feel of the ice cubes melting against your skin. You're allowed to moan, Ashleigh. I love it when you purr."

"Austin!"

"Okay, okay, baby. Do you shower or take baths?"

"Hot baths." She had to wonder if this was his way of heating her right back up. For that to happen, she'd first have to cool down. "How about you? What's your preference?"

"Cold showers are the in thing for me since meeting you on the ship. I can't think about you without becoming aroused. I'll go back to hot showers when you decide to take one with me. Think that'll ever happen, Ash?"

"Anything's possible, Austin. We'll have to wait and see."

"Not exactly a promise, but I can live with whatever decision you make. At least you didn't shoot me down. I'm grateful for that. What kind of shampoo do you use? I thought I smelled papaya mixed with a light floral scent. How close am I?"

"Well, it is a tropical scent. Coconut is the right answer, but my conditioner is what smells so good. I have no clue of what's in it, but it's light and fresh. You use one of the Ralph Lauren scents, but I'm not sure which one."

"Safari and Polo are the two I use most. You must have a smart nose, but how did you know it was a Ralph Lauren product?"

She laughed heartily. "Seeing it in your cabin helped my smart nose out a bit."

"Very clever, young lady. But you should've kept me guessing. Never give a man too much too soon. We have a tendency to take a woman like that for granted. Men love a good game of intrigue, Ashleigh."

"Have I given too much too soon? Am I in danger of completely blowing the intrigue?"

"Not even close, Ashleigh Ayers. Don't worry, though, I won't let you do that. I want us to take our time with each other. The crescendo already promises to be a mind destroyer. I'll give you my heart and soul, but just don't play with my mind. In this instance I want us to love both the player and the game."

Ashleigh looked at the clock. "How soon can you get here? I got a sudden urge to experience all that you've described. You got me burning for you."

From the plausible silence, she guessed that Austin was speechless. She laughed inwardly, knowing he'd fallen right into the trap she'd set for him. He had been doing all the talking; now she wanted to see his delivery to her challenge.

"Thirty-five minutes or so from Houston to Galveston isn't too bad. What do you want me to bring to sleep in?"

All Ashleigh could do was laugh. Austin had just turned things back around on her. "Your skin," she flirtatiously taunted.

"Baby, you don't know how much that works for me. Sheets are the only clothes allowed on or in my bed. What else do you desire?"

"To end this crazy conversation we've been having for the last thirty minutes. I'm tired. Aren't you still fatigued after such a long trip and endless activity, Austin?"

"I'm worn out, but I could never tire of you. However, I don't want to wear you out. Find peace in sleeping next to my heart, Ash. That's where I'm going to hold you all night. Sleep peacefully, sweet angel."

The line went dead, making Ashleigh instantly wish she hadn't dared to mention how tired she was. Fatigued or not, she was going to stay awake until she went over every detail of their conversation. Ashleigh slid down farther in the bed and closed her eyes. Then a light knock came on the door. A sweet rendezvous with her memories would have to be put on hold for now, but she had every intention of a reunion before the night was over.

Lanier popped into the room. "Was it Austin?"

Ashleigh smiled. "You only get one guess."

Chapter 3

As Austin and Ashleigh sat quietly in the sparsely furnished living room inside Haven House, she found it hard to believe that he was once again seated next to her. From what he'd told her, he had called the apartment for her and Lanier had told him that she had gone over to their newly acquired property to do some work. For all the talking and flirting they'd done over the phone the previous evening, an uncomfortable silence now hovered between them.

Smiling inwardly, Ashleigh thought of the past and recent days when she and Austin had talked so freely with each other. As she closed her eyes, she could almost smell the freshly cut lawn at the Carrington ranch. The lovely image of an orange-, yellow-, and black-speckled butterfly flew into her haze of thought, as Tyler, the family dog, chased after the fluttering creature in vain. Angelica, beautiful, elegant, also crossed the path of her consciousness. She could envision

Austin's mother looking like a fresh breath of spring air in a bright blue loose-fitting dress.

Then, the deep resonance of Beaumont Carrington, Austin's father, cut into her soundless thoughts, filling her up with a bubbling champagne-like glee. When Beaumont smiled at Ashleigh, she recalled how it had seemed that he smiled at no one else in the room but her.

"Sariah," Austin called out to her, "are you okay?"

Slightly startled, Ashleigh quickly opened and closed her eyes to shut out the name she'd once been called by. Her middle name certainly hadn't come in just her thoughts. Somewhat dazed, Ashleigh looked at Austin, wanting to reach out to him, to have him tenderly embrace her. But no, that wouldn't work. During the restless night she had once again convinced herself that Austin came from a different world, one that she'd come so close to knowing: the loving world that she'd been kicked out of without the slightest warning. Something about the memory of him at the port with the queen of debutants made her fear anew the society and circle of wealth that he moved about in. Ashleigh's world was far less prominent than his in the eyes of many.

Slowly, Ashleigh arose from the worn sofa. Moving like a zombie, she walked into one of the bedrooms and picked up the paint roller to resume her work. Tears slid from her eyes as she whitewashed the wall, wishing she could do the same with her bad memories of yesteryears. Her hands shook, but she kept on painting, kept on praying for deliverance from the agony burning within her like a red-hot poker. The bad memories often made her a prisoner of the past.

Austin walked up behind her and took the roller from her anguished hands and returned it to the paint pan. His hands lightly gripped her waist as he led her from the back room and up to the front of the house. After seeing her comfortably seated in the chair, he knelt down before her, taking both of her hands in his. "You don't have to fear anything or anyone anymore, especially not *us,* Sariah. We've been so happy together since the first moment we ran into each other. Granted, we experienced some choppy waters aboard the cruise ship, but our sail off into the sunset is not yet complete." *Don't you remember that we promised to be forever valentines?*

Her eyes blinked hard. "That's all easier said than done, Austin. Changing gears is hard for me. I've practically lived my whole life being shifted around. Now that I've found a comfortable spot to operate within I do as little shifting of gears as possible. By the way, continue to call me Ashleigh. Sariah no longer exists, Austin. She's dead. Let her rest in peace."

He nodded, eyeing her curiously. The ice-cold tone in her request concerned him. "Okay, Ashleigh, I won't ever call you that again. But, Ashleigh, no one should ever stay in one mode forever. Taking risks is all about initiating growth. Without growth, we'd stay stuck in the mundane and never have anything to look forward to. Life is exactly what you make it. Whether you realize it or not, you have shifted gears, you have grown, tremendously. We've clicked in a wonderful way on the cruise and I don't want us to ever grow apart. I've already explained to you why you were taken away from us. But that's all over for us now. So much time has passed."

Ashleigh cut her eyes at him. "Don't you mean *sent* away?"

He shook his head. "No, Ashleigh, you weren't sent away. Just as I said before, you were taken away from us. I thought we'd settled this issue already."

She put her hands over her ears. "I don't want to hear this again from you, Austin. I don't want to hear it from anyone. What's done is done. It won't erase the pain and it won't heal the scars. You'll never know what I've been through and it doesn't matter anymore."

He looked crestfallen. "It'll always matter to me. You have always mattered to me whether you want to accept it or not. My family found it so easy to accept and love you."

Ashleigh was looking at him, but she couldn't see or feel anything but the memories of pain, hunger, and deprivation. Unsettling memories had assailed her, unsavory memories of living in numerous foster homes, filthy ones. The faces of the people who'd taken her in only to abuse her and strip away her self-esteem loomed before her. Being orphaned at birth had seemed like an excellent excuse for grown people to mistreat her, to make her feel less than human, then to toss her away like day-old newspapers. She'd been recycled in foster home after foster home, each one enforcing her belief that she was unworthy of love, that she'd always be unlucky in it.

If the Carringtons hadn't loved her back then, they couldn't possibly love her now. She was no longer the innocent, shy little girl they'd taken into their home so long ago. She was altogether different now, severely jaded by the cruelty of adults that should've protected her, hurt deeply by those who should've known better. The holiday cruise was over and reality was back.

Austin touched Ashleigh's face, bringing her back from the hell she'd lost herself to. "I can't force you to listen to me. But we should try to find peace within ourselves. We've spent so many incredible days making new memories, unbelievable ones. Though having you arrested was the craziest thing I've ever done, I thought you'd finally come to terms with what you mean to me, what we mean to each other. I don't want the rebuilding of our relationship to stop. Can we just hang out with each other and see what happens? That's all I'm asking for right now."

Ashleigh's heart swooned at his remarks, but her head didn't share in the sentiment. Her head often had a way of screwing her up, causing her to hold on to things she should let go of. But those things in her past had become her shield, protecting her from ever again going through the horror she'd already experienced. It now seemed to her as if she'd been just an observer on the cruise. The old her, Sariah, had stood in the shadows and watched the new Ashleigh flirt, dazzle, and fall in love all over again with her hero. Just as Sariah had fallen for him when she was too young to know the true meaning of love. Ashleigh shook herself hard, as if she were trying to shake off the musty dust from the past and to rid herself of such unhealthy thoughts.

This is here and now, a new beginning. The day you've so often dreamed of, she mused.

Unable to deny him anything, Ashleigh smiled at Austin. "Hanging out with you sounds like we might be in for more fun." She then looked as if she'd been surprised by her own words.

Austin grinned, sighing inward with relief. "Then it's settled. More fun wins out."

Clearly seeing that her own answer had surprised her, Austin was glad that her heart had won out over her head on this one. He hoped that her head would one day soon surrender total control to her heart. If not, he didn't know how he'd ever win his heart back from her. Ashleigh, as Sariah, had stolen his heart from him long before now. Though he'd only recently realized it, the heart transplant had been performed twelve years ago. From all indications, it had been a successful operation. Ashleigh definitely held his heart within hers. But the fear that she might now decide to reject the love that his transplanted heart carried for her had him worried.

Despite his worries, he was elated with her response, one

that would hopefully give him more time to win her over. Austin got to his feet. "Come on, girl, we've got some serious painting to do. I'm going to help you all I can with the repairs on this big house."

Looking astounded, Ashleigh watched him leave the room and head toward the back of the house. She shook her head and smiled. Well, his help was needed. The truth was that she and Lanier needed a lot of help in making the house visually presentable and comfortably livable for its future residents. Having Austin to help out was a huge blessing, one that she wasn't going to ignore or turn down. If she had nothing else to call her own, she had humility. Remaining humble throughout all her ordeals was a miracle in itself.

Austin was using the paint roller when Ashleigh entered the back bedroom. Watching him make light work of one wall, she picked up the paintbrush and joined in. The look on his handsome face was one of contentment. His expression held the type of peace she longed for.

Two bedrooms were completely painted after several hours of steady work. Speckled with paint from head to toe, Ashleigh and Austin stood together, smiling at their handiwork. Although they'd worked in near complete silence, they'd made a surefire emotional connection.

Austin rubbed a paint chip off the tip of Ashleigh's nose. "What do you have to eat?"

Ashleigh frowned, stretching out her hands, turning her palms upward. "Mother Hubbard's cupboards are completely bare and the new refrigerator hasn't even been delivered yet. I'm sorry I can't offer you anything to eat, but I do have some cold drinks in the cooler I brought along with me. It's in the kitchen."

Austin's boyish grin caused Ashleigh to suck in a deep breath. He was so handsome.

"This brother is a little more than thirsty, Ash." He looked at her mouth, wishing he could taste the moisture from her sweet lips. She had been far too reserved for him to attempt any intimacy with her, yet he couldn't block out all the memories of their numerous intimate encounters aboard the *Forever Fantasy.*

The last night of the cruise was an unforgettable memory, the most sensuous of their rendezvous, one that would live on and on in his heart. He quickly snapped himself out of his reverie; it was already hard enough to withstand his desire for her. Reliving the memories of those passionate nights made him want her all the more, but Ashleigh had once again erected a brick wall between them. Prayer, his love, and constant patience were the only things that would allow him to climb up the wall and make it over to the other side.

"Let's clean up a bit and I'll take you out for a late dinner."

Ashleigh looked hesitant although she desperately wanted to spend more time with him.

He lifted her chin with his forefinger. "You have to eat. Eating together is often a part of friends hanging out with each other. Will you please hang out with me for a while? If you're not hungry, you can watch me satisfy my ravenous hunger. That should keep you a bit amused."

A smile brightened her eyes, erasing the doubt. "You're right and I am starving. I know a great little seafood place down at the end of the pier. They have the best fried shrimp."

He grinned. "Captain Abe's, right?"

"You know the place, huh?"

He nodded in the affirmative. "Just as you said, it's a great place to eat. Let's get moving before it gets too crowded in there. The place is crazy with customers on Friday nights."

"Okay. I brought a change of clothes with me because I

knew I'd look like a paint ball when I got through. It'll only take me a couple of minutes to pull it all together. Be right back."

Austin had her in his arms before she could turn around good. It was hard for him not to kiss her. He needed to, so badly. Instead of kissing her, he brushed her hair back from her face. "Mind if I wash up in the downstairs bathroom? I always keep a gym bag with me, and a couple of changes of clothes are stored inside the trunk of my car. Most of us athletes stay prepared."

"Help yourself."

For several very tense seconds they just stood there gazing into each other's eyes. Ashleigh wanted to be kissed as much as Austin desired to kiss her. Instead of her lips, it was the loving expression in her topaz eyes that made the intimate connection with his.

As Ashleigh took a quick shower, she thought about the seafood place, wondering if she'd ever missed Austin by minutes or seconds on any of the numerous times she'd eaten at Captain Abe's. She'd never seen him there, but knowing that he'd patronized the place had her wondering what she would've done had she run into him. She probably would've run scared.

Ashleigh pulled on a fresh pair of denim jeans and a red and gray Texas Wrangler's sweatshirt bearing Austin's number, 7. A quick facial makeover was completed before she returned to the downstairs area, where she found Austin seated in the living room. He looked comfortable and that made her smile. She wanted him to feel right at home.

Upon seeing her athletic gear, Austin laughed heartily. He had on the same identical sweatshirt she wore. "So you *are* a true fan of mine. I love it. Looks almost as good on you as it does on me, Ash." His eyes flashed with the joy he felt inside at seeing her wearing his number.

Ashleigh looked embarrassed even though she'd had no way of knowing what type of clothing Austin would change into. Her wearing his team number was a dead giveaway, as far as her being one of his biggest fans. She hadn't given that a single thought when she was busy putting it on. She had so many different types of Texas Wrangler sports gear, all of it with his number on it. She wore each one proudly. Whether he knew it or not, Ashleigh was his number-one fan, win, lose, or draw.

Her expression was sober. "Would you like me to change? I didn't think about what I was putting on. This Wrangler's sweatshirt is one of my favorites."

His heart filled with an emotion he couldn't begin to explain. "I'm glad it's your favorite." *And you are definitely mine.* "I wouldn't think of having you change."

Ashleigh released a sigh, happy that he didn't seem to mind them dressed like twins.

The little seaside restaurant was cozy with a relaxing ambience. Lifelike replicas of starfish, lobsters, crabs, and other creatures of the sea were trapped in large fishing nets hanging from the rustic wood-beam ceilings. A variety of colorful oil paintings featuring all kinds of boats and coastal residences completed the sleepy fishing-village-like décor.

It appeared to Ashleigh that Austin was a regular customer. Everyone seemed to know the local hero, the Wranglers' starting quarterback, yet Austin was given his space. Waves and a host of welcoming shouts came his way, but not one person physically approached him.

Ashleigh spotted the owner, Captain Abe, as he came from

behind the counter. Once Ashleigh and Austin had seated themselves on the bar stools at the high but small round table near a window, Abe walked up and took their orders. The silvered-haired Abe was a kind old soul and he loved to put his customers at ease by telling them a joke or two. Ashleigh fondly remembered the many times that Abe had entertained her with his adventurous pirate stories.

After Abe left the table, Ashleigh and Austin talked quietly while waiting for their food to be served. Passersby could be seen walking the pier and others were visible as they studied the menu posted on the inside of the large window.

Ashleigh pointed toward the boat moorings. "Have you ever taken the clipper boat around the island or taken a leisurely ride on the ferry?"

"Many times, but not lately. One of my teammates owns a forty-foot yacht. I've been out to sea with him numerous times. I like the water, but I'm not much of a sailor."

Ashleigh sighed. The mention of the yacht was just another indication of them being worlds apart. A yacht no less. In her dreams. "Sailing on a yacht must be a thrill a minute. Is it a smooth ride?"

Austin shrugged. "All depends on the condition of the gulf. It can get pretty choppy out there. Interesting that you mentioned boats. Clifton Norris, the best wide receiver in the business, is having a party tomorrow aboard his yacht. Want to hang out with me? We don't have to call it a date. Just another way of saying there won't be any strings attached. Interested?"

"I like the idea. But if you're taking me around a bunch of rich, snooty people, strings will be attached. That means you can't stray very far away from me. I'm easily intimidated with wealth since I've lived in near poverty all my life. The last thing I want to do is embarrass you."

Pain clouded his eyes. Thinking of Ashleigh being hungry and cold made him feel sick inside. But sympathy was something she wouldn't tolerate, least of all from him. Putting his painful thoughts aside, he began to revel in the idea of them being attached the entire evening. Things between them were getting better all the time, he mused, remembering all they'd shared during the last big boat ride. Ashleigh seemed a tad more comfortable than she did earlier.

"Are you regretting asking me to go along with you?" Her sweet voice pulled him from his thoughts. "You're mighty quiet over there, Austin."

He raised an eyebrow. "No way, girl. I'm ecstatic that you've accepted the invitation. This group of friends isn't at all snooty. In fact, they're probably a little more wild and daring than you might be used to. They're harmless, though. I'll have your back."

"Dress code?"

"Strictly casual. Wear something warm, similar to the thick sweatshirt you have on. We already know how cold it can get out on the water, especially when the sun starts to go down."

"Is the party going to last until the late evening?"

"Pretty much so, but they'll start heading back in before it gets too late. Is that a problem for you, Ash?"

"Not if I take my Dramamine along. I'm getting a little queasy just thinking about it. A yacht is much smaller than a cruise ship. There won't be several decks between the bottom of the ship and the water. I'll probably feel every single movement the yacht makes."

Austin chuckled, recalling all the days aboard the ship that she had looked green. "Maybe we should take in something a little more tame than sailing, like a movie or bowling. I'm sure hanging out on dry land is more appealing to you. You think?"

Seated in a dark theater with Austin, their thighs touching, hands entwined was so appealing to her, but it was far too romantic an atmosphere than she wanted to find herself in with the man she desired more than just romance from.

"I'm now all excited about the yacht, Austin. I'll do just fine." Ashleigh spotted Abe approaching the table. "Our food is here."

Abe set the food down, smiling at Ashleigh. "Want to hear something funny?"

Sure that Abe was about to tickle her funny bone with one of his jokes, Ashleigh nodded.

"On many of the occasions I've seen you in here having dinner alone, I couldn't help thinking of what a great lady you'd make for this here tough guy. He always comes in here alone, too." Abe grinned at Austin. "Tough guys like him need something soft and pretty to help tone them down. I think you can smooth out his rough edges. It's amazing to see you two together like this. I had no idea you even knew each other. You're a perfect match."

Austin and Ashleigh laughed yet both looked thoroughly embarrassed. On the other hand, it seemed that Austin hadn't brought Sabrina there for dinner. That bit of news thrilled Ashleigh. It was probably too crude a place for the rich socialite to be seen in, Ashleigh thought.

Austin faked a punch at Abe. "Did you have to embarrass us like that, Captain? For your information, Ashleigh and I go way back."

"And! What does that have to do with now?"

Austin shrugged, grinning boyishly. "Give us a minute, Captain Abe, we're taking time to get reacquainted. It's been a long time for us, partner."

"Just don't take too long," Abe advised Austin. "You're both prime candidates for some man or woman who's looking for a permanent situation. For you to end up with someone else would be such a shame, especially since you two look like you were made for each other."

Austin briefly thought about how he'd barely escaped a permanent situation, one that had never really had the slightest chance of working out, nor had it been a match made in heaven.

"Enjoy your dinner." Without further comment, Abe winked at the couple as he left.

Ashleigh's eyes flickered with amusement. "He's certainly a shy one!"

"The captain's a great guy, Ash. He meant well. I hope you don't think I was offended by his remarks. I wasn't." *I hope you weren't bothered by it either; he was making perfect sense.*

A smile spread across Ashleigh's face. "I'm relieved to hear that. I was worried about how you'd take his less-than-tactful comments. I enjoy Captain Abe's humor. Let's eat."

"I guess we should, before it gets cold." Austin bowed his head and blessed the food.

The shrimp were huge and the fillets of white fish were chunky and flaky, fried in a light beer-batter crust. The plump French fries and homemade creamy coleslaw accompanied the delicious-looking meals. Pink lemonade had been the choices in beverages.

Ashleigh picked up the bottle of malt vinegar and sprinkled it over her seafood. She then offered the condiment to Austin. He used it and then returned it to the red basketlike holder. Without giving it any thought, Austin stuck one of his fries up to her mouth. While her eyes locked into his, she took a bite of the crispy potato. He then popped the rest of it into his mouth.

Ashleigh and Austin easily settled into a companionable silence while eating and enjoying every bite of their delicious dinner. A thick slab of carrot cake was shared between the two of them before the meal was completed.

Their short walking tour along the pier, hand in hand, gobbled up a few more minutes of amicable silence.

Before long, Austin had delivered Ashleigh safely to the front door of her apartment, with the promise of picking her up at ten o'clock the next morning. The *Kristina Elise* was due to set sail at 11:00 a.m. The light kiss he'd left her with wasn't nearly enough to satisfy their desires, but neither of them pushed the issue.

Ashleigh wished that Lanier were at home as she slipped off her jeans and sweatshirt. After moving into the bathroom, Ashleigh began brushing and flossing her teeth. While looking into the mirror at her image, she wondered why she hadn't been born beautiful and smart like the type of women she thought might run in Austin's circle of friends. Even though she'd never met any of his female acquaintances, she imagined them as lovely puffs of softness clad in expensive designer labels, drenched in costly perfumes, with beautiful hair styled in the finest salons.

Ashleigh began to fool around with her hair, trying different styles, hoping to bring about a touch of elegance and sophistication to her unruly locks. Worried about what she'd wear the next day, she went back into the bedroom and looked through her wardrobe. Seconds later, feeling despair, she closed the closet door. She then looked at the clock. An hour and fifteen minutes before the mall closed. Ashleigh redressed herself in a hurry.

Excited about her purchase, even though the designer outfit cost way more than she cared to think about, she dressed for bed in eager anticipation of the time she was to spend with Austin. Nestled comfortably in bed, ready to fall into what she hoped would be a deep sleep, Ashleigh closed her eyes. Before she could lose herself in the sweet dreams she wanted so badly and needed desperately to have, unpleasant memories of her youth came at her from every way.

"Get in here and clean this nasty toilet, girl," Mrs. Mack had yelled at her. "You think you're on holiday or something? When you get through cleaning all the bathrooms, the kitchen needs a good sweeping and mopping."

Ashleigh heard and then felt her skin crack beneath Mrs. Mack's stinging backhand.

"Don't look at me like that, you little ungrateful witch. Remember who feeds you."

"The state," Ashleigh recalled mumbling under her breath. Ashleigh was too stubborn to cry. Ashleigh never wanted Mrs. Mack to know how much she'd hurt her so badly, both physically and emotionally. Mrs. Mack already seemed to find joy in seeing Ashleigh in pain.

Memories of the Saturday morning before Easter Sunday came to Ashleigh's mind. It was easy for her to recall how all the smaller foster children had gotten new church outfits that she'd helped to pick out. Outfitted in frilly dresses, done in different shades of pastels, Jasmyne and Kimberly looked like fresh spring blooms. Terry, Leroy, and Emmett, her darling little foster brothers, looked so cute in their brand new navy blue two-piece suits and crisp white shirts.

Ashleigh had wanted a new Easter outfit, too. Mrs. Mack had said there wasn't enough money left over to buy her anything, yet before leaving the shopping center, her foster mother had purchased for herself a new suit of clothes along with shoes and a bag to match.

Tears slid down Ashleigh's cheeks as she recalled standing in front of the full-length mirror in Mrs. Mack's bedroom while the older woman pinned and tucked one of her old spring dresses to alter for Ashleigh to wear for Easter. Lavender with dainty white flowers, the simple dress wasn't that bad on the eyes, but all Ashleigh could think about was that it wasn't brand-new. She hadn't had any new clothes since leaving the Carrington house. Accustomed to wearing only hand-me-downs, Ashleigh felt deprived, unwanted, and ugly. *Stupid* and *Dummy* had become her new names—and she hadn't liked them any more than she liked the abusive Macks.

A soft knock on her door pulled Ashleigh out of her doldrums. After sitting up in bed, Ashleigh called out to Lanier to enter.

A smiling Lanier popped into the room and stretched out at the bottom of Ashleigh's bed, loving the feel of the white down comforter beneath her body. Though it held very little color, Lanier loved Ashleigh's room. Everything was done in white with the exception of the peach-colored throw pillows. Lanier was aware of why her friend desired to have everything around her so sterile. Because Ashleigh had lived in such filth all of her life, the color white made her feel clean and fresh, she'd once told Lanier. The bright whiteness also lent an airy feel to the room.

Lanier propped herself up on her elbows. "Why are you in bed so early, Ash? It's just a little after ten. Did you get anything to eat yet?"

Ashleigh's eyes glowed with laughter. "I have an early morning date. I ate at Captain Abe's earlier."

Lanier's curiosity was aroused by the look in Ashleigh's eyes. "With who?"

"Who indeed! The famous Wrangler QB."

Lanier sat straight up, nearly falling out of bed in the process. "So, Austin did come over to the house to see you. After I told him where you were, he didn't say if he'd intended to go over there or not. I'm glad he showed up."

Ashleigh grinned, rubbing her hands together. "In the flesh, looking hot as ever."

Lanier bubbled with enthusiasm. "That's fantastic, Ash." Then Lanier's expression quickly turned to a serious one. "I'm glad that you and Austin are going to continue seeing each other, but what's he going to do about his fiancée? It doesn't appear that Sabrina is ready to let go of him."

"Ex-fiancée! Like you told me on the ship, she's his problem, not mine. Austin swears that's it's over for them. He has certainly found a few unique ways to convince me of that."

"Have you two talked any more about what happened back then, why you were taken away from their home, Ash?"

"Since we talked about it on the ship, I didn't feel as if there was anything else to say. However, Austin did try to discuss it with me earlier, but I refused to talk about it. His friend and neighbor, Barry, told a lie to his mother about Austin, which resulted in Barry's mother calling social services to tell them that Austin had been talking about molesting me. It's hard to believe that someone could be that cruel and to dare tell such a bald-faced lie. According to Austin's account, that's exactly why I was removed from the Carrington home. I never told you that I was taken from the Carrington ranch, because I was angry about it and ashamed of it. I'm no longer angry, but I'm still a little ashamed that no one wanted me back then."

"If Austin wanted to discuss it earlier, why didn't you let him?"

"I guess I'm not prepared to go back into the past. I know the truth now, so there's no reason to revisit the dark period in my life. It somehow seemed easier to deal with when I didn't know one way or the other."

"Now that you know the Carringtons are innocent, you do hold them blameless, don't you, Ashleigh?"

"I don't think I ever really held them accountable. I no longer feel any of the bitterness I normally felt when I thought about that day. I didn't know what role the Carrington family may've played in it, but it was hard for me to accept or believe that they wanted rid of me. Their wonderful treatment of me belied that theory. It's still hard hearing the truth from Austin, but it's also comforting to learn that they had nothing to do with me being taken away."

"I'm happy that you guys have gotten past that difficult time. Now, let's talk about this date of yours for tomorrow. What exciting happenings are on the agenda?"

"A yacht party."

Eyes bulging, Lanier screeched with excitement. "Go ahead, Miss Girlfriend!" Lanier's smile suddenly turned down in a frown. "Aren't you worried about getting seasick, like you did on the big ship? You were a mess, girl."

"Dramamine has my back, Lani. Besides, if I swoon, Austin will be there to catch me, just as he did on the ship. I often thought of faking a few fainting spells just to have his arms wrapped around me." Both women laughed. "I'm no actress. He would've seen right through me and my pitiful charade."

"You are quite transparent where he's concerned. This is some change that's come about. It seemed to me as if you'd made up your mind not to involve yourself in a love affair with him, especially when you didn't return any of his phone calls. If I loved someone the way you love Austin, I couldn't have held out as long as you did. If he hadn't taken matters into his own hands, I'm not sure you would ever have called him back."

Ashleigh shook her head. "Yeah, how foolish of me. I can't believe I held out so long, either. Fear can make you do strange things. But Austin and I aren't going as far as having a love affair, at least not yet. Tomorrow's outing isn't even a date, though that's what I called it. We're just going to hang out with each other and become good friends."

Lanier sucked her teeth. "Yeah, right! You're already crazy in love with Austin and he's no less than crazy about you." Lanier took a minute to think about what Ashleigh had conveyed. "Perhaps by trying it as friends you'll really come together as lovers. There's no doubt in my mind that you and Austin Carrington are going to end up jumping the broom. You two were made for each other."

Ashleigh's smile was soft, brightening her eyes considerably. "You're the second person to say that today. Captain Abe said the same thing to us at the restaurant. We both nearly perished from embarrassment. Maybe you and Captain are right, but I'm not going to set myself up like that. There's still the vast difference in our two worlds. I don't see that ever changing. His world simply dwarfs mine and I don't want to get lost in a world that's capable of swallowing me whole."

While Ashleigh's mouth was saying one thing, her eyes expressed how much she'd love to have Austin as a lifetime partner. If he could somehow step out of his world, and allow them to find a new world all of their own, they could possibly endure forever. But that wasn't likely to happen. Austin Carrington was a superstar who belonged to the world that created his popularity and the million-dollar contracts despite the fact his family already had loads of money. His was a household name in his native Texas. Although the patrons had kept their distance at the restaurant, Ashleigh clearly saw the reverence his fans held for him. Austin was a man of position and wealth, the two things that intimidated her the most.

Ashleigh couldn't help wondering if she could ever overcome their vast differences.

Chapter 4

Similar to large white puffy clouds, the yacht's sails were raised, billowing wildly in the heavy cool breeze. The air was clean and crisp but with the distinct smell of brine. The hull of the large boat gleamed under the brilliant rays of the golden sun. It was a gorgeous morning, a perfect day for sailing, a perfect day for romance and falling deeply or deeper into love.

Dressed in a FUBU-designed navy blue and white hooded jacket and matching pants, Ashleigh looked chic. Though extremely nervous, she smiled radiantly, her Nike-clad feet keeping in step with Austin's long strides. As he took her around the yacht and introduced her to his numerous friends, several women, all of them beautiful, tossed envious glances her way. However, the majority of the stunning ladies greeted her with genuine friendliness, which helped to put Ashleigh more at ease. Elaine, as Austin had called the statuesque brunette, extended her hand to Ashleigh while giving her a warm welcoming smile.

After a couple of minutes of friendly chitchat, Austin steered Ashleigh away from the giggling group of females. "Let's go find Clifton, the owner of this floating beauty. He's anxious to meet you."

Ashleigh looked puzzled. "He is? Why would he want to meet me?"

Austin bumped her playfully with his shoulder. "He'd heard from some of the other guys about our romantic rendezvous aboard the cruise ship. When he asked me about you, I promised him I'd make sure that he got to meet you one day. I had no idea it would happen this soon, if ever, but I'm glad that it is." Austin chuckled. "My excitement over you is what made Clifton anxious to meet the woman who'd obviously done a serious number on my head and heart."

"I'm happy you're getting to keep your promise to Clifton. Thanks for letting me hang out with you and your crew, Austin." *Your head and heart weren't the only ones compromised.*

"My pleasure, Miss Ayers. I can't think of anyone I'd rather hang out with."

Flattered by his sweet comments, Ashleigh let her glowing eyes slowly rake over his sexy body. Austin was an impeccable dresser. His tall, lithe frame looked magnificent in the gray and red fleece jogging set. The gray polo he wore beneath the jacket was open at the collar, exposing tufts of thick chest hair. Her eyes were then attracted to his curly head of hair. The wind rustling through his thick curls was somewhat of a physical turn-on for Ashleigh. While the slightly unshaven look gave him that sexy, bad-boy appearance, his soft eyes and generous mouth were what had her heart doing jumping jacks. He often had a boyish yet extremely confident look about him, the total male package.

Her eyes on him made him hot. His desire to kiss her flared

up inside him with a burning sensation. Austin wasted no time in leading Ashleigh to a quiet, uninhabited spot, far from the partying crowd. Immediately, his mouth hungrily sought out hers, making her gasp with pleasure. The thought to fight her desires for him had dissipated the same moment his tongue connected with hers. The kiss was long and deep as his hands roved and caressed her body with tenderness and warmth. His hips slightly grinding against her lower body made her crazy with longing. Her body responded ardently, as her mouth coupled with his in a sexually arousing kiss. If they were alone, Ashleigh could easily imagine what delicious coupling would occur next.

In the same instant Ashleigh finally made the decision she'd been wrestling with since the day they'd first reunited. She and Austin would become lovers very soon. It was no secret that they'd desperately wanted to make love to each other, and the time was drawing closer for them to act upon their strongest desires. They'd come so close to consummating their feelings on the cruise ship. Though deeply reluctant, they managed to hold back. Ashleigh silently vowed not to hold back much longer what they both obviously wanted and needed from each other.

Just as Austin steered Ashleigh toward another group of men and women, a shrill voice pierced the air. Recognizing the whiny voice, Austin stopped dead in his tracks. Looking down at Ashleigh, he shrugged his shoulders. "Whatever you do, Ash, don't let her get to you. I can assure you that that's why she's here. I seem to have a spy inside my crew."

Ashleigh had no idea what he was talking about. Then she spotted the beautiful woman that had come to the Galveston port to meet the cruise ship. Pounding inside her ribs with force, Ashleigh's heart raced recklessly inside her chest as

Sabrina Beaudreaux entwined her fingers with Austin's as she kissed him on the mouth. With her heart breaking in two, Ashleigh quickly turned her head away. This was another sight she didn't want to see or memorize.

With ease, in one quick motion, Austin freed his fingers from Sabrina's. It hurt him to see Ashleigh looking as if she were sick inside. But it wasn't in him to treat Sabrina with disrespect; he didn't think Ashleigh would want him to act like that, either. "Hello. How are you, Sabrina?"

Sabrina snorted, eyeing Ashleigh with open contempt. "Don't you stand here and put on that innocent act with me, A.C. You walked out on me at the port, which was bad enough. But since you've been back home, you haven't bothered to return any of my calls. Why's that?"

Austin bit down on his lower lip. "I think you know the answer to that, Sabrina. At any rate, we aren't discussing my reasons for not calling. Not here, anyway," he said calmly. He took Ashleigh by the hand. "Ashleigh, I'd like to introduce you to Sabrina Beaudreaux, my head coach's daughter."

Ashleigh extended her hand to Sabrina, but Sabrina acted as if Ashleigh didn't even exist.

"Coach's daughter, my foot! For your information, lady, in case he hasn't enlightened you, I'm A.C.'s fiancée. Furthermore, I don't care who in the hell you are, but Austin Carrington is already spoken for. If either of you has thought differently, I've now set the record straight." Sabrina's smile came with discernable falseness. "Ashleigh, I'm glad to see that you're a gracious loser. Austin, will you please get us girls something to drink? I think a toast is in order."

"Sabrina, don't do this," Austin practically pleaded. "Please don't."

"Do what? Now that your friend here and I understand each

other, I think we should get better acquainted. We certainly have at least one thing in common. *You*."

Austin thanked his lucky stars that the *Kristina Elise* had not yet set sail. There was no way he was going to subject Ashleigh to a full day and evening of Sabrina's petty show-casing. "Excuse us a minute, Sabrina. I see that I need to make Ashleigh aware of a few things, but I'd like to do it in private. That's only fair. We'll see you in a few minutes."

"I'm glad you're starting to see things my way again, A.C. No one has to get hurt in this if you come clean with her up front. I'll be down below when you finish breaking it down to your little friend. Better luck next time, Ashleigh. Remember that the best woman always wins."

Without further ado, Austin led Ashleigh through the throng of gossiping whisperers and gawking onlookers. It appeared to Ashleigh that no one seemed a bit surprised by what had just transpired. After talking briefly with Clifton, the host, Austin whisked Ashleigh off the yacht. He didn't slow his pace or look back until they were well away from the now slowly moving yacht.

While holding on tightly to Ashleigh's hand, Austin ducked into a shoreline restaurant. Inside the comfortable establish-ment, he asked for two seats out on the waterfront terrace, which extended a short distance out over the Gulf of Mexico.

The waiter appeared rather quickly and wasted no time in taking their breakfast orders. His retreat was as hasty as his appearance.

Completely floored by the activities of the last several minutes, Ashleigh passed several uneasy glances in Austin's direction. Her eyes were full of questions, but her mouth felt as if it were frozen shut. Ashleigh couldn't help recalling the thoughts she'd had just a few minutes prior to Sabrina's unexpected appearance; contemplating how near the time was for them to finally make love. Sabrina's actions had had the same effect on Ashleigh's fiery desires as that of a cold shower. The fire of her desires had been thoroughly doused with a bucket of ice water.

Looking a bit chagrined, Austin covered Ashleigh's hand with his. "I know there's nothing that I can say to make you feel any better about what happened aboard the yacht, so I won't try to diminish your feelings. Just know that I'm sorry. I would never have intentionally put you in such an awkward position. I had no idea that Sabrina would show up uninvited."

"I would hope not," Ashleigh replied coolly. Ashleigh knew she had no right to be upset about anything since she and Austin were supposed to be just hanging out as friends. *Keep your emotions detached from all this drama,* she told herself. *You're simply an outsider looking in.*

"Ashleigh, I haven't lied to you about anything. Let me re-iterate my position. I'm no longer engaged to Sabrina. I told you the wedding was called off long before the cruise."

Ashleigh's heartbeat quickened at the distressed look on his face. The desire to take Austin into her arms and hug him was strong. He looked as if he needed comforting. "She certainly doesn't act as if it's over between you two. Did you somehow forget to tell her, Austin?"

"Anyone would think so by what just occurred on the yacht. But, no, I didn't forget to tell her. And Sabrina hasn't forgotten it, either. Believe me, she knows it's over for us. Someone from my crew must've told her about the yacht party and that I'd be there. No one knew that I was bringing you along. So her showing up like that had nothing to do with you."

Despite her deep love for Austin, Ashleigh felt horrible for both him and Sabrina. "I'm sorry that my being there with you kept you from trying to work things out with her."

His eyes swept over Ashleigh with firelight warmth. "There's nothing for us to work out or work on, Ashleigh. It's over, finished, kaput. Sabrina and I are not meant to be. I'm really sorry that I didn't go with my first instinct about her. I knew she was spoiled rotten. But that's not her fault. Parents are to blame for giving in to their kids' every demand. I just couldn't meet all of Sabrina's demands, had no desire to meet most of them. I don't have a hole in my back for a hand to slip through, nor do I have a spot anywhere on my anatomy for someone to attach strings. Sabrina needs a flesh-and-blood puppet. A hand puppet I'm not. I had to leave that unattractive job up to the people who created the puppeteer, her extremely well-to-do family."

"The decision to break your engagement must've been a difficult one. I'm really sorry for both of you, Austin." *If that's the case, then why do I feel so much joy?* Ashleigh felt guilty for her joyous feelings, but she couldn't lie to herself. She had no desire to hurt Sabrina, but outside of his wealth and prestige, Ashleigh saw Sabrina as the only other obstacle that stood in the way of her and Austin having any kind of long-term future. Still, she felt bad for the other woman.

"I hated hurting Sabrina, but a divorce would've hurt more. It's better this way. Sabrina will come to see that in time. I'm simply not the man for her because I can't be controlled. She has to be in control of every situation. She needs way more than I can give her, Ash."

The waiter brought their breakfast orders and set the plates of hot food before them. Austin had ordered eggs, pancakes, and sausage; Ashleigh had ordered scrambled eggs and toast, no meat. Freshly squeezed orange juice had been both their choices in beverages. The moment the waiter took his leave Austin said the blessing.

While taking a bite of her egg, Ashleigh eyed Austin with a mixture of curiosity and reverence. He sounded as if he had already totally detached himself from Sabrina, but she had to wonder, since their engagement had only been broken a short time ago. She was also in awe of his courage in taking the necessary steps to ensure his own happiness when he recognized he wouldn't have it with Sabrina. It couldn't have been easy for him to break such bad news to the woman he'd promised to marry. He was too sensitive to hurt someone recklessly and selfishly. Austin had to be hurting, too. She silently prayed that he wouldn't suffer any more needless pain.

"Perhaps Sabrina needs you to be tough on her, have you lay down the law to her, Austin. Maybe she really doesn't want to have her own way all the time and just needs someone to challenge her into learning how to accept *no* for an answer. You think?"

Austin smiled at Ashleigh's valiant attempt to patch things up with him and Sabrina. Her heart wasn't in it, though. He was glad for that. It just might mean that she felt more for him than she was letting on. In fact there was no doubt in his mind that Ashleigh had deep feelings for him. The vast amount of time they'd spent together on the cruise had let him know that much. He was only concerned that she might not allow herself to act upon what she felt. Being back on dry land had somehow quelled her overt passions. Her deep-seated fears were not lost on him.

He laid his fork down and stared right into Ashleigh's eyes. "Not! Sabrina can't be raised again. I'd need another millennium to straighten her out. I don't have that long to live. Someone will come along and make her see the error of her ways. She'll someday learn to love someone other than Sabrina. I desperately want that for her. Everyone deserves to be happy and in love."

Ashleigh shook her head. "Doesn't just thinking of her with another man make you a bit jealous, Austin? I find it so hard to believe that you're not feeling any of this. It also scares me."

"Not even the slightest twinge of jealousy. I don't want to seem callous, but like I said before, Sabrina and I aren't meant to be. Honesty can be scary. I'm only trying to keep it real."

Austin shoved his plate across the table. He then got up and took the chair right next to Ashleigh's. After scooting his seat even closer to hers, he put his arm around her shoulders. "Now you and I are an altogether different matter. If you're trying to talk me back into Sabrina's arms because you're afraid of what you feel for me, it's not working, Ash. Not in the least."

Looking into her eyes, Austin planted a kiss behind her ear. "When are you going to stop fighting the idea of us being together? The only thing that has changed for us is location. We can have the same thing on dry land that we had out on the open sea."

Her questioning eyes connected with his. "Can we, Austin?"

He fingered a loose strand of her hair. "Despite your fears, we can have it all, Ash."

Hoping to make Ashleigh believe that they could have it all, he claimed her mouth with his in a riveting kiss. Ashleigh trembled inwardly as their tongues came together and the kiss deepened.

While losing her fingers in his hair, Ashleigh made a silent promise to herself. If Austin was really over Sabrina Beaudreaux, she vowed to do everything in her power to be the kind of woman he could love forever. Austin Carrington was the only man in this world for her; she now had to make sure that he'd come to see her as the only woman in the universe for him.

Once the hair-raising kiss ended, Austin couldn't seem to find the strength to pull away from Ashleigh. Those super-magnetic drawing powers of hers had never failed to work on him yet. Like a magnet to metal, he wanted to cling to her forever. With his arm firmly in place around her shoulder, he placed a gentle kiss in the center of her forehead. "Since we blew the yacht party, do you have any suggestions on how you want to spend the rest of the day, Ash?"

The back of her hand tenderly grazed the side of his face. "I'll leave that up to you."

He grinned. "You might not want to leave our itinerary up to me, girl. I've only had one thing on my mind since we first bumped into each other."

Ashleigh raised an indignant eyebrow. "Is that all you men think about?"

Not seeming to care that he was a popular public figure, he captured her lips with his. "I don't concern myself with what other men do or don't do. I just know what I want to do with you."

Ashleigh wished the outdoor terrace came equipped with air-conditioning. It was getting a little steamy for her. With Austin in such close proximity, she was feeling his sexual heat. Combined with hers had it mighty hot. "I won't ask you to spell it out for me since what you're talking about is obvious." She looked a tad injured. "I hope having sex isn't the reason you wanted to continue seeing me. If so, you're in for one big disappointment."

It was now his turn to look wounded. "Ashleigh, how do you keep jumping to the wrong conclusions? I wasn't talking about sex. Maybe you're the one with lovemaking on the brain. Is it possible that you're projecting your own physical needs and desires? Girl, it sounds to me like you can't wait to get me into bed. The glowing lust in your eyes isn't the least bit subtle."

Ashleigh looked mortified. The deep color staining her cheeks gave away the depth of her embarrassment. "You can't say that kind of stuff about me or to me. I've never given you any such impression, Austin Carrington." *Have I?*

Though amused by her reaction to his comments, he was careful not to reveal it. He wasn't sure how serious she might be taking things, but he couldn't pass up the opportunity to find out. "Are you saying you've never thought about an entire night in bed with me, never imagined us locked together in a sexual fantasy?" With bated breath, he waited for her answer.

Ashleigh's cheek color deepened even more. "Do you really expect me to answer those questions, Austin? If so, you've got a long, long wait, boyfriend."

He'd had an idea that she'd dodge the questions, but he had hoped she'd admit to having sexual fantasies about him. He had certainly had his share of sweet fantasies about her.

He grinned. "I can see that you're chickening out. I've got nothing but time, especially since I'm in off-season. Now, back to my original question. What do you want to do for the rest of the day? I'm all yours."

Anxious to change the subject, Ashleigh took a moment to ponder his question. She then snapped her fingers. "I'd like to browse the furniture stores for beds." Her color rose again. "Ugh, I can't believe I went there."

Austin laughed. "You see? I was right. You've got nothing but thoughts of bedroom magic and raw sex on your mind. But that's okay, Ash." He winked at her. "I'm always open to erotic suggestions, but only to those coming from you."

Ashleigh feigned a punch in his direction. "I was talking about beds for Haven House. You're purposely misinterpreting my remarks. I'd love to browse through a few furniture stores to select furnishing for the bedrooms at Haven House. Does that clarify things for you?"

"Yeah, but I have to admit to being a little disappointed. What I was talking about earlier was spending time alone with you, not getting you into bed. From the moment we first met, I could only hope that there'd come a time when I might have you all to myself. All I could think of on the cruise was being alone with you. I love spending time with just us. I was hoping I could take you out to my little ranch so you can see where I live. I remember how you loved the horses on my parents' property. I only have four horses and two of them are palominos. Q.B. and T.D. are mighty beautiful animals. Texas and Wrangler are my work horses. I'm sure they'd love to meet you, Ash. Think I can change your mind about the shopping spree?"

She smiled radiantly. "If you promise to take me shopping another day. I'm sure the two horses' initials stand for quarterback and touchdown. Right?"

"On the money. Believe it or not, T.D. is the female. As for taking you shopping, that's a promise that I can easily keep. Once I pay the check, we can be on our way." He paused for a second, looking at her intently. "I have something important to say to you, Ashleigh. I feel the need to say it right now, before we take another step forward. Willing to listen to me?"

Ashleigh nodded, though fearful of the serious expression he now wore on his face.

He shook his head. "I don't think I can go backward, Ash."

She looked puzzled. "What do you mean, Austin?"

He momentarily nuzzled his nose into her shiny hair and

deeply inhaled the fresh coconut scent of her shampoo. "We became so close and shared so much intimacy on the ship, Ash. So much so that I find it hard to act like we're nothing more than friends. Ashleigh, I'm definitely your friend, but I want to be more than that to you, need more than friendship from you. You seem to be on the fence about what kind of relationship you want us to have. I know you still have fears about us, but there's no reason for you to have any fear where we're concerned. I've made my intentions clear. I have to know up front, Ashleigh. I know what I said earlier about just hanging out as friends and . having no strings attached, but that's clearly not the direction I want to see us go in. Just friends, or are we friends that desire to build a serious personal relationship? Plainly speaking, are we or are we not destined for a love affair? I need to know right here and now what it's going to be like for us so I can begin to play strictly by the rules. I believe you already know what I want. But you're the one who gets to make the call, Ash."

His comments made her feel somewhat frightened, not to mention them sounding a bit threatening. It seemed as if Austin was prepared to withdraw from her his loving affection if she only wanted them to be friends. *How awful would that be?* This wasn't something she could leave to chance or even put off for a later discussion; he wanted an answer, forthwith.

Ashleigh leaned into him and lazed the pad of her thumb across his full lips. She then brought his face close to hers. In the next instant she drew his bottom lip into her mouth and sucked on it gently. As her hands entwined in his hair, she kissed him fully on the mouth. Thinking of all the places she wanted to touch him but couldn't, since they were in public, made her blood pressure go sky-high. Ashleigh moved slightly away from him and looked into his eyes. "I just made the call, Austin, but you get to interpret it all on your own."

Beaming from head to toe, Austin let his eyes dart all around the terrace. "If we were alone, I bet your challenging remarks wouldn't be so bold and spicy. Furthermore, I don't think you'd be able to handle the wild responses to my interpretation of your call."

Ashleigh flicked her tongue against his ear. "Let's go to your place and find out."

The warm spring weather had already weaved its magic over the vast acreage of Austin's not-so-little ranch. In direct contrast to the description he'd given earlier of his place, Austin owned what Ashleigh saw as a big Texas spread. At first glance, the entire property appeared to her as a wonderful work of magnificent artistry. The massive ranch-style house was certainly an impressive one-story structure.

The interior's blend of modern, contemporary, and country-style furnishings was extremely tasteful. Though done in different styles, each lent a warm and welcoming feel to the place, as well as a cozy one. Beautiful ceramic tile and hardwood floors were adorned with ornate handmade rugs. Three of the ten rooms had brick fireplaces: family room, audiovisual-game room, and master suite. Surrounded by a variety of magnificent evergreen trees, making it appear even more magnificent, Austin's home had been erected smack dab in the center of the property. The continuous floor-to-ceiling glass windows offered a panoramic view.

Ashleigh and Austin now sat astride the two beautiful golden palominos, Q.B. and T.D. Austin had tied a large pink bow around the shiny flaxen tail of T.D., the horse Ashleigh was riding. When he'd shown up with the horses in tow, her lilting laughter at seeing the bow had electrified the atmosphere.

The magnificent animals trotted slowly around the grounds while their riders engaged in light conversation, which included plenty of humor. When Austin suddenly challenged Ashleigh to a race, she took off before he could set the rules. Because her horse had taken off like a rocket, Austin didn't think Q.B. stood a chance of catching up to T.D. and Ashleigh. Ashleigh threw her head back in laughter when Austin finally reached her. Teasingly, he accused her of cheating.

After spending the next couple of hours exploring a large portion of the twenty-acre ranch on horseback, Ashleigh was ready to call it a day.

Once Ashleigh told Austin she was ready to pack it in, he left her seated in the ornate gazebo while he returned the horses to the nearby stables. Feeling so much peace, she sat perfectly still on the gazebo's bench seating, watching him in adoration until he disappeared into the stables. Austin was such a nice, safe person. Even if she wasn't in love with him, she felt that he would be a very good friend to her. Her romantic feelings for him had nothing to do with friendship, yet she was very much afraid that it might complicate the relationship if a love affair didn't come into being. While she desperately desired him as a lover, his friendship was every bit as important to her.

After a light supper of grilled lamb chops, fresh spinach, and other mixed vegetables, lemon meringue pie for dessert—all but the pie was prepared by Austin—Ashleigh and Austin's evening began with them stretched out in front of the nonburning fireplace. While the couple looked out at the property through the continuous window in the family room, soft, romantic music played on Austin's state-of-the-art audio equipment.

Though it hadn't been her intention to emote, Ashleigh found herself telling Austin about how fragmented her life had become, after she was taken from the Carrington home. While he was very sympathetic to her, he wanted nothing more than to see her move forward with her life. Austin hated seeing her stuck in her awful past, which couldn't be erased no matter what.

He took her hand in his. "I know you've endured a lot of pain, incredible hurt, Ash, but what's making you hold on to it? What's keeping you from letting go of the past?"

Ashleigh appeared stunned by his questions. She blinked hard as she thought about what he'd asked. "I don't know. I want to, but it's my guess that I don't know how to let go of it. Sometimes I don't believe I'm worthy of feeling anything other than this gut-wrenching pain. That's certainly what I've been taught to feel through the dialogue and actions of my foster families. Maybe I'll start to feel validated once I accomplish my goals for Haven House. I see it as a new beginning for me, one that will take away the pain and replace it with a sense of belonging. I've never felt as if I belonged anywhere or to anyone, Austin. You can't even begin to imagine what that feels like, since you've always been loved, have always been protected and kept safe. You had parents to take care of your every need and fulfill your every whim. I'm sorry, Austin, but it's never been like that for me. I wish it had been."

"You're right, Ash, I can't imagine it. I'm terribly sorry that you've had to live your life in that kind of pain. Sorry for everything you've had to go through. Do you somehow begrudge me the kind of life I was fortunate enough and blessed to have?"

Her eyes widened. "Of course not! I wouldn't wish my life on my worst enemy. I have yet to be validated in this cold, cruel world, but I'm still praying and hoping."

"Sweetheart, you can't look to others for validation. You have to validate yourself. No one can do that for you. You are exactly what you think you are." He pounded his heart with a closed fist. "It's all in here, girl. It's what you feel inside."

Ashleigh's heart pounded unnaturally. "That's part of the problem. Half of the time I don't feel anything inside."

Austin looked frustrated. "But you've already accomplished so much. You're a college graduate, a licensed social worker, and now a homeowner. If those things aren't validations in your life, I don't know what else you're after. How can you effectively minister to a bunch of brokenhearted kids if you haven't yet come to grips with your own painful past as one of them? Maybe you're not as ready for this huge undertaking as you think you are. If you're not mentally and emotionally prepared for this challenge, you're being grossly unfair to the kids you want to help. And failure is guaranteed if your negative way of thinking doesn't change."

Ashleigh felt hurt and was slightly agitated by his assessment of her. It hurt her even more knowing he'd hit the nail on the head. His concerns about her were not much different from hers. "You just don't understand, Austin. I don't think it's possible for you to since you've never been in my shoes. Maybe we should change the subject. This one hurts. A lot."

"Thanks for making my precise point. It will always hurt. Until you learn to deal with your past and move on, you can't expect it to do anything but cause you pain. Why can't you live in the moment? Why do you refuse to accept the rewards and accolades for all that you've accomplished thus far, Ashleigh? They're only staring you right in the face."

She studied him intently. "You sound as if you're angry with me, Austin. Are you?"

The forlorn look in her eyes cut deep into his heart.

Although he wanted to gently shake her into reality, he instead pulled her to him and kissed her eyelids. "No way, Ash. I'm just feeling a little frustrated. I want to help you, but I can't do it without your participation." *How can I get through to this beautiful woman who has accomplished so much despite how rough things were?* He believed time healed all wounds, but so much time had already passed her by without the slightest mending of her broken heart and damaged spirit. Talking to her about wounds healing with time would be fruitless, especially after she'd already endured twenty-four years of nothing but pain and anguish.

Ashleigh glided the back of her hand down the side of his face. "Good, because that's not what we came here for. Austin, have you forgotten why you brought me here in the first place?"

Knowing she was taking the initiative in changing the subject, he shook his head in the negative. "Have you, Ash?"

Her mouth claimed his in a fiery kiss. "I'm extremely interested in knowing if I can handle your interpretation to my earlier call. Are you as anxious as I am to find out?"

In order to keep her from feeling rejected, Austin had to tamp down his biggest fear. Her running away from him, should they reach the point of no return, scared the dickens out of him. There were great risks involved should this sweetly challenging rendezvous end up in a wildly passionate lovemaking session; any degree of regret on her part was his greatest concern.

Deciding that even the slightest hint of rejection from him was the worst thing of all for her to experience, Austin fought off his fears. As he brought her body fully against his, he allowed the anxiousness in his lips and roving tongue to answer her last question. With her every breath quickening, he unbuttoned the top of her jeans and slowly pulled down the zipper until her lace bikinis were completely exposed.

Wanting desperately to make her feel comfortable and totally relaxed, he was careful not to make it seem as if he was in a rush. In his opinion, foreplay wasn't something a man should ever rush his partner through.

Ashleigh arched into him as his fingers gently probed the opening to her moist flower. They'd come this far before, but she desperately desired them to go all the way this time. He had already made his position crystal clear; a love affair was what he wanted most.

His fingers inside her caused her to writhe with wild abandon. Not an ounce of self-consciousness rushed in to ruin the highly charged moment. Ashleigh experienced a quick moment of fear when Austin suddenly withdrew his fingers from inside her. Her belief that he was having second thoughts was immediately quashed when he whisked her up into his arms and carried her into his bedroom.

After positioning her on the king-size four-poster bed, he stripped out of his clothes and then lay down beside her. Having her in his intimate space made him smile as he drew her in closer to him. While rubbing his thumb tenderly across her lower lip, Austin looked deeply into her eyes. "If we reach a point where you want to stop, please don't hesitate to tell me. I definitely won't want to end our lovemaking prematurely, but I promise you that I will. Okay?"

Ashleigh raised herself up, lifted her sweater over her head, and then tossed it aside. This was one time she was going to trust her heart and totally disregard her head. The time had come for her to risk it all. Making love to Austin was a matter best left to her heart and soul, not to mention the needs of her body. Something about directing his head to her breasts caused her heart rate to go berserk. Her nipples had grown taut from the eager anticipation.

As he laved an erect nipple, her bold gesture in bringing him close to her breasts was having no lesser impact on him. His tongue circled and flicked at each of her aureoles, causing her to tighten her grip on his hair. As his mouth trailed kisses lower and lower on her anatomy, her inner thighs felt as if they'd turned to jelly. Ashleigh knew that a climax was possible without the act of penetration, but she had no idea that it could happen to her just by him sucking her breasts. Ashleigh was glad the room was dark, glad that she could hide her embarrassment by keeping her face buried into his chest.

Knowing there was no turning back for them, Austin reached for a foil packet.

As impassioned moans and soft purrs escaped her lips, while her body shook with the force of unexpected spasms, Austin slowly slipped inside her. Though he could easily lose himself in his desire to keep the fires of their desires burning hot, he was mindful of the need to be delicate with her during the initial act of penetration.

Lovemaking was the ultimate in intimate acts, one that shouldn't ever be rushed. He wanted Ashleigh to have with him the most wonderful sexual experiences possible. Although they'd come terribly close to making love on the ship the last night of the cruise, this was his very first time inside her, a fantasy fulfilled.

Chapter 5

Ashleigh couldn't believe that the beautiful and elegant Angelica Carrington actually stood at the front door of Haven House. The perfect picture of health, her ebony eyes warm with vibrant life, the five-foot-eight Angelica was slender and chic. Though her dark brown hair was now frosted with numerous strands of gray, it didn't make her look a bit older. She was as striking as ever, wearing the smile of an angel, possessing a flawless caramel-brown complexion.

Stunned, dirty, and disheveled from housecleaning, her mouth agape, Ashleigh couldn't seem to find her voice. How many times had she dreamed of this very thing happening? She had often imagined Angelica coming to rescue her from every awful place she'd ever lived. Just seeing the smiling Angelica brought back a wave of wonderful memories. Ashleigh wanted desperately to hug Austin's mother, squeeze her tight, but she didn't know if her affection would be welcomed. It had been such a long time since she last shared a loving embrace with Angelica.

As though she'd read Ashleigh's mind, Angelica briefly brought the younger woman into her embrace. "Hello, Sar…Ashleigh." Angelica had suddenly remembered Austin telling her that Sariah now referred to herself as Ashleigh; truly preferred the name Ashleigh over Sariah. "My, my, you've grown into such a stunning young woman. I always knew that a swan resided inside you. But you were always beautiful to me. Is it okay if I come in, Ashleigh?"

Ashleigh slapped her forehead with an open palm, embarrassed by her own rudeness, though unintentional. "Of course you can come inside." As she stepped inside for Angelica to enter, Ashleigh didn't know what name to call her by; Mommy had been most appropriate back then. Angelica and Beaumont were the only foster parents she'd ever fondly referred to as Mommy and Daddy. "I'm sorry. I guess I'm still a little stunned at seeing you after all this time."

Ashleigh looked so nervous that Angelica felt compelled to take her into her arms and give her another hug. "Oh, Ashleigh, we thought we'd never see you again. When Austin called to tell us he thought that it was you who was on the same cruise with him, Beau and I could barely wait for confirmation. We were beside ourselves with joy when Austin finally confirmed to us your true identity. We were so glad to know that you weren't suffering from amnesia."

Warmed by Angelica's sweet Texas twang, Ashleigh laughed as she led Angelica into the living room and over to the badly worn sofa. "I see that Austin has already told you he thought I had amnesia in the beginning. Our initial meetings were very interesting ones."

"Though you hadn't revealed it to him, he was so sure you

were our precious Sariah. He also thought you may've blocked out the pain of all your past emotional harm. Austin didn't want to pressure you to remember if you'd truly forgotten him or had erased the tough times."

Ashleigh's shoulders sagged with the weight of her unhappy past as she turned to face Angelica. More nervous with Angelica than she was with Austin, Ashleigh bit down on her lower lip. She didn't realize how hard she'd sunk her teeth into her bottom lip until she tasted the blood. "I didn't set out to deceive Austin, but that was exactly what I ended up doing. I just didn't know how to tell him who I was when we first came face-to-face. Then, things between us quickly progressed to the point where I became scared to tell him the truth. I didn't think he'd understand, but I was wrong. I even thought Austin might end up hating me for not telling him, yet I knew he wasn't a hate-filled man."

Angelica smiled gently, tenderly patting the back of Ashleigh's hand. "My Austin could never hate anyone, especially you. Austin loves you, Ashleigh. He always has. The pain he endured after you were taken away from us was immeasurable. I'm glad you know the truth of what really occurred back then. Nosy neighbors can sometimes be a blessing, but ours acted maliciously and without caring who got hurt. Terribly jealous of Austin and angry that Austin had been given his starting quarterback position, Barry Akins lied on Austin. His mother believed her son's lies because, in the throes of a nasty divorce, her own personal life wasn't a happy one. Spreading misery to others is often a common goal of miserable people."

"Austin told me all about what happened. I know firsthand how malicious some people can be. It seems that I've encountered more bad people than good ones. It's been frightening."

"Thank God that's all over for you. We can move on now.

You're back in our lives and we couldn't be happier about it. When can you come to the ranch? Beau is very anxious to see you. I know it's short notice, but can you come for dinner this evening? Austin will be there."

Ashleigh fought the rising color in her cheeks, to no avail. The latter mention of Austin's name had instantly brought to her mind the delicious memories of their previous night of sensuous lovemaking. She had spent the entire night and the first few hours of dawn in Austin's arms and in his bed. Glad that Angelica couldn't read minds, Ashleigh smiled. "Perhaps we should first find out if Austin minds me being there. What he thinks is important to me."

"We've already discussed it. Like Beau and me, our son is hoping you'll accept the invitation. If you decide to come, is six-thirty a good time for you, Ashleigh?"

"That's fine with me. That'll give me time to do a little more work on the house. After I'm finished here, I'll go back to the apartment and get cleaned up. I still remember the address to your place, but I'll have to go online to map out the directions. How should I dress?"

"Comfortably, the only way to be dressed when eating Beau's barbecue ribs. As for directions, I'm sure Austin will want to pick you up. I'll have him call you. Is that okay?"

"It should be fine. However, I'll need to see my roommate before I go out."

Angelica laughed softly. "I hear that your roommate holds our Dallas's personal interest. Dallas told us a lot about Lanier Watson before he left for spring training camp. Beau and I are looking forward to meeting her. If she's free this evening, we'd love to have her come with you. Dallas would approve of the invitation, though we haven't spoken to him in a few days."

Ashleigh grinned, remembering how hard Lanier had

fought her attraction to Dallas. "If Lanier is free, and not running late, I'm sure she'd love to come with me. I'll talk to her and then let you know if she can make it. I'm sure you'll want to know how many guests to prepare for."

"There's always enough food in the Carrington home for extra guests and the healthy Carrington appetites." Angelica looked around the room. "I'd love to see the rest of the house if you don't mind. If this room is any indication of the others, the house appears to need a lot of work. Austin told us you're trying to raise money for your wonderful project. I've taken the liberty of sending out a few personal notes to several of the local social and business organizations. I think your money problems can be addressed and solved rather quickly."

Ashleigh was overwhelmed with Angelica's letter-writing generosity on behalf of Haven House. "Thank you so much for your thoughtfulness. I'd love to show you the rest of the house."

Angelica got to her feet. She then put Ashleigh's hand in hers. "I noticed that you haven't called me by my name once. I know it's been a long time, Ashleigh, but I've never stopped thinking of you as my child. If you're uncomfortable with Mommy, Mom, or Mother, please call me Angelica. Mrs. Carrington is far too impersonal for the kind of love we share."

Ashleigh squeezed Angelica's hand. "Thank you for the kind gesture. I'd love to resume calling you by one of the maternal names you've mentioned, but it may take me a short time to get used to it again. If it's okay with you, I'll just call you Ms. C for now."

"I'm for whatever makes you comfortable. I guess we'd better get on with the tour."

Ashleigh failed to hide her nervousness. Being in such close proximity to Beaumont Carrington had her insides quivering.

This was the fearless, tall, dark, and handsome man she had once called Daddy, the same man she had loved and trusted without question. He was a big man, as gentle as he was big. She was so glad that her voice hadn't quivered when she'd introduced Lanier to the Carringtons. Ashleigh saw that Lanier wasn't the least bit nervous around Dallas's parents, but then again, she was never a shy one. Lanier met people easily.

Beaumont bear-hugged Ashleigh for the third time in just a matter of minutes. He couldn't get over her actually being there in the flesh after so many years of his family not knowing what had happened to her. "Gosh, you're beautiful, Ashleigh. You're the butterfly we've often imagined you as. You have no idea how many hours Angelica and I spent wondering and worrying about you, hoping we'd one day see you again." He stroked Ashleigh's cheek with gentle fingers. "We've really missed you, honey. Welcome home."

Emotionally full, Ashleigh could only nod. Her voice had yet to be found. A noise from somewhere behind her caused her to turn around. Her body immediately relaxed at the sight of Austin. He had a way of bringing instant calm to her existence. She knew serenity with him.

Austin quickly made his way to Ashleigh's side, entwining his fingers with hers. Bending down, he kissed her forehead. "Hi, Ash. Are you okay?"

"I'm doing great. Seeing you has put me a little more at ease." Seeing Lanier so comfortable with the Carringtons also helped to ease the tension she had over their first meeting.

"That's nice to know. I'm glad you were able to find the ranch. I was worried about you, concerned that you might get lost coming way out here in no-man's land."

"I did just fine. Still, I wish I had let you pick me up at the apartment. Since Lanier was running late, as usual, I didn't want to make you late, too. I thought we'd be running way behind. I'd rather be an hour early than one minute late. Lanier's not as much into punctuality as me."

As a phone bell rang in another part of the house, Austin watched after his parents as they left the room. He then looked down at his watch. "You're not late, as was obviously anticipated. You're actually seven minutes early. I'm just happy that you got here, period." Smiling, Austin eyed her from head to toe, his eyes flirting wildly. He loved the way her jeans hugged her curves. She looked comfortable in the lightweight sweater she wore. "You're looking mighty good, girl."

Ashleigh ached to kiss him. She was still so amazed at how considerate he was of her, at how easily he could bring a smile to her lips and to her heart. He was looking pretty great himself. Austin was also casually dressed in denim jeans and a nice and stylish dark blue sweater.

Beaumont and Angelica came back into the room. Each looked a bit anxious. Mr. Carrington cleared his throat, interrupting the special moment between his son and the young woman he loved like a daughter. Beaumont then took his wife's hand as he moved into the center of the room. "I'm afraid I have some bad news, family. According to the call I just received from Dallas, he incurred an injury to his right ankle a few days ago. The team physician has placed him on the injured reserved list. Dallas didn't call any sooner because he needed time to come to grips with his situation."

Ashleigh saw how alarmed Lanier looked. Though Lanier wouldn't voice it aloud, Ashleigh knew that her friend would worry about the man she'd come to care about.

"How serious an injury?" Austin asked, thinking of the wincing pain he'd endured during the same time frame. The excruciating pain had been in his right ankle, too.

It wasn't unusual for multiples to often feel the same pain and the deep emotions of their siblings. It had happened to Austin and his brothers many, many times. All three of the brothers were very aware of their heightened senses where their siblings' physical, mental, and emotional stability were concerned. Austin said a silent prayer in his brother's behalf.

Beaumont rubbed his hands together. "It's been determined that he has a fracture. He'll be out of the game for a good little while. Dallas will be recuperating here at home. As we speak, Houston is on his way to pick Dallas up at the airport. They're coming straight here."

Lanier's state of alarm had now turned to deep concern and fear. She was able to hide her anxiety from everyone but Ashleigh. "Is surgery indicated?" Lanier asked.

The slight twitching of Lanier's left eye was a sign that Ashleigh was very familiar with. It only occurred when Lanier was emotionally troubled or angry. Since there wasn't anything for her to be angry about, Ashleigh figured that Lanier's personal involvement with Dallas was hard at work on her emotions.

"That doesn't appear to be the case, Lanier, since he's flying home," Beaumont responded. "I don't know all the facts, but Dallas didn't mention a thing about being out the entire season. I think he would've told me about it if that were the case."

"I'm sure you're right, Dad. They would've operated immediately had surgery been warranted," Austin offered. "But then again, swelling can often prevent a definitive diagnosis."

Angelica sighed as she took hold of her husband's arm. "No use in us speculating. We won't know all the details until Dallas fills us in. Let's go to the table. We can choose a different topic of discussion over dinner, one that's a little less stressful. We'll know soon enough."

Austin wedged himself between Ashleigh and Angelica, as he took each of them by the hand. "Good idea, Mom. Your oldest son, that is, by several minutes, is only starving to death."

Beaumont held his arm out to Lanier. "Austin, 'starving to death' isn't the best choice of words coming from a man who's never had to miss a meal in his life," Beaumont berated his son in a gentle tone. "There are far too many hungry and homeless people in the world for us to even make joking references about starving."

Austin looked slightly chagrined. "You're right, Dad. I apologize. Let me rephrase that. I'm as hungry as a hibernating bear, one who has just awakened from a long winter's nap."

Everyone laughed at Austin's comment as they seated themselves around the long mahogany dining table. Seated at the head of the table, Beaumont passed the blessing.

Seated directly across from her friend, Ashleigh kept watchful eyes on Lanier. Ashleigh was sure Lanier was more worried than she was letting on. Her feelings for Dallas had grown considerably since the cruise. Their nightly conversations kept Lanier floating on cloud nine. Austin kept Ashleigh way up high on a cloud, too. He had a way of saying all the right things and making all the appropriate gestures. It wasn't just for show either. Austin was a sincere man, one of the things Ashleigh loved most about him.

Following Austin's lead, Ashleigh picked up a rib bone and put it up to her mouth. Her eyes closed expressively as her lips made contact with the cooked-to-perfection meat. How could anyone ever forget Beaumont's delicious sauce? Thick, spicy, zesty, and very tasty. Ashleigh moaned aloud. "I see you still make the best ribs in Texas. The sauce is divine!"

Beaumont grinned in appreciation of Ashleigh's compliment. "The very best," he proudly boasted, smiling at Lanier.

"Licking your lips and your fingers is definitely allowed in the Carrington house. Don't be ashamed to make an absolute pig, as well as a mess, of yourself."

Laughter and female giggling rang out.

Angelica took the lid off a casserole dish. "Don't forget these. No barbecue is complete without baked beans. These delicious little brown nuggets are from my own special recipe."

Austin smiled adoringly at his parents. "Mom and Dad should've gone into the restaurant business. They both can throw down in the kitchen."

"You got that right, big brother," Houston chimed in while entering the dining room.

On crutches, Dallas hobbled into the room right behind Houston. "Hey, Carringtons," Dallas greeted cheerfully. "I'm here. Not all in one piece, but I'm too blessed to be stressed."

Angelica jumped up and hugged her two sons. Austin and Beaumont followed suit.

Dallas then caught a glimpse of Lanier from over his mother's shoulder. His eyes flashed with the brightness of a midnight star. "Hey, girl, look at you," he said softly, grinning from ear to ear. "Nice to see you seated at the Carrington family table." Gingerly Dallas worked his way over to Lanier and kissed her full on the mouth. "Hmm, delicious! This is such a nice feeling."

Though it took him a while, Dallas managed to lower himself into the seat next to Lanier. "Now that we're all present and accounted for, let's eat." Dallas leaned into Lanier and bumped her with his shoulder. "Surprised to see me, huh?"

Lanier shook her head in the negative, smiling smugly. "Not at all. I knew you'd do whatever it took to see me before spring training was over. Just didn't expect you to go to such drastic measures as fracturing your ankle."

Along with everyone else, Dallas laughed heartily. "You're not the only one, Lanier Watson. However, I'm here and so you are. How about that?" He winked at Lanier as he kissed her on the tip of her nose. Dallas turned to Ashleigh. "Since I haven't had the opportunity to tell you before now, we're all happy to see you, ecstatic to have you home again. We're a family again. Welcome back, Ashleigh."

"Just so you'll know, Ashleigh, I'm happy to have you home again, too. I also welcome you back with open arms," Houston chimed in. "We *are* your family."

Ashleigh's eyes glistened with unshed tears. "*My family.* I love the sound of that! Thank you, Dallas and Houston, a heartfelt thanks to the entire Carrington clan. It's an honor to have all of you welcome me back this way. I've never stopped loving this family, not for a second."

Ashleigh had successfully stemmed her desire to break down and cry. She was thrilled to be home again, happy to be among the Carrington family, blessed to be considered one of them. This was one of her many dreams that she'd always hoped would come true. If only another of her lofty dreams could come true. To be a part of the Carrington family permanently. Marrying Austin was certainly one way to accomplish that.

Austin smiled at Ashleigh as he lifted her hand and kissed the back of it. "Welcome home, sweetheart, welcome back to the place you've always held in my heart," he whispered, silently praying that Ashleigh would never again leave his side. They belonged together. To finally have his forever fantasy fulfilled would be his dream come true.

"Ashleigh and Lanier, Austin tells us that you young ladies hope to have your grand opening for Haven House during the week of Kwanzaa celebration," Beaumont mentioned. "Is there anything Angelica and I can do to help you prepare for it?"

Ashleigh looked over at Lanier and smiled. "There are tons of things that we need help with. The first thing we must accomplish before anything else is to get all the repairs done. The old house needs to be completely overhauled, a major undertaking. However, things are coming along slowly but surely. We'd be truly grateful for any offer of help you can give us."

Beaumont's eyes encompassed each of his sons. "Hey, guys, are you up to the challenge? We can all pull together and get these tasks done in record time, especially if you're willing to solicit the help from a few of your teammates, Austin and Houston. Dallas's team is away and he's not in any shape to help us out with the physical labor. What do you boys think?"

"I'm definitely in." Austin looked to Houston for his input and Houston nodded his approval. "It looks like we can count on Houston, too," Austin remarked. "We'll need to have a meeting so we can get organized and come up with a manageable work schedule."

Dallas laughed. "Maybe I can't contribute to the hard labor, but I'm one heck of a supervisor. Helping to supervise the workload at the house will give me something else to do besides sitting around and thinking about my ankle injury. You can count me in, too."

For the next forty-five minutes the Carringtons and their special guests gorged themselves on Beaumont and Angelica's superbly prepared feast. The needs of the house were discussed between bites and the brothers had a great time as they entertained the others with their colorful jokes and light ribbings of each other. Ashleigh saw that Angelica looked very comfortable surrounded by her family of men. Ashleigh couldn't help remembering when she'd been their only girl, their precious little lamb.

Beaumont got up from the table when the doorbell rang.

"Dad, you sure you don't want me to get that?" Dallas joked.

Beaumont laughed along with the others. "I'm sure, son. I don't think we want to leave the visitor or visitors outside quite that long. Perhaps you can run interference for me once you learn to get around better on those twin sticks of wood."

Angelica had begun showing her female guests some old photos of the triplets when Beaumont came rushing back into the dining room. Ashleigh took note of the troubled expression on Beaumont's face, wondering why he looked that way, so anguished.

"Son," Beaumont said, looking at Austin, "I need to see you in private. This is something only you can handle. Please excuse the intrusion, Ashleigh."

Austin looked puzzled as he got up from his seat. "I'll be right back, Ash."

Before Austin could move another muscle, Sabrina waltzed into the dining room, smiling sweetly, acknowledging everyone at the table but Ashleigh and Lanier.

Austin sat back down and took Ashleigh's hand, squeezing it gently. "Hang tough, now. I'm going to let her have her way for now," Austin whispered to Ashleigh. "Are you with me?"

Ashleigh merely nodded, wishing away the butterflies flitting about in her stomach.

Sabrina held center stage for the next half hour while Ashleigh studied the expressions of the others. Ashleigh saw faces of dismay, disappointment, and disbelief, only to name a few. Angelica was way too polite, which was also too obvious. It was unlike her to embarrass someone or to be rude to a guest in her home, but Angelica's dislike of Sabrina's unsavory antics clearly showed on her lovely face. The frantic way that she clutched at her husband's arm, once he'd reseated himself at the table, indicated her determination to practice restraint.

Beaumont kept quiet, looking totally unnerved by Sabrina's unattractive behavior. His concern for Ashleigh was apparent in the nervous glances he periodically shot her way. Dallas, Houston, and Lanier appeared to be in a state of shock. The tension in the room was as thick as a foggy morning on the Gulf of Mexico and was felt by everyone present. Sabrina was the only one who seemed totally at ease with her dramatic performance. She knew without a doubt that Sabrina Beaudreaux held everyone's rapt attention, that she was the star of the show.

Not once did Sabrina look at Ashleigh or even bother to take a glance in the direction of where she sat. It seemed as if Ashleigh was totally invisible to Austin's ex-fiancée. As Sabrina began to talk about the wedding, as though Austin hadn't called it off, Austin's impatience with the situation came through in the language of his body. He only allowed a couple more tense minutes to pass by before he jumped up and excused himself and Sabrina.

It looked to Ashleigh as if another showdown between Austin and Sabrina was imminent.

Houston moved into Austin's seat next to Ashleigh before Austin even cleared the doorway. It didn't surprise Ashleigh to see that the triplets had each other's back and that they really knew how to cover for one another.

Feeling that Ashleigh could use a breather about now, Houston suggested that he show Ashleigh around the place so she could get reacquainted with the Carrington home. His well-meaning intentions were apparent to the others. Grateful for the suggestion, Ashleigh left the room with Houston, confident that Lanier would be just fine if she was left on her own. At any rate, Lanier had the handsome Dallas and the elder Carringtons to keep her company.

As they moved down the long corridor, Houston looked

over at Ashleigh. "I know this isn't an easy situation for you to find yourself in. That's why I thought you could use a minute or two away from everyone. Are you doing okay?"

Ashleigh looked flushed. "I'm fine, Houston. Thanks. I just hope Austin's going to be."

Houston laughed. "The QB is a big boy. He can take care of himself. Austin knows what he's doing. Don't worry."

Houston guided Ashleigh into the floor-to-ceiling-windowed solarium, where they both took a seat. Ashleigh sat on one of the leather sofas and Houston sat in the matching chair.

Ashleigh wrung her hands together. "I'm not worried, but do you think I should be?"

Houston shrugged. "About Austin, no. Sabrina, now that's a good question. I feel that you should be more cautious than anything. She's used to getting her way. That is, with everyone but Austin. When they were together, he never let her get away with much of anything."

Ashleigh looked curious and also reluctant. "I want to ask you a couple of questions. If you're not comfortable about answering, I'll understand."

Houston hand-gestured his approval for her to proceed.

"Is your family upset about the breakup? Do they still want Austin to marry Sabrina?"

A tad nervous about the nature of the very pointed questions, Houston scratched his head. "You gave me a way out of this—and I should probably take it, but I think you have some rights in this matter since you and Austin are romantically involved. The answers to both questions are a resounding *no*. Our parents were never comfortable with the relationship. None of us believe that he can be happy with Sabrina. We finally accepted and then had to respect his choice for a wife, but there were plenty of heated arguments about it in the beginning. There were far too many cons for us to even try and weigh them against the pros. Bottom line is this—Austin's decision. We stand behind our brother, our parents always support their sons."

"Thanks for being so candid. I promise to keep this conversation between us."

Houston shook his head. "That's not necessary. I want Austin to know what we've discussed. That's the way it is between all of us. This isn't something we have to try and hide from him. I think your questions were valid ones and the answers I gave you were honest. Knowing Austin as well as I do, not only will he understand our discussion he'll recognize our reason for having it. The Carrington brothers do not keep secrets from each other."

"I see all the points you've made. I wouldn't want to promote deception in any form, and certainly not between the Carrington triplets." Ashleigh smiled. "You and Dallas surprised me when you welcomed me back into the family. But it was so nice to hear it."

"Ashleigh, it really is good to have you back in our lives. I know I didn't pay as much attention to you as Austin did when you lived with us, but it wasn't lack of caring. I was just full of myself in those days. It was always obvious to us that Austin was very protective of you. It now seems to us that he'd also accurately visualized what you might look like one day. Four years in age isn't that big a difference. For example, when you're twenty-one and twenty-five. Twelve and sixteen is unacceptable. That's just the way it is in our society."

"You're honest and understanding, too. I appreciate that, Houston."

Houston slapped his hand down on his thigh. "I probably shouldn't say this, but I'm going to. Austin is in love with you.

While keeping that in mind, don't let anyone come between you two. My brother knows what he wants. His love for you won't allow him to let you down."

Ashleigh's heart was filled with warmth. "That's so nice of you to say, Houston. Thanks for the reassurances. While I'm not worried about where I stand with Austin, I am concerned about his feelings. He seems to be awfully sensitive."

"He is, has always been. But that doesn't mean he's weak and that he can't take care of himself. Austin Carrington is one of the strongest men I know. He'll do more to spare Sabrina's feelings than his own, but he's not going to let her go too, too far. Contrary to what some believe, sensitivity and stupidity are not synonymous. My brother will be just fine."

Austin stepped into the room and leaned his body against the doorjamb. "I think I'd have to agree with that assessment, little brother." Austin came over to the sofa and sat down next to Ashleigh. Gently putting her face between his two hands, he pressed his lips into her forehead. "I hope I don't need to defend myself to you. I'm sorry if you've been hurt again."

She stroked his face. "You don't. And I'm not hurt. Are you okay, Austin?"

Houston stood up. "I think I'm hearing an exit cue. See you two later." Before leaving the room, Houston bent down and kissed Ashleigh's cheek. "Don't jump ship. You wouldn't want him to drown trying to rescue you. No doubt he'll try. That's what heroes do."

Ashleigh smiled up at Houston. "I love being around so many heroes. Thanks for rescuing me when I needed it most. Also, thank you for all the great advice."

Austin waited for Houston to clear the doorway and then he turned back to Ashleigh. "To answer your question, Ash, I'm fine." Looking frustrated, he shrugged. "I just don't know what to say about all these unexpected appearances from Sabrina. When we're not on the road, we all have dinner with my parents once a week, which usually occurs on a weekend day or a day in the middle of the week. So there's no mystery in her finding me here this evening. Still, her constantly showing up wherever I am with you is unnerving. I don't know what to do about it."

Ashleigh laid her head on his shoulder. "I don't expect you to say or do anything. This is obviously something you have no control over. When we come to understand that we have no control over what other people do and say, we'll be better off. As it pertains to the relationship between you two, I think you've made your position clear to Sabrina. I just don't think she can accept it. That's not your fault."

He looked surprised by her comments. "I'm stunned to hear you say that, but I'm glad you feel that way. That you believe I've been honest with you from the start means a lot to me. I don't know how I can convince Sabrina that we're really over, but I have no desire to do it in a malicious, hurtful way."

"Then you shouldn't resort to that. You don't have to go against your nature to get your point across, Austin. Under the circumstances, kindness and patience are the right tools to use."

He appeared thoughtful. "From the immature temper tantrum she just threw in my parents' den, after I explained that I've moved on with my life and that she needs to do the same, I don't see her accepting the facts any time soon. That alone makes me wonder what this all means for us. How her irrational behavior might affect our relationship is a big concern for me. I don't want to see you caught up in the middle of this emotional firestorm, Ashleigh. From all indications, the road for us to move forward on is not going to be an easy one to travel."

Ashleigh felt extremely apprehensive. "It sounds like you're saying our future looks mighty grim. Is that what I'm hearing from you, Austin?"

Austin cracked his knuckles to ease the tension he felt. "I don't know what I'm saying, Ash. I'm seriously groping for a solution to a very real problem. How do you see things after hearing what I've said?"

Ashleigh gulped hard. "It's not so much what I see rather than what I feel. I'm feeling terrified. Austin, we just made love for the very first time, and now I'm feeling as though I may've made a big mistake." A single tear escaped the corner of her eye. "I don't know what to do about this complicated situation any more than you do, but I'm hurting emotionally over it."

He opened his arms wide. "Come here, Ash. The last thing I want you to feel is hurt and regret. I know how long you've been running away from my perfectly thrown passes." He hugged her tightly. "I remember you telling me on the cruise that you didn't know whether to catch my forward pass, run with it, or fumble. Now that you've caught my pass and have decided to run with it, it probably seems to you that I'm suddenly asking you to drop the ball. Do you remember what I told you that night on the ship?"

She closed her eyes. "If you decide to catch it, bring it in close to your body, hold it near and dear to your heart so a fumble won't occur. If you run with it, don't look back—just run for glory. When you step into the end zone, fall on your knees in celebration. Whatever you do, be careful not to give another the opportunity to intercept what was only intended for you. How did I do, Austin?"

He was amazed. "Perfect! You recited my remarks words for word. How did you remember all of it?"

"People have a tendency to remember what's important to

them. Your comments were very important to me. I can never forget what you said that night. It touched me that deeply. I still don't want an interception to occur, Austin. I still want you."

He kissed her full on the mouth. "You have me, Ash, always and forever. Will you come back to the ranch with me tonight? We still have a lot to talk about."

"I'll come home with you, but only on one condition."

"Name it, Ash."

"No talking, just action."

Chapter 6

Dressed in one of Austin's team jerseys, wearing nothing beneath it, Ashleigh felt sexy and uninhibited, something she hadn't felt before. While standing in front of the mirror in Austin's bathroom, she searched the depth of her eyes. Although she saw deep concern and also a touch of uncertainty there, the look of being in love shined the brightest.

Love was exactly what she felt for Austin. Not only did she love him, she was deeply *in* love with him. She had to wonder if she was being fair to him or even to Sabrina. That the estranged couple still had unfinished business was obvious to everyone that knew them.

Was it callous and coldhearted of her to get into bed with him and make love to him knowing of the dilemma he was already faced with? Ashleigh believed he was over Sabrina, yet she still thought that he might need more time to make a complete emotional break. Although he'd told her time and time again that that wasn't the case, Ashleigh still wasn't sure that he knew with certainty what he needed at this point. On the flip side, if he truly needed her, wouldn't it be just as wrong for her to deny him access to her love and affection?

So many questions, so few answers. It was frustrating.

Placing the cool cloth to her heated flesh felt good. Upon closing her eyes, she began to breathe in deeply, exhaling slowly. She needed to be more relaxed before facing Austin again. He would be waiting for her, in his bed, where she'd promised to sleep the entire night through.

Austin couldn't take his eyes off Ashleigh as she came out of the bathroom and walked toward the bed. The closer she got to him, the faster his heart began beating. The impassioned look in his eyes further fueled her need for him. Ashleigh suddenly realized that second-guessing what they felt for each other wouldn't solve a thing. He was the only one who knew which woman he truly desired to be with. Since she was the one sharing his bedroom with him, his choice should've been clear. Still, she had niggling doubts. Sabrina seemed to feel that what they had was worth hanging on to. Could it have been all that bad, since he had asked Sabrina to marry him? Perhaps he was still hurt over the things he'd overheard Sabrina saying and that he needed more time to heal from such a devastating blow to his heart and his ego.

It was no secret that Ashleigh wanted them to come together as one, emotionally and physically. Were they inevitable? If so, she had to stop trying to make decisions for him, had to stop trying to make a case for him and Sabrina to stay together. As Houston had told her earlier, Austin was a big boy. He knew how to take care of himself and how to choose his own destiny.

Just as Ashleigh was about to climb into the huge four-poster bed, Austin reached out to her, lifted her up, and carefully pulled her across his lap. Far past the anticipation of being inside her, Austin kissed her breathless. *No talking, just action,* he recalled her saying.

Ashleigh's request was an easy one for him to fulfill. Talking to her with his eyes, hands, and lips was the kind of communication he could accomplish with ease. Ashleigh would be able to easily interpret the type of sensuous communication he had in mind. For the body language he had in mind to use, she would definitely not need a translator. The romantic atmosphere was already set. The lights had been turned down low, while Kenny G's greatest hits sweetly strummed the air, flowing from the speakers like white magic. The only other kind of communication necessary was the tender, loving language spoken by their entwined bodies.

While rediscovering what gave Ashleigh extreme pleasure, Austin quickly found out that sucking on her earlobe made her squirm about quite a bit. Every time she made the slightest movement, her bottom rubbed against his lower anatomy, increasing his desire to completely nix the arousing foreplay. Austin was more than ready to get on with the main event, but his sensitivity toward her had him wanting to give her a preview of things to come by tenderly priming her with an erotic opening act.

His free hand slowly snaked under the team jersey she wore and cupped a full breast. A fingertip to her naked flesh eventually met with a hardened nipple. His hand roamed from one breast to the other while his tongue explored the sweetness of her mouth. Ashleigh suddenly shifted her body around until she straddled his lap. With that provocative, unexpected move of hers, the hardness of Austin's sex strained against the silk of his boxers, making their desire for each other nearly uncontrollable. Biting down on her lower lip was all she could do to keep herself from begging him to get on with it. It was hard not to tell him exactly what she wanted from him and how she wanted it, wild and hot.

No talking, just action, she reminded herself.

Ashleigh's small hands roved over Austin's broad chest, heating up his flesh even more. Lifting his hand to her lips, she kissed his fingertips, then drew his forefinger into her mouth, sucking on it ardently. Austin couldn't help imagining her sweet mouth elsewhere on his anatomy. Desiring to feel the soft flesh between her legs, Austin pushed her jersey up around her waist. The slow insertion of his fingers caused Ashleigh to moan huskily with pleasure. As she conjured up an image of his tongue in the hot spot where his fingers nested, her heart raced painfully inside her chest. Ashleigh had to shut out the arousing image or deal with a premature release. The early climax didn't work for her since she wanted all night long with him.

It wasn't long before hands and legs became just as entangled as the bedsheets.

The intensity of his kisses made her hotter and more intimately wet. His next kiss turned her need into an inferno of desire. He was harder; harder than before, if that was possible. Her hand showed no mercies in tenderly stroking his maleness. While it was her pleasure, it was nearly his undoing. Ashleigh loved to touch him this way, loved to see the pleasurable agony in his eyes. Taking his hand, she guided it back between her legs, to where the moisture had already begun to flow. Hot, wet, insane with lust, she was ready for him to rock her entire being.

As Austin's fingers began to once again tease her treasure

trove of sweetness, biting down on her lower lip was all Ashleigh could do to keep from screaming out his name. Her body twitched as his fingers probed deeper into her sanctuary of hot, wet flesh. To savor the feeling of being on the very edge, Ashleigh brought his lips to hers, drawing his tongue into her mouth.

Using the tip of her fingernail, she traced his hardened nipples and then moved downward to the crown of his maleness. *If only I was bold enough to stroke him there with my tongue. One day, one day soon.* To ward off her nearly uncontrollable desire to taste all of him, she instead kissed him deeply, lazing her finger up and down the inside of his thighs. Drawing her head back, she gave him a taunting smile. "Are you ready to explode?"

Austin kissed her softly on the mouth. "Lady, I explode every time you touch me. All you have to do is look at me, instant orgasm. It's the kind of release that's felt everywhere on my anatomy. My brain even explodes with the thoughts of loving you until you beg me to stop. My hands detonate as they slip inside you and my lips burst into flames every time we kiss. Is that enough of an explosion for you?" Austin anxiously eyed the condom on the nightstand, wishing he didn't have to put it on, yet knowing that it couldn't be any other way.

She smiled smugly. "Perhaps. But then there's another kind of explosion, the kind that occurs when you're deep inside me. You know, that indescribable feeling, the one when you're right on the edge, but you're not ready to detonate because it feels way too good."

"Hush, baby, even your taunting words cause an explosion inside me." His head lowered, his mouth went to her thighs, drawing closer and closer to the core of her passion.

As his lips made contact with her sweetness, she screamed

out, loving the exotic way in which his mouth caressed her in such an intimate way. *Help,* she cried inwardly, *help me keep my sanity a few minutes longer.* "Yes," she cried out, as his hands and tongue warmed her through and through.

Moaning with pleasure, he briefly pulled himself away to sheath himself with protection.

In one unbelievably smooth motion, Austin lifted her up from the bed, just high enough to complete the act of penetration. Ashleigh gasped as his granite maleness completely filled up her inner sanctum, bringing them together as one. Colorful fireworks went off inside her head as his hungry mouth closed over hers with reckless yearning. Her hunger matched his own as she kissed him back, abandoning anything tantamount to reserve. If this was a dream, she didn't want to wake up any time soon. But it wasn't a dream. Austin was deep inside her, every hardened inch of him. As Austin made love to her, tenderly, sweetly, pulling back, reentering her, time and time again, she could no longer hold back her pleasure-filled screams.

Then the racking sobs of her utter fulfillment came way too soon.

Depleted of most of his physical energy, Austin held Ashleigh tightly in his arms. With her head pressed onto his chest, Ashleigh's fingers were splayed in his thick chest hair. Her energy was all but nonexistent, too, yet she felt vibrant with life. The lovemaking had been wild and daring but so fulfilling. Always concerned as he was about protecting them, taking full responsibility for their physical well-being, she loved Austin for once again stopping in the height of passion to put on a condom. Though she always appreciated his special concern for their health, she'd nearly gone insane while waiting for him to garner protection.

Austin stroked Ashleigh's hair. "Since we've mostly had the action without a lot of talking, are we allowed to converse a little more now?"

Ashleigh looked up at him and smiled. "Maybe we should wait awhile longer?"

He scowled. "What for, may I ask?"

"Talking also uses up a lot of energy. We need to save up some oomph for later." She looked over at the illuminated clock dial. "There are several more hours left before morning, Austin. I don't know about you, but I'm entertaining thoughts of a few encores."

He threw his head back and laughed. "You're becoming a little sex fiend, but I like the way you think," he joked. Closing his eyes for a brief moment, savoring the wonderful feeling of her being in his arms, he kissed the top of her head. Heaven couldn't be any better than this.

Ashleigh turned up on her side, supporting her head with her elbow and hand. "That's not true, Austin. I'm no fiend. I was just having fun. My body is completely out of commission at the moment, but my mind is tireless when it comes to making love to you inside my head. I've only been doing it that way most of my adult life. The reality of it all is so much better than the fantasies. If you want to talk, I guess I have enough energy left for that."

He kissed the tip of her nose. "You're being a little incorrigible right now, but I love it. Outside of the unexpected interruption, did you have a good time at my parents' home?"

Ashleigh smiled broadly. "I had a divine time. If your mother hadn't come to the house earlier, I'm not sure I would've been as comfortable. Her visit definitely broke the ice. I was made to feel right at home and I'm still reeling from the joy of seeing everyone. I'm also excited about the upcoming fund-raiser that one of her social clubs is putting on in behalf of Haven House. She told Lanier and me all about it while you guys were playing poker. The entire evening was wonderful and everyone made me feel so good, so welcome. Sabrina wasn't able to put much of a damper on our time together. Despite her attempts, the evening still turned out to be a great one. I'm so happy I accepted the invitation to dinner."

"Everything to do with the family is all very sincere. No one has to put on an act about how they feel about you personally. You're so easy to care about, Ash, easy to love. Lanier seemed to enjoy herself, as well. Mom's thrilled about her club members wanting to help you raise funds for Haven House. Over the next couple of months, I'm sure you'll have all the finances that you need and more. I noticed that you and Lanier had a little private chat before we left. How's she handling Dallas's ankle injury?"

"Of course she's worried, but he told her that she didn't need to be. He also told her he'd change his plans about staying at your parents' place if she'd come to his house and take care of him. Can you believe that?"

Austin chuckled. "Of course I can! Dallas Carrington is no fool. He can get all the sympathy and pampering he needs from Mom, but I'm sure he'd much rather have Lanier fussing over him. That big old Texas boy loves to be coddled. What was Lanier's response?"

"No way is she going to stay at his place, but she admitted to entertaining the idea for a minute or two. For one thing, it's too far for her to drive to work every day. His answer to that was for her to take a leave of absence and he'd pay her salary. In listening to her talk about his offers, it seems that he'd thought of everything. She's not going to stay at his place, but she'll visit him at your mom's as often as she can. You Carrington boys are absolute charmers."

"What if I was hurt and proposed the same thing to you? What would be your response?"

"Boy, you wouldn't have to ask me but once. I'm not that easy, but staying with you has its fringe benefits."

Grinning, he eyed her curiously. "What type of bennies are you talking about?"

Her eyes went straight to his manhood. Her hands instantly followed. "Do I need to get vocal with my response, Austin?"

His eyes instantly filled with passion. "Ash, your wonderful hands are communicating just fine. They feel so good on me, so warm and tender. Oh, baby, do you even know how much I want and need you? Do you have any clue as to how good you make me feel? All the time, not just when we're making love."

"I think I have an idea, but you can always show me. I like being reassured, Austin."

"Since you promised to spend the night with me, I have plenty of time to reassure you. I never want you to have doubts, Ash. Come here, sweetheart, so we can get this fire started."

"And keep it going all night long," Ashleigh breathed.

Ashleigh was in absolute awe of the beauty surrounding her. The terrace off of Austin's bedroom offered an excellent view of the ranch. Only steps away from the master bedroom, an in-ground Olympic-size swimming pool and Jacuzzi carried the bluest water she'd ever seen. Stark-white fencing made a nice contrast to the abundance of greenery that appeared to sprout from every square inch of earth. Countless trees and a vast variety of shrubs and plants graced the entire property. Colorful wildflowers and flowering bushes seemed to have free run of the grounds. A riot of bougainvilleas, bursting with color, climbed a dozen or so white trellises.

While having breakfast out on the terrace, with Austin seated right next to her at the frosted-glass patio table, Ashleigh had already relived several times the entire previous night. The whole evening and most of the night had been so beautiful, so fulfilling. She loved that she and Austin were growing so intimately close, that time seemed to stand still for them when they looked into each other's eyes. But once again problems had arisen for them. Once again their serenity had been terribly compromised.

Sabrina had become an annoying intrusion to both Ashleigh and Austin. She'd shown up at Austin's in the middle of the night begging to talk with him, pleading to be heard. Though reluctant to do so, he had indulged Sabrina in her whims for more than an hour, trying to show respect for her. His bad decision had only resulted in another extremely unpleasant scene. Ashleigh was all the way in the back of the huge house, still lying totally nude in Austin's bed, but from way up in the front of the place echoes of Sabrina's cursing and screaming had reached her ears with crystal clarity. Ashleigh had had the presence of mind to get up and lock the bedroom door just in case Sabrina got away from Austin's control.

Ashleigh was relieved that Sabrina had never learned that she was in the house with Austin, glad that Lanier had driven her car back to the apartment, which had allowed Ashleigh to ride home with Austin. Had her car been in the driveway for Sabrina to see, Ashleigh could only imagine what might've happened. Just the thought was daunting.

Because of all the emotionally draining stuff that had occurred with him and Sabrina, Austin had slept fitfully, tossing and turning the entire night. In the wee hours of the morning, when sleep had become impossible for him, he'd wakened Ashleigh to tell her that he felt as if he were caught between heaven and hell. Ashleigh was his heaven. Emotionally drained, with his head resting in the well of her arm, Austin had finally fallen into a deep sleep.

Ashleigh reached across the table and put her hand over Austin's. "Are you going to end up breaking my heart, Austin?"

He looked at her intently, his heart breaking over the fear in her voice. Then a soft expression filled his eyes. "Ashleigh, I plan to take very good care of *our* heart. Don't you remember that my heart is beating inside your chest? Do I need to say more?"

Her eyes became as brilliant as a million stars. "I love you, Austin Carrington."

Emotionally full from her sincerely spoken words, Austin had Ashleigh in his arms before she inhaled her next breath. He kissed her until he had to come up for air, unable to believe that she'd finally confessed on dry land her feelings for him. She had told him she loved him upon the high seas, but she hadn't said it since. His entire world had suddenly righted itself.

His hands tenderly cupped her face. "I love you, too, Ashleigh Ayers. Now and forever." He stroked her hair. "I know you're upset about last night. So am I. I keep trying to handle this in a diplomatic manner, but it's getting impossible. Do you want to hear my take on it?"

The last thing in the world that Ashleigh wanted to talk about was Sabrina, especially during this special moment, but she could clearly see Austin's need to get a few things off his chest. He'd had one horrible night and it looked like his anguish might not come to an end any time soon. She silently vowed to be there for him, no matter how long it took. "I'm listening."

His ebony eyes made direct contact with Ashleigh's. The brief glint of sadness she saw in his dark gaze made her heart flinch. If only she could kiss all of his emotional pain away.

"Sabrina is not in love with me, because she's simply incapable of that emotion. I realize that more and more each day, especially after each episode of sheer drama. Had she broken things off with me, everything would be just fine and dandy. This is all about her need to control everything and everyone around her and to win at all cost. I need tenacious people like her out on the football field, those with a win-at-all-cost mentality, but I don't want that in my personal life. But as long as she's venting on me and not you, I'm going to give her the opportunity to wear herself completely out, hoping she'll get tired real soon. Her endless tantrums have to be as physically and emotionally draining on her as they are on me. This has to end soon."

Ashleigh frowned. "I hope you're right. But I'm not convinced that it's going to end soon or on a pleasant note. There are people in the world that may not even want a person anymore, but they don't want anyone else to have him or her either. I think we need to be very careful as to not flaunt our relationship in front of her. To me, Sabrina seems emotionally and mentally fragile."

"You may have something there, but why should we have to do that, Ash? I don't see us being together as flaunting anything in her face. We're together because we choose to be, not to make her miserable."

"As long as we know what we have and that we're in love with each other, we can find comfort in that. If she's present, or shows up unexpectedly, we have to make a conscious decision not to rub her nose in it. The question of whether she truly loves you or not isn't relevant here. She's hurting. It

doesn't matter if she's created her own pain by her bad be-
haviors, because this is apparently how she's always been.
She's still in pain. Until she sees the glaring defects in her own
character, she's not going to get it. My biggest fear is of her
responding like a wounded animal to the person that she holds
responsible for inflicting such devastating pain upon her. That
would have to be you, Austin. I don't know that she's a dangerous person, but I heard the desperation in her voice. As you
once told me, desperate people do desperate things."

Ashleigh had certainly given him a heaping helping of food
for thought, but he didn't dare speak upon the fact that Sabrina
held her responsible for breaking them up. "If you hadn't met
that little conniving witch on the cruise, we'd still be together.
This is all her fault. She'll get hers in the end." It was apparent
to Austin that Ashleigh hadn't heard every word spoken.

Frustrated to no end, Austin pushed his hand through his
hair. "I guess we should move on to other topics. This isn't
the nicest thing we could spend such a glorious morning discussing." To try and keep his hands from shaking, he picked
up his glass of orange juice.

Ashleigh nodded. "I agree, but I have a couple of questions
before we move on. How long were you engaged to Sabrina
and how long after you two met did you get engaged?"

"I resisted Sabrina's not-so-subtle advances for over a year.
I wasn't even attracted to her—and that was even before I saw
how badly she conducted herself. To this day I don't know how
I let myself get caught up like I did. I'm not a weak man. But
I didn't show much strength in this situation. Pretty much like
she's doing now, every time I turned around, Sabrina was there,
smiling and flirting, never accepting no for an answer from me.
I really disliked this girl, a lot, but six months later I ended up
engaged to her." A moment of plausible silence came.

His laughter was derisive. "The funny thing is that I never asked Sabrina to marry me, nor did I purchase the ring. She presented the ring at the same time she asked me to marry her. A year and a half of Sabrina's tantrums and controlling ways is more than any one person should ever have to deal with. I'd like to think I didn't get involved with her or say yes to the proposal of marriage to please my new head coach, but there's no other explanation for it. It certainly wasn't youth. I was certainly old enough to know my own heart and make my own decisions."

Austin had to laugh to ease the tension he felt. Just thinking of how he'd gotten so tangled up with Sabrina made him cringe. After Austin's first head coach had been fired in midseason, the newly hired coach, Pete Beaudreaux, arrived in Houston with his family. Pete had taken an immediate shine to his star quarterback. Shortly after he'd settled in came the introduction of his wife and daughter. Sabrina had instantly decided that she wanted Austin. What Sabrina wanted was what Sabrina got. Pete Beaudreaux always saw to it that Daddy's little girl had whatever her little heart desired, even a lot of the things that weren't good for her.

Their relationship had been all but forced upon him by Sabrina and both of her parents. They had pulled him into practically all of their family plans and had constantly invited him to dinner at their home, often done under false pretenses made up by his coach. Team business was the one reason most often used. Austin and Sabrina were thrust together by her parents at every turn. Sabrina had to have Austin for however long she could be contented with him.

The rest was history.

Desperate to make a physical connection with Ashleigh, Austin took Ashleigh in his arms and kissed her thoroughly. "Did you get enough to eat, baby?"

Ashleigh nodded. "I'm full." Her eyes lit up. "Thanks for letting me cook us breakfast in your kitchen. I've never before cooked on such modern appliances. Everything is so shiny and new. I've loved working about in your kitchen. It was a thrilling experience."

The anguished pangs in his heart were nearly unbearable. That something as simple as cooking on new appliances could thrill Ashleigh silly was so hard for Austin to comprehend. This was the most humble woman he'd ever met, completely opposite of the woman he'd once been engaged to. Although Ashleigh had a good-paying job, she'd scrimped to save every thin dime to make her dream of Haven House come true, depriving herself of all luxuries to do it.

Austin suddenly saw the birth of his children in Ashleigh's topaz eyes. The next image was of them as a family. The sheer beauty of it blew him away. While praying for him and Ashleigh to have a lifetime of wonderful experiences, Austin engaged her in another lingering kiss. This was the woman he wanted eternity with. He was making no mistake about it this time.

Ashleigh nudged Austin out of his dream world. "I guess we should get dressed so you can take me home. I know you have tons of things to do."

He kissed her deeply, hoping that the dramatic events of the previous night weren't scaring her off. "Have you forgotten your promise to ride with me out to the lake? The horses love to graze out in the pasture where the grass grows high. The lake is only a hop, skip, and jump away. Sudden change of heart?"

Cupping his face in her hands, she kissed him gently. "We've already showered, so let's get inside and dress so we can get the show on the road, cowboy."

* * *

The magnificent lake was only a stone's throw away and the engaging tunes of nature were clear and distinct. Bees buzzed about and birds sang a soft lullaby from their treetop homes. The light breeze was cool, the air smelled clean; the grass was long and green. The picture-perfect setting was idyllic for lovers.

As Mariah Carey's "Through the Rain" played on Austin's portable CD, Ashleigh and Austin held hands, seated on the blanket Austin had spread out on the grass. The words to the sad but inspiring song practically mirrored the feelings Ashleigh had experienced throughout her life. The rain had kept on coming, but she had fought hard to stay strong, struggled to keep her head above water, battled with everything in her to keep the dark shadows at bay. The sunshine had finally arrived with Austin. If he were to take the sun away, she knew she'd once again find the strength to go on, but her heart would never recover. At this wonderful moment in time, she didn't dare to think of what life would be like without Austin.

All Ashleigh could do was pray that Sabrina would find someone to love her the way she needed to be loved, a strong person that she couldn't dominate, a special person that would make her want to leave her selfish ways behind. It could happen. Miracles often did. Proof of that was having Austin seated next to her, holding on to her hand.

Ashleigh truly had high hopes for the same kind of miracle to happen for Sabrina.

Austin suddenly looked troubled. He then let go of Ashleigh's hand. "I know this is too beautiful a setting for me to bring up Sabrina again, but last night is weighing heavily on my mind. Can you indulge me another few minutes? There are a few things I still need to say."

Ashleigh nodded her approval, though she thought his timing was terrible. A serene place such as this one wasn't an appropriate setting to discuss topics of utter turmoil.

Austin plucked a blade of grass and pressed it between his thumb and forefinger. "Ash, I know this situation is so unfair to you. I haven't handled Sabrina the right way. In trying to spare her feelings, I know that I'm doing it all wrong. As long as I continue to indulge her, she's going to think there's still a ghost of a chance for us. I don't want to give her an ounce of false hope."

Ashleigh took his hand. "I know you don't, Austin. You have your work cut out for you."

His eyes burned with intensity. "As for you and me, Ashleigh, I know we can have a great future. I don't have the least bit of doubt about us. We have what it takes to go the distance, but I need you to understand a few things about me. I'm a professional athlete, but I don't see me staying in the game until I'm too beat up or too old to do anything else. Sacrificing your body on the field week in and week out for six months out of the year is no joke. I want to be healthy enough to enjoy my retirement years…" He appeared reluctant to go on.

Ashleigh looked puzzled. "What are you really trying to say, Austin? I get the feeling that you're reluctant to say more because you fear I may be offended. Am I right?"

Ashleigh was right; he was very hesitant to ask her all the questions he'd never asked Sabrina. But there was no way to find out where she was coming from if he didn't make the necessary and hard inquiries. He couldn't make the same mistakes a second time.

Austin dug his fingers into a patch of soft earth and let it sift through his fingers. His eyes captured hers once again. "Working the land is what I do best, Ash. Mucking out the stables, planting and plowing, mending fences, and pitching hay are chores that aren't beneath me. I'm a Texas rancher at heart, a football player by profession. What I do today is only securing my future for the tomorrows to come. I'm a real low-key guy who cares nothing for all the flashy and glitzy stuff. What I need to know from you is this—can you be content with a rancher versus the heralded football star? Can you truly be happy with a mere Texas cowboy, Ashleigh?"

Ashleigh's expression grew somber. "Life with a cowboy? You've got to be kidding! If you're saying that a future with you means that we're not going to live high on the hog, travel to exotic places, and spend money like it grows on trees, I don't think so. I can't imagine us not dining in fancy restaurants, staying in the finest hotel suites, and taking cruises at least four times a year. Oh, no, I don't think I can be content with the lifestyle you're talking about. Considering my humble beginnings, I'm sorry, but I want more, so much more than what you've described."

Austin looked absolutely crestfallen. As though he couldn't believe what he'd just heard, he shook his head. Could he have been that wrong about Ashleigh? She had sounded just like Sabrina. But that couldn't be. It was downright impossible for him to be so far off the mark.

Laughing hard, Ashleigh leaped on Austin and pushed him back on the blanket. "Ask me an offensive question and you'll get nothing less than an insulting answer. I'd be content with you if you were a stable boy. The profession he's in should never measure the worth of a man. Neither should it measure the heart of one."

Austin kissed her hard on the mouth. "Don't even joke with me like that." He swiped at the sweat on his brow. "You had me scared stiff. You were so convincing, expressions and all."

Playfully, she popped him on the shoulder. "I've never had

much, Austin, and I know how to be content with very little. If mucking out the stables is good enough for you, it's fine with me. I'm not a bit scared of hard work. I love working with the earth too, planting things and watching them grow. I'd make an excellent ranch hand and cowgirl."

Austin grinned. "With that said, there's going to be a season ticket on the fifty-yard line with your name on it! Will you be there at all the home games for me, Ash?"

She scowled hard. "Isn't that where Sabrina sits?"

He took her in his arms. "Not to worry, sweetheart. Sabrina wouldn't dream of sitting with the other team girlfriends and wives. She loves to watch the game from her imperial position upon high in the owner's skybox. Let me whisper to you a little, not-so-nice secret." He put his mouth to her ear. "Sabrina *hates* football."

They both had a good laugh at that.

Austin held Ashleigh slightly away from him and kissed her lightly on the mouth. "Baby, thanks for confirming for me that you're the perfect cowgirl for this cowboy. Am I the perfect cowboy for you, Ash?"

He received her answer to his question in her passionate kiss.

Listening to Austin had only further confirmed for Ashleigh that he was a man whose direction was quite clear. The pride he felt in his ranch was evident. That he wanted to take care of his land and his animals himself was remarkable, especially when he could afford to hire someone to do it for him. It had pleased her to hear that he didn't want to spend his millions on a lavish lifestyle, that he wanted to live a simple life. She was impressed with her rancher cowboy. The one thing she had feared most was that she wouldn't fit into his high style of living.

Being dead wrong in this instance was a welcome sensation for Ashleigh.

Chapter 7

Ashleigh had never before been to a country club in her life, yet here she was seated in one of the most prestigious clubs in Houston, Gulf Coast Meadows. Lanier and Angelica were already there at the head table with Ashleigh; Beaumont was expected to show any minute. Three additional name placards were on the table in reserve for the other Carrington men.

As the three women waited, with bated breath, for the fund-raising talent show/auction to begin, they sipped on refreshing drinks. Ashleigh looked exotic dressed in a chic black pantsuit with sheer sleeves. The onyx and gold butterfly choker and earrings were a striking complement to her stunning attire. Lanier had chosen to wear a long navy blue skirt, matching jacket, and white silk shell. Natural pearls were her choice in jewelry. Always the epitome of class, Angelica wore an elegant jade silk dress. Exquisite emerald gemstones graced her neck and ears.

Several single professional athletes and other business professionals, men and women alike, would be auctioned off as a luncheon date to the highest bidder. All funds raised were to be donated to Haven House. While the triplets weren't a part of the auction, they were scheduled to participate in the talent show. Although Ashleigh had never heard Austin speak of any other special talent, she was sure he'd be darn good at whatever he decided to try his hand at.

Ashleigh nearly dropped out of her seat when the MC walked toward the microphone, Sabrina, beautiful Sabrina, with the bad temper and mean spirit. Ashleigh looked around the room, as though she was looking for a sure way out. Seeing Sabrina had her trembling.

Lanier's hand instantly covered Ashleigh's hand in a comforting manner. "Be cool. I got your back. Nothing is going to go down that you and I can't handle. Austin is your man simply because he proudly claims himself as such. Don't forget what you two mean to each other."

Angelica and Beaumont exchanged uncomfortable glances, each concerned for Ashleigh.

Ashleigh listened intently as Sabrina went on and on about why they were there and what a good cause she thought it was. It sounded to Ashleigh like Miss Beaudreaux was trying to win a few Brownie points with the Carringtons. Ashleigh wondered if her speech came off as phony to those who really knew her. It was clear to the average ear that she was a whiner and complainer. Her mean spirit came through in her MC duties, as she complained about how hard it was to get some of the guys to participate despite the worthiness of the cause. She even told the audience that she saw those who had refused their services as selfish and uncaring of others.

In short, Sabrina had no compunction about voicing her high-handed opinions.

Ashleigh had never felt more relief than she did when Sabrina announced the opening act and left the stage. She didn't think her ears could've taken another word from her whiny mouth.

Willie and Woody, a professional ventriloquist-comedian and his adorable little wooden sidekick, were the first performers. Ashleigh recognized the duo from seeing them on *BET Comic View, Jay Leno,* and memorable appearances on several other television shows. She made a mental note to try and engage them for the gala open house and Kwanzaa festivities.

The final act to appear onstage was none other than the famous Carrington triplets. Each triplet was dressed to the nines in matching double-breasted suits. The silk shirts were fashioned in different colors but their ties were identical. Crooning with magnificent voices in a perfectly blended harmony, hitting with precision both high and low notes, some like Ashleigh had never before heard, the guys did a medley of songs recorded by Boyz II Men. Their sultry rendition of "I'll Make Love to You" had both Ashleigh and Lanier in tears. "On Bended Knee," "I Will Get There," and "It's So Hard to Say Good-bye" had everyone emotionally full.

With his fine-as-wine brothers flanking him on stools, Dallas looked positively adorable seated in his wheelchair. Ashleigh couldn't help noticing the glow on Lanier's face as she looked at Dallas as if he were her knight in shining armor. Love had definitely blossomed in her eyes.

The grand finale, featuring "A Song for Mama" and "One Sweet Day," had the crowd on their feet. Angelica and Beaumont beamed with pride at the fabulous jobs their sons had pulled off. No parents had ever been prouder of the children than were the Carringtons.

Within seconds of the brothers leaving the stage, Austin re-appeared and took his place front and center. Much to Ashleigh's total surprise, he picked up the microphone and perched himself on one of the two high stools, the one that gave him a perfect view of the woman he loved like crazy. The other stool was whisked away as soon as he'd seated himself. She'd heard him sing before and hum along with songs, but never anything akin to these performances. Austin had been as poised in his role as a singer as he was in his position on the football field. The transformation from quarterback to crooner was an incredible one. When he made a dramatic showing of removing his tie and opening the first few buttons on his shirt, Ashleigh had to draw in a deep breath. She nearly screeched like an overzealous fan when he tossed the tie in the direction of where she sat. The fashionable piece of silk landed right in her lap.

For the next half hour Austin nearly drove Ashleigh insane as he crooned songs by one of her favorite balladeers, Latin sensation Marc Anthony. Ashleigh hadn't known what to expect, but Austin giving a mini concert to raise money for Haven House wouldn't ever have crossed her mind. Whether it was his intent or not, he appeared to sing only to her.

The audience couldn't help dancing in their seats as he sang the funky upbeat tunes "I've Got You" and "I Need to Know." As soon as the lights dimmed, he slowed the pace, making an art form of working on Ashleigh's already fragile emotions, continuing to belt out her favorite Marc Anthony songs: "Love Won't Get Any Better," "I Swear" and "I Reach for You."

Austin finished the set out with Ashleigh's very favorite, "My Baby You."

Ashleigh was definitely the reason Austin was flying so high these days.

Before leaving the stage, Austin said I love you in both English and Spanish, blowing kisses until he disappeared in the wings. The women were going crazy, screaming and shouting for an encore. Much to their dismay, Austin didn't reappear, but only in the interest of time.

Sabrina looked like an angry typhoon when she came back to the microphone, practically snatching it from its base. For a moment, she just stood there, looking out over the crowd, as if she were seeking someone out. She appeared dazed and somewhat lost.

It looked to Ashleigh as though Sabrina had tears in her eyes. Unable to stop herself from feeling sorry for the woman who seemed to have everything she'd ever wanted, everything but Austin's love, Ashleigh felt a twinge of sympathy for her. "Better luck the next time. Remember the best woman always wins," she recalled Sabrina saying during one of her malicious taunts.

So much for Austin not flaunting his love for her in front of Sabrina, Ashleigh mused, cringing at the glaring look she was receiving from Sabrina. Ignoring Sabrina was so easy now.

Sabrina finally lifted the microphone to her lips. "With the talent portion of our show now over, it's time to get on with the rest of our evening, ladies and gents." Sabrina's voice came out syrupy sweet, not so surprising for a woman with dual personalities. But the fire of the rage in her eyes was easy to see as she explained the auction rules. "We're about to bid on some of the finest men and most beautiful ladies in all of Texas. The highest bidder gets to have a luncheon date with one of our wonderful participants. Shall we get the bidding started?"

The audience cheered and clapped in response.

She looked down at the white index card she held in her hand. "Our first participant…" Her voice trailed off as she watched Austin sit down at the table with Ashleigh. Several moments of pregnant silence came next. Then Sabrina smiled, which came off as more of a smirk.

The devilish look on Sabrina's face had Austin worried. It also caused him to take Ashleigh's hand. *Something's up.* There was no doubt in his mind that Sabrina was about to cause him major embarrassment. He inhaled a few deep breaths to brace himself.

"Ladies, before the bidding begins on our first participant, let me set the record straight. Austin Carrington, quarterback for the Texas Wranglers, is my fiancé. I'll be very generous in loaning him out for a lunch date should one of you outbid me, but don't get your hopes up too high. The Beaudreaux pockets are deep." She winked. "Should you be lucky enough to win, lunch date only, mind you. All of his extracurricular time and his loving belong to me. I'll open the bidding on Austin Carrington at five hundred dollars but he's worth five million."

Under any other circumstances Austin would've challenged Sabrina, but there was too much at stake. He didn't want to undermine Ashleigh's cause or embarrass his mother by refusing to participate in the auction. He was a public figure and was held to high standards. Sabrina had counted on that. The date wouldn't happen, at any rate. He vowed to donate to Haven House whatever ridiculous amount of money Sabrina won. He didn't doubt for a second that she was playing to win. Austin was also sure she'd outbid everyone else.

Austin's strides were slow and burdensome as he made his way toward the stage.

As screams thundered throughout the room, Ashleigh looked around at all the smiling, eager females. There didn't appear to be one woman, young or old, who didn't want to land the date with Austin. Ashleigh was bewildered. Seeing that her man was in such popular demand was too incredible for words. But were they enthralled with the man, or was it his profession?

The very next bid jumped all the way from five hundred dollars to a whopping fifteen hundred bucks. The bidding war was on with the dollar amounts rising rapidly. Sabrina found great pleasure in raising the stakes, looking dead at Ashleigh each time she made a higher bid.

Looking as though she'd just stepped off the cover of a high-fashion magazine, a stunning sienna beauty stood up and raised her hand as high as her bid. Audible gasps swept through the room, including a few loud ones from Ashleigh.

The smug look on Sabrina's face instantly turned hateful. When Sabrina topped the offer by five hundred dollars, Ashleigh was not surprised. If Sabrina thought of Ashleigh as her competition, her heart had to be crashing inside her chest just thinking of the model-type stunner sharing a date with Austin. Ashleigh was willing to bet on that.

For the next several minutes Sabrina and the other woman, whom someone had referred to as Kelly while cheering her on, held their own bidding war. The numbers were so high that no one dared to continue since there were so many other eligible men.

Ashleigh was amused but also a little envious. If she had that type of money, she'd bid on him, too, even though she thought him to be priceless. At any rate, she'd be bidding against her own cause. Haven House needed every dime that could be raised. If Sabrina won, Ashleigh had to wonder if she'd actually fork over the cash. She somehow doubted it, which would make a mockery of the auction. However, Austin wasn't the only person on the auction block.

As much money as Sabrina had, she had to shrink away from Kelly's ten-thousand-dollar bid, which turned out to be the final one. Smiling beautifully, the gorgeous woman clapped her hands as she reclaimed her seat. Sabrina instantly disappeared, looking none too happy.

Looking thoroughly embarrassed, Austin returned to the table where Ashleigh was seated. After several minutes of listening to his brother's merciless ribbings about him being bought and paid for, Austin excused himself to go to the bathroom.

Ashleigh looked after Austin as he walked toward one of the exits. Her heart palpitated fervently with her love for him. His confidence in himself was easy to discern. The man had a captivating presence. Ashleigh's heart nearly skipped a beat when she saw Kelly get up and follow Austin out of the room. While stealing a glance at Sabrina, who had taken to the stage again, Ashleigh saw that Sabrina looked livid. That Sabrina didn't also follow along behind Austin and Kelly came as a big surprise to Ashleigh. Deciding that it was best to take all her mind off the unpleasantness, Ashleigh turned her attention on her companions.

Lanier was in a world of her own, her eyes fastened on Dallas. Houston and Dallas appeared to be involved in deep conversation with their parents. It became apparent to Ashleigh that Angelica and Beaumont were scolding their sons for making light of a very bad situation, one that had caught everyone completely off guard. The triplets sincerely apologized to Ashleigh, after realizing that she, too, was a victim of Sabrina's cruelty. They hadn't meant any harm in ribbing Austin in front of Ashleigh, and each brother hugged Ashleigh to show his sincerity. Ashleigh was embarrassed yet graciously accepted the apologies.

Just as Austin had done, Dallas and Houston had chosen

to participate in the talent show over the auction. Both Austin and Dallas had declined the auction idea out of respect for the women they were deeply involved with. Houston simply wasn't the type of man to be chosen by anyone, nor was he in any hurry to give his heart away or have it stolen. If he were to go out on a lunch date, Houston Carrington would be the one to choose his companion.

Though the cause was a great one, not a single one of the three brothers had been keen on the idea of auctioning himself off to the highest bidder. However, each one had agreed that participation in some capacity was a must. No one wanted Ashleigh and Lanier to make a success of Haven House more than the Carrington triplets did.

In the absence of Austin, Ashleigh suddenly felt so alone again. Feelings of abandonment were never really far away. It was so easy to retreat into her old shell and fall back into reliving the memories of when she'd resided in hell.

Austin wore a brilliant smile when he finally came back to the table. He looked more relaxed and content than when he left. Ashleigh was dying to know what he and Kelly had discussed, if anything. She couldn't be sure that Kelly's intention of leaving the room was to be with Austin, but it had looked that way to her. The fact that they'd returned to the room together made Ashleigh feel that she was right. He had also seen Kelly to her table before he'd made his way back to Ashleigh.

With her insecurities once again ruling her thoughts, Ashleigh made no attempt to greet Austin. Though it was so unlike her, she actually gave him the cold shoulder. After Sabrina's latest stunts and thoughts of his upcoming lunch date with Kelly, Ashleigh had already convinced herself that she'd had enough of this. She couldn't take any more. Sharing her man with any other woman wasn't her idea of a safe place to fall. Her dream of one day living happily ever after with Austin was rapidly slipping away. It had been proven once again that the places they resided in were worlds apart. The realization of it all broke her heart into a million pieces.

Once the benefit was over, Ashleigh vowed that it would also be over for her and Austin.

Austin had tried to make conversation with Ashleigh during the entire drive to her place, but he was never able to get more out of her than a few curt responses. It wasn't that he didn't know exactly what had her so upset; he just didn't know how to get her to talk about it.

At the door of her place, when Ashleigh told Austin she didn't want him to come in, he refused to leave her alone with things unsettled between them. Taking control of the situation, he took her firmly by the arm and marched her inside the apartment and on into the living room. When he dropped down on the sofa and tried to plant her next to him, she jerked away and seated herself on a nearby chair.

Although he understood her attitude, Austin didn't like Ashleigh acting the least bit out of character. It simply didn't become her beautiful spirit. He knew she had to be hurting, because he was hurting for her. Sabrina had hurt him, too. Like Ashleigh, he'd also had enough of her.

"Please talk to me, Ashleigh."

She glared at him. "About what? Your favorite subject, Sabrina! No matter what we begin to talk about, she always ends up being the focus of our conversation. I'm sick and tired of living in her shadow. I won't do so for another day."

Austin flinched at the anger in her voice. "Why are you

acting this way with me, Ash? You're being as stubborn as one of Dad's oldest mules."

Ashleigh rolled her eyes. "Haven't you been listening? I'm fed up. I'm beginning to think you're enjoying all of Sabrina's sick attention. You may find it flattering but I don't."

He was taken aback. "Aren't you the same person who told me she was hurting and not to flaunt our relationship in front of her?"

Ashleigh put her hands on her hips and looked him dead in the eye. "One and the same. I did tell you that and it was horrible advice. But I've changed my mind, a woman's prerogative. I'll be here when you're really single and free. If you truly love me, don't make me wait too long, 'cause I'm ready to move on without you. 'No more Mr. Nice Guy' should quickly become your motto from here on in, especially when it comes to your ex-fiancée. Sabrina has controlled you, and our relationship, every step of the way. She has dogged your every move long enough. I know it's difficult for you to see behind you, but I'm going to let you in on a little secret. You have footprints all over your back from Sabrina walking all over you."

The expression on his face had turned from bewilderment to deep anger. "Is that how you see it? And were those ultimatums you just handed me, Ash?"

"Plain and simple. I can't make myself any clearer. I'm not blind. These eyes can see."

"It seems to me that you're starting to be a little controlling yourself, Ashleigh. At least, that's what it sounds like to me."

Ashleigh got up from the chair and advanced on the sofa until she stood over Austin. "If taking cheap shots at me is your only defense, it's a weak one. People have been taking potshots at me all of my life. I'm used to it. My heart has been bulletproof for years. There's nothing hurtful that you can say to me that won't just bounce off my chest." Liar, liar, she screamed inwardly. *Nothing he has ever said or done has bounced off of you.* There was no type of shield in the world that could protect Ashleigh's heart against Austin.

Ashleigh bent down and kissed him on the mouth. "Good-bye, Austin. I love you." She hated to walk away from him, but she had to. As long as he let Sabrina control their lives, they'd never have any peace or happiness. Austin needed a wake-up call.

It was now or never for them.

"Ashleigh," Austin shouted after her, "please don't walk out of my life until you've heard me out. I need you to listen to what I have to say one last time. We can get this right. I know it."

Ashleigh could no more deny his request than she could stop loving him. Without uttering a word, she sat back down in the chair.

Austin came over to the chair and knelt down before her and took her hand. "I love you, Ashleigh, and I believe you know that. I admit to not taking firm control of this situation and bringing it to a sudden death, like I would do in any football game that went into overtime. It's hard for me to hurt people, even those who get pleasure out of hurting others. In a lot of ways I feel responsible for the way things are between Sabrina and me. It was wrong for me to ever have gotten involved with her knowing I could never love her, especially the way she wanted to be loved. Once I had gotten in so deep, I didn't know how to back away without making an emotional mess of her life. If that makes me weak, so be it. I made excuses for her and sacrificed my feelings when there should've been no excuses or any sacrificing. Zero tolerance is how it should've been. It wasn't like that and I can't go back and change it. But I am going to end it. Once and for all."

Austin lowered himself to the floor and pulled Ashleigh down onto his lap. Prepared to beg her not to give up on them if he had to, he looked deeply into her eyes. "What about us, Ash? Are you sure you're ready to end it, that you're ready to throw in the terrible towel? Do you really want to give up what we have so much of? Love overflowing. Our lives are only just beginning and we love each other something fierce. Please don't throw away what we have on a mere technicality. I fumbled the ball and I'm desperately trying to recover it. As my teammate and soul mate, will you continue to block for me and run interference until I can get the ball back? Once we recover the fumble, Ash, will you help me get it and *us* into the end zone so we can celebrate this glorious win together?"

Tears fell from Ashleigh's eyes. "You just scored the winning touchdown! Since we're already in overtime, Austin, you won't need to make the extra point."

Austin kissed her passionately. "I love you more than you'll ever know, sweet Ashleigh Ayers. I don't ever want to try imagining my life without you. I love you."

"And I love you just as much, Austin Carrington, my very own rancher cowboy."

With his eyes as full of tears as hers were, Austin presented Ashleigh with an engagement ring, the very same brilliant diamond she'd admired in the Caribbean jewelry store. He didn't even get to pop the proverbial question because Ashleigh was already screaming, "Yes, I'll marry you," over and over again, at the top of her lungs. Their mouths collided in a joyous, passionate kiss, thus sealing their fate forevermore.

Chapter 8

Month after month came in and flew out like an unstoppable whirlwind. So much productive activity had occurred, all of it happening in the midst of numerous people involving themselves in the complete renovation of Haven House. All sorts of donations had come in. Stripping floors, laying carpet and tile, installing new plumbing, exterior and interior painting, updating the heating and cooling systems, scrubbing, cleaning windows inside and outside, waxing, landscaping, preparing the ground for planting flower and vegetable gardens, wallpapering, interior decorating, and a host of other necessary chores were tackled on a regular basis by the Carrington triplets, several of their teammates, and many other gracious volunteers.

True to his word, Dallas had made a great supervisor. However, he eventually tried to get in on the heavier action. In helping to move some furniture, he slipped and fell on his

healing ankle, which caused serious damage, putting him out
for the entire season. His team had made it into the postsea-
son, but they didn't win the pennant race. The doctors at one
time felt confident that he'd be ready to play long before then,
but then came the new injury. While it had been a terrible blow
to him, the staff, and members of his baseball team, he'd
taken it all in stride.

Lanier had taken very good care of him throughout his
season-ending ordeal.

Though there was still a lot of red tape to untangle before
tenant occupation could actually occur, as far as kids moving
in, Ashleigh and Lanier had finally moved into the refurbished
and newly furnished house, which looked brand-new. All the
boundless labors of love had produced a magnificent outcome.
Haven House had been transformed into a place where any
child and teenager would be more than happy to live. Ashleigh
and Lanier had given so much of themselves and had made
countless sacrifices to make their dream come true.

Looking beautiful and exotic, dressed in brightly colored
African attire, Ashleigh was pleased that so many of her
personal acquaintances and coworkers had showed up for the
open house and Kwanzaa celebration. Ashleigh hoped that
this was only the first of many celebrations to be held at
Haven House in honor of foster kids all over the world.

The house had come to life with an amazing Kwanzaa
theme that Ashleigh and Lanier had begun working on even
before the cruise. The dynamic duo had pushed their celebratory plans into high gear right after Thanksgiving. The girls
had chosen the sixth day of Kwanzaa to have the open house
so their guests could partake of the traditional Kwanzaa
Karamu feast.

All of the downstairs rooms had been decorated with an

African theme, featuring African art and timeless artifacts. The large family room had been set up for the actual feast. Several tables lined against three of the four walls featured every kind of hors d'oeuvres and soul food imaginable. Located in one corner of the room, a table dressed in *kente* cloth held the *kinara,* a candleholder; the *mishumaa saba,* the seven candles, one black, three red, three green; a *mkeka,* the straw place mat; and a *kikombe cha umoja,* the communal unity cup. The *mazao,* fruits and vegetables, were placed in a beautiful wicker basket. A straw basket held the *vibunzi,* the ears of corn that represented the number of children in the household. This basket was overflowing with corn to reflect the number of children Ashleigh and Lanier hoped to one day have living inside the walls of Haven House.

Watching Angelica and Beaumont interact with her wealthy benefactor, Thomas Early, gave Ashleigh great pleasure. They appeared to get along well, after having shared several outings already. Thomas was a dignified, well-built, extremely good-looking older gentleman, a spry sixty-two. Thomas had brought along a very attractive date, fifty-eight-year-old Meredith Hemsley; Ashleigh couldn't be more thrilled. For him to find someone who really cared about him and not his money had been hard for him to achieve; Meredith was wealthy in her own right.

Darius Early had come with his uncle but in his own car. Ashleigh noticed that he hadn't wasted any time in finding a group of people he could relate to. As good-looking as he was, and single, a flock of women had already drifted his way, including her coworker, Bethany Marlton.

Houston hadn't showed up yet, but all the social workers from the cruise couldn't wait to see him. They'd been giggling over his expected arrival for the last half hour or so. Dallas had been over to the house the entire morning and Lanier had driven him home to change clothes.

The regular football season had come to an end and Austin's team had made it into the playoffs. The Texas Wranglers were heavily favored to go all the way to the Super Bowl, only a few weeks away. All games were in the sudden death phase, lose, you go home. Ashleigh hadn't missed a single home game during the entire regular season, but she'd missed one playoff game because of the flu, the one where Austin had racked up 360 yards passing, not to mention the thirty yards rushing; mighty impressive quarterbacking.

Ashleigh couldn't wait for Austin to get back. There were several of her friends and coworkers that he had yet to meet and everyone was eager to make the personal acquaintance of her handsome and very famous quarterback.

Ashleigh didn't have to turn around to know that it was Austin's hands on her shoulders, squeezing them gently. It also explained the loud oohs! and ahs! she'd just heard. It was as if he'd appeared on cue. Tilting her head back, Ashleigh gave Austin a smile that caused his heart to soar. The love she felt for this man was indescribable. He felt the same way about her.

He grinned, kissing her softly on the mouth. He then took a cursory glance around the room. "How are things going here, baby? We sure have a full house."

Before Ashleigh could respond to Austin, she turned around to see what all the female screeching was about. *Unbelievable!* Ashleigh could hardly believe her eyes, as her jaw dropped.

Sabrina, recently recovered from a near mental breakdown, smiling all over herself, had just entered the room on the arm of a heralded black athlete, another NFL quarterback. As if that wasn't shock enough for the guests, Dallas and Lanier came into the room right behind them.

Ashleigh couldn't help laughing at all the stunned expressions as they spotted Dallas. Then she thought of Austin and what he might be feeling over seeing Sabrina after such a long spell. She stole a glance at him, only to see that he was also smiling, summoning his brother to where he stood. Austin didn't seem to be the least bit affected by Sabrina and her new man.

Ashleigh felt instant relief. The last time Austin had seen Sabrina was the worst time in his life. Putting the final word down to her regarding their relationship being over hadn't come without a major incident. Her emotions had spun out of control, so much so that she threatened suicide. It was then that Austin went to her parents and told them Sabrina needed help. As parents sometimes are, they were in total denial about the seriousness of her mental state.

If the screeching had been loud before, the women were now out of control. Seeing Houston come in had been way too much to take, especially after seeing all the other superstars. It was now Ashleigh's turn to be shocked silly. She fought hard to keep herself from screaming when she saw who was on Houston's arm. But that didn't stop all the women from rushing him.

Ashleigh looked back and forth between Austin and Houston several times before Austin finally came over and pulled her off to the side.

She shook her head in disbelief. "What's that all about? How did he get with her?"

Austin blew out a ragged breath. "I'm so glad I can finally get this out in the open. I've been keeping this secret for what seems like an eternity. When I make a promise, I really try to keep it. During the auction, after Kelly Charleston, that's her name, won the bid, she came out in the lobby and told me a little secret. She then asked me to keep it to myself…."

"What secret?" Ashleigh screeched. "You're killing me with the suspense."

Austin laughed. "It seems that Kelly and Sabrina knew each other in college. Sabrina didn't like Kelly and had tried to make her life miserable every chance she got. However, that's not why Kelly bid against Sabrina. Kelly is very interested in Houston."

Ashleigh gasped, her laughter following. "This is too much for me to begin to fathom!"

"I know the feeling, Ash. I felt the same way. She didn't want to win a lunch date with me; she only wanted to meet my brother. She met him a while back, but only briefly. I've been trying to get my pigheaded brother to go on the lunch date with her for months, but he wasn't having any of it. I think the boy's scared of falling for her. He mentioned to me how fine she was after the auction. Well, he finally decided to go out with her, but only after I told him I couldn't get the money for Haven House until after the lunch date had been fulfilled. That's why he finally conceded. They had the lunch date only yesterday."

"Was that true about the money?"

Austin looked chagrined. "I lied. He knows that now. But it looks as if it might've paid off. Houston would never bring a woman to a gathering with so many other women present, not unless he was really interested in her. For him, that would be like bringing sand to the beach. As you've already heard him say, repeatedly, Houston loves to be loose and free. He doesn't misrepresent himself to anyone. He's not ready to settle down and he makes no bones about it. They should make an interesting pair. She's a sport physician, of all things."

Ashleigh had never asked Austin about the date with Kelly because she hadn't wanted to know anything about it. She was surprised to learn that it had never happened. She was certainly pleased about it, but not because she felt threatened. Kelly was not only stunning, she was a doctor, too, but Ashleigh knew that Austin wasn't interested. He loved her. He made that perfectly clear every chance he got. What had happened on Christmas Eve was proof enough of that.

Austin grinned. "Speaking of the devil, here he comes now. Look how cool he is. The women just love his charming behind. That's my little bro. He thinks he's never going to get caught by the fairer sex. But I got news for him. He hasn't met anyone like you yet."

Ashleigh blushed as she kissed Austin in response to his generous remarks.

"Hey, sis." Houston kissed Ashleigh on the cheek. He then embraced her with a huge hug. "Kelly, this is Ashleigh, Austin's brand-new wife. They got married on Christmas Eve at our parents' ranch. The intimate ceremony, family type, was beautiful. It was off the hook."

Kelly smiled brilliantly. "Congratulations! So you're newlyweds. I'm happy for you two. That is surprising news. I can't believe it didn't make all headlines all over the country."

Ashleigh looked up at Austin in adoration. "Thanks, Kelly. It took me by surprise, too, when he suggested it. We've been married an entire week. It was what we both wanted, so we took the leap. It didn't make the headlines because only our little family and close friends knew of our plans. We're announcing it this evening." Ashleigh kissed her husband gently on the lips.

Wishing they were somewhere alone, Austin kissed her back. "Lanier is trying to get your attention. You'd better get on over there. It looks like it may be speech time, Ash. Now it's my turn to cheer you on, baby. Go do your thing. I'm rooting for you all the way."

Ashleigh accepted a hug from her husband and brother-in-law before leaving their side.

Ashleigh and Lanier met up and chatted with each other for a couple of minutes. Joining hands, they made their way behind the makeshift podium. The two young women took turns at the microphone, welcoming their guests, sharing all the important details of why Haven House had come into existence, what they hoped to accomplish, and how they appreciated all the help they'd received through donations, time, and efforts from their friends, family, community leaders, and everyone else who had contributed in some way.

Ashleigh accepted the mike from Lanier. "Both Lanier and I are thrilled to see this long-awaited day. We would each like to share with you why we chose the week of Kwanzaa to hold our open house. Lanier will go first."

Feeling extremely nervous, Lanier cleared her throat. "As many of you may know, Kwanzaa was created to restore the people's roots in African culture. It also serves as a regular communal celebration to reaffirm and reinforce the bonds among Africans as a people. It is also designed as an ingathering to strengthen community and reaffirm common identity, purpose, and direction as a people and a world community. The seven principles of Kwanzaa are observed from December twenty-six to January one. Today is the sixth day of Kwanzaa and also New Year's Eve. Ashleigh and I have our reasons for wanting to celebrate this day differently than we've done in the past. My reason for doing so is as a young child, I was taken out of the home and placed in foster care during the week of Kwanzaa, never to return." Lanier's voice had suddenly cracked. She took a moment to compose herself. An encouraging smile from Dallas helped her go on.

"While my family didn't observe the African celebration

back then, we still should've been in the Christmas spirit. Alcohol played a part in my being removed from my home, when a terrible fight between my parents ensued on the twenty-sixth day of December, the day after Christmas. This was a sad time for me every year. When the celebratory season rolled around, I felt not an ounce of joy. It is our desire to change this, not only for ourselves, but also for the children who will one day call Haven House home. At Haven House, we will celebrate both Christmas and Kwanzaa every year."

Lanier moved back and Ashleigh stepped forward.

"My story is a tad different, but no less sorrowful. My father was killed during the week of Kwanzaa, as he repaired a storm-damaged Texas highway. Instead of a wedding taking place that week, my mother had to bury my father on the day their wedding ceremony was to take place. Because my mother had no money to take care of me, she left me at the Angels of Mercy orphanage. Had she been married to my father when he was killed, she would've received death benefits. My mother ended up taking her own life. Alcohol played a part in this tragedy as well. A drunken, speeding motorist hit my father with his car, killing him instantly."

Gasps were heard throughout the room as each woman had shared her story.

As Ashleigh wiped the tears from her eyes, Austin came to her side and put his arms around her shoulder. "But that was back then and this is here and now. No longer will Lanier and I wallow in our sorrows during the holidays. We will see to it that Haven House is filled with celebration every holiday season and we hope all of you will join us each year."

Ashleigh looked up at Austin and smiled. "We're so happy to have you all here to celebrate new beginnings and fresh starts for Lanier, the soon-to-be occupants of Haven House, and to celebrate the sixth day of Kwanzaa with the Karamu feast. However, we'd also like you to join in another kind of celebration, our recent marriage. Not wanting to wait another year to fulfill our long-ago fantasy, Austin and I exchanged vows on Christmas Eve."

The cheers, hand claps, and whistles filled the room. Shouts of congratulations echoed off the walls. Beaumont kissed Angelica, long and hard. Dallas warmly embraced Lanier, and Houston gathered up all the women he could get his long arms around, including his date, Kelly, and the social workers from the cruise. Thomas Early had the look of a proud papa on his face.

Smiling broadly, Austin took hold of the mike. "With that said, let's get this long-awaited celebration started. We're so glad that you're all here to also help us celebrate our marriage and the beginning of the rest of our lives."

At the very vocal prompting of the crowd for the groom to kiss the bride, Austin took his wife in his arms and kissed her passionately. Ashleigh Ayers Carrington lost herself in the loving embrace of her handsome husband, her once upon a time *forbidden fantasy.*

As the entire Carrington family moved forward to embrace the bride and groom, the other guests formed a line so they, too, could offer their sincere congratulations to the happy couple. Flashing cameras captured the happy images of Ashleigh, Austin, Houston, Dallas, Angelica, and Beaumont holding hands. The loving pose was perfect for capturing a family portrait.

Ashleigh had finally been reunited with her old family and she and Lanier couldn't wait to start their new one. She and Lanier were as much a family to each other as were the others.

These two young women would never again want for a real family and a loving home.

Ashleigh and Austin's fantasy of long ago had now been utterly fulfilled.

"Happy Kwanzaa!" Ashleigh and Austin shouted. "Let the Karamu feast begin!"

SOMEONE TO LOVE

Michelle Monkou

Chapter 1

Dear Daddy

I miss you so much. Tomorrow is my birthday. Tomorrow was one of my spelling words. I will be eight years old Daddy. Mommy misses you too. I think that she needs a friend. She cries too much because you are gone. A nice friend can stop her from crying. I will help her. Daddy I love you for ever and ever.

Patti Stone folded her handwritten note into a neat square and slid it under her favorite pillow with the dancing teddy bears. She'd already said her prayers, so the angels could continue helping her dad.

No sounds came through the house. Patti slid off her bed, tiptoed to the door, and peeked out. In the direction of the stairs, the darkness eerily covered everything. She gulped at the thought of what could come out of the shadows. Never mind. She shook her head to chase away the fear, she had to keep an eye on her mother. It was her duty and she took it seriously. On the opposite end, she looked over at her mother's bedroom. That end of the hallway was bathed in a soft light from the partially opened bathroom door.

There was no light under her mother's door. Good. At least, her mommy had stopped crying. If she cried too long, then Patti would knock and make up an excuse to sleep next to her. It used to be every night, but now it was more like once a week. On really bad days, her mother cried at a movie or a song playing on the radio.

Patti sighed. Nights made her mother sad. During the day, she smiled, talked, and sometimes even played games with her. But one night after they had said their good-nights and her mother had tucked her into bed, she'd discovered that her mother suffered with deep sadness.

A soft, sleepy yawn overcame Patti. One more quick survey just to be on the safe side. She returned to her bed and slid under the comforter, surrendering almost immediately.

The birthday party wound down now that the clown and most of the games had been played. Patti looked around the basement, glad to see that her mother had returned upstairs. Only a few of her friends remained, but she really wanted her favorite pals, Dwayne, Donna, and Mike, to turn up before it was all over.

Right now would be a good time to escape. Her mom wouldn't be gone for too long. She had to put her plan in motion before she didn't get another chance.

Imagining that spies chased her, Patti made a zigzag path around her friends toward the back door. Twice she looked over her shoulder, just like her favorite action hero. No one followed and her mother had still not appeared.

Her blue dress with the stupid, starched, white frill around her neck and legs didn't match the seriousness of her mission. The black jeans with her new red blouse would have been better. But her mother wouldn't budge from making her look like one of those stuck-up, silly girls. At least her mother had allowed her to wear a ponytail, rather than a bunch of curls like a little girl.

Patti headed over to one of the folding chairs that had a balloon tied to it. As fast as she could, she unfastened it, making sure to keep a tight hold. Then, after checking that she was still unnoticed, Patti unlocked the sliding door and slipped out.

What was the big deal about going outside without an adult?

On New Year's Day, the air carried a stinging bite. Patti gritted her teeth, aware that her breaths formed wispy puffs of smoke. Her eyes watered and for a second she regretted not wearing her coat.

She studied the backyard, wondering about the best launch site. Not that the area was very big, but she had a small swing set in one corner, while her mother's vegetable garden was in the other corner. The deck off from the dining room provided wonderful shade in the summer, but it could prevent her mission from occurring. Her best bet was to head to the edge of the yard near the wooden fence.

One of her friends had suggested this balloon trick to make a wish come true. Pulling a small slip of paper from her shoe, she tied it to the balloon string. She'd written her secret in such neat, crisp letters that Miss Brown, her teacher, would be proud.

Just in case, she had also made the same wish when she'd blown out the eight candles stuck in her birthday cake a few minutes ago. "Please, please, please work."

From her vantage point Patti looked through the sliding doors where her guests chased each other. She saw her mother cut the birthday cake that had a ballerina doll standing on tiptoe with her hands over her head. As her mom cut, she placed the pieces onto small plates and handed them to those standing nearby.

Patti kicked at the gravel near the garden patch with her new shoe. No one knew about her wish. She'd worked on it without anyone's help. Hopefully all the words were spelled correctly. But it filled her with dread at the thought of someone reading it and then laughing at her. Or worse, someone feeling sorry for her.

Her mom would do neither.

She was cool like that. But since the wish was about Patti's mother, she couldn't include her in the plans at all.

Patti gazed at her mom and her heart swelled with pride and love. Her mom treated her with respect and didn't talk down to her. It wasn't unusual for her to spend weekends with her mother watching movies and eating popcorn. When she was in first grade, her mother came on every school field trip, something her school friends still talked about because none of their parents ever came as chaperones.

This afternoon her mom deserved all the credit for a wonderful birthday party. Along with all the games she'd organized, the big surprise happened to be the magician who dressed as a bunny. For all her mom's effort, though, Patti only wanted her mom to smile more and to stop her crying late at night.

"One, two, three." Patti swung up her small arm and released the balloon. It sailed slowly away from her outstretched hand and then dipped with the gentle breeze. "Please make it come true," she whispered into the air.

"Patti, get in here. It's too cold for you to be standing out there with no coat." Her mom stood at the sliding door, waiting for her to come in.

Patti took one last look at the balloon, which had floated over their fence into Mr. Jackson's yard and toward his deck. Satisfied that her plan unfolded as she'd hoped, she ran to her mom, hardly put off by her disapproval. She hit her mom at full speed and wrapped her small arms around her mom's hips in a big hug.

That's all it took for her mom's smile to radiate. Patti allowed herself to be fussed over as her mom vigorously rubbed her arms to warm them.

"Time to play musical chairs, honey. Then it's gifts."

"It's almost over?" Patti looked at the clock and watched a new number drop into place. She wondered how long it would take for the wish to come true.

"Yes, it is, and everybody's having a wonderful time."

Patti nodded. Why did birthdays have to happen only once a year? There were lots of wishes to be made.

Chapter 2

T.J. opened his vertical blinds, adjusting them to see what Patti planned to do with her balloon. From the door leading to his deck he had the perfect view into his neighbor's yard.

"Uncle Thane, when are we going?"

Thane tousled his niece's curly mop of hair. Her upturned face marked with impatience made him smile. "Soon, honey. I'm expecting a call from work. By the way, where are your brothers?" Thane returned his attention to Patti.

Each time the little girl pulled at her frilly dress, he chuckled. Knowing Patti, she would rather run around in pants and a shirt. Then she'd have the freedom to do cartwheels, her trademark outdoor activity.

It was her focus on the balloon that hooked his attention. Her expression puzzled him, though, so solemn and deliberate, as if she was offering the balloon as a valuable gift to someone. Fascinated with the entire ritual, he watched the balloon and what looked like a small piece of white paper tied to its string.

The balloon's journey arced and soared before smoothly floating past his deck and over the railing. Its string dragged along the wood planks before becoming entangled. The balloon continued to dance under the slight breeze straining to get on its way, but hopelessly stuck between the floorboards.

Thane waited until Patti had gone back into the house. Then he stepped out onto the deck and began to unwind the string.

"Uncle Thane. Uncle Thane."

Thane ran back inside toward the sounds of his niece's voice. "Donna?" His heart raced when he saw the front door standing wide open. Running and sliding along the floor, he skidded headlong through the foyer.

"Boo!"

He gasped just as his feet hit the edge of the welcome mat and slid out the front door, landing with a thud on the porch. His two nephews and niece, Dwayne, Mike, and Donna, showed no sympathy as they crowed over their fallen uncle.

"Gotcha." Donna giggled.

"I think it's time you go to Patti's party."

"Yay!"

Thane rolled onto his knees, grimacing as he slowly rose. He wondered how many neighbors witnessed the spectacle. God love the little rascals. Four, six, and seven years old, his niece and nephews were the loves of his life. They kept him on his toes.

Once he had dropped them off at the party, he returned home. There would be a call from work on whether he had to report for night duty, since it was New Year's Day. The staff on duty at the firehouse was a small one. His chances for a free night were not good.

Out of the corner of his eye, he noticed that the balloon still bobbed from being stuck on the deck. Returning to his task, he performed his rescue mission on the balloon.

A paper had been twisted like a candy wrapper around the string. Making sure that Patti hadn't returned outside, he read the note, frowning at the simple request. Its message touched an emotional note with him.

Witnessing a little girl's love for her mother tugged at his heart. Growing up with lots of siblings and relatives, he had enjoyed the love and support he received. Family feuds did occur, but the familial bonds were stronger than any petty disagreements. From what he'd noticed, Patti was an only child and her mother was a single parent.

He untied the paper and shoved it in his pants pocket. An idea formed. There might be a way to help Patti with her quest. He took the balloon to the edge of the deck and let it go, watching it clear the pine trees lining the wooded perimeter fence in his backyard. Chances were the balloon would not make it over the small wooded area behind his property. Well, at least he had the important part to the entire package.

His phone rang, ending his musing.

It was the job. Everyone had reported to duty. He wouldn't be needed until tomorrow. Good news.

There was a birthday party waiting for him and a little girl who would have the best birthday gift. A little kernel of doubt set in. The *best* birthday gift might be overstating it. He was willing to concede that it would be a unique gift.

His mind easily returned to thoughts of Patti and her mother, Jennifer. His quiet neighbor never gave him the opening to muster the nerve to ask for a cup of sugar, a glass of lemonade, much less a date. Jennifer only managed a "hello" or a "fine, thank you" to his greetings. Once he'd remarked about the weather and she merely waited for him to finish speaking, offered a shy smile, nodded, and went into her home without a second glance.

That's when he decided to use his nephews and niece to get closer to his shy neighbor with the big brown eyes. They'd followed Patti to her house after hearing her tell about her new video game. Knowing that getting them to leave would be difficult, he readily gave his permission. As the concerned uncle, he reminded them that he had to check in on them once or twice while they played.

But his few attempts to stick around fell flat. Jennifer always managed to gush over them, feeding them wonderful candied treats, while looking at him with a frosty gaze. But good gracious, she had an adorable pair of lips with her signature earth-toned lip gloss emphasizing their fullness.

He played with the note in his pocket. Here was his chance to enter that no-fly zone with Jennifer. A madcap idea continued to form out of his original Good Samaritan plan. He grinned at his brilliant creativity. "Damn, I'm so good!" Before heading for the front door, he grabbed his old firefighter hat and jacket and headed for the party, whistling a fifties show tune.

Chapter 3

Jennifer handed her departing guests their coats, scarves, and gloves. "Thank you for coming to Patti's birthday." She looked over to where Patti sat sulking because her party was over. "Patti, don't you want to say thank you?" Jennifer pasted a plastic smile on her face and tried to communicate her displeasure at her daughter's behavior using her "angry" eyes.

Patti walked over with her eyes downcast, her feet dragging across the carpet. Jennifer bit back an exasperated sigh. "Say goodbye, Patti."

"Goodbye. Thank you for coming."

Jennifer waved after her daughter's schoolmates and parents. She closed the door, breathing a sigh of relief that it was over. No more celebrations until the summer when Patti had her slumber party for the second year.

Right now, she had to deal with her daughter's dark mood. Part of her dramatic behavior was her loneliness as an only child. "There's no need to sulk. You should be grateful that so many friends came to celebrate. Why ruin the end of your day? Besides, your buddies, Donna, Dwayne, and Mike came."

Jennifer walked into the kitchen and retrieved a large green plastic trash bag from under the sink. "Why don't you gather up the gift paper lying on the floor downstairs?"

Patti took the bag and reluctantly went down to the basement. Jennifer bit back the easy tendency to scold.

In no time, the gift paper and paper cups and plates were picked up. Patti balled the last of the paper into a great big ball before tossing it into the bag. "Do I get to stay up late tonight?"

Jennifer didn't pause in her cleaning up, but shot a sideways glance toward her daughter's profile. Wow. Her baby was growing up. Where were the days when she could put her down at seven or eight o'clock and she would sleep until the next morning?

What about the long hours she'd spend playing with her dolls? Now, it was the latest adolescent girl sitcom on any of the cable networks.

Not only did Jennifer have to deal with her daughter's growing pains, there were other bittersweet moments beyond Patti's control. As her face matured, every year she looked more like her father. It was the small things like her ears, nose, or the shape of her face. Jennifer remembered holding Patti's hands and admiring the long tapered fingers. Oh so similar to those strong ones that had gently caressed and kneaded away her tiredness. The sad tone of her memories played against the sad pangs of her heart. It ached at the mere thought of how she and her husband would've been sharing in their daughter's birthday celebration.

She bit her lip to stem the tears, so readily at the surface. Completely unexpected, she'd lost the only man she'd ever love. Jennifer wiped a tear, knowing that if she didn't fight for control, she'd be a weepy mess in a few minutes. She'd promised herself, no emotional breakdowns during the day for Patti to witness.

"Mommy," Patti called, "I didn't mean to make you sad."

Jennifer bit her lip harder, embarrassed that her daughter had seen her weakness.

Her daughter's small hand touched her arm tentatively, and Jennifer's heart fluttered and melted. She looked down into the dark brown eyes framed with thick, long lashes that reflected love and so much trust. "I'm not sad." A tremulous smile hovered on her lips. "When we're done, let's curl up in my bed and watch one of the movies you got for your birthday."

A big toothy smile lit Patti's face. "Oh, boy!" She practically skipped around the basement with renewed energy. Her ponytail bobbed in time with her bouncy antics.

The doorbell rang.

Jennifer paused, glancing at the clock. She couldn't imagine who could be visiting. The party was over. She motioned with a flick of her hand for Patti to continue with her task before running upstairs.

At the front door, she pressed her face against it, peering through the peephole. The view only showed an elongated face with a familiar, bright smile already in place. Jennifer stepped back from the door with her answering smile.

Her neighbor was such a flirt. For the most part, she treated him and his playful attempts to get her attention with her usual blow-off style. Lately, she noticed a new directness that didn't offend her. Instead, she had to admit to a certain level of anticipation in hearing him greet her or show up at her doorstep with his niece and nephews in tow. She guessed he used whatever means necessary.

"Who is it?" she shouted from behind her closed door. A giggle erupted and she clamped her hand over her mouth.

"Hi, Jen. It's me, Thane."

Jen?

She mouthed the shortened version of her name. New. Different. But not uncomfortable. She bit her cheek to refrain from another giddy urge to giggle.

A grown man stood less than a foot away from her. All she had to do was open the door. A simple act, but that wasn't the problem. It scared her that her defenses were more show than reality. Pretty soon, he would be able to wear her down and then she'd want to be in his company.

That wasn't an option. *Just remain focused and send him on his merry way again.* There would be no harm done because she wasn't looking for a man. And it would surprise her if he had any serious interest in a single mother.

Her daughter thundered up the stairs. Jennifer looked over her shoulder and saw Patti drop the bag of trash near the kitchen door.

"Who is it?" Patti ran over to the front-facing windows and pulled aside the curtain to peer out the window. "It's T.J.," she shouted.

Jennifer was at somewhat of a loss at how her daughter practically sang "Tee-Jay" as if he were her long-lost friend.

"It's T.J., Mommy." Patti pushed her way in front of her mother to fiddle with the locks.

"Hold on, young lady. I'll get the door. It's only our next-door neighbor." Jennifer shifted Patti's little body away from the door. Was she a hypocrite because the nervous energy zipped through her with traitorous sparks as she pretended to be calm and even slightly dismissive? She unlocked and opened the door. "Bit late, aren't you?"

Thane stepped in with a big grin, swooped toward Jennifer, and brushed his cheek against hers. "Sure looks like I'm late. Anyway, I'm here to collect my little hellions. You look wonderful, but a little tired around the edges."

His warm gaze slid along her face, which had heated under his attention. Then there was the spot on her cheek that touched his unshaven face. If she were alone, she'd touch the spot that still felt warm and tingly.

It didn't appear that Thane suffered a similar reaction. He wore his trademark grin, but otherwise remained unchanged—normal. As a matter of fact, she was the one whose emotions rolled up and down like an annoying yo-yo. This maddening surge to her pulse and weird flip-flops in her stomach had to be some bad side effect to dealing with life without her husband.

Gosh, she hoped that she wasn't turning into a horny, middle-aged woman.

"Plus, I was summoned."

"What? Who summoned you?" What was this man up to?

Patti danced around her mother and pushed herself between Thane and her. "Hi, T.J."

"Hey, girlie." He swung her up into his arms and spun her around. "I got your wish. You know, the balloon…" When he set her down, he lowered himself to one knee so she would be comfortable and could look him eye-to-eye.

"Oh." Patti stopped dancing around and glanced up at her mother. "I…I didn't…um." She turned her full attention back to him, although her gaze shifted between the two adults.

"Remember the balloon?" Thane prompted.

"What balloon?" Jennifer didn't like feeling left out, especially when it came to her daughter. "Patti, talk to me." Her tone held no room for negotiation.

"Patti had a simple wish—to make her mother happy."

Jennifer raised her gaze from her daughter's unhappy face to Thane, who now stood at her level. His deep warm brown eyes bored through her. It made no sense for a man to have such long, dark eyelashes. She'd deal with those eyes later. Right now, clearly an issue was about to unfold. "Patti?"

"Yes," her daughter responded. Her small chin buried itself onto her chest, eyes downcast. "I wanted to see you smile."

Her daughter's words plainly spoken carried so much weight that wrapped itself around her heart and tugged for attention. How to answer her child's plea? A small smile shakily appeared.

"Not like that. I want to see you smile like you used to. Like when you and Daddy used to on the videos. Remember when I was Cinderella? Daddy taped you laughing and laughing." Patti offered her small hand to Thane. "Come on, can you make my mommy happy again?"

Now that Patti had cleared up why Thane was at her front door, Jennifer wasn't sure she wanted to rely on him to bring her daughter any happiness. Of course, she worried about what method he'd use. Tall, wide shoulders, dark and unforgivably handsome, he served as eye candy—nothing more.

"Come on in and have a seat. I have to hear this." She stepped back as he trudged past her. What was another hour of distraction? "Would you care for coffee, water, soda?"

"Nope. I'd like to get under way with my mission."

"Again with the mission?"

"I'm here to make you happy."

If happiness meant looking at his sculpted face with square jaw, high cheekbones, and dark brown eyes, then she should be screaming for joy. "I'm listening."

"Patti," he called. When the little girl came next to him and stood, he placed his hand on her shoulder. "I'll be your genie and grant you three wishes."

"This is too much." Jennifer popped her head out of the kitchen where she was preparing a cup of coffee. "I'm not sure about this game." The last thing she needed was for Patti to think that Thane really was a genie. It was one thing for her body to react to the smooth deep voice like a hormonal teenager, but when it came to her daughter, it was all business.

"Mom!" Patti exclaimed.

"No, it's okay, Patti. Your mom is absolutely correct. Your mom and I are at the beginning of the getting-to-know-you stage. Although I can honestly say that in those few minutes, I can recognize a remarkable mother and woman." He grinned. "I'm sure that she may not feel as comfortable."

Jennifer figured she'd better get a pair of knee-high rubber boots to wade through the mushy compliment.

"Pretty. Kind. Loving with her daughter."

"Enough." She handed him the coffee, noting the devilish twinkle in his eyes. Her face flushed under his praises. Besides, she was feeling particularly pleased that he'd noticed her, just as she had him. "Tell me about yourself."

"Not much to tell. I'm a firefighter and that's my life. No wife. No kids. No significant other." She caught his message in his intense gaze: single and available.

"I was outside washing my car. I met Patti when she was riding her bike one afternoon. You were jogging with her, but she'd ridden ahead. We struck up a conversation until you arrived."

"I remember when Patti rode on ahead, but I don't remember meeting you."

"That's because we didn't meet. You were too busy being

winded and scolding Patti for leaving you behind to notice me scrubbing my wheels."

"Oh." He would have had to be hunkered down by his car to pass her scrutiny. Little did he know that she had made it her business anyway to know his routine—when he headed out to work on the graveyard shift, when his lady friends came and went, none of whom had a lasting relationship with him. "So, why the fancy getup?"

"I was hoping that Patti's friends were still here and I could make a big deal about being her personal genie." He looked around the room. "Guess I missed them. Looks like my sister picked up the little hellions, too."

"You didn't miss them by much. And they are sweethearts. But getting back to your little game here, what's the next step?"

"I will grant Patti three wishes."

"I know what my first one is," Jennifer offered, with an eyebrow cocked at him. This insanity had to come to an end.

"I don't think I want to hear what yours is. Besides, since it's Patti's birthday, she should decide."

Jennifer's back stiffened. "I'm her mother and it's up to me." The protective juices had kicked in. Balancing her neighbor's devilishly handsome proposition with her daughter's wishes conflicted with her need to keep her feelings private.

"My fault." Thane raised his hands in surrender.

Jennifer looked over to her daughter, who wore a smug grin. "Mommy, you're going to like this. I'm going to write down my wishes and give them to you, T.J." Patti ran, leaving Jennifer to entertain their guest.

Most people would pretend to look at the surroundings or make inane conversation to while away the time. Thane didn't follow this philosophy. Instead he pinned her with a frank, assessing gaze that had her like a jittery girl on a first date. Jennifer wished that her eight-year-old didn't leave her alone with this muscle-bound giant.

At a loss to provide significant conversation, she sipped her coffee while hoping that Patti would hurry up. Her daughter's footsteps overhead marked her hurried progress down the hall into her bedroom and then back again down the stairs.

"Here ya go, T.J." Patti had a paper with her handwriting all over it.

Jennifer tried to see what was written, but Thane deliberately moved it from her line of vision. With a confident smile, he folded the paper and tucked it in his pocket.

Jennifer didn't feel any bad vibes with Thane and she wasn't really worried about her daughter's friendship with him. Call it mother's intuition. She'd managed to get a few interesting details from his sister, who had picked up her kids after many of Patti's play sessions.

"All this is cute as long as you don't get in my way. You hear me, Patti?" Jennifer opted for the strong-arm tactic, hoping that it would get Patti to cave in and tell her what was really going on in that overactive mind.

"Yes, Mommy."

"Me, too. Scout's honor."

"Were you a Scout?" Jennifer looked suspiciously at Thane, imagining him sporting a khaki shorts uniform. It was difficult to see the teenager in him. What stood before her was all man, stocky with a thick muscular layer.

"Yes, I earned the highest honor as an Eagle Scout."

"Hmm." This six-foot wonder in close quarters scrambled her thoughts. Thinking proved to be difficult when her imagination rolled like a movie as he provided information to fuel it. He had to go before she lost control of the little sense that she had. She reached for his cup, hoping that he would get the message that it was time to leave.

He did.

"See you, Jen. See you, Patti."

Jennifer escorted him to the door and watched him walk down the stairs. He did it again with the name thing. He sure had nerve, that's for certain. Instead of meeting his familiarity with indignation, she remained tongue-tied.

Jen.

Even thinking about it seconds later made her feel cozy.

Closing the door with a firm click, Jennifer blamed her behavior on lingering loneliness that had overcome her since the second anniversary of her husband's passing. This warred with her deepest fear that it was wrong to replace the wonderful, loving relationship that she had shared with her husband.

Chapter 4

T.J. stared out the window from the back seat of the limo. If he could only get rid of the nerves, maybe he could enjoy himself. A glance at the bouquet of flowers and he again questioned what the heck he'd gotten himself into.

"Sir?"

T.J. cut off his meandering thoughts to acknowledge the driver.

"Should I circle the building, again?"

T.J. looked at his watch. The one thing he hadn't factored into his plan was Jennifer's decision to work late. "Yes, Sam. One more time." He studied the tall building with tinted windows, granite, and chrome. Its cold exterior made him glad for his choice of professions away from cubicles and conference rooms and having to breathe in stale air. "What if this building has another exit?"

There was a parking garage on the opposite side. A steady

flurry of cars entered and exited. He really didn't know the details of her commuting and worried that several of the doors on the sides of the building could be used as main exits by the employees.

He pulled out his cell and dialed. "Hey, Patti, have you talked to your mom? Sure she's in there?"

"Yep, T.J. She says that she's leaving in ten minutes."

Thane heard the phone being handed over to Patti's aunt. "Thelma?"

"Hi, T.J., you know that I think you're crazy."

"I know."

"Anyway, when Jennifer says that she'll be coming out in ten minutes, then that really means that she'll be coming out in twenty or thirty minutes."

"Thanks, Thelma." Thane pinched the bridge of his nose. "I'm not trying to disrespect your brother," he blurted. No rule existed on how long a wife should grieve for her deceased husband or how a sister should, for that matter. In his little plan, he had not considered having to deal with Jen's sister-in-law. The awkwardness felt like an itchy wool coat.

"I hear you. Bye, T.J."

Thane hung up, not sure if he'd offended Thelma with his harebrained idea. Not long after, the doubts crept in and he leaned over ready to tell the driver to forget it.

The cell phone rang.

"Hello."

"Don't worry about me. Go for it." The call ended abruptly and Thane silently thanked Thelma's forthrightness.

"Stop the car. I'm going in to get her." He stepped out into the path of the rush-hour foot traffic heading for a subway station a block down the street.

He couldn't imagine this constant whirlwind of activity

with no emergency as the cause. The picture of penguins walking in formation came to mind as men and women walked with uncanny precision while talking to each other or on cell phones. At the height of the winter season, there was no splash of bright colors. Navy blue or black suits appeared to be the preferred uniform under matching woolen coats.

Thane let out a shudder. Nope. He wasn't buying any of it. Taking a deep breath, he walked into the expansive lobby, past the attendant, to the chrome elevators.

As he rode up the elevator car alone, his cool bravado oozed from him. He rubbed his palms together, feeling the moisture. His mouth grew dry, making his throat painfully parched. If he didn't get out of the elevator soon, he'd hyperventilate.

On cue the doors opened with a swoosh and he stepped forward, aiming for the receptionist. For once, he was glad that he had dressed in a suit. One of a few suits that he reserved for special church services, weddings, and, in a few cases, funerals. The upscale, expensive wall decorations and New Age furnishings demanded a certain clientele.

"Hi, I'm here for Jennifer Stone." He tugged at his tie and smoothed it against his shirt. Maybe he should've picked the black-and-silver tie.

"Your name?"

"Thane Jackson." Thane didn't have time to think about the wisdom of giving his name. There was no plan B if Jennifer refused to see him after he was announced. He watched the receptionist's face closely for any signs that he was being dismissed.

"No answer. Was she expecting you?"

Thane shook his head. So much for being a genie. No magical powers and he couldn't even fake it. What to do next?

"Thane?" Jennifer hesitated, wondering if she was mistaken. Holding her briefcase and coat over her arm, she was drawn to the familiar shoulders, strong and broad, the ramrod-straight posture, and slightly bowed legs that brought a smile to her face.

"Jen."

He sounded relieved, yet his presence puzzled her. Could it be that he had a date in his fine dark suit with Tricia or maybe the new girl every man lusted after? "How are you?" She smelled his cologne as she approached, marveling at the suave transformation to a *GQ* cover model, albeit he did look a tad uncomfortable.

"Fine. Fine. I'm here to see…um."

Great. Maybe it was Tricia, the ex-Wizards cheerleader, who worked two offices down from her. He wouldn't be the first athletic, macho guy to want the doll-like figure and high-fashion-model features.

"You. I'm here for you."

"Me!" Damn. Did it have to sound like a squeak?

Thane fumbled with his cuffs, a smile quivered and disappeared with the appearance of a quick frown. "Would you do me the honor of going to dinner with me?"

Jennifer gulped. So this was the plan. His eyes shifted over to the receptionist, who gaped between the two. How many times had anyone picked her up from work to take her to dinner? She didn't need both hands to count. Heck, she didn't even need one hand or a finger. No one had ever done something like this.

Dressed in his svelte black suit, crisp white shirt, and razor-sharp creased pants, Thane took her breath away. Jennifer couldn't stop the instant attraction. He had snared some part of her. It thrilled but equally scared her to be so caught up in outward appearances.

A dreamy sigh escaped from her. She gulped at the audible faux pas.

"I won't keep you out late, weeknight and all. Oh, by the way, Patti's with Thelma."

Her daughter's name dragged her back to reality, which tumbled its way into her consciousness. "Patti? Thelma? They knew about this?" Her scalp prickled as embarrassment washed over her face. This had to be a first where an aunt was in cahoots with her eight-year-old niece to fix up her widowed sister-in-law.

"Yep, and if we don't hurry, we won't make the reservations."

"I can't do this." Jennifer had to run after Thane's retreating figure. His open, long black coat whisked outward like a dark bird with his long strides. "Thane, I said you could do whatever it was you and Patti planned as long as it didn't get in my way. I've got things to do this evening."

Thane punched the elevator button and stood in front of one of the elevator doors. "It's Monday." He kept his focus on the silver-plated doors. "That means that you go grocery shopping, and then you go home to help Patti with her homework. Then you work until about midnight before you go to sleep."

He had to be guessing, or spying. Whatever it was, there were many nights that sleep eluded her. She'd stay up late watching TV or reading.

The elevator doors slid open and he stepped in. Jennifer hesitated; her instincts told her that if she threw away caution, there was no turning back. The doors began closing and Jennifer stared at Thane, her pulse keeping time with the passing seconds to bolster a few nuggets of courage to follow what her heart screamed for her to do.

Jennifer blew out a breath. What the heck, she deserved a night on the town. She slipped her hand in between the doors, halting their progress. "Fine, I'm all yours."

When Thane answered with a wide boyish grin, she felt the tension ease from her limbs.

She turned her back on him and stared avidly at the numbers of each floor flashing as the car descended. She felt so unequipped for this evening. What could she possibly talk about that would be of interest to an oversized bear of a man? Besides, was this a humanitarian effort on his part? His eyes, oh, Lordy, those soft, melting dark chocolate eyes got her every time. Well, not only that, but those long legs that swung out as he walked. She remembered that even in high school, slightly bowlegged boys earned a few pages in her diary.

She got off the elevator, but stepped aside for his lead. The way he strode through the lobby with his broad shoulders and arms swinging to match his wide gait drew inquisitive glances. From the women, it was more like admiring gazes, some drooling, and lots of throat clearing.

Oh, too bad for them. Or not.

Personally she liked the way he parted the way as he barreled toward the door.

"Um…where're we going?"

"A place called B. Smith's. Union Station." He looked over his shoulder.

Jennifer shrugged, recognizing that he expected her to protest. It would be too difficult pretending to dislike her favorite dishes at the famous hot spot. "Oh, my gosh. Is this for us?" She pointed at the shiny black limo, amazed to see a uniformed driver step out around the car and approach them. His tailored black suit and chauffeur's cap were delightful touches to her afternoon of fantasy.

"Ma'am." The chauffeur nodded to her. He opened the back door and waved his hand in a grand gesture for her to enter.

Jennifer stared openmouthed at the fairy-tale scene playing out in front of her. Thane's light touch to her elbow prompted her and she willingly slid into the car.

At the soft click of the closing door, Jennifer entered another world. One filled with luxury that made her feel as if she had stepped into a privileged class. The plush interior sported tan leather upholstery and a black lacquered finish. Across from where she sat, a fully stocked minibar, compact stereo, and television console fit in the wall separating them from the driver.

"This isn't you," she stated. It wasn't a criticism, simply a noticeable fact. Thane didn't appear to be a man who needed airs and graces for his identity.

"It's not for *me*."

Jennifer nibbled at her bottom lip to solve the puzzle that popped into her mind. "All this for me? It's a bit much and frankly, that makes me uncomfortable. I'm a plain girl, Mr. Jackson."

Thane cocked his head to the side. His eyes never left her face, but flicked back and forth as if reading a message.

"What're you looking at?"

"Just wondering what has you spooked."

Jennifer laughed, or more like snorted. "Tell me why I shouldn't be spooked. My neighbor, whom I don't really know, shows up at my job, although I never gave him the address, to go to a popular restaurant in a snazzy limo with heavily tinted windows, as if I'm a celebrity."

During her speech, Thane had helped himself to a club soda. He prepared one and offered the glass to her when she was finished. There was no answering smile, no intense stare, nothing that revealed how he had taken her honesty. Jennifer started doubting the harshness of her words. She hadn't meant to offend him, just to set him straight. No expectations spelled no disappointment.

"You're a lonely woman, Jen." He touched her hand. "Hear me out. Patti, Thelma, and probably any one of your friends would want you to relax and enjoy the evening. Don't read anything into my actions. Once you get to know me, you'll realize that I have no problem saying what's on my mind." He took a long swallow of the drink.

Jennifer watched his Adam's apple bob. What a beautiful neck, holding up a gorgeous head. Several responses came to mind, but her heart and mind had declared war.

Chapter 5

They rode to Union Station with no conversation between them. Several times she felt the limo brake from the heavy spots of afternoon rush-hour traffic and hordes of pedestrians marching to the subway and commuter trains. They passed the corner of Louisiana Avenue and Constitution Avenue, which framed one side of the capitol building. The historic architecture of the nation's political strength prominently marked the skyline. After years of working in the District of Columbia, Jennifer barely looked at the famous landmarks, noteworthy statues, or stately buildings.

The alternative meant facing Thane eye-to-eye, blushing like a schoolgirl. She settled on deliberately focusing on the Japanese-American memorial on her left.

The limo pulled up to the busy station's curb. Thane exited first, waving aside the chauffeur's assistance.

She gently pulled her hand away from his after she stood

on the sidewalk. No such luck. He tightened his grip, guiding her hand through the crook of his arm. After a quick pat on her hand, he tossed a smile her way. "Don't worry, the night of torture will be over soon enough."

Jennifer giggled, a mix of nervousness and embarrassment, and allowed her shoulders to relax. They headed for the west end of the station past boutique shops and other restaurants.

Obviously other diners had the same idea to have dinner at the highly reviewed restaurant. Thane spoke directly to the maitre d', his tone too low for her to discern. Within a few minutes, they were seated in a corner away from the bustling traffic of waiters and patrons.

"Welcome to B. Smith's. I'm Brett, your waiter this evening. Is this your first time dining with the B. Smith family?"

Jennifer waited to see if Thane admitted to making the restaurant his favorite hangout place. Instead he nodded and only then did Jennifer nod also.

"Wonderful. You've come at a good time."

Jennifer listened with half an ear as Brett filled them in on the details about catfish, Cajun ribs, and various appetizers.

She refocused enough to order an iced tea with lots of ice. To keep from looking at Thane she reread the oversized menu, although she had already selected the louisiana she-crab chowder.

"Are you on one of those diets?" Thane lingered over her face, down her chest, to the remaining portion of her body, before the table blocked his view. "Your face is a little thin, but you're filled out elsewhere."

Jennifer gulped the tea along with an ice cube. A throat-tickling cough erupted. Of all the nerve. She didn't know whether the thin face or the "filled out" comment offended her more. When her cough subsided to a minor throat scratching, she glared at her companion.

"And another thing, you get huffy easily." Then a huge grin broke out and he chuckled. "It means that it's easier to get under your skin."

Jennifer had to smile from his infectious banter. "How many siblings?"

"Three sisters, two older." He twirled his glass of beer. "They gave me hell, but then I got bigger and faster." He chuckled, and Jennifer realized that the sound had an immediate cheering effect. "And the younger one wanted to date my friends." He spread his hands with a victorious smile.

She raised her iced-tea glass to his and nodded. The only boy in the lot. Probably spoiled by his father and doted on by his mother.

"What're you thinking about?" he asked.

Jennifer blinked and shook her head.

"Oh, I thought you were thinking about me." His mouth lifted with a quirk as he boldly winked at her.

Brett arrived in time with their meals. No need to address the last remark.

As Jennifer thought about what to say next, she studied Thane sawing his meat off the spice-rubbed barbecue short ribs with fervent gusto. In between the mounds of meat, he popped forkfuls of mashed potatoes and greens into his mouth. It was easy to see why his appetite matched his solid, massive frame.

Meanwhile her chowder had a wonderful cream base with andouille sausage and heavy Cajun seasonings. She spooned the thick broth into her mouth, enjoying the spicy flavor.

"I bet you're overprocessing this evening." He looked at her as he paused with his glass halfway to his lips.

"I think I'm within my right to do so." She dabbed at her lips with the napkin. "It's not every day that I'm picked up at my job and taken to dinner."

"That's too bad." He pinned her with a stare. "Is that by your choice?"

Good question. It was by her will. What kind of mother would she be to go cavorting all over town with a man? "My daughter is my life."

He nodded. "She's a beautiful little girl. She thinks about you a lot."

Something in his tone caught her attention. "What has she said about me?" She didn't mean to ask the question in such a sharp tone, but she wasn't willing to apologize for it, either. Thane had touched a nerve and she could feel herself curl defensively against his gentle probing.

"Coffee or dessert?"

Jennifer didn't know whether he was deliberately ignoring her, but she answered with a shake of her head for neither choice.

Thane signaled to the waiter. "We'll take the check." He dug into the inner pocket of his jacket. "Patti worries about you. About whether you're happy."

"Go on." Her hands fidgeted, balling up the napkin. She leaned forward with her muscles as taut as her nerves.

He stilled her hand with his hand. "She just thinks that you should smile a bit more. Have fun. Go on trips like her other friends' parents."

Jennifer's stomach knotted and she exhaled with a soft hiss. "There won't be any trips. My husband died two years ago…." Her voice trailed into uncomfortable silence.

Thane's only immediate response was to rub the top of her hand with his thumb.

Brown skin next to brown skin, she noticed that they matched perfectly. She admired his short trimmed nails. Long fingers. Thick veins snaked up his hand leading to a muscled wrist.

What struck her even more was the warmth of his touch and its soothing effect. While she focused on his hand, she didn't have to acknowledge any signs of pity in his eyes.

"I can only imagine what you're feeling." His voice dropped to a soothing deep timbre. "I think Patti has high hopes for you. Not necessarily with me, mind you," he added hurriedly when she jerked away from his hand. "For her, happiness means sharing your joy with someone."

"I'm sharing it with her and only her. And that's the end of this discussion." Jennifer wanted to retreat. She stood to give the signal that the evening was over. She slipped on her coat, placing her entire concentration on buttoning the full-length wool blend.

She raised her hand when he stood. "I'll see myself home. Thank you, Thane. I'll tell Patti that I had a wonderful time."

"Sounds like you'll be lying." His eyes narrowed and he gestured for her to proceed to the exit.

"Not at all. It was a pleasure," she said placatingly. He didn't understand that it was more than pleasure that warmed her. Grateful that he was walking behind her, she allowed the small smile to linger.

Outside, the evening bustle of patrons hadn't subsided. The temperature had a frigid bite and Jennifer pulled her coat tighter around her. She looked up and down the street for a taxi, praying that she wouldn't have to swallow her pride and ask for a ride.

On cue, a black-and-white cab pulled up and Jennifer exhaled a grateful sigh. She turned to offer Thane an apology and a departing speech.

Thane signaled to his driver, who was parked across the street. The limo pulled up behind the taxi.

"Thane—"

He touched her arm. "You win, Jen. I'll let you call an end to this evening. Maybe, the next time…? I still have two more wishes to fulfill."

Jennifer opened the taxi door and stepped in before opening the window. "No more wishes. I played along and I appreciate all of this." She tilted her head at the limo and the restaurant. "But I don't want you to get the wrong idea. Nothing will come of this."

Thane hadn't moved a muscle. She couldn't understand why he stood there staring at her. Maybe she had something stuck on her face.

"Jen."

"Yes?"

"Get over yourself. It was a fun evening for you and for me." He turned and walked over to the limo and got in.

Jennifer's face burned with embarrassment and it didn't help that the taxi driver actually snickered. She gave him her address and settled back, keeping her eyes averted from his rearview mirror.

Much later that night, after Patti was in bed, she retreated to her room and stayed up looking at one of the late-night talk shows. No doubt about it, she'd really loused up the night.

She listened with half an ear to Angela Bassett talk about her latest movie. Bits of tonight's conversation replayed in her head. Maybe later, after a few more months, she could appreciate everyone's efforts. But she couldn't dismiss the traitorous thoughts that it was too soon since her husband's passing. Besides, her daughter did need her. Damn it. She punched her pillow before readjusting it behind her.

She parted her hair into small sections and fastened the edges of her hair around rollers.

Her life had been so different two years ago. In a snap, she could no longer take her routine for granted.

The doctors had told her that her husband had died of an aneurysm. A freaking blood clot at thirty years old.

Eight years of marriage and an extra four in college, those were the days and memories that she clung to each day.

Her parents had enrolled her in a support group. Thelma, her sister-in-law, had moved in with her for a few months when her depression was at its worst. Guilt snapped at her conscience at the thought of Patti not being able to rely on her mother at such a critical time. Slowly she had revived her energy to continue and to be a mother to her only child.

Jennifer rolled the last section of hair around the pink roller and snapped it into place. The credits rolled for the talk show, marking another night that she was up late into the early hours of the next day. She took the silver-framed picture on her night table and stroked its surface, wishing that she could feel the contours of Wilfred's face once more. Tears welled. The lump in her throat made her gulp repeatedly as she struggled to control her emotions.

Wilfred faced the camera with a broad smile and outstretched arms. He'd called out to her to join him in front of the Toronto Zoo sign. The deep timbre of his Bostonian roots popped up in certain words and she loved the way he called her Jenny.

The unshed tears blinded her. She snuggled down beneath the covers, and blinked to allow the tears the freedom to run their course off to the side of her face, wetting her pillow.

Jen.

She heard, or more like imagined, her name being called. A strong image of Thane sitting across from her at the restaurant with a huge grin replayed in her memory. She could hear the deep voice say her name with his touching familiarity.

There had to be something wrong in fantasizing about one man and at the same time thinking about her deceased husband.

Plumping her pillow, she tossed and turned to her other side. Thane Jackson would have to take his one-man show to someone who could appreciate the attentions. As for Patti, she must buy a doll or something to keep her little girl focused on other things, instead of her mother's love life…or lack thereof.

Chapter 6

Thane hadn't seen his neighbor since that fateful night. He sensed that she took extreme measures to avoid him, even while he aimed for every advantage to bump into her. Even Patti wasn't outdoors for him to get a report of the home front.

He'd told himself that he was only doing a favor for a little girl. Yet, the moment that he saw Jen and the way her face lit up when he popped up at her job, he threw out his altruistic intentions. Pure and simple, he wanted Jen all to himself.

"Yo, man."

Thane snapped back to the present. "I'm listening." He took a swig of his beer and let the bitter, smooth liquid cool the length of his throat. He cast a sideways glance at his buddy. "You're still crying about the bet you lost to Willie."

"I wouldn't be crying if I'd just ignored your messed-up prediction."

Thane grinned at Malik. Ever since the Super Bowl game,

Malik never failed to remind him on a daily basis that he'd lost a sizable bet to their other work buddy, Willie.

Thane signaled to the bartender. "Get another beer for my friend, will ya?"

"You think that will shut me up?"

"Nope, but for a few seconds you've got to close that yap to drink."

Malik took the green-tinted bottle and kissed the brim before taking a long drink. He burped and then popped a few peanuts into his mouth. "So, who's got you all tied up in knots? You keep spacing out on me. What's up with that?"

"Man, you won't believe it. Lots on my mind." Thane filled his friend in on his latest volunteer job as a little girl's human-sized genie.

"Get the hell outta here." Malik's laughter rumbled loud and clear, drawing the inquisitive stares of the bar's patrons. "Wait till Willie and the guys hear about this." He slapped the bar counter, punctuating the roar of his laughter.

Thane groaned and took a sip. The men at the station would be riding his back after Malik delivered his colorful version.

"That's the cute but definitely uptight one who moved in a few months back. Figured you'd be hittin' on her sooner than later."

Thane growled. "Don't be so crude. She moved there after her husband died. Guess she couldn't live in the same house. Wanted a brand-new start."

"Man, that whole husband dying thing is deep." Malik patted his chest and then rubbed his stomach, shaking his head. "To be so young. Damn." He chugged a long drink, followed by his customary burp. "You know that means it'll be difficult to get close to her. If you do it too fast, then you'll come off looking like a dog in heat. If you do it too slow…I guess there's nothing wrong with taking your time. But you know how women are."

"That would be your department, player. One expensive ex and three women on rotation, I should get my notebook when your class is in session."

"Laugh all you want to, but I know you want to be like me." Malik drained his beer. "Okay, let's go to your place."

Thane paid the tab and slid off the barstool. "You're not coming home with me."

"Whatever. See ya there." Malik jingled his car keys and headed for the exit.

Thane chuckled.

On the drive home as he followed Malik, he was always thankful that he had such a loyal friend. They were more like brothers and it was Malik's protective nature that saved him from the gut-wrenching effects of his share of bad relationships. Malik came armed with cynicism, while he held on to the old-fashioned notion that every man had a special someone out in the world for him.

Malik constantly called him a fool for his romantic notions. Scolding him soundly for not paying attention to the high divorce rates. Maybe that's why he didn't bother to admit to his friend how much he looked forward to seeing Jen and her daughter. He had no reservations when he decided to embark on his self-appointed mission. As a matter of fact, an unusual cockiness gave him the courage to roll out the first phase of his special-ops procedure at a restaurant—neutral territory.

Unable to slow down his feelings once he made the commitment, Thane had spent last week wondering what Jen did during the day and in the evenings, when he saw her laden with grocery bags and Patti skipping at her side. He had even tried getting his nephews and niece to come over so that he would have an excuse to see her. But they had violin lessons. He would've taken them from class early and headed for Jen's, if facing his sister's wrath didn't give him pause.

Malik pulled into the parking lot in front of the town houses. Thane automatically looked up at the windows of the end unit. Jen's lights were on. He glanced at his watch as he walked up to his door, wondering if it was her dinnertime.

"Yo, man. Go knock." Malik stood at his door, waiting for him to approach.

"Shh. Keep your voice down. I'm not going over there. She made it clear."

"You know, sometimes you can be such a wimp. Big man and no bite." Malik stomped off and headed for the familiar rust-brown door. "Take a few pointers from me."

"Malik," Thane hissed.

It was only six o'clock, but with the end of daylight saving, it was already dark. Only a few residents were out walking their dogs. He didn't want too many witnesses when Jen would turn those dark brown baby-doll eyes on him. In her no-nonsense voice she'd set him in his place. It had never happened, but he had a feeling.

He hurried after Malik, who sped up his pace toward the door. "Malik, this isn't funny. I knew you would do some mess like this."

"Don't I stop you when you're about to do something stupid?" Malik threw over his shoulder.

Thane wanted to slap the bald head in front of him. Malik was at the door and had turned around with a wide, mischievous grin. "Don't you think that it's odd that I'm helping you get this woman?"

Thane's heart pumped, the adrenaline racing through his body. He didn't really care what Malik had to say.

Silently, he urged Malik to knock before he lost his nerve and retreated for his house. In the meantime, he'd continue pretending.

Malik folded his arms, looking like a stocky wrestler. "I see what she does to you when you talk about her. You get a little giddy, looking like a space cadet. Man, you wear your heart on your sleeve. Not always a good thing. Take me for instance—"

The door snapped open. Jennifer stood in the doorway. Her gaze immediately fastened on Thane. "Gentlemen, I'm not sure why you feel it necessary to have your discussion on my front steps." She turned her attention toward Malik. "And who're you?"

Malik grinned, overtly sizing up the full length of her. "I'm Malik, Thane's brother, who was abandoned by the family. Didn't he tell you?" Malik offered his hand and pumped Jennifer's.

"No, he didn't. And from the sound of things, you like being the center of attention."

"Yep. May we come in? It's cold out here."

Jennifer stepped back, opening the door wider. She didn't bother to look at Malik when he walked past her. Thane hoped that she would not only look his way, but that her look would not harbor any of the irritation that was now directed at his friend's aggressive behavior.

However, disappointment nagged when she kept her eyes downcast. He slowly walked past her. His eyes never left the top of the ponytail holder, willing her to meet his gaze. Her soft floral scent perfumed the air and he inhaled to keep a small part of her close at hand. "Hi, Jen," he all but whispered.

She raised her head, but her eyes never quite climbed to meet his. "Hi, Thane."

"I'll just sit over here," Malik piped up from across the

room. He was already sprawled in the middle section of an L-shaped sectional couch.

Thane waited until Jen took her place at one end. "Where's Patti?" He looked toward the hallway, expecting his pint-sized friend to emerge.

"She went to the library with Thelma and her kids." Jennifer looked up at the wall where an old-fashioned clock hung with a swinging pendulum. "She should be home soon."

"Well, in that case, I'm going to say so long and mosey on outta here." Malik stood and boldly winked at Thane. "It'll give you two kids a chance to talk over a few things." He turned to Jennifer. "Nice meeting you. I hope that you'll join us for game night over at Thane's parents'. It's a once-a-month thing."

"Malik." Thane could have kicked his friend, who wasn't born with a filter over his trap. "Jen…Jennifer may not want to come. I…I may not even go this month." His family, especially his sisters, had put several of his past girlfriends through some serious mind games. None had survived. No loss there.

"Cut it out. You know darn well that your mother would have a fit if you didn't show up. You'll go, won't you, Jennifer?" He pointed at Thane. "He wouldn't be any good if you didn't come. I mean, like right now, he walks around the station like he lost his best friend. You—"

Thane sprang up from the couch. "That's enough." He grabbed Malik by the arm and pushed him toward the door. "It's time for us to go."

Malik might have thought he was winning over Jennifer, but Thane could see the look of puzzlement on her face. As far as he was concerned, Jennifer appeared to be newly suspicious of him. He gave his friend an extra shove out the door.

"Thane," Jennifer called, "would you stay? Please."

Thane didn't speak. The fact that he remained while Malik waved from the sidewalk spoke volumes.

Jennifer ran a nervous hand over her hair. Thane's back had stiffened when she called him. Not a very good reaction. But she had to tell him that she'd changed her mind about him, about them. The fear of getting in over her head still controlled her.

Each morning when he headed out for work, she wanted to call out to him. Instead she remained silent behind the sheer curtain, with her thoughts running through such a scenario in her head.

Somehow, in that one evening, over a candlelit dinner, a tiny bit of magic had occurred. The stirrings of some buried emotion had poked its head through the muck of her depression and anger. Rational behavior couldn't be expected when she'd tossed logic aside.

Not to mention the physical reactions that left her guilty and overflowing with embarrassment. She had no control over the warm tingly sensations that flooded her deep in her stomach to her lower regions. All it took was his gaze, like now. "I'm almost finished cooking. Would you stay for dinner?" She licked her lips and blinked to break the moment.

"Thank you, but I don't want to intrude." He offered a rueful grin. "I guess it's too late for that."

She smiled back and shrugged, beckoning him to follow her to the kitchen.

"I won't stay for dinner, but I don't mind keeping you company in the kitchen." He moved to the other side of the kitchen to sit at the countertop.

"I owe you an apology." Jennifer opened a medium-sized pot and stirred the contents. Her spaghetti sauce had thickened nicely. In another pot, the pasta bubbled. A few more minutes and it would be ready. She wished that he'd stay for dinner.

"Why?"

She started, for an instant wondering if he was questioning her sudden longing for him to stay put. "I realized that I was very rude after everything you'd done."

"Yes, you were." He winked to soften his remark. His stomach growled. "Okay, I accept your dinner invitation."

Got him. Jennifer promptly pulled out an extra bowl with spoon and fork. "No arguments from the peanut gallery."

"You're very assertive after a full day's work."

"Maybe it's because I had a glass of this fabulous wine that I bought last week." She opened the refrigerator and pointed. "Want a glass?"

Thane shook his head. "I've had a beer and that's enough for me, thank you."

Silence descended on the couple. Jennifer bustled back and forth from the kitchen to the table. She shooed Thane's offer of assistance. Finally finished with the table setting, she stepped back to survey the scene. Everything was in its place.

"Food looks great."

"Thanks."

Just then the front door swung open and Patti came running into the house. Along the way, she dropped her coat, then gloves and hat. She pulled up short when she saw Thane.

"T.J.!" She ran and jumped into his waiting arms, which enclosed her in a bear hug.

Jennifer witnessed the tender scene, forbidding any thoughts of what could be. She only wanted to live in the present. And in the present, she was quite contented.

"Hey, lady," her sister-in-law greeted.

Jennifer hugged Thelma and then her niece and nephew.

In a matter of minutes, the once quiet house was filled with constant chatter and warmth that could only be generated by a close-knit family.

Out of the corner of her eye, Jennifer noticed Thane shifting uncomfortably before sliding off the stool. "Please don't leave. Not yet."

Thelma stopped her conversation with her children and craned her neck around the tall potted plant. "Thane? Didn't know you were here. Why are you hiding in the corner?"

Patti had detached herself from Thane, but with everyone's attention zeroed in on him, she came over to save him.

"We're about to have dinner. Are you staying?" Any other night Jennifer would be grateful for her sister-in-law's company. Tonight wasn't the case, especially after she had worked up the nerve to invite him to dinner. Heck, the real challenge had been to listen to Malik and Thane's discussion in front of her door. She had had to take several deep breaths before opening the door.

Thelma looked over to Thane. "Nope, we won't be staying."

"Aw, Mom, but it's spaghetti," Thelma's daughter complained.

"I'll make spaghetti, okay? Now, go and get in the car."

"That's okay, Mom," her son replied. "Yours isn't like Aunt Jenny's."

"Well," Thelma huffed, a small smile twitching on her lips. "Come on, guys. For that remark, no one's sharing my peanut brittle. Thane, it's nice to see you…here." She gathered up her family, kissed her niece, and left.

Jennifer stared at the door, waiting for her embarrassment to subside. Thane had his crazy friend, Malik, to deal with and she guessed that on her side, she had to deal with Thelma.

"Let's eat." She sat at the head of the table and watched

Patti constantly offer smiles to Thane. It made Jennifer happy to see her daughter's face light up. It would seem that the Stone women had fallen under the spell of the neighborhood firefighter.

Chapter 7

"Thanks for staying."

"Patti's down?"

"Yep." Jennifer handed Thane a mug of coffee and settled in the chair across from him. "I want to talk about the other night."

Thane sipped his coffee, waiting.

"Why did you do it? Take me out." She looked down at her naked hands, no jewelry or nail polish. There wasn't much time for those things. Who was she fooling? She had no desire to be stylish beyond her work needs. Coming home to a dark house and sleeping in her bed with no familiar body to snuggle against sapped her motivation.

"Because I wanted to."

Thane had moved closer and Jennifer automatically stiffened. "That makes no sense."

"May I?" Thane turned her chin until she faced him.

Jennifer's heart thumped, anticipation building. He lowered his face toward her, hesitating for a brief instant. When she felt his lips touch hers, a gasp stuck in her throat as her body tingled with its own electricity. Surrendering to his probing tongue, she enjoyed his exploration, hoping that he had no intention of stopping soon.

Just when she thought that she would pass out in a puddle on the living room floor, he pulled her into a tight embrace. Jennifer threw back her head, gasping from the sweet sensation of his soft kisses on her lips trailing down her throat. He pulled away from her.

Jennifer blinked to clear her head and to stem the raw physical response that Thane's kiss elicited.

She wanted him now in her living room. She was ready to throw down and get busy with Thane. Even though he was only stroking her hair aside, she pushed him away. "Whoa. I think it's time for you to leave."

Thane didn't seem surprised by her request. "No prob. But there's more where that came from. I want to get to know you, Jen. Don't run from it." He tapped the tip of her nose.

The first thing was to get used to Thane's bluntness. Jennifer escorted him to the door. The desire for this broad-shouldered hunk of man hadn't subsided. She wondered how she'd sleep tonight.

"May I call you?"

"Sure." Jennifer couldn't handle the body contact, but she wasn't ready to relinquish the budding relationship.

Instead of her usual cotton nightdress, Jennifer slipped on her silk nightie that came to just below her behind. The soft, slippery material draped her body, clinging to her breasts and hips. She turned off the light beside her bed and then snuggled under the covers.

A few minutes later, she kicked off the covers with a frustrated sigh because sleep was so far away. Instead, she couldn't get her mind off the dark brown handsome face of her neighborhood firefighter. Jennifer bit her lip as the unfamiliar quivering between her legs ignited a yearning, so sexual and new that she rolled her pillow over her mouth to subdue a moan.

What was the matter with her that all it took was to picture his square jaw, full bottom lip, and pencil-thin moustache that framed his top lip to make her nipples tighten?

In slow motion she pulled up her negligee, and her fingers trailed a seductive path up her thigh. The primal hunger that her body felt drove her to distraction. She could pick up the phone and invite Thane over, or tiptoe over to his place for a late-night booty call.

Her breasts ached at the fantasy and she circled a taut nipple with her finger, playing with the silk fabric against the sensitive mound. Between her thighs, deep within her, she continued to pulsate, alive and wanting for attention.

With the same boyfriend-turned-husband, Jennifer didn't possess a wide sexual experience. Not that she was complaining. What she had shared with her husband was mutually satisfying, comforting, and sweet.

As her hand brushed against her underwear, playing with the laced fringe around the waist, Jennifer boldly stepped up to the new phase. In her new enlightened place, she had to take charge and go after her destiny, even if she didn't have a clue how to do this.

Jennifer balled up the comforter and squeezed it between her legs. She looked over to the nightstand, hesitating. Safely locked in her drawer was a birthday gift from one of her friends, batteries included.

"Oh, what the heck!" She leaned over, turned on the light,

and unlocked the drawer. With the bright gleam of the hundred-watt bulb, she squinted fiercely at the bumpy length of the vibrator. "I hope there're instructions."

She pulled out the sex toy, turning it around for inspection. Spying the on/off button, she flicked it.

"Aaah!" Jennifer dropped the vibrator on her lap, amazed at the actual feel and sound. She turned it off to give herself a minute to stop the erupting fit of giggles.

She flicked off the light, preferring to do her business in the dark. Once she'd regained some semblance of control, she slid out of her underwear. Flicking on the vibrator, Jennifer had to calm her rapid breathing and then refocus on Thane's muscular body to get back into the mood.

"Mom?" Patti opened the door. "Can I sleep with you? I had a nightmare." She pushed open the door wide. The hallway light surrounded her little frame in an angelic glow.

Jennifer hurriedly turned off the now offending object. Her hands shook, her face flushed.

"What's that noise?"

"Nothing. Probably the heater."

Patti ran over to the bed and jumped on while Jennifer switched the vibrator to the hand closer to the edge of the bed. Keeping an eye on Patti she let it fall under the bed. She'd better remember to pick it up before her inquisitive daughter played treasure hunt.

Her daughter slid under the covers and tossed and turned on the other side of the bed, getting comfortable among the pillows. Meanwhile Jennifer felt around the bed for her underwear. Her hand closed around the small item and she scooted out of the bed and headed for the bathroom.

Under the unforgiving bathroom light, she leaned against the sink looking into the mirror. Her dark eyes shone back at her in a face framed with pink sponge rollers. Suddenly, she laughed softly. "Well, I tried," she told her reflection. "That's got to be worth something."

Jennifer fought the stray thoughts about why Thane hadn't called her. She looked down at the papers in front of her. Work still had to be done and she had the upcoming regional banking conference in Chicago to host.

Her phone rang. She read the display and swallowed a curse. "Hey, Sylvia. What's up?" She wondered what HR wanted.

"Got some good news for you," Sylvia said. "You got the interview at the Jacksonville location."

Jennifer didn't respond.

"They will fly you out at month's end."

Jennifer glanced at the calendar, mentally counting the days—fifteen days away. It had been three months since she'd applied for the director of membership at the company's other site in Florida. With Thane on her mind, she had swept those plans out of sight.

"Any questions for me?" Sylvia prompted.

"Um…no. I'll need to make arrangements for my daughter."

"I'll find out the details and let you know, as soon as I can."

Jennifer hung up the phone and stared at her computer monitor. A half-written letter awaited her attention. She groaned and then shook her head. This job meant a more secure future for Patti and her. She typed a couple of words to the letter soliciting a sponsor for the conference.

The cursor blinked at her, waiting for her input. She didn't owe Thane anything. If he called her, she would go out with him. But her plans were hers. She had to remain focused and dismiss the new feelings that rose despite her attempts for self-control.

* * *

Thane pulled out the worn piece of paper from his pocket. Patti had slipped it to him when he was at dinner at her house. She hadn't lost faith in his ability to make her mother happy. He envied her optimism. He knew that Jennifer struggled with herself when it concerned him. But even though he knew this, it didn't stop him from kissing her and he loved every minute of it.

Her sexy brown eyes sucked him in, making him feel short of breath. Nothing tasted sweeter than her beautiful mouth.

"Enough! Damn!" Malik smacked Thane on the back of his neck. "I know you're thinking about that woman again." He soaped up the front of the fire truck in wide sudsy circles.

"Mind your business," Thane growled. He dipped the stiff bristled brush into the bucket and scrubbed a tire.

"Yo, Willie, I think somebody has whipped our boy, if you know what I mean."

Willie and some of Thane's other coworkers gathered. With no emergency calls, the firehouse had to be cleaned. The other firefighters rotated the duties of cooking, cleaning, washing. Thane preferred washing the fire trucks. It fulfilled a childlike passion and fascination with the powerful machines. When his father had brought him to the station, he immediately ran to the trucks and climbed in, imagining the day when he would ride out of the firehouse.

Now the men took an impromptu break to hear Malik's story. "Fill us in."

Thane turned a threatening glare at Malik. Too bad his friend was bald, he would have loved to shave a path right down the center of his head when he fell asleep. But he could do the same with one eyebrow.

For the next half hour, he endured his coworkers' teasing.

Even the women didn't show any mercy, declaring that they wanted to meet the woman who had managed to capture Thane's heart. He waved off their ribbing and walked away to find a quiet spot, opting for an empty ambulance in the bay.

"I'm not washing this truck by myself, Thane. Get your butt over here," Malik shouted over the din of the water hose rinsing off the truck.

Thane merely waved at him, justified that this was perfect punishment for Malik.

His mind worked hard to find a way to make Patti's second wish come true. The child had a wonderful imagination, but it sure did challenge him. He sighed and refolded the paper.

Think, Thane.

Chapter 8

Patti liked helping her aunt Thelma with the dishes. Next to her home, she enjoyed visiting her aunt's home. Her house looked like all the other houses on the block, but her aunt had planted lots of neat flowers along the driveway and then prickly green shrubs along the front of the house. In the backyard, there was a swing set with a sliding board, monkey bars, and a tire at the end of a thick rope.

Hearing her cousins laugh, Patti peeped into the family room. Brother and sister lay on the floor watching a cartoon of a rabbit running away from a man with an axe. Patti wrinkled her nose in distaste. She was too old for that nonsense.

"Hey, Patti, want to help me?"

Patti turned a grateful smile to her aunt and headed into the kitchen. Her aunt was the neatest person and always talked to her like a real person, not like a little kid. Besides, it was fun talking with Aunt Thelma. Patti could tell her things that she couldn't tell her mother.

"You know that your mother won't be picking you up until seven. She had to work late tonight, kiddo." Thelma took the soapy plate from her niece and rinsed it before setting it on the drain board.

"It's okay. Mommy works hard. Sometimes I think she works too hard." Patti soaped a glass, being careful since it was slippery from the suds. "I know she's tired, even though she pretends."

"I know what you mean. She's lucky to have you be there for her."

Patti thought about that statement for a moment. She had to agree with her aunt because although her aunt was alone, her husband was still alive. Her aunt had told her that they had a divorce, but her cousins still belonged to both of them. Lucky. "Sometimes I think that I'm getting in her way. I try to do everything that I'm supposed to. I wonder what I could do to make it better. Could I have helped Daddy if I told him that I loved him lots and lots of times?"

Thelma stopped wiping the plate in her hand and studied Patti. "You are a marvelous little girl. Your mother's lucky to have you in her life."

"Really?" Patti's face radiated with the thought that her mother could be proud of her. Aunt Thelma always made her feel special. Chatting with her aunt was like having a little part of her daddy. They resembled each other, but what she liked most were the childhood stories Aunt Thelma shared about her daddy.

"Oh, honey, give me a hug. You're like a daughter to me. I would do anything for you, even getting Thane and your mom together." She nudged Patti and winked. "By the way, how's that going?"

With the last dish washed and stacked, Patti followed her aunt into the family room. Her aunt's routine was to look at the seven o'clock game shows. Although she couldn't answer any of the questions, she would sit quietly on the couch as her aunt twirled her finger around the fat plaits in her head and played with her children, making sure no one felt left out.

"Aunt Thelma, I gave T.J. his second wish and he said it was hard. He hasn't called my mom yet." Patti worried over whether she should change her wish.

Thelma gave her a quick hug. "He'll figure out something. What was it, by the way?"

"You know how the prince has to kiss the princess awake?"

Thelma nodded.

"That's what he has to do."

"Aah." Thelma kissed her forehead. "He's right. That's going to be a doozy, knowing your mom. But I can't wait. Good for you."

Patti glowed under the praise. Maybe she should start thinking about the third wish. She settled in the crook of her aunt's arms and listened to the game show host talk about the parting gifts.

"Get your butt out of that ambulance." Malik thumped on the door. "I need to get to Gaithersburg and I'll need a ride."

"What the heck happened to your car?"

"Brenda's got it."

"Why do you let these women that you barely know hold on to your car?" Malik couldn't help being the generous guy, but it inevitably got him into trouble. "One day I won't be around to bail you out."

Thane pulled up to his town house after shuttling Malik from one place to the other. Most families were in for the night and the parking lot was full. No lights were on at Jen's. He wondered where she was. It was a weeknight. Patti had school tomorrow. She couldn't be at work at this time of the night.

"It's not my business," he muttered as he walked into his house. He switched on one light and aimed for the refrigerator for a cool beer. Dinner didn't appeal to him. Taking his beer, he sat at the dining table and began opening his mail, then separating it into various piles. An opened bag half-filled with potato chips tempted him. He grabbed a handful and chomped. So much for dinner.

A worn envelope caught his eye. Actually it was the familiar tight, short handwriting. His father's. Thane stared off into the distance, thinking about when he last saw his father. Their final argument had not been resolved over the last six months.

Thane tore the end of the envelope and tapped the hand-written letter into his hand. As he began to read, his shoulders relaxed and his frown evaporated. His mother had taken the high road to be the go-between and she had started the letter off with an admonishment for him holding a grudge.

But it was more than a grudge. His father wanted him to quit his profession. The only career that he'd ever wanted and worked so hard at to be a success. It didn't matter with his father, who couldn't understand why he didn't want a desk job, to wear a designer suit, or be on somebody's board chewing on a cigar.

His eyes read over his mother's loving words and then he came to his father's choppy style. There weren't any of the terms of endearment that decorated his mother's words. Instead his father came to the point. Thane had to come home for dinner at the end of the month to make amends.

One thing he could count on from his father was his stubborn will. He flicked aside the envelope with an exasperated sigh. He'd think on it.

A muffled intermittent ringing distracted him. He looked up, wondering what was the source of the sound. Getting up from the table, he grabbed his beer and looked out the windows facing his backyard. Nothing out of the ordinary caught his attention as he surveyed the balcony with the barbecue grill and outdoor dinette set.

"Damn!" he swore, dropping the bottle at his feet.

The upturned bottle leaked its contents unnoticed onto the floor. Thane ran out of his house, his heart already pounding in rhythm with his feet. He leaped over the three steps leading up to Jennifer's house.

The smoke alarm still blared. Thank goodness there was no sign of smoke. He sniffed the air and pounded on the door. No response. Trying the doorknob, he knocked again, this time calling her name.

Not waiting any longer, he made his way to the rear of the house. The balcony door was opened and a small whiff of black smoke curled and danced away in the air. He ran up the stairs leading to the balcony and entered Jennifer's dining room.

"Jen!"

"Thane!" Jennifer's voice sounded overhead before he heard her run down the stairs. "What are you doing here?" Overcome by a fit of coughing, she stumbled onto the balcony. "Can you do something with that smoke alarm?"

Thane walked over and disabled the alarm. "What happened here?"

Jennifer looked over her shoulder. "I wanted to heat up a frozen pasta packet. So I put it in the pot to boil and went to take a shower."

Thane walked into the kitchen, waiting for the story that would explain the chaos that he saw before him.

"When I came out of the shower, the alarm was screaming. I ran into the kitchen only to see that the wrong burner was turned on and my plastic cutting board was a toxic inferno."

"At least you had a fire extinguisher." Thane shook his head as he picked up a few charred remnants of the board. The acrid smell of smoke tickled his throat and he had to blink rapidly to ease the burning in his eyes.

Jennifer coughed and walked over to the balcony, breathing deeply. "You could hear the alarm?"

"Yes. I'm glad to know that your alarm works."

"Spoken like a true firefighter. Well, looks like all the excitement is over." She pulled her robe closed.

The sound of light footsteps running down the hall made them turn their heads.

An idea formed and quickly took hold in Thane's head. "Look, Jen, do me a favor."

Jennifer turned, waiting for him to continue.

"Lie on the floor. Right there." He pointed at a spot in front of the kitchen. "Hurry. I'll explain later."

"Mommy?" Patti's voice called hesitantly from the top of the stairs.

Jennifer looked at Thane and then up at the stairs.

"Shh," Thane urged. He motioned for her to come over. "Lie down." Thane looked up and saw Patti's feet appear on the steps. He leaned over Jen's face. "Close your eyes. Work with me."

She gave a slight nod, and a look of understanding marked her face.

"Mommy?" Patti now ran down the remaining stairs. Her voice grew worried. "Mommy? Thane? Where's Mommy?"

She looked down and after the sight of her mother on the floor sank in, she leaped off the steps to the bottom.

"Mommy, wake up."

Thane tapped Jennifer's face. "She'll be okay. See? Touch here, near her neck. Feel her pulse. It was just a little too much smoke."

"Well, blow in her mouth." Patti looked up at Thane, her dark eyes filled with worry.

"Hmm. Think that will work? She's breathing on her own. Maybe she's just asleep. I wonder what could wake her up."

Patti settled next to her mother and took her hand. She rubbed it, talking softly to her. Thane recognized a poem that Patti had learned from school.

"A kiss. That's what she needs."

Thane looked surprised. "Are you sure? I wouldn't want to waste a kiss if your mother doesn't respond." He looked down and saw the edge of Jennifer's mouth lift slightly. "Besides, what if she has bad breath?" Thane wrinkled his nose.

Patti giggled. "Mommy never has bad breath. She eats lots of those little white mints. They look like aspirin to me."

"Okay, then. I'll take your word for it and kiss her. But if she's got garlic breath and I fall over from the smell, I'm going to get you." He leaned all the way over Jennifer's face, holding his face a few inches above her. "Lips look a bit chapped," he complained. "Hope I don't cut my lips on that!"

Patti scrambled up and ran into the kitchen to the cupboard next to the fridge. Thane wondered what she was up to until he saw her pull out the Crisco tin.

"Here, this might help."

Thane bit back a chuckle. "How innovative of you." He opened the tin and scooped out a large fingerful of the vegetable shortening. "Now, let's see." He liberally coated Jennifer's lips, noting that she was peeping under partially closed eyes. "All done. I think she looks fantastic."

"Yuck. I wouldn't want to kiss her now."

"I know what you mean. I don't, either. But I must save her. By the way, this would be the second wish."

Patti nodded.

Thane kissed Jennifer, keeping it chaste since her eight-year-old daughter was propped on her elbows, stretched on the floor paying close attention.

Jennifer fluttered her eyes with exaggerated effect. She groaned and moved her head from side to side, muttering. Thane leaned back on his knees, enjoying Patti's look of concentration.

"I think you've got to kiss her again. The first one only worked a little bit."

Thane didn't particularly relish the thought of having the shortening on his lips. But he wouldn't pass up the opportunity to experience that giddy quiver of excitement when their lips touched. "Let's try on her forehead."

He offered a soft kiss in the middle of her forehead. "Hmm. I may have to do a special thing."

"What's that?" Patti craned her neck, her eyes wide with wonder.

"You'll see." Thane winked at the little girl and then bent over and blew gently in Jennifer's right ear.

A giggle erupted from the prone figure.

He blew again.

This time Jennifer crunched her body, twisting to get away from Thane. She rubbed her ear against her shoulder. "Stop. I'm revived. Honest."

"Mommy." Patti flung her body over her mother and they collapsed on the floor.

Thane chose a chair nearby and watched the tender scene.

More than once, he observed mother and child, noting their bond and fierce loyalty to each other.

Patti's resemblance to her mother was remarkable. As they found each other, he admired Jennifer's profile and matched Patti's younger features to her mother's. If it wasn't inappropriate, he would have slid over to the couple and shared the family hug with them.

"Okay, ladies, it's time to clean up the mess."

"Oh, Thane, thank you for coming over and saving the day. And thank you so much for the shortening on my lips." Jennifer grimaced at Thane. "This smell is awful. Now that the smoke has cleared, would you fix the smoke alarm?" She fanned the air.

"Sure. How about coming to my place?" Thane shifted his weight, feeling suddenly nervous. "I've got beds in the other rooms. You know, for my nieces and nephews." He jammed his hands into his pocket, his heart hammering against his chest. He wished that she would say something. Actually, he hoped that she would say yes.

"I don't know, Thane. I don't want to inconvenience you."

"Oh, Mommy, let's do it." Patti jumped up and started dancing around the room.

If he wouldn't look foolish, Thane would have joined Patti's exuberant team and jumped around pleading for Jennifer to say yes.

"Okay, okay," Jennifer relented, eyes locked with Thane's while Patti whooped and ran upstairs to get a change of clothes.

Jennifer made sure that Patti was settled in bed before tiptoeing out of the room. Thane had invited her to share coffee and conversation with him in the living room. Sleep eluded her and there was the more obvious reason that she wanted some quiet time with him. And here she was on his turf.

"Is Patti comfortable?"

Jennifer walked over to where Thane sat. A coffee tray with cookies and a carafe sat on the center table. "She's knocked out. Poor thing, all this excitement…" Jennifer shook her head.

"Help yourself. I'm glad you took me up on my offer."

Soft lights, jazz playing in the background, Jennifer felt the tense moments from earlier ease away. She sank into the love seat, the same one where Thane sat, and busied herself with making his coffee.

"You've got a good sense of style. I like your decorations."

"I wish I could take the credit. It's my sisters who came in here and made it into what you see." He sipped his coffee. "Of course, I gave them my credit card and now I'm still paying the bill."

Jennifer chuckled. "Well, I think it's great." She meant it. The copper tones and gold accents with tan-colored furniture captured the manliness of its owner, but also added a touch of elegance.

Thane set down his coffee mug and placed a warm hand on the back of her neck. Jennifer could have purred under this attention. "I think we should talk," she began, her voice a mere whisper.

"Go ahead." His fingers kept up their magic on her muscles.

"Is this a game to you? You know. The dinner date thing, then getting close to my daughter. I don't know if I want or need someone in my life." She turned to him, her knee touching his in the confines of the love seat. "However, I do know that I'm not up to playing games."

"I'm not going to lie. I find you attractive. And I want to kiss you every time that I see you. But that's not all. From the way you handle your affairs and your daughter, I see glimpses of a wholesome woman, with a good head on her shoulders and a generous heart."

Jennifer's throat tightened, her emotions running high. Her breaths came out shaky. "So what do we do from here?"

His answer was to cup her head and pull her face close to his. She inhaled his cologne and parted her lips, ready to accept his gift of a sweet, tender kiss. Upon the touch of his lips, Jennifer's arms came up and encircled his neck.

Should a kiss feel so good? Her mouth devoured and was being devoured all at the same time. When Thane moved down her neck, she sucked in deep breaths of air. Each searing kiss battled against her attempts to get fresh air into her lungs.

Drowning didn't have to be only by water. From where she sat under the onslaught of Thane's kisses on her breasts, she was going down for the third count. Thane's hands slid under her blouse and worked their way under her bra. A soft moan escaped as his hands cupped her breasts and massaged them, flicking his thumb over each nipple.

Her body responded, arching against Thane's arousal. Jennifer didn't know where she was heading, but she wasn't ready to stop. If her mind would stop the warnings from buzzing, she could relax and go all the way.

Thane pulled her leg up and rested it on his shoulder. He kissed her thigh and rubbed his cheek against her skin. There was a point of no return and she was fast approaching it. If she were on a ski slope, this would be a double diamond for experts only.

"Thane," she finally uttered, "I can't do anything on a casual basis." The moist haven between her legs ached for his attention. If she followed her heart, she would surrender to Thane without a second thought. "Thane."

He stopped and gingerly set her leg down, pulled her skirt back to its original place, and fussed with her hair, moving it out of her face. "I can give you what you want, Jen. I won't push you...for now." He smiled and kissed her on her cheek. "I'll wait, but in the meantime I do have one more wish to fulfill."

Jennifer didn't trust herself to say anything intelligible. She stood and headed for the stairs to the room where her daughter slept. "Good night." She left Thane on the love seat without turning around. Hopefully, it wouldn't take long for her pulse to stop its racing.

Chapter 9

Thane pulled into his parents' driveway. His sisters had already arrived. Their cars lined the street, while a spot on the driveway was left for him. There were perks to being the only boy in the family.

The all-brick ranch captured so many childhood memories and family celebrations. The block looked the same with manicured lawns, kids skateboarding or hanging out in someone's driveway with the trademark basketball hoop attached over the garage door.

Raised voices and much laughter escaped from the house. He loved these family dinners when his mother would issue an edict that she wanted everyone over for dinner. It usually meant that something had happened to someone in the family and this was her way of showing family support. Whatever the reason, he loved the familiar surroundings and home-cooked meals.

"T.J., you're here."

"Hi, Mom." He kissed his mother's soft cheek. She wore her signature scent of lilac. At seventy years old, she looked fit with a slim figure and a salt-and-pepper bob.

The sister that looked most like his mom stepped into the foyer where he was still locked in his mother's embrace.

"Hey, you two, break it up."

"Hey, Charlene. Mom won't let go."

"That's because my baby's home. With that job of his, you never know what tomorrow will bring."

Thane had heard this line before and he held his tongue. Nothing would change his mother's mind. She hated his job as a firefighter. He kissed his sister's cheek and followed the two women into the kitchen.

The remainder of the family, including brothers-in-law, nieces, and nephews and even some faces that he didn't recognize, occupied the family room, spilling into the kitchen. He made his way around the area, kissing, hugging, and tickling the younger kids' necks.

His other sister playfully punched his arm.

"T.J., did you bring the ice?"

Thane snapped his fingers. "Oh, crap, Bonita. I completely forgot."

"I'll go."

Bonita's son popped from behind his mother. "Could I go get it in your car, Uncle T.J.?" His deep teenage voice penetrating Bonita's scolding of Thane.

Thane hesitated. "Um…when did you get your license?" He critically looked over the gangly youth.

"He got it yesterday," Bonita answered. "I have some other things to get, so I can go with him."

"And that's supposed to make me feel better." Bonita was always the wild one. She'd smashed both parents' cars. Thane saw his mother grinning at them and he threw his hands up. "Fine. If you put one dent on my car, I'll wring your necks."

Thane cringed when he heard the squealing tires scream out of the driveway.

"I wouldn't have given in," Joe, his brother-in-law, offered. "I got a similar request when we were coming here, but I drove." He held up his key ring and jingled the lot. "And these are not leaving my fingers." He walked past him toward the refrigerator. "Wimp!"

"That's why your team didn't win the Super Bowl. Has-been!" Thane playfully pushed Joe's massive frame. He loved teasing him about his former professional football days.

An hour later, the entire family surrounded the large dining room table. A smaller, kiddie-sized version was set up in the corner of the room for the three pint-sized family members.

Thane's stomach rumbled as his eyes roved over the colorful dishes: collard greens, corn pudding, macaroni and cheese, sweet potato soufflé, two baked chickens and two honey-baked hams, a garden salad, and freshly baked bread. Even with such a sumptuous feast, his wandering gaze lit on the side table where his second, eldest sister, Cassie, displayed her baking talents with three sweet potato pies, two apple pies, and his favorite peach cobbler.

"Don't worry, honey. I've got your favorite ice cream," his mom reassured him. "Who's saying grace?"

"Wait a minute!" His father limped into the room, eyebrows furrowed deeply. "I go upstairs for a second and you hungry bellies are ready to eat me out of house and home."

The younger children giggled, used to their grandfather's gruff, lovable ways.

"Hey, Pop." Thane waved from his seat. "Looks like you're getting around."

His father sat down heavily at the head of the table. He stuck out his right leg to the side. A painful grimace gripped his face, mouth thinned, as he gingerly moved his foot from side to side. "I don't think the doctor knows what he's doing. My foot hurts more." He gritted his teeth.

"Cedric, if you would stay off your feet, maybe you wouldn't be hurting so badly," his wife scolded. "Now that you've interrupted us, the family would like to begin."

His grandchildren around the little table giggled. He winked at them before puffing out his chest and glaring at his smiling wife. "Okay, you may begin."

Thane enjoyed his quirky family, who loved each other and defended each other with loyal ferocity. He wondered how Jen would fit in with his sisters and parents, even his nieces and nephews.

"What do you think, T.J.?" Charlene broke into his musings.

"Hmm?"

"What's up? You're daydreaming like a lovesick puppy. Is it Jennifer?" his mother asked.

"Who's Jennifer?" Cassie, his youngest sister, dropped her fork, staring at Thane, a slow grin spreading across her face.

Thane's face grew hot and he shook his head at his mother's question. "A friend." With his feelings in full-blown confusion, he wasn't ready to discuss Jen. From Charlene's guilty expression, he guessed that she had told their mother.

Charlene snorted. She leaned forward and rolled her eyes dramatically. "What an understatement! He's all wrapped up with Jennifer and her daughter."

"Patti's my friend," Thane's six-year-old niece piped up.

"Daughter?" His father turned an inquiring look at his son.

"Jen is married, Dad." Thane recognized his father's concern since he believed in the traditional family.

"You're messing with a married woman?"

"Now, now, Cedric. Not at the dinner table." Thane's mother nodded toward the younger children. "Thane can explain himself after dinner."

"I can't wait," Cedric said, his characteristic scowl in place. He shoveled in a piece of sweet potato soufflé and poked a thick elbow into Thane's side.

"She's a widow." Nothing like being teased to bring back his teenage years. But he didn't want to suffer under his father's critical glare or his mother's worried glances. "Her daughter, Patti, is eight years old."

"That's unfortunate." His mother tutted. "Poor child. When will you bring her to meet the family?"

"Mom." Thane dragged out his protest. "We're just friends. You know…getting to know each other."

"There was a time that you had to bring your friends to meet the family," his father said. "I met all your sisters' husbands."

"A nightmare, if you ask me," Joe whispered under his breath.

Thane lowered his head and bit his lip to refrain from smiling.

"I heard that, boy. My foot may be broken, but not my hearing." He waved a fork toward the kids. "You'll see when it's your turn." Cedric ate several mouthfuls of chicken and macaroni and cheese, his eyes never leaving Thane's figure. "Does she know what you do?"

Thane nodded. He tensed, sensing the direction of his father's question.

"She doesn't have a problem with it?"

"No." Thane tried to let the matter drop, but his job as a firefighter was the central point of conflict between his father and him.

"Time for dessert." Charlene and her sisters popped up

from the table and started to clear the table. His brothers-in-law promptly rose to help their wives.

Thane understood the sudden unease since it was not the first time that this discussion had escalated to a heated exchange. He took comfort in his mother's quiet support, which lay in sharp contrast to his father's brooding disapproval.

Dessert was served. Immediately the strong, enticing aroma of his slice of peach pie made his mouth water. The familiar scents of allspice and cinnamon wafted under his nose, tantalizing his tastebuds. There wasn't much conversation across the table. Thane concentrated on his pie, lingering over the sweet, smooth taste of the peaches.

Later, after everyone was settled down in the family playing cards, watching TV, or cleaning up the kitchen, Thane glanced at his watch, wondering what Jen was doing. She'd told him that she would take Patti to see the latest Disney movie as a reward for coming in second in her school spelling test.

Thane followed his father, who was limping down the hallway to his home office, his father's domain. The dark chestnut furniture was balanced with splashes of deep gold borders framing the room. A small desk with a desktop computer and printer sat in a corner. This was probably the only item that belonged to his mother, a retired accountant.

More than likely, she had to make an appointment to enter his father's sanctuary. His father guarded his room like a wolf with his territory. A large reclining chair sat off-center in the office facing a wall-to-wall entertainment unit that all his children had pitched in on and bought for his last birthday.

Thane sat on the leather couch against one wall and watched his father ease himself into his reclining chair. He decided to give his father the lead to begin the conversation as he retreated into defensive mode.

"Tell me about this lady."

Thane filled him in, discussing his relationship with Jennifer using basic facts without coloring them with emotional baggage. It wouldn't help his case with his father if there was someone else to be affected by his career.

"Sounds like she's special to you."

Bingo. His father had seen through his attempt. "I'm not sure what her feelings are." He realized that was very true. Jennifer appeared to enjoy his company. However, there was no strong sense that she wanted to be more than friends.

"Do you think it wise to be a part of her life? You, the firefighter, facing constant danger. Plus, her husband who is dead? I can't see her wanting or needing that again in her life."

Those truths nibbled at his conscience, but on the surface, he pretended the dark fear hadn't burrowed its way into his heart. "Aren't you a part of Mom's? You, the firefighter."

Thane maintained eye contact with his father. He didn't need an observer to tell him that he resembled his father. Before the surgery, they had walked alike, with a smooth, confident swagger. While his father had a paunch and a slightly rounded face, Thane's body was in tip-top shape partly because of the rigors of his job and also because he liked to work off the stress of his profession in a gym filled with free weights.

"But I didn't come from a pampered life where opportunities to do better flooded my way. I am a man from the streets and I used these hands in more than one way to get out of the streets." His father held out his beefy hands. Thick veins wound their way up his muscular forearms like vines around a tree trunk.

"Why do you think that your passion for adventure, the adrenaline rush to give it your all, the urge to fight are only for you? Maybe it's in the genes."

"Bull! You were supposed to go to college, like your sisters. Become a doctor, dentist, gosh darn it." He pointed toward the door. "Look at them, Bonita and Cassie are happily married."

Thane leaned his head back against the couch. He stared at the ceiling trying desperately for a way to convey what his job meant to him. Words failed him, or rather he was too embarrassed to launch into a snappy confession about how his father was the only hero he knew and his only role model for fashioning his life. "So is Mom."

"Stop talking about your mother. That's not the point," his father growled. "You're a hardhead. Why can't you do what I say and quit?"

"Because you never taught me how to quit." Thane raised his head and refocused on his father. "I'm proud that you're a firefighter and maybe if you weren't so good, I wouldn't have wanted to walk in your footsteps. But here it is, I'm a firefighter. I really don't know what it will mean with Jennifer, but then again I don't know if it will matter, because it's not as if she's breaking down my door."

His father rocked in the chair, grinning broadly. "You were never the smartest one of the bunch. Bring your lady friend home and I'll be able to tell whether she's got you on her mind."

Thane exhaled noisily for more than one reason. His father had retreated from a continued fight about his profession, and a new pressure had mounted at the thought of leading Jennifer as the willing victim into the family circle. Being the last single one in the family meant that everyone would assume it was his responsibility to give a stamp of approval.

Later Thane headed home a little lighter from the burden of his father's disapproval. They had talked until nightfall, when his sisters knocked on the office door to say their good-byes. He chuckled. They probably wanted to know why it was so quiet. There were many relieved smiles when they saw him sprawled on the couch across from his father, still reclining in his chair watching his favorite movie star, Morgan Freeman.

Chapter 10

Jennifer entered her office, groaning at the stack of papers in neat piles on her desk. Her company's first conference of the year was in a few weeks. It was time for her to take care of the final details before heading out of state for a week.

The phone rang.

She hated to start her day without a steaming mug of coffee. "Good morning. ATB. Jennifer Stone speaking."

"Ms. Stone, this is Human Resources in ATB-Chicago. I wanted to let you know that we've scheduled your interview."

"Oh, I hadn't heard anything."

"Well, it took some time with everyone's schedule. You'll meet the president and the heads of operations and membership."

"Wow!" Her stomach responded with its signature flip-flop. "When?"

"By the way, I'm sorry the Jacksonville location didn't work out. For this job, we figured that you could tag it onto your trip for the annual meeting since it's here in Chicago. How does that work?"

"Sounds good to me." Her stomach protested. But it wasn't only her stomach that had reservations, her conscience was ready for a riot. She hadn't discussed the move with Patti, not even a mere hint. When she'd originally decided on the move, it was mainly due to Patti having a difficult recovery time.

With Thane entering the picture, she had pushed this move to the back of her mind.

"Ms. Stone?"

"I'm here."

"I'll e-mail you the details. Looking forward to seeing you. You'll do just fine."

"Thank you." Jennifer hung up the phone, already preoccupied with what her next move should be.

After getting her coffee and bagel, she settled down to lighten the pile on her desk. The morning passed with the phone pinned between her shoulder and cheek, as she ironed out last-minute hitches with the hotel, travel agency, and speakers. Her to-do list slowly diminished as lunch approached.

In her office, she paced the length of the room, biting the end of her pen. She had to write a letter to one of their competitors. Despite the mutual dislike, both companies realized the benefit of hosting a meeting together. However, Jennifer was determined that ATB would take the lead and she wanted to start the partnership with that clearly stated.

A knock on her door caught her in midpace. "Come in," she responded, irritated at the interruption. She waited with her hand on her hip for her intruder to enter.

"Sorry, Ms. Stone, got something for you." Her assistant bustled in with an armful of flowers.

The opening sentences to the letter flew right out of Jennifer's mind. She retrieved the flowers and buried her face in the soft petals, loving the bouquet of scents. "Is there a card?"

"Right here." Her assistant pointed to the card stuck among the stems.

Jennifer pulled out the minisized envelope and then the little note card. A small smile crossed her lips upon reading the bold signature. She looked over the top of the envelope and cocked an eyebrow at her assistant. Thankfully, the young lady caught her pointed hint and excused herself.

Jennifer dropped the flowers into a vase on her bookshelf. She'd get water as soon as she read the note. *Jen, take a look out your window. All yours, T.J.*

In an instant, Jennifer ran to the oversized window and pulled up the blind. Not sure what she was looking for, she searched the sky. Thane would be the type of boyfriend—a giggle escaped at the easy reference—who would skywrite a message to her. Not seeing any sign of a plane, she shifted focus to the building directly across from her. Most of the blinds were closed and the few that were drawn up revealed people busily working at their desks.

She glanced down at the note again. She shook her head and tapped the note against her cheek.

Tires squealed below, drawing her attention. The road was a busy thoroughfare of cars, trucks, and buses. Messengers wound zigzag paths on their bikes, cruising past the dense traffic. She leaned forward, resting her head against the windowpane.

On the same curb as her building was a black limo. No one was in sight next to the car. Could it be Thane?

Well, she'd soon find out. She flung open her door and ran to the elevator, punching the buttons. This was no time for the elevator to take forever. She kept punching the buttons, tapping her foot to the irritated beat in her head.

Finally it opened and she punched the lobby button, hoping that it would take her there without a stop on each floor.

The elevator obliged her plea and she promptly ran out into the lobby upon its arrival on the ground floor. She'd left her coat in her office, but the crisp air did little to hinder her from her goal. She didn't slow down until a few feet away from the limo. The tinted windows didn't reveal its occupants and Jennifer made her way around to the driver's side.

The back window slid open and a familiar face poked out with a toothy grin. "Wanna have lunch with me?"

Jennifer leaned against the limo and chuckled. "I don't know, I'm not supposed to talk to strange men in cars."

"But I'm not a stranger."

"You're saying that you know me."

"Yup." Thane extended his hand with a little Godiva chocolate in his palm.

"Wicked man. Using bribes to get me in your car?"

"What if I proved that I know you."

"I'm listening."

"I'll work my way up." He grinned and replaced the Godiva with a small plate with one shrimp and cocktail sauce.

Jennifer stared at the plump shrimp, already imagining the cool meat dipped in spicy cocktail sauce. Shrimp first, and then Mr. Thane Jackson.

"You have a small scar on your ankle from when you fell off the bike after your father took off your training wheels. You have beautiful calf muscles that your trainer dutifully conditioned. On your inner thigh, you have a birthmark in the shape of Florida, and Miami points to that wonderful patch of—"

"That's enough from you, pervert." Jennifer blushed, her

face quite warm, while another traitorous part of her responded to Thane's acknowledgment.

He opened the door and slid over to the other side. "Welcome, my darling," he drawled. He pressed a button and the privacy panel rose up.

The limo pulled away from the curb.

"Where are we going?"

"A drive around the city while we have lunch. Peanut butter and jelly sandwich?"

"Where's the shrimp?"

"Oh, there's only one shrimp and that was for a prop." He grinned and planted a wet kiss on her mouth.

"You're so crazy."

He kissed a path down her neck, running his fingers through her hair. "Mmm. Crazy about you. What's wrong, Jennifer?" He kissed the tip of her nose. His hands had already found its mark, gently stroking her nipple.

She shivered and licked her lips to maintain some dignity instead of moaning like a sex-starved woman. "I can't talk if you're going to keep doing that."

"Then I guess there won't be any further words." He unbuttoned her shirt and pushed it down her shoulders.

"The driver," Jennifer gasped. It took a lot of effort to get out those two words. She squirmed in Thane's embrace, feeling her bra loosen. "The limo."

"I knew you were smart. Yes, we do have a driver and his name is Phil. Yes, this is a limo and I think if we keep our legs bent, we'll fit." Before she could answer, he played with her nipple before flicking the sensitive peak with his tongue. Jennifer's hand lashed out against the window, her head thrown back. She prayed no one could see in as her eyes rolled up in her head from his passionate ministrations.

"I've never done this before."

Thane leaned up, his eyes twinkling mischievously. "How'd you get Patti?"

"You know what I mean." Jennifer had never felt so alive, even her scalp prickled from Thane's attention.

Aching for his lips to touch hers, she arched up to meet their softness. Hungrily she wrapped her tongue around his, drawing him into her with a teasing swirl.

Her hips rose to meet his in an erotic rhythm, rubbing, grinding, squirming in a sensual dance. A guttural moan escaped. "Thane, are you sure it's soundproof?" she managed in a husky whisper.

"Think so."

Jennifer giggled. "My mother would die."

"Mine, too." He propped himself above her. "No more talk about mothers. It kills the mood."

She nodded and pulled his head back down to hers.

Thane pulled on his protection. Now he was ready to get busy.

"I'd say this was premeditated." Jennifer nipped at Thane's bottom lip.

He hugged her tightly. "Yep. Ever since you wore that god-awful print mumu dress when you moved in." He kissed her forehead, her nose, and lingered on her lips.

Their dance continued soft and slow. Jennifer deferred to Thane's lead, enjoying the long strokes against the most sensitive part of her body.

The touch of his fingers between her legs, playing with her soft folds, quickened her breathing. Her body craved satisfaction. She gripped his hips tightly between her thighs, arching up to encourage his deep strokes, opening and tightening against his penetration.

Jennifer gripped his shoulders and prayed that she wouldn't

scream as their momentum built. Her hunger knew no simple satisfaction and she worked her passion into a frenetic beat. Her lower region quivered, pressure building, for that complete fulfillment that was so close at hand. "Please don't stop." Later she would scold herself for being selfish. At this moment, it was all about her. She wanted him to lead her to the peak and let her world explode.

And, boy, did she blow up!

The orgasmic explosion erupted repeatedly. Each wave sent trembling shock waves from her head through to each toe. She buried her face into his shoulder to muffle the cries of ecstasy until the last tremor died into a shuddering whimper.

She stretched like a cat, smiling at the exhaustion on his face. "How about that peanut butter and jelly sandwich?"

Chapter 11

The phone rang, jarring Thane awake. He rolled over, cracking an eye open at the offending instrument. The clock emitted enough light for him to see the phone in the otherwise dark room. It was barely past midnight. Thane urged his body to follow his mind's instructions and pick up the receiver. "Hello," he croaked.

"T.J.? It's Malik. We need you down here ASAP."

Sleep fled. A wild rush of adrenaline surged. He jumped out of bed and pulled on his clothes. Malik had told him that a three-alarm fire blazed through several townhomes in the downtown area.

His heart pumped. Its fierce echo pounded in his head. He ran downstairs two at a time, grabbed his keys and headed for his car.

Within a few minutes he squealed into the parking lot of the firehouse. His coworkers had already taken out two trucks, along with the ambulance. The third truck waited, its engine revving. Thane waved to the driver and slipped on his gear.

As the truck's siren cleared the early morning traffic, Thane barely noticed the scenery whizzing past him. Fires in homes, especially when people were more likely to be asleep, filled him with dread. He had to focus on saving people to keep down the sickening nausea from the brutal realities.

The fresh air filled his lungs and he continued to take deep breaths until the truck pulled up alongside the other trucks. He jumped out ready to take on the blaze.

"Pumper One on the scene at 5700 Cherry Lane, three-town-house unit. Heavy smoke showing from southern windows." Thane listened to the pumper officer. At any moment, his chief would give instructions to begin. "We are laying a three-inch supply line to the front of the residence and advancing an attack line into the building."

Thane worked for an hour battling the flames and, just as deadly, the smoke that belched from the windows. There was still a small chance that they could dampen the inferno and focus on the other nearby units. Eventually, he exchanged his air tank with the driver of the tactical support unit. Exhaustion flooded his entire body, considering the massive weight of his protective gear. But it was all part of the job he enjoyed.

A mother stood on the curb with an infant in her arms. The nearby medical sector area where the firefighters treated any casualties was a hyperbed of activity. A paramedic approached and tried to lead the mother toward the ambulance. She resisted, gripping the crying infant even closer to her body.

Thane ran past her, leading his men to the end unit, which had only begun to burn. The chief was also having crews begin to overhaul the building. Physically demanding chores had to be completed by opening walls and ceilings to look for any hidden embers that might reignite the fire.

"My son. Sir, my son is still up there. I could only get the baby," the mother wailed. "Help him. Please help him." She ran forward and grabbed Thane's hand.

"It'll be okay, ma'am," he reassured her.

Precious minutes passed, but he wanted to give the young woman hope. Looking up at the old building, he saw the flames with thick black smoke curling out of the top windows.

"Where is he?"

"His room is on the second floor. I was downstairs in the kitchen feeding the baby. I didn't mean to leave him. I didn't mean it." A fresh wave of sobbing racked her body. Thankfully the paramedic took over and gently guided the woman toward their area.

"We'll do all we can." Thane allowed a small reassuring smile before heading into the house. He kept a lookout for any signs of smoke as he led the way up the stairs, casting searching glances to locate the boy. He hoped that the little boy wasn't hiding from them, as they probably made a frightening sight in full gear and masks.

Following the mother's directions, he turned to the door with animals painted on its front. Thankfully, the knob turned easily and he perused the room before fully entering. His men ran past him and headed for the stairs to tackle the flames above him.

"Jamal? Are you here? It's time for us to go." Thane dropped to his knees and looked under the bed. No luck. He pulled open the closet door and poked around under the hanging clothes. "Jamal? Please answer me. This is a dangerous place and we need to leave." There was no sign of the boy and Thane worried that he may have run up to the third floor.

His men ran back down the stairs. "We've got to get out.

The fire is out of control up there. Looks like it might be an efficiency apartment."

"Gas stove?"

"Yep, and worse, it was a painter's studio." His own alarm bells clanged in his head. The buildup of gases and heated materials in the burning building created a very dangerous environment.

"Ladder Three," the chief called out. "Secure a hand line and protect the east exposure. Ladder Four, ventilate the roof over the fire."

His men's actions provided him with a few more precious minutes. Good news. Thane continued on his mission. He had to find the boy, but first he had to see to his men's safety. "Go ahead and do what you can from outside. I'll continue looking for the boy."

"We're staying with you. We can help."

Thane didn't have time to argue. Besides, time was running out. He nodded and directed them toward different parts of the house.

When the room revealed no clues, he grabbed the knob to close the door. Just then he noticed that there was a toy box under the window. Hope overcame the dread that had bogged down his spirit. He ran over and flipped open the cover.

"Jamal?" Relief washed over him and he pulled up the little boy, who silently watched him with big, frightened eyes. "I'm here to take you out of the house to your mom." At the mention of his mother, the boy blinked, his little lips trembled. "You're a very brave boy, Jamal."

A creak from above was all the warning he got as the ceiling caved. Instinctively he pulled Jamal to him and used his back to shield the burning chunks of the third floor as they fell.

Jamal emitted a shrill scream before the sound was smothered under Thane's body. A thick heavy beam landed on the back of Thane's head. A white shaft of pain flared behind his eyes before dimming under the cover of a sleepy haze. As if floating above the macabre scene, he saw the flames greedily make their way from his hand up his arm.

He closed his eyes, silently offering his apology to Jamal for failing to get him to safety.

Jennifer walked through the hospital burn unit. Her low heels clicked against the floor. Although the ward was busy with concerned relatives and friends and bustling medical staff, she could only see the long white hallway ahead of her. Opened doors of patients' rooms were like short paths to painful recoveries. She pulled her coat closed and focused on the signs that directed her to her goal.

The first recognizable face was Charlene's, who turned as she approached. The usual impish smile didn't emerge and her round eyes were red from ever-ready tears. Jennifer gritted her teeth, fighting to be strong.

"Thanks for coming, Jennifer."

"Thanks for calling me. I wondered where he was. I'd gotten used to him greeting me in the morning…" Her voice betrayed her as it quivered. "He'd bring me a flower every day."

"You must be Jennifer."

Jennifer nodded at an older woman who she guessed was his mother.

"I'm pleased to meet you, ma'am."

"Call me Kathleen. I'm his mother." She wrapped her arm around Jennifer's shoulders and brought her toward the other family members.

After the introductions, Jennifer wandered back to the room of clear glass. She'd avoided looking at the prone figure, afraid of what she would see. A nurse tended to the beeping equipment. She was covered with protective garb, including a face mask.

"It's to keep the room sterile. Infection is the enemy right now."

Jennifer nodded upon hearing his father's voice.

"He's a strong one, though. He'll be courting you in a couple of weeks."

Jennifer blushed. She wondered how much Thane had told his family about them. So far, she thought his family was loving and welcoming. Casting sidelong glances at his father, she could see the emotional strain on the older man's face. Even his shoulders appeared to be carrying a burden as he leaned heavily on his cane. A long shuddering sigh escaped, before he turned away from the window and limped back to the small waiting room.

A doctor came into the room. "Are you Thane's family?"

They all nodded. Jennifer didn't nod, but she hoped that she blended in with the family.

"His vitals are looking good. We'll keep him in critical care overnight, just to monitor him. By tomorrow, we can transfer him to intensive care."

"How is he, Doc?" Charlene asked the question that preyed on everyone's mind. Jennifer slowed her breath so she could hear every word that the doctor said about his condition.

"His arm is badly burnt and a few spots along his shoulder and back. Right now we have him on antibiotics and pain medication, which is why he's really not in any condition to communicate. I can allow two of you to go and see him, though."

Charlene took charge. "Mom and Dad, you go see him."

Kathleen nodded, dabbing at her eyes with tissue. She gripped her husband's hand tightly, her lips moving silently.

The doctor cleared his throat. "By the way, your son and brother is a hero. He saved a little boy's life. He shielded him from danger and because of it, the boy is with his mother instead of in a hospital room."

Jennifer resumed her seat in the corner of the room. She'd leave after she heard Thane's mom come back to report. In the meantime, she popped a piece of gum to keep her mouth busy while she waited. Conversation was at a minimum among the sisters. Everyone appeared to be deep in thought.

After five minutes, Thane's parents rejoined them. The family encircled them and Jennifer stood respectfully apart, but close enough to hear.

"He squeezed my hand," Kathleen sobbed against her husband's shoulder. "His eyes never opened, but when I told him that I loved him, he squeezed my hand."

Cedric cut a path through his family and pinned a stare on Jennifer. "Honey, he asked for you. His mouth moved when I was leaving and I leaned down to hear what he said. He was asking for you, Jen."

A sob bubbled up in Jennifer's throat and tears trailed down her cheeks. The iron front that she had tried to exhibit had evaporated. "But the doctor said—"

Cedric waved his hand, dismissing the doctor's rule. "I say that you should go to see him."

Thane's father exuded a quiet strength that Jennifer clung to as she walked toward the room on shaky legs. Her clenched hand tightly held a soggy wad of tissue.

As she stepped through into the sterile world, Jennifer looked down on the man who held her heart. More tears spilled. She loved him. It was that simple and that quick.

She'd give anything to be greeted annoyingly by him like he did every morning at the house. Instead he looked like a mummy with his limbs heavily bandaged. His face remained pristine. His peaceful expression could have been mistaken for contentment if it wasn't for the immediate circumstances.

Jennifer began to doubt Cedric's claim about Thane calling her name. Yet he had called her Jen, just like Thane usually did.

She reached out to touch the uncovered fingers of his right hand, but hesitated. "You'd better get yourself fixed up and ready to go, Thane." Surrendering to the urge, she lightly touched one finger, admiring the strength of his hand and long tapered fingers. That hand had touched her face with tenderness that had sent tingles through her skin.

Jennifer walked around the bed until her back was to the window for privacy. She raised a shaky hand to her face and swiped away a tear. The fear that she'd held at arms' length galloped toward the surface at full speed and a shuddering sob racked her body before she could contain herself. "Thane, can you hear me?" She slipped her hand under his and waited for a sign, no matter how small, from him.

It was twenty-three months ago when she had come to this very hospital to pay her last respects to her husband. Their family and pastor stayed until the end. For several months they'd turned their attention to her, but she'd held up to the pain. From the time of his diagnosis to his death, she had had no time to grieve.

After the funeral, she'd fallen into a depression, wondering how she would ever make it with her little girl. The responsibility weighed on her shoulders and she dedicated every waking minute to giving Patti a normal life.

She'd mastered shutting out people, their opinions, attention, and concern. Getting a good-paying job was her priority to make sure her daughter enjoyed all the things that she and her husband had planned. In this tunnel of focus she had stayed until Thane Jackson chipped away and poked his head through with his trademark comic tenacity.

The machine tracking his heartbeat emitted a rapid sequence of beeps before returning to normal. Automatically her breath caught and she stared at Thane's face, wishing for a twitch.

There.

She couldn't be mistaken.

His lips moved, slowly, with long breaths. Eyelids flickered and opened sleepily to watch her.

"Thane?" Jennifer was torn between alerting his parents and not losing one minute away from him.

"Jen." His eyes searched the room before settling on her. "I'm in the hospital?"

She nodded. "Your family is outside. I'll go get them."

"Okay." His eyes closed and she wondered if he had sunk into unconsciousness. "Thanks for coming, Jen."

Jennifer blew him a kiss and went to get his family.

The two-person rule didn't apply when the entire Jackson clan rushed into the room. Happy exclamations filled the air. With a sigh, Jennifer opted to head home to her family.

Jennifer took Patti to Thelma's house the night before she had to leave. The worst part of the new job, if she got it, would be the large percentage of her time she would spend traveling. Her first priority when she relocated would be to find a live-in nanny.

Her sweet daughter was so understanding of her schedule right now that it made her guilt heavier that she had to leave. Back at her house, she added a few more toiletries to her carry-on luggage and locked the suitcase. Looking around her bedroom for anything that she may have forgotten, she spotted a silver-framed photo of Thane posed in front of the George

Washington Monument. A warm flush spread through her as she thought of their lunchtime ride through scenic downtown.

She picked up the photo and rubbed her thumb over the glass surface, imprinting to memory every feature. He knew that she was going to Chicago on business, but didn't know that she had intentions of moving.

It never seemed like the right time and despite her weak attempts to put distance between them, the minute he kissed her or spoke tender words to her, she was lost. She replaced the photo, determined to follow through on her sudden decision. Grabbing at her house keys, she went to visit her neighbor to give her the travel itinerary, as she'd keep an eye on the house.

Chapter 12

Thane looked forward to getting back to work without bandages and little pain. The skin grafts would come later, but, for now, he was only too happy to be right alongside his co-workers riding off to another adventure.

Dressed in his work pants and sweatshirt, Thane felt less like a recent patient. He couldn't stand the pitying looks and constant attention from his coworkers, which wasn't as bad as how thick his family poured theirs on him.

At least there was one sane person in the bunch, as he thought of Jen. He credited her distance to understanding his need to be treated in the normal, regular way. They clicked in so many ways that he wanted to push it further, make their relationship more open. More than anything else, he wanted to share his feelings with Patti. After all, she'd trusted him to help her mother find a special someone.

Greedily, he now wanted Jen for himself.

Maybe later this week he would talk to Jennifer and then Patti. Thane pulled open his sock drawer. Since adolescence it had served as his hideaway. With his numerous nephews and nieces who felt his house was one big treasure hunt, he had to squirrel away any secrets.

Under his ankle-length whites, he retrieved a small ring box. He could imagine Jen freaking at the thought that he was proposing. Pushing open the hinged top, he looked down on the small garnet ring. There could be no doubt that this was a friendship ring. No need to rush, but he wanted to nudge her into committing to their possible union.

To Thane, this token of his feelings for her went beyond friendship. Knowing that garnet was her favorite stone, he wanted to give her a more permanent gift. Even if she didn't love him right now, he'd wait. She was all that he needed.

His doorbell chimed. Replacing the ring, he headed for the door. A wide grin emerged and he flung the door open. Grabbing his hostage in a bear hug, he planted a wet kiss. Without releasing her, he kicked closed the door and propelled a giggling bundle to the living room.

"What's gotten into you?" Jennifer playfully punched his arm.

He loved to see her eyes shining from excitement. After a quick kiss on her perky nose, he tried his best to settle down.

Surveying his clothing, she nodded. "I see you're off to work. That would explain the giddiness."

"You're not giving yourself any credit. You have me in a docile state of obedience." He stuck out his tongue and panted. "See? And if you scratch my belly, I'll be your best friend."

"Ooh."

He pulled her toward him by her shirt until their foreheads

touched. Angling his head, he kissed her, pulling gently on her bottom lip.

Jennifer turned her head away and took a deep breath. "This is so hard for me." She placed a restraining hand against his chest.

"What?" Thane frowned, but his hands remained busy under Jennifer's blouse.

"I'm leaving town."

"I know. Patti told me about your conference."

"I'm going to a conference, but I'm also going on a job interview," Jennifer explained further.

Thane's hands dropped from their busy work. All he wanted to see were Jennifer's eyes. Then he'd know the extent of this decision. A decision she didn't share with him or even hint at.

"Thane, please don't look at me like that." Jennifer raised her hands as if to touch him, but then hesitated and dropped them.

"I don't mean to make you uncomfortable. It's a shock, that's all." He walked away and headed for the couch, where he could sink into something that would support him. Meanwhile his mind roared that in such a brief amount of time his world had been tipped. "Is it definite? I just don't understand. Why? What about us?" He shook his head for some clarity to filter through his confusion. "I just don't understand," he repeated.

"I—I wanted to tell you. It's not about you or anything you did or said. I loved being with you." Jennifer came and sat next to him. "But I've got to think about my future. Patti's future. I guess…sacrifices have to be made."

"What?" Thane didn't mean to shout. "I can take care of you and Patti. I love both of you." He pulled her hands into his. "Do you hear me, Jen? I love you."

Jennifer twisted her arm out of his grasp. "Oh, God, you're making this so difficult." A sob caught in her throat. "Thane, I know you're an honorable man and would take care of me.

But I have to be honest. I was so scared standing in that hospital looking down on you when they first brought you. I felt like I was reliving the most nightmarish part of my life when I sat at my husband's bedside until he passed." Tears now freely flowed down her cheeks, hanging in a precarious balance from her chin before falling into her lap. "I don't have the strength to have vigils, hoping that you will come back to me."

Thane rested his head in his hands. It had crossed his mind that his job would conflict with Jennifer, but he'd hoped or, rather, willed her to accept this lifestyle. She'd lost someone dear to her, so how could he expect her not to have that fear?

"You have given me a wonderful boost, but it's time to move on. I don't want you to throw away your profession or who you are for me."

"I thought I was more than a boost," he countered, his voice softened from the hurt of her easy reference. "You're blowing me away. I think you're afraid of the next phase of your life, a life with me."

Jennifer didn't object; instead a stubborn light entered her eyes. "I'm leaving tonight."

When the door closed, Jennifer walked away from Thane's house with a heavy burden weighing on her heart. With Patti at Thelma's, she entered her empty house alone. Her footsteps echoed as she walked through to pick up her suitcases.

The taxi that she'd called showed up on time. Its horn honked to alert her. Jennifer took a deep breath and headed to the airport for Chicago.

The airport buzzed with its usual activity. Jennifer endured the long lines through the security lanes, glad that she had packed her laptop in her checked luggage, instead of having to boot up the system for an eagle-eyed officer.

Since she'd arrived early and her flight wasn't due to depart for another forty-five minutes, Jennifer wasn't distressed at the long line in front of her going through the X-ray gate. Instead she glanced around to see if any of the nearby little shops sold books. With a five-hour flight and one transfer, she'd need something to keep her mind busy from worrying about Patti and wondering about Thane.

"Jennifer."

An electric jolt shot through her entire body. The voice, oh so familiar, caused warm tingles. "Thane, what are you doing here?"

"I came to change your mind. I guess it's my last chance."

He grinned at her and Jennifer had to shift her gaze to his shoes to keep the facade that she was emotionally distant.

"Would you have a drink with me?" He pointed at the bar to their right. "Please."

The woman standing in front of her in the line turned at his plea. She looked at him before turning her attention on Jennifer.

Jennifer read the silent message to give Thane a chance, or maybe it was guilt prodding her.

"Okay. You've got ten minutes." Jennifer loathed getting out of the line, especially when she saw the additional foot traffic join the queue.

"I'll hold your spot," the woman offered.

Thane led the way. His broad shoulders cleared a natural path while Jennifer followed in his wake. The bar was filled with people awaiting friends and relatives mixed with those waiting for a connecting flight. Occasional warnings about unattended luggage and boarding information played over the intercom system.

They sat on the edge of the bar's seating area. Jennifer sat facing the security area to keep an eye on the activity. She was determined not to miss this flight, regardless of what Thane's plans happened to be.

Jennifer placed her drink order, along with Thane's. In a few minutes, the drinks arrived, breaking the mutual silence between Thane and her.

"Talk, Thane." Jennifer looked at her watch to make a point. He made her feel defensive, which had her call up her stubborn nature for reinforcement.

"You never said you loved me."

"What?"

"I want you to say it before you leave for your trip."

"It wouldn't really make a difference."

"Then say it."

"I love you." Jennifer drained her glass and set it down with a sharp tap. "Satisfied?" She gathered up her pocketbook and her trench coat. "I've got to be going."

"What if I told you I'd resign?"

"I told you that wouldn't do it. I know that you love your profession. But more than that I don't have the energy to depend on anyone."

"You're being a coward."

The truth hurt. Her pride didn't enjoy the harsh stab of honesty. With less than twenty minutes before her plane left, she would take this opportunity to get going before Thane could break through her barriers.

Jennifer stood. "Goodbye, Thane. I'll be back in a few days and maybe we could still be friends. That is up to you. But we can't go on as before."

"See you, Jen." Thane remained seated. "You're pretend- ing to be this unfeeling woman, but I know better. I've gotten in past the ice maiden routine and seen a loving mother and a vibrant, seductive woman."

"I wish you wouldn't. It's unnecessary."

"Unnecessary to voice natural emotions? Your husband is gone, Jen."

Jennifer sucked in her breath and mumbled a soft curse. "You have no right to tell me how long I should mourn." Underneath it all, she felt as if she had unfairly put Thane up against her husband. The last thing she wanted to do was strip herself bare of her fears and insecurity in the sterile confines of the airport.

Without a backward glance, she headed for the line where she had stood. Tears hovered on the brim, but she'd be damned if she would cave in and bawl for everyone to see.

When it was her turn to walk through the gate, Jennifer finally managed a quick glance over her shoulder in the bar's direction. The table where she'd just sat, having probably her last conversation with Thane, was newly occupied with another couple.

Jennifer swallowed the huge lump in her throat, biting her cheek to keep back the swell of emotion that threatened to bring a new onslaught of tears. She headed for the gate and boarded the plane for the place she could be calling home soon.

Chapter 13

Patti moved around in the background. She didn't want to be noticed or her aunt would make her go to her room. A few steps to the left, she settled on the floor between the huge plant with wide, shiny green leaves and the dining room wall.

The little girl propped her chin on her knees drawn to her chest. Auntie Thelma, T.J., and Malik sat in the living room talking about her mother. She hoped they would raise their voices just a little or she would have to find a new hiding place closer to them.

What did her mommy do?

T.J. looked sad and Auntie Thelma and Malik were listening to him. Nobody asked her what she thought. Because if they did, she would tell them that T.J. shouldn't give up.

Mommy liked T.J. She liked him a lot. The only time that Mommy had cried recently was when T.J. was in the hospital.

But then, even she had cried. But she didn't want to think about that right now. It made her eyes sting.

"Look, Thelma, I already said that I'd quit."

"I don't know why you're quitting. This is your life, Thane."

"Malik, I love this woman more than anything else. She's walked out of my life. Ever since then I don't know whether I'm coming or going."

"Thane, calm down. I've talked to Jennifer today."

"And…"

"And she said that her interview went well." Thelma put a reassuring hand on Thane, who blew out an exasperated sigh and leaned back in the chair. "She thinks that she might have a follow-up interview on her last day when they'll make the offer."

"Thelma, why are you telling him this?"

"I'm telling him because he needs to know what he's up against, okay?"

Patti crept forward to see T.J.'s face. It sure didn't sound as if Mommy and T.J. would be together. He looked so sad and tired. Watching the grown-ups talk, Patti didn't feel they would be able to figure out what to do. It had been a while, but Patti knew the one person she needed to talk to.

She scooted to the edge of the room, slid her body upright against the wall, and tiptoed to the front door. Looking over her shoulder to make sure that no one had noticed her, she turned the doorknob and stepped out onto the porch.

The Saturday afternoon sun was still high in the sky. A few kids from the neighborhood rode their bikes up and down the sidewalk. Their bikes gave her an idea. She walked around the entire unit of town houses until she was behind Aunt Thelma's. She walked into the backyard and saw her bike propped against the sliding door with her helmet on the handle.

Stuffing her braids under the helmet, she fastened it under

her chin. Then she wheeled her bike to the front and mounted the bike. Wavering slightly at first, she pushed the pedals until she got the easy rhythm and then steered her way out of the parking lot centered in front of several town-house units.

Patti remembered the path her mother's car took out of the neighborhood. In the car, it was a quick ride along the twisty road with its hills. But on her bike, Patti was already breathing heavily. Sheer determination kept her small legs pumping as her forehead broke out in a sweat.

Ahead was the big hill that always made her tummy flip-flop when her mommy drove down, just before she turned onto the main road. Patti smiled, hoping that the thrill would be the same. She wished that she wasn't wearing a helmet, but didn't want to stop to take it off. There was no telling how soon Aunt Thelma would come looking for her.

The hill proved to be more than she could handle. Disappointed, Thelma got off her bike and walked up the steep incline. She looked up at the sun, which had sunk a little. A worried frown imprinted itself on her forehead. She'd be in big trouble if nightfall came before she got back.

With second thoughts flooding her mind, she paused and looked back, weighing whether she should give up. But this was something that she wanted to do, had to do, for everyone's sake. Taking a deep breath, she faced the hill and started on her journey.

Cars had whizzed by, but she heard a car slow behind her. Panic raced through her body. All of her mom's warnings went off in her head.

"Don't look around," she told herself. "Please just go away."

The car continued to follow and then there was a short honk. The sharp trumpetlike sound startled her. Patti sped up her pace, ready to let her bike fall and run. She didn't have any friends in this part of the neighborhood or she would run to their homes.

Another honk made her jump again.

She couldn't take it anymore. Slamming down her bike, she spun on her heel to stare down the driver of the annoying car. Her mother had told her not to speak to strangers in the playground, but she didn't give her any warnings on how to handle a nasty driver.

The car pulled up alongside Patti.

She exhaled, her legs shaky and weak. "Malik, it's you."

"Yes, little one, it's me. T.J. went in the opposite direction through the baseball fields. Your aunt is back home, just in case you were still in the neighborhood. She's going out of her mind, worrying about you. Where are you heading, anyway?"

"I'm on a mission." Patti's heart had stopped racing and now the old courage had come easing back.

"You know I have to take you back."

"I'm not going."

"Look, young lady, you don't have a choice."

Patti made a face.

"At least tell me where you were going."

"To see my father."

"Oh. Want to make a deal?"

"Go ahead."

"How about if I take you to see your father after I tell Thelma that I have you?"

Patti thought about it, noticing that the sun had sunk even farther. Plus, there was still that hill to climb. "What about my bike?"

"I'll put it in the trunk."

"Okay."

Malik placed the call on the cell phone. Patti heard him tell

Aunt Thelma over and over again that she was okay. She breathed a little easier when she heard Malik say that he'd take her to see her father.

Before long they were on their way with Patti directing him. The ride did seem a little long. She couldn't imagine how she would have been able to do it on her bike.

"How's T.J.?"

"His basic problem is that he's lost his head—" Malik stopped talking.

"It's okay, I understand what you mean. T.J. is crazy about my mother and it's making him crazy."

"Yeah, something like that."

"You don't like it, though."

"I have nothing against your mother."

"But you don't want him to get all googly over my mom." Patti looked at Malik. "You've never been in love."

"And I've managed to stay sane."

"Grouchy."

"Excuse me?"

"Sane and grouchy. You need love to soften you. You wouldn't look so mean, because you're cute for an old man."

Malik looked at Patti with his mouth opened, eyes round with wonderment. "Are we close?"

Patti looked out the window. "Turn here."

They came upon Eternal Meadows Cemetery and rode through the open gates. Patti continued to direct him toward her father's resting place, as her mom referred to it.

Malik parked and Patti paused with her hand on the door. She wasn't sure what she would say. She looked over to him. "Could you watch me from here?"

Malik nodded. He stepped out of the car and leaned against the hood. "Go on, little lady."

Patti walked between the headstones. She concentrated on not looking at any of the words or names. Counting six deep, she stooped and read the headstone. *Wilfred Stone—loving husband and father. Gone too soon.* Patti traced the letters with her finger. "Hello, Daddy."

A few birds flew out of the tree that provided partial shade. Patti looked up as they circled before flying off. She saw them as a welcome sign from her father.

"I have to talk to you, Daddy. A lot is happening. My genie fell in love with Mommy. And I think Mommy may like him a lot, too, but not as much as you, Daddy." She hoped he didn't get mad. "But I need you to let me know it's okay that Mommy and T.J. kinda get together. He's sad. I know she'll be sad again. And, well, Daddy, I will feel sad, too." Patti waited for his response, hoping that it wouldn't take too long.

Footsteps approached and Patti turned to see Malik. "We've got to get going, Patti. It's getting late."

Patti nodded, disappointed that her daddy hadn't given her his answer. She stood and silently said goodbye to him. Glancing down, she saw a white feather by her feet. Patti picked it up and touched it to her face. She looked up, but there was no sign of the birds. In her heart, she knew that this was the sign. The beautiful tiny feather was his approval. Patti's face broke into a wide grin. "I'm ready to go home."

Jennifer didn't like hearing that her daughter had taken it upon herself to go visit her father. It made it all the more important that she be there for her. Thelma had filled her in on the details. Although there was only one person she wanted to hear about. She steeled herself from asking Thelma.

A couple of times she had picked up the hotel phone to call Thane. The routine of hearing his voice early in the morning had soothed her nerves and gotten her started for the day ahead. It was a habit that she would have to break.

Even though she had said they could be friends, that sounded good in a speech. The reality did not have room for that arrangement.

She picked over her order of eggs and nibbled at her English muffin. Thane may not have realized it, but their brief time at the airport was their official goodbye.

Jennifer drained her coffee cup, stuffed the remainder of the muffin in her mouth. Then, she slipped on her suit jacket and walked over to the full-length mirror. Her reflection showed a fairly tall woman in a navy-blue designer suit. The unique skirt was a straight cut with a small slit in the back, just enough to have a peekaboo effect with her calves. She tied her hair back and pulled it into a neat ponytail. Her hair gleamed from the additional oil treatment. With a touch-up of lipstick to her lips, Jennifer felt ready to face the interview team.

Later that morning, she sat across from five of the company's executives and other senior management. She had to keep her hands folded to keep the trembling from their view. Whatever she said at this time would determine her future, one without Thane. Jennifer took a deep breath, pasted on a smile, and waited for the grilling to begin for the next sixty minutes.

Chapter 14

Thane waited in the limo. The digital readout of the clock imbedded in the entertainment console showed that it was ten minutes after Jennifer's flight was due in.

What was he thinking? Jennifer had called Thelma to tell her the great news that the company had made an offer. Ever since she'd left, he'd suffered from heartburn. When he'd heard that she accepted the offer, he had to pop two tablets to soothe the burning sensation in the pit of his stomach.

"Sir, I think I see her over there."

Thane looked in the direction of where the driver pointed. Sure enough, Jennifer stood waiting for Thelma. She looked even more beautiful with her hair filled with bouncy curls draping her shoulders.

"Pull up in front of her."

Thane nodded. He felt like a young boy going on his first

date: hands sweaty, heart racing, and concentration zapping from one place to the next.

The car door opened and Thane slid across the seat awaiting Jennifer's entry.

"Hi, Thane." She stepped into the car and sat back. "This is a surprise."

Thane nodded, not liking how crisp her voice sounded. He'd hoped that she would have greeted him with her usual wide smile and big hug. It would be tougher than he'd thought.

The limo pulled out and smoothly joined the heavier traffic on Interstate 95. They cruised at an easy pace toward Silver Spring. A soft jazzy tune filled the interior.

"Are you going to tell me what's going on? You know, you can stop with the limos."

"Actually I know the owner." He laughed all by himself. "I wanted to be here when you came back."

"Nothing's changed, Thane." She folded her hands on her chest. "As a matter of fact, I've taken the job in Chicago."

Instead of answering, Thane pulled out a long-stem red rose from the bouquet sitting on the table. "For you."

"Thank you." She took the single rose and brought it to her nose. "Smells wonderful." A smile briefly wavered.

"Champagne?"

"What are we celebrating?"

"Your daughter's last wish." Thane retrieved a small envelope from his pocket. "She wanted me to give this to you."

Jennifer frowned and took the envelope. "What is it?" Concern touched her face. "Is she hurt?"

Thane shook his head.

"You're not telling me something. Either you tell me or stop the car." Jennifer, in a full-blown panic, tossed the rose aside and grabbed her pocket book.

"Jen, it's okay."

She ignored him and pulled out her cell phone, punching the numbers in with intensity.

Thane listened to her side of the conversation. He knew there was no calming her down until she had talked to Patti or Thelma. The conversation was short, but he saw that she had calmed down. Unfortunately, the panic was now replaced with open irritation.

"Obviously Thelma knows what you're up to." She opened the envelope and pulled out the handwritten note. Her eyes moved quickly over the words. Occasionally she bit her lip, but her eyes never wavered. Once she'd read it, she refolded the note and inserted it back in the envelope. "Do you know what the note said?"

Thane shook his head. He didn't know if that was a good thing.

"It's from Patti." Jennifer gulped. "I think I'll take that glass now."

Thane handed her a full glass and watched her gulp it. "Was it bad news?"

She shrugged. "It's one of those good news, bad news scenarios." She looked out the window, trying to read the green signs overhead. "Where are we?"

"Do you want to go home—"

"Home."

"Or go somewhere special with me?"

"I'm going home, Thane." She sighed.

"Then it means that I have approximately twenty minutes to change your mind."

"Change my mind about what?"

"I want you to realize that you need to spend the rest of your life with me."

She raised an eyebrow. "Aren't you being a little overly dramatic?"

"For the normal person, I'd say no. But you're a very special woman who likes putting me through the wringer. I now have to be the knight in shining armor to slay your dragon."

"My dragon?" She handed back her empty champagne glass. "And what or who is my dragon?"

"Being afraid to love…me."

She shook her head. "Nope. I love you." She threw her hands up. "See? I'm not afraid to say it."

"But that's all you can do. Say it. Actively loving me means dealing with the good and bad, kind of like wedding vows."

Jennifer didn't give him a quick reply. Obviously his words had penetrated, but if he thought she would come over to his side of thinking, then he'd have to try harder.

"Jen," he called softly. He moved closer to her, amused to see her nervous shifting in the seat. "I don't want to browbeat you all the way home."

"Ah…too late."

He admired her, running his eyes over her body. He noticed that she'd crumpled the note, twisting it between her hands.

"Was it bad news?"

"No." She dropped the note in his lap.

Thane hesitated, wondering if the note would derail his plans for the evening. His hand hovered over it.

She picked it up and placed it in his hand. "Read it."

The limo exited at the Connecticut Avenue exit heading toward Kensington. Thane was running out of time and this note could be the final stroke to end his pursuit of Ms. Jennifer Stone. Taking a deep breath, he began.

Mommy,

It's Patti. Your daughter. Mommy, T.J. loves you. He told me that he loves you. He is telling the truth. I went to see Daddy. He gave me a sign. You can love T.J. Daddy understands and so do I. Please love T.J. before he loves someone else.

"Jennifer, thank you for sharing this with me. Patti is a very special girl and I wish that you would let me be part of her life in a more meaningful way. I told you that I would resign from my job. I've interviewed with a consultant firm that is hired by the local government for safety programs. I'll do whatever it takes to have your heart. I'll even move to Chicago. I'll do all this for more than physical attraction. I truly love that beautiful shy person inside who has brightened my life when I thought that no one could."

Thane hadn't looked at Jennifer through his entire speech. He didn't want his last memory of her to be of the cool detachment she showed when he expressed his feelings. Now as he took in her delicate features, he saw the tears glistening in her eyes. He leaned over and kissed her cheek, softly.

When she held his head in her hands and raised her lips to his, his heart soared.

"Thane," she whispered, before hungrily kissing him, "I could never leave you. I tried." She laughed while the tears spilled down her cheeks. "Oh, God, how I tried." She hugged him tightly, resting her chin on his shoulder. "I couldn't stand it if anything happened to you and I can't stop myself from thinking that way."

"Shhh. Honey, I can't control my life, but we will work through this together."

The limo pulled up in front of the town house, but neither made a move to open the door.

"Take me away, Thane. Take me away."

Thane instructed the driver, then poured another glass of champagne. "I've got something to show you." He slipped a videotape into the VCR and turned on the television.

The tape was fuzzy for a few seconds and then a clear picture emerged of Thelma, Patti, and Malik.

"Turn up the volume."

Thane obliged, glad to see the tears had dried up.

Thelma spoke: "Hi, guys. If you're watching this, then I guess it's all worked out. Have fun and I want to hear all the details, PG-rated version, though."

Patti spoke: "Hi, Mommy. Hi, T.J. We did it. We did the last wish. You're driving off into the sunset with each other. See you on Sunday. I promise to do all my homework."

Finally, Malik spoke: "Jennifer, you have a great man there. He'll make you happy, but now he's going to be all wimpy. Yuck."

Jennifer grinned at him. "All this was planned, including the note?"

"No, I didn't know about the note. The tape was just a final touch."

"So where are we going for the last wish?"

"We're riding off into the sunset with me kissing my beautiful African-American princess."

"You *are* wimpy."

Thane growled before pulling her into an embrace. His kiss held all the love and passion that he would share with her forever. For always.

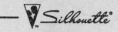

SPECIAL EDITION™

Silhouette Special Edition brings you a heartwarming new story from the *New York Times* bestselling author of *McKettrick's Choice*

LINDA LAEL MILLER

Sierra's Homecoming

Sierra's Homecoming follows the parallel lives of two McKettrick women, living their lives in the same house but generations apart, each with a special son and an unlikely new romance.

December 2006